PETER PAN

彼得·潘

(英)詹姆斯·马修·巴里
James Matthew Barrie

盛世教育西方名著翻译委员会
主　　任：黎小说　高民芳　林敬贤
美术编辑：赵　旭
插　　图：赵　旭
本册委员：章　杰　屠　彬

世界图书出版公司

上海 · 西安 · 北京 · 广州

图书在版编目（CIP）数据

彼得·潘：中英对照／（英）詹姆斯·马修·巴里著；盛世教育西方名著翻译委员会译.—上海：上海世界图书出版公司，2009.1（2014.3 重印）
(中英对照全译丛书)
ISBN 978-7-5062-7737-2

I. 彼… Ⅱ.①詹…②盛… Ⅲ.①英语－汉语－对照读物②童话－英国－近代 Ⅳ.H319.4：I

中国版本图书馆 CIP 数据核字（2008）第 170575 号

彼得·潘

（英）詹姆斯·马修·巴里 著
盛世教育西方名著翻译委员会 译

上海世界图书出版公司 出版发行
上海市广中路 88 号
邮政编码 200083
北京中科印刷有限公司印刷
如发现印刷质量问题，请与印刷厂联系
（质检科电话：010-84897777）
各地新华书店经销

开本：787×1092　1/32　印张：10.75　字数：585 000
2014 年 3 月第 1 版第 2 次印刷
ISBN 978-7-5062-7737-2/H·624
定价：16.80 元
http://www.wpcsh.com.cn
http://www.wpcsh.com

前 言

通过阅读文学名著学语言，是掌握外语的绝佳方法。既可接触原汁原味的外语，又能享受文学之美，一举两得，何乐不为？

对于喜欢阅读名著的读者，这是一个最好的时代，因为有成千上万的书可以选择；这又是一个不好的时代，因为在浩繁的卷帙中，很难找到适合自己的好书。

然而，你手中的这套丛书，值得你来信赖。

这套精选的中英对照名著全译丛书（注：《小王子》一书还附有法文版本），未改编改写、未删节削减，书中配有精美手绘插图，图文并茂，值得珍藏。

要学语言、读好书，当读名著原文。如习武者切磋交流，同高手过招方能渐明其间奥妙，若一味在低端徘徊，终难登堂入室。积年流传的名著，就是书中“高手”。然而这个“高手”，却有真假之分。初读书时，常遇到一些挂了名著名家之名改写改编的版本，虽有助于了解基本情节，然而所得只是皮毛，你何曾真的就读过了那名著呢？一边是窖藏了五十年的女儿红，一边是贴了女儿红标签的薄酒，那滋味，怎能一样？“朝闻道，夕死可矣。”人生短如朝露，当努力追求真正的美。

本套丛书的外文版本，是根据原版书精心挑选而来；对应的中文译文以直译为主，以方便对照学习，译文经反复推敲，对忠实理解原著极有助益。

读过本套丛书的原文全译，相信你会得书之真意、语言之精髓。

送君“开卷有益”之书，愿成文采斐然之人。

目录

Chapter 1
第一章

Peter Breaks Through

All children, except one, grow up. They soon know that they will grow up, and the way Wendy knew was this. One day when she was two years old she was playing in a garden, and she plucked another flower and ran with it to her mother. I suppose she must have looked rather delightful, for Mrs. Darling put her hand to her heart and cried, “Oh, why can’t you remain like this for ever!” This was all that passed between them on the subject, but henceforth Wendy knew that she must grow up. You always know after you are two. Two is the beginning of the end.

Of course they lived at 14 (*their house number on their street*), and until Wendy came her mother was the chief one. She was a lovely lady, with a romantic mind and such a sweet mocking mouth. Her romantic mind was like the tiny boxes, one within the other, that come from the puzzling East, however many you discover there is always one more; and her sweet mocking mouth had one kiss on it that Wendy could never get, though there it was, perfectly conspicuous in the right-hand corner.

The way Mr. Darling won her was this: the many gentlemen who had been boys when she was a girl discovered simultaneously that they loved her, and they all ran to her house to propose to her except Mr. Darling, who took a cab and nipped in first, and so he got her. He got all of her, except the innermost box and the kiss. He never knew about the box, and in time he gave up trying for the kiss. Wendy thought Napoleon could have got it, but I can picture him trying, and then going off in a passion, slamming the door.

Mr. Darling used to boast to Wendy that her mother not only loved him but respected him. He was one of those deep ones who know about stocks and shares. Of course no one really knows, but he quite seemed to know, and he often said stocks were up and shares were down in a way that would have made any woman respect him.

Mrs. Darling was married in white, and at first she kept the books perfectly, almost gleefully, as if it were a game, not so much as a Brussels sprout was missing; but by and by whole cauliflowers dropped out, and instead of them there were pictures of babies without faces. She drew them when she should have been totting up. They were Mrs. Darling's guesses.

Wendy came first, then John, then Michael.

For a week or two after Wendy came it was doubtful whether they would be able to keep her, as she was another mouth to feed. Mr. Darling was frightfully proud of her, but he was very honourable, and he sat on the edge of Mrs. Darling's bed, holding her hand and calculating expenses, while she looked at him imploringly. She wanted to risk it, come what might, but that was not his way; his way was with a pencil and a piece of paper, and if she confused him with suggestions he had to begin at the beginning again.

"Now don't interrupt," he would beg of her.

"I have one pound seventeen here, and two and six at the office; I can cut off my coffee at the office, say ten shillings, making two nine and six, with your eighteen and three makes three nine seven, with five naught naught in my cheque-book makes eight nine seven, – who is that moving? – eight nine seven, dot and carry seven – don't speak, my own – and the pound you lent to that man who came to the door – quiet, child – dot and carry child – there, you've done it! – did I say nine nine seven? yes, I said nine nine seven; the question is, can we try it for a year on nine nine seven?"

"Of course we can, George," she cried. But she was prejudiced in Wendy's favour, and he was really the grander character of the two.

"Remember mumps," he warned her almost threateningly, and off he went again. "Mumps one pound, that is what I have put down, but I daresay it will be more like thirty shillings – don't speak – measles one five, German measles half a guinea, makes two fifteen six – don't waggle your finger – whooping-cough, say fifteen shillings" – and so on it went, and it added up differently each time; but at last Wendy just got through, with mumps reduced to twelve six, and the two kinds of measles treated as one.

There was the same excitement over John, and Michael had even a narrower squeak; but both were kept, and soon, you might have seen the three of them going in a row to Miss Fulsom's Kindergarten school, accompanied by their nurse.

Mrs. Darling loved to have everything just so, and Mr. Darling had a passion for being exactly like his neighbours; so, of course, they had a nurse. As they were poor, owing to the amount of milk the children drank, this nurse was a prim Newfoundland dog, called Nana, who had belonged to no one in particular until the Darlings engaged her. She had always thought children important, however, and the Darlings had become acquainted with her in Kensington Gardens, where she spent most of her spare time peeping into perambulators, and was much hated by careless nursemaids, whom she followed to their homes and complained of to their mistresses. She proved to be quite a treasure of a nurse. How thorough she was at bath-time, and up at any moment of the night if one of her charges made the slightest cry. Of course her kennel was in the nursery. She had a genius for knowing when a cough is a thing to have no patience with and when it needs stocking around your throat. She believed to her last day in old-fashioned remedies like rhubarb leaf, and made sounds of contempt over all this new-fangled talk about germs, and so on. It was a lesson in propriety to see her escorting the children to school, walking sedately by their side when they were well behaved, and butting them back into line if they strayed. On John's footer (*in England soccer was called football, "footer" for short*) days she never once forgot his sweater, and she usually carried an umbrella in her mouth in case of rain. There is a room in the basement of Miss Fulsom's school where the nurses wait. They sat on forms, while Nana lay on the floor, but that was the only difference. They affected to ignore her as of an inferior social status to themselves, and she despised their light talk. She resented visits to the nursery from Mrs. Darling's friends, but if they did come she first whipped off Michael's pinafore and put him into the one with blue braiding, and smoothed out Wendy and made a dash at John's hair.

No nursery could possibly have been conducted more correctly, and Mr. Darling knew it, yet he sometimes wondered uneasily whether the neighbours talked.

He had his position in the city to consider.

Nana also troubled him in another way. He had sometimes a feeling that she did not admire him. "I know she admires you tremendously, George," Mrs. Darling would assure him, and then she would sign to the children to be specially nice to father. Lovely dances followed, in which the only other servant, Liza, was sometimes allowed to join. Such a midget she looked in her long skirt and maid's cap, though she had sworn, when engaged, that she would never see ten again. The gaiety of those romps! And gayest of all was Mrs. Darling, who would pirouette so wildly that all you could see of her was the kiss, and then if you had dashed at her you might have got it. There never was a simpler happier family until the coming of Peter Pan.

Mrs. Darling first heard of Peter when she was tidying up her children's minds. It is the nightly custom of every good mother after her children are asleep to rummage in their minds and put things straight for next morning, repacking into their proper places the many articles that have wandered during the day. If you could keep awake (but of course you can't) you would see your own mother doing this, and you would find it very interesting to watch her. It is quite like tidying up drawers. You would see her on her knees, I expect, lingering humorously over some of your contents, wondering where on earth you had picked this thing up, making discoveries sweet and not so sweet, pressing this to her cheek as if it were as nice as a kitten, and hurriedly stowing that out of sight. When you wake in the morning, the naughtiness and evil passions with which you went to bed have been folded up small and placed at the bottom of your mind and on the top, beautifully aired, are spread out your prettier thoughts, ready for you to put on.

I don't know whether you have ever seen a map of a person's mind. Doctors sometimes draw maps of other parts of you, and your own map can become intensely interesting, but catch them trying to draw a map of a child's mind, which is not only confused, but keeps going round all the time. There are zigzag lines on it, just like your temperature on a card, and these are probably roads in the island, for the Neverland is always more or less an island, with astonishing splashes of colour here and there, and coral reefs and rakish-looking craft in the offing, and savages and lonely lairs, and gnomes who are mostly tailors, and caves through which a river runs, and princes with six elder brothers, and a hut fast going to decay, and one very small old lady with a hooked nose. It would be an easy map if that were all, but there is also first day at school, religion, fathers, the round pond, needle-work, murders, hangings, verbs that take the dative, chocolate pudding day, getting into braces, say ninety-nine, three-pence for pulling out your tooth yourself, and so on, and either these are part of the island or they are another map showing through, and it is all rather confusing, especially as nothing will stand still.

Of course the Neverlands vary a good deal. John's, for instance, had a lagoon with flamingoes flying over it at which John was shooting, while Michael, who was very small, had a flamingo with lagoons flying over it. John lived in a boat turned upside down on the sands, Michael in a wigwam, Wendy in a house of leaves deftly sewn together. John had no friends, Michael had friends at night, Wendy had a pet wolf forsaken by its parents, but on the whole the Neverlands have a family resemblance, and if they stood still in a row you could say of them that they have each other's nose, and so forth. On these magic shores children at play are for ever beaching their coracles (*simple boat*). We too have been there; we can still hear the sound of the surf, though we shall land no more.

Of all delectable islands the Neverland is the snuggest and most compact, not large and sprawly, you know, with tedious distances between one adventure and another, but nicely crammed. When you play at it by day with the chairs and table-cloth, it is not in the least alarming, but in the two minutes before you go to sleep it becomes very real. That is why there are night-lights.

Occasionally in her travels through her children's minds Mrs. Darling found things she could not understand, and of these quite the most perplexing was the word Peter. She knew of no Peter, and yet he was here and there in John and Michael's minds, while Wendy's began to be scrawled all over with him. The name stood out in bolder letters than any of the other words, and as Mrs. Darling gazed she felt that it had an oddly cocky appearance.

"Yes, he is rather cocky," Wendy admitted with regret. Her mother had been questioning her.

"But who is he, my pet?"

"He is Peter Pan, you know, mother."

At first Mrs. Darling did not know, but after thinking back into her childhood she just remembered a Peter Pan who was said to live with the fairies. There were odd stories about him, as that when children died he went part of the way with them, so that they should not be frightened. She had believed in him at the time, but now that she was married and full of sense she quite doubted whether there was any such person.

"Besides," she said to Wendy, "he would be grown up by this time."

"Oh no, he isn't grown up," Wendy assured her confidently, "and he is just my size." She meant that he was her size in both mind and body; she didn't know how she knew, she just knew it.

Mrs. Darling consulted Mr. Darling, but he smiled pooh-pooh. "Mark my words," he said, "it is some nonsense Nana has been putting into their heads; just the sort of idea a dog would have. Leave it alone, and it will blow over."

But it would not blow over and soon the troublesome boy gave Mrs. Darling quite a shock.

Children have the strangest adventures without being troubled by them. For instance, they may remember to mention, a week after the event happened, that when they were in the wood they had met their dead father and had a game with him. It was in this casual way that Wendy one morning made a disquieting revelation. Some leaves of a tree had been found on the nursery floor, which certainly were not there when the children went to bed, and Mrs. Darling was puzzling over them when Wendy said with a tolerant smile:

"I do believe it is that Peter again!"

"Whatever do you mean, Wendy?"

"It is so naughty of him not to wipe," Wendy said, sighing. She was a tidy child.

She explained in quite a matter-of-fact way that she thought Peter sometimes came to the nursery in the night and sat on the foot of her bed and played on his pipes to her. Unfortunately she never woke, so she didn't know how she knew, she just knew.

"What nonsense you talk, precious! No one can get into the house without knocking."

"I think he comes in by the window," she said.

"My love, it is three floors up."

"Weren't the leaves at the foot of the window, mother?"

It was quite true; the leaves had been found very near the window.

Mrs. Darling did not know what to think, for it all seemed so natural to Wendy that you could not dismiss it by saying she had been dreaming.

"My child," the mother cried, "why did you not tell me of this before?"

"I forgot," said Wendy lightly. She was in a hurry to get her breakfast.

Oh, surely she must have been dreaming.

But, on the other hand, there were the leaves. Mrs. Darling examined them very carefully; they were skeleton leaves, but she was sure they did not come from any tree that grew in England. She crawled about the floor, peering at it with a candle for marks of a strange foot. She rattled the poker up the chimney and tapped the walls. She let down a tape from the window to the pavement, and it was a sheer drop of thirty feet, without so much as a spout to climb up by.

Certainly Wendy had been dreaming.

But Wendy had not been dreaming, as the very next night showed, the night on which the extraordinary adventures of these children may be said to have begun.

On the night we speak of all the children were once more in bed. It happened to be Nana's evening off, and Mrs. Darling had bathed them and sung to them till one by one they had let go her hand and slid away into the land of sleep.

All were looking so safe and cosy that she smiled at her fears now and sat down tranquilly by the fire to sew.

It was something for Michael, who on his birthday was getting into shirts. The fire was warm, however, and the nursery dimly lit by three night-lights, and presently the sewing lay on Mrs. Darling's lap. Then her head nodded, oh, so gracefully. She was asleep. Look at the four of them, Wendy and Michael over there, John here, and Mrs. Darling by the fire. There should have been a fourth night-light.

While she slept she had a dream. She dreamt that the Neverland had come too near and that a strange boy had broken through from it. He did not alarm her, for she thought she had seen him before in the faces of many women who have no children. Perhaps he is to be found in the faces of some mothers also. But in her dream he had rent the film that obscures the Neverland, and she saw Wendy and John and Michael peeping through the gap.

The dream by itself would have been a trifle, but while she was dreaming the window of the nursery blew open, and a boy did drop on the floor. He was accompanied by a strange light, no bigger than your fist, which darted about the room like a living thing and I think it must have been this light that wakened Mrs. Darling.

She started up with a cry, and saw the boy, and somehow she knew at once that he was Peter Pan. If you or I or Wendy had been there we should have seen that he was very like Mrs. Darling's kiss. He was a lovely boy, clad in skeleton leaves and the juices that ooze out of trees, but the most entrancing thing about him was that he had all his first teeth. When he saw she was a grown-up, he gnashed the little pearls at her.

彼得·潘闯了进来

除了一个孩子，所有的孩子都会长大成人，并且他们很快就会意识到这一点。温迪是这样意识到的：她两岁的某一天，在花园里玩，摘了朵花，拿在手里，跑到妈妈那里。我想她的样子一定非常惹人喜爱，因为达林太太把手放在胸口，大声地说：“唉，你要是一直像这样不长大该有多好啊！”事情的经过就是这样。从此，温迪就知道她是注定要长大成人的。通常人们过了两岁就会明白这一点——两岁，既意味着结束，也意味着开始。

温迪一家住在大街上十四号房子里，温迪出生前，妈妈是家中的首要人物。她是个有趣的太太，头脑爱幻想，嘴巴甜蜜但爱捉弄人。她那爱幻想的脑袋，就像是来自神奇的东方世界的小盒子，一个套一个，无论你打开多少个，里面总还藏着一个。她那张甜蜜、爱捉弄人的嘴上总是挂着一个温迪永远都得不到的吻，尽管它就很明显地挂在右边的嘴角上。

达林先生是这样追到太太的：当达林太太还是个小姑娘的时候，就有很多男孩子不约而同地喜欢上了她。他们长大成人后都跑去她家向她求婚，而达林先生却租了辆马车，抢在他们前头来到她家里，就这样娶走了达林太太。达林先生得到了她的一切，除了她最里面的那个小盒子和那个吻。他从不知道那个小盒子的故事，最后也放弃了想要得到那个吻的念头。温迪想，拿破仑应该可以得到那个吻，不过我可以想像即使拿破仑曾尝试着想要得到它，最后也只能怒气冲冲地甩门而去。

达林先生常常向温迪炫耀说，达林太太不仅爱他，还很尊敬他。他学问高深，懂得什么是股票和红利。虽然没有人真正了解这些事情，不过达林先生看起来确实像是知道这些东西的。他常常说，股票涨了，红利跌了。某种程度上，这让所有的女人都尊敬他了。

达林太太结婚时，穿了一身雪白的婚纱。刚开始，她觉得记账就像玩游戏一样愉快。她家中的账都记得非常详细，连一颗小包菜都不遗漏。可是不久之后，就连整棵整棵的花椰菜都被漏掉了，取而代之的是一些没有面孔的婴儿的图画。在应该结账的时候，她画了这些小娃娃——他们都是达林太太想像的样子。

第一个来的是温迪，接着是约翰，然后是迈克尔。

温迪出生后的头一两个星期里，他们还不知道自己能否养活她，因为又多了一张要吃饭的嘴。达林先生为温迪的到来感到非常高兴。不过他是个实在人；他坐在达林太太的床沿上，一边握着她的手，一边算着开销费用，而达林太太则用哀求的神情看着他。不管发生什么事情她都想要冒一冒险，可是达林先生并不想这么做。他想做的就是拿支笔跟一张纸仔细盘算。如果达林太太提什么意见来干扰他，他就会从头再算一次。

“不要再打断我！”他恳求道。

“我这儿有一镑十七先令，在办公室还有二先令六便士；我可以取消办公室的咖啡，那样就可以省下十先令，加起来就有两镑九先令六便士。加上你的十八先令三便士，总共有三镑九先令七便士，我的支票本上还有五镑，总共八镑九先令七便士——是谁在动？——八九七，小数点进七——别说话，亲爱的——还有你借给上门来的那人的一英镑——安静点，孩子——小数点进，宝贝——你看，还是被你给搅和了——我刚才是不是说九九七来着？没错，我说的是九九七。现在的问题是，我们能不能试着靠这九镑九先令七便士过一年呢？”

“当然可以，乔治。”达林太太大声嚷道。她当然偏爱温迪，不过达林先生说的话更有分量些。

“别忘了得腮腺炎还要花钱，”达林先生几乎用威胁的语气警告她，然后又接着算下去，“算治疗腮腺炎花个一镑，我先记下这个数，不过我敢说差不多要花三十先令——别说话——麻疹要一镑五先令，德国麻疹要半个几尼，总共要两镑十五先令六便士——别摇你的手指——百日咳算十五先令。”——他就这样一直算着，每次合计的结果都不一样。不过最后温迪还是熬了过来，腮腺炎减少到十二先令六便士，两种麻疹并作一次处理了。

约翰出生时，也发生过同样的骚动，迈克尔遭遇的危险更大。不过这两个终究还是养活了，而且很快你就看见姐弟三人排成一排，在保姆的陪伴下，到福尔萨姆小姐的幼儿园上学去了。

达林太太喜欢安于现状，达林先生却非常喜欢事事向左邻右舍看齐；因此很自然地他们请了一位保姆。但是因为他们家很穷，而且孩子们喝牛奶花费太多，所以他们家的保姆只是一只纽芬兰犬，叫作娜娜。在达林夫妇雇用她之前，她并不属于任何人，不过她总是把孩子看得很重。达林一家和她是在肯辛顿公园里认识的。她把大部分的消遣时光都花在那儿，把头伸进婴儿车里偷看。那些粗心大意的育儿保姆十分讨厌她，因为有时候她会跟着她们回家，向她们的女主人打小报告。她确实是块当保姆的料：洗澡的时候，她总是做得一丝不苟；夜里不管什么时候，只要她照看的孩子发出轻微的哭声，她就会一跃而起；当然她的狗舍就在育儿室里。她有一种天赋，知道有时候小孩的咳嗽是不能掉以轻心的，咳嗽时该用袜子围着脖子。自始至终她都相信老式的治疗方法，比如用大黄叶治病；每次听到别人谈论细菌之类的新名词时，她都会发出不屑的声音。看她护送孩子们上学是一门礼仪课程。当孩子们表现得规规矩矩时，她就安详地走在他们身边；当他们乱跑乱动时，她就会用头把他们推回队列里。在约翰踢足球的时候，她从不会忘记带他的毛线衣；而且她常常会用嘴叼把伞，以防下雨。福尔萨姆小姐的幼儿园里，有一间地下室，保姆们都在那里等候着接孩子们放学。她们都坐在长板凳上，只有娜娜卧在地板上，这是她和她们之间惟一的不同之处。她们假装没有看到她，自以为娜娜配不上她们，其实，娜娜才鄙视她们那种喋喋不休的唠叨。她不喜欢达林太太的朋友们来参观育儿室，可是如果她们真的来了，她就会先迅速扯下迈克尔的围涎，给他换上那件带蓝花边的，然后抚平温迪的衣裙，再匆忙梳理一下约翰的头发。

没有哪个育儿室能比这儿更井然有序的了，达林先生非常了解这一点，可有时候他还是难免会担心街坊的闲言碎语。

他不能不考虑他在城中的声誉地位啊。

但另一个方面，娜娜也让达林先生很烦恼，有时候他会觉得娜娜不尊敬他。“我知道她是非常敬佩你的，乔治。”达林太太向他保证说，然后就示意孩子们要特别尊敬父亲。接着，就跳起欢快的舞蹈。他们另一位也是惟一的女仆莉莎偶尔会被允许参与进来。莉莎穿着长裙，戴着女佣帽；虽然当初被雇用时，她发誓自己早就过了十岁，但她还是显得那么矮小。这些调皮的小家伙们玩得多快活呀！最高兴的当属达林太太了，她踮起脚尖疯狂的旋转着，你能看到的只有她的那个吻。这时候如果你扑了过去，一定可以得到这个吻。如果没有彼得·潘的出现，世界上再也没有比他们更朴素更和睦的家庭了。

达林太太第一次听说彼得这个名字，是在她整理孩子们心事的时候。凡是好妈妈，晚上都有一个习惯——当孩子们睡着以后，彻底搜查他们的脑海，把白天散乱的物品放回原位，让第二天早晨的事情变得井井有条。如果你能醒着不睡（当然你肯定做不到），就能看到你妈妈在做这些事。你会发现，她就像是在整理抽屉一样，真的很有趣。我想你会看见她跪在那儿，饶有兴致地翻看你脑海里的东西，很好奇你究竟是从哪儿拣到这些东西的；她会发现有些东西很可爱，有的则不那么可爱。她会把某样东西当成可爱的小猫，贴在脸上；而把另外一些慌忙地收起来，放在一个看不到的地方。早上醒来的时候，你临睡时内心里那些淘气的念头和不快的情绪都被叠得小小的，压在你脑海的最下面；而在上面则整整齐齐地摆放着你那些美好的心思，供你在这一天享用。

我不知道你有没有见过人大脑的图像。有时候医生画你身上其他部位的图像时，你自己的图像会变得特别有趣。但是当你碰巧看到他们画一张孩子头脑的图像时，你会发现，那张图不仅杂乱无章，而且始终旋转不定。上面有弯弯曲曲的线条，就像你体温的曲线图，这些线大概就是岛上的道路吧。因为梦幻岛或多或少像个岛屿，上面到处洒满了惊人而斑驳的色彩。附近的海面上有一片珊瑚礁，漂浮着轻快的小船。岛上住着野蛮人；还有几个荒凉的巢穴；上面还有土地神和许多裁缝；有河流穿过的洞穴；有排行老七的王子；有一间快要倒塌的小棚屋；还有一个长着鹰钩鼻的矮小的老太太。如果只有这些东西，这张图并不难画。但是那里面还有第一天上学的情形，有宗教信仰、神父、圆形水池、针线活、谋杀案、绞刑、与格动词、吃巧克力布丁的日子、穿背带裤、数到九十九、奖励自己动手拔牙的三便士等等。这些东西不是岛上的一部分，就是画在另一幅画上。总之，一切都混作一团。特别是因为，这些东西没有一件是静止不动的。

当然，每个人的梦幻岛又各不相同，例如，约翰的梦幻岛里有一个湖泊，上面飞着许多火烈鸟，约翰正用箭射它们。迈克尔年纪尚小，他的梦幻岛上也有一只火烈鸟，上面飞着许多湖泊。约翰住在一只翻倒在沙滩上的船里，迈克尔住在一间小棚屋里，温迪住在一间用树叶巧妙缝成的房子里。约翰没有朋友，迈克尔在睡梦中有朋友，温迪有一只被父母遗弃的小狼崽。不过大体说来，他们的梦幻岛还是离不开家庭的模式的。如果让他们安静地站成一排，你会发现他们的鼻子大同小异，等等。孩子们在这些神奇的海滩上游戏，总是驾着小舟靠岸登陆。其实我们也到过那个地方，如今我们还能听到海浪拍岸的声音，尽管我们无法再次上岸。

在所有令人愉悦的岛屿里面，梦幻岛是最舒适、最紧凑的了。地方并不太大，也不太分散，从一个冒险到另一个冒险距离恰到好处，十分紧凑。白天你用椅子和桌布玩游戏时，一点也不会感觉到它的存在；但是在你入睡前的两分钟，它就会变得非常真实，因此晚上要点夜灯。

有时候达林太太在孩子们的脑海里漫游时，会发现一些令她无法理解的事情，其中最让她困惑的就是彼得这个名字。她不认识叫彼得的人，但是在约翰和迈克尔的脑海里，到处都是这个名字，温迪的脑海里更是写满了。这个名字比别的字要粗大，要醒目，当达林太太盯着它看时，觉得这名字有种奇怪的傲气。

“是的，他确实非常傲慢。”当她妈妈质问她时，温迪遗憾地承认道。

“可他是谁啊，宝贝？”

“他叫彼得·潘，你知道的啊，妈妈。”

刚开始达林太太根本就想不起来有这么一个人，但是在她回想

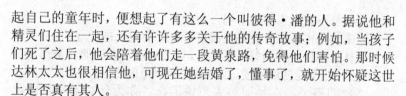

起自己的童年时，便想起了有这么一个叫彼得·潘的人。据说他和精灵们住在一起，还有许许多多关于他的传奇故事；例如，当孩子们死了之后，他会陪着他们走一段黄泉路，免得他们害怕。那时候达林太太也很相信他，可现在她结婚了，懂事了，就开始怀疑这世上是否真有其人。

“况且，”她告诉温迪说，“即便这个人真的存在，现在他也该长大了吧。”

“噢，没有，他没有长大，”温迪自信地告诉妈妈，“而且还跟我一样大。”温迪的意思是说，彼得的身心都和她一样大。她也不知道自己是如何得知的，反正她就是知道。

达林太太就此事询问了达林先生，不过达林先生只是不屑地笑了笑，说：“听我说，这肯定是娜娜对他们胡说八道的，只有狗才会有这种念头。别管它，这事儿自然会被淡忘的。”

可是事情并没有被淡忘，不久之后，这个讨人厌的男孩竟然让达林太太吓了一大跳。

孩子们常会有许多前所未知的奇遇，而他们自己并不因此劳神费心。例如，事情发生一个星期之后，他们可能会想起来说，他们在林子里遇见了死去的父亲，还跟他一起玩游戏。有一天早上，温迪就是这样漫不经心地说出了一件让人心神不宁的事，就是她发现育儿室的地板上有几片树叶，而头天晚上孩子们上床睡觉时明明还没有的。正当达林太太觉得事有蹊跷时，温迪却笑嘻嘻地说：

“这肯定又是那个彼得干的！”

“你这话是什么意思，温迪？”

“他真淘气，玩完了也不打扫干净。”温迪叹了口气说道。她是个爱干净的孩子。

她像真有其事似的解释道，她觉得有时候彼得会在夜里到育儿室来，坐在她的床脚边上，吹笛子给她听。可惜她从没有醒来过，因此她也不知道自己是如何知道的，反正她就是知道。

“你在胡说些什么，宝贝！没敲门谁也进不了屋。”

“我想他是从窗户上爬进来的。”温迪说。

“亲爱的，这里可是三楼啊！”

“树叶不就在窗脚跟前吗，妈妈？”

这确实不错，树叶就是在离窗子很近的地方被发现的。

达林太太也不知该怎么说才好，因为这一切在温迪看来都显得那么自然，你不能随随便便说她是在做梦，而把这事儿给糊弄过去。

“我的孩子，”她妈妈大声说道，“你为什么不早告诉我呢？”

“我忘了。”温迪毫不在意地回答着，急忙跑去吃早饭。

啊，她一定是在做梦。

可是另一方面，树叶的的确确就在那里。达林太太仔细检查了一番这些树叶，那是些干树叶，不过她敢肯定，这些绝不是从生长在英国的树上掉下来的叶子。她趴在地板上，借着烛光仔细查看地面，看看是否有陌生人的脚印，用拨火棍慌乱地捅烟囱，敲墙壁。她从窗口放下一根带子，窗子到地面的距离足足有三十英尺，而且墙上甚至没有一个可供攀爬的水管。

温迪一定是在做梦。

可是温迪并没有做梦，这在第二天夜里就被证实了，孩子们非同寻常的冒险经历可以说就是从那一夜开始的。

那个夜里，孩子们又都上床睡觉了。碰巧那天晚上娜娜不在家。达林太太给他们洗澡，又给他们唱歌，直到他们一个个放开她的手，进入了梦乡。

一切都显得如此安宁舒适，达林太太不禁嘲笑起自己的多虑，于是静静地坐在火炉旁，做起衣服来。

这是给迈克尔做的，等他过生日的时候就该换衬衫了。炉火暖洋洋的，育儿室里点着三盏夜灯，朦朦胧胧的。没过多久，针线活就掉在了达林太太的腿上，她睡着了，头优雅地上下晃动着。看看这四个人，温迪和迈克尔睡在那边，约翰睡在这边，而达林太太睡在火炉旁。本来应该有第四盏夜灯的。

达林太太睡着之后做了一个梦，她梦见梦幻岛离她很近很近，一个陌生的男孩从那里冲了出来。这男孩并没有吓到她，因为她觉得自己曾在一些没有孩子的女人的脸上见过他；也许在一些已为人母的女人的脸上，也可以看到他。但是在她的梦里，这个男孩拨开了遮掩着梦幻岛的那一层薄雾，她看到温迪、约翰和迈克尔正从那条裂缝向里张望。

这个梦本微不足道，但是就在她做梦的时候，育儿室的窗子被风吹开了，果真有个男孩落在地板上。跟随在他身边的是一团奇异的光，那光还没有拳头大，在房间里四处乱飞，像是有生命一样。我想，肯定是那团光把达林太太惊醒了。

她忽然尖叫着站了起来，发现了那个男孩。不知为何，她立刻知道这人就是彼得·潘。如果当时你或我或温迪就在那儿，我们会觉得，他像极了达林太太的那个吻。他是一个可爱的男孩，穿着用干树叶和树浆做成的衣服。不过他身上最让人着迷的地方是他那一口乳牙。当他发现达林太太是个大人时，就咧着满口珍珠般的牙齿愤怒地看着她。

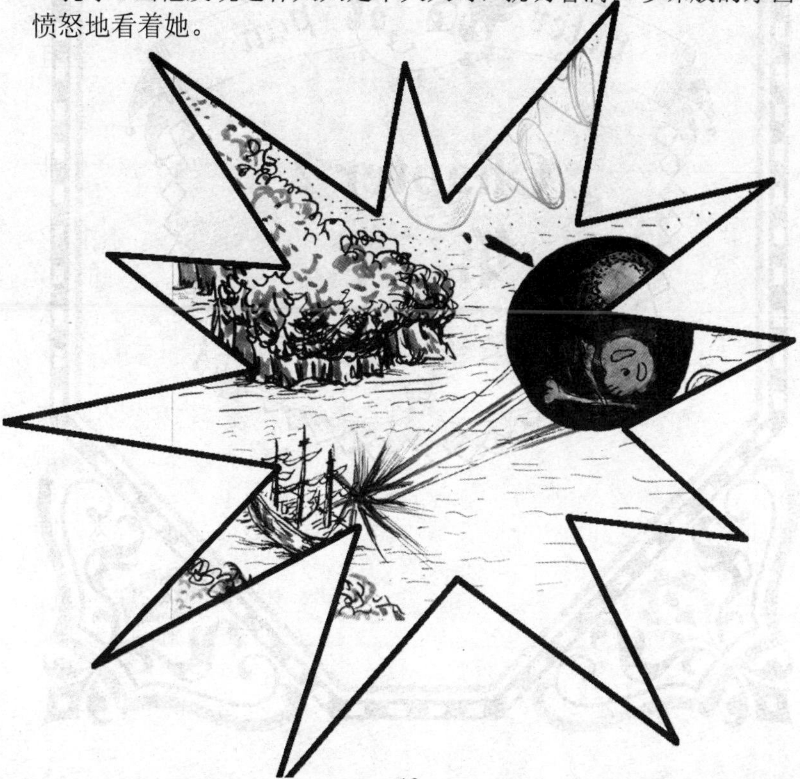

Chapter 2
第二章

The Shadow

Mrs. Darling screamed, and, as if in answer to a bell, the door opened, and Nana entered, returned from her evening out. She growled and sprang at the boy, who leapt lightly through the window. Again Mrs. Darling screamed, this time in distress for him, for she thought he was killed, and she ran down into the street to look for his little body, but it was not there; and she looked up, and in the black night she could see nothing but what she thought was a shooting star.

She returned to the nursery, and found Nana with something in her mouth, which proved to be the boy's shadow. As he leapt at the window Nana had closed it quickly, too late to catch him, but his shadow had not had time to get out; slam went the window and snapped it off.

You may be sure Mrs. Darling examined the shadow carefully, but it was quite the ordinary kind.

Nana had no doubt of what was the best thing to do with this shadow. She hung it out at the window, meaning "He is sure to come back for it; let us put it where he can get it easily without disturbing the children."

But unfortunately Mrs. Darling could not leave it hanging out at the window, it looked so like the washing and lowered the whole tone of the house. She thought of showing it to Mr. Darling, but he was totting up winter great-coats for John and Michael, with a wet towel around his head to keep his brain clear, and it seemed a shame to trouble him; besides, she knew exactly what he would say: "It all comes of having a dog for a nurse."

She decided to roll the shadow up and put it away carefully in a drawer, until a fitting opportunity came for telling her husband. Ah me!

The opportunity came a week later, on that never-to-be-forgotten Friday. Of course it was a Friday.

"I ought to have been specially careful on a Friday," she used to say afterwards to her husband, while perhaps Nana was on the other side of her, holding her hand.

"No, no," Mr. Darling always said, "I am responsible for it all. I, George Darling, did it. *Mea culpa, mea culpa.*" He had had a classical education.

They sat thus night after night recalling that fatal Friday, till every detail of it was stamped on their brains and came through on the other side like the faces on a bad coinage.

"If only I had not accepted that invitation to dine at 27," Mrs. Darling said.

"If only I had not poured my medicine into Nana's bowl," said Mr. Darling.

"If only I had pretended to like the medicine," was what Nana's wet eyes said.

"My liking for parties, George."

"My fatal gift of humour, dearest."

"My touchiness about trifles, dear master and mistress."

Then one or more of them would break down altogether; Nana at the thought, "It's true, it's true, they ought not to have had a dog for a nurse." Many a time it was Mr. Darling who put the handkerchief to Nana's eyes.

"That fiend!" Mr. Darling would cry, and Nana's bark was the echo of it, but Mrs. Darling never upbraided Peter; there was something in the right-hand corner of her mouth that wanted her not to call Peter names.

They would sit there in the empty nursery, recalling fondly every smallest detail of that dreadful evening. It had begun so uneventfully, so precisely like a hundred other evenings, with Nana putting on the water for Michael's bath and carrying him to it on her back.

"I won't go to bed," he had shouted, like one who still believed that he had the last word on the subject, "I won't, I won't. Nana, it isn't six o'clock yet. Oh dear, oh dear, I shan't love you any more, Nana. I tell you I won't be bathed, I won't, I won't!"

Then Mrs. Darling had come in, wearing her white evening-gown. She had dressed early because Wendy so loved to see her in her evening-gown, with the necklace George had given her. She was wearing Wendy's bracelet on her arm; she had asked for the loan of it. Wendy so loved to lend her bracelet to her mother.

She had found her two older children playing at being herself and father on the occasion of Wendy's birth, and John was saying:

"I am happy to inform you, Mrs. Darling, that you are now a mother," in just such a tone as Mr. Darling himself may have used on the real occasion.

Wendy had danced with joy, just as the real Mrs. Darling must have done.

Then John was born, with the extra pomp that he conceived due to the birth of a male, and Michael came from his bath to ask to be born also, but John said brutally that they did not want any more.

Michael had nearly cried. "Nobody wants me," he said, and of course the lady in the evening-dress could not stand that.

"I do," she said, "I so want a third child."

"Boy or girl?" asked Michael, not too hopefully.

"Boy."

Then he had leapt into her arms. Such a little thing for Mr. and Mrs.

Darling and Nana to recall now, but not so little if that was to be Michael's last night in the nursery.

They go on with their recollections.

"It was then that I rushed in like a tornado, wasn't it?" Mr. Darling would say, scorning himself; and indeed he had been like a tornado.

Perhaps there was some excuse for him. He, too, had been dressing for the party, and all had gone well with him until he came to his tie. It is an astounding thing to have to tell, but this man, though he knew about stocks and shares, had no real mastery of his tie. Sometimes the thing yielded to him without a contest, but there were occasions when it would have been better for the house if he had swallowed his pride and used a made-up tie.

This was such an occasion. He came rushing into the nursery with the crumpled little brute of a tie in his hand.

"Why, what is the matter, father dear?"

"Matter!" he yelled; he really yelled. "This tie, it will not tie." He became dangerously sarcastic. "Not round my neck! Round the bed-post! Oh yes, twenty times have I made it up round the bed-post, but round my neck, no! Oh dear no! begs to be excused!"

He thought Mrs. Darling was not sufficiently impressed, and he went on sternly, "I warn you of this, mother, that unless this tie is round my neck we don't go out to dinner to-night, and if I don't go out to dinner to-night, I never go to the office again, and if I don't go to the office again, you and I starve, and our children will be flung into the streets."

Even then Mrs. Darling was placid. "Let me try, dear," she said, and indeed that was what he had come to ask her to do, and with her nice cool hands she tied his tie for him, while the children stood around to see their fate decided. Some men would have resented her being able to do it so easily, but Mr. Darling had far too fine a nature for that; he thanked her carelessly, at once forgot his rage, and in another moment was dancing round the room with Michael on his back.

“How wildly we romped!” says Mrs. Darling now, recalling it.

“Our last romp!” Mr. Darling groaned.

“O George, do you remember Michael suddenly said to me, `How did you get to know me, mother?'”

“I remember!”

“They were rather sweet, don’t you think, George?”

“And they were ours, ours! and now they are gone.”

The romp had ended with the appearance of Nana, and most unluckily Mr. Darling collided against her, covering his trousers with hairs. They were not only new trousers, but they were the first he had ever had with braid on them, and he had had to bite his lip to prevent the tears coming. Of course Mrs. Darling brushed him, but he began to talk again about its being a mistake to have a dog for a nurse.

“George, Nana is a treasure.”

“No doubt, but I have an uneasy feeling at times that she looks upon the children as puppies.”

“Oh no, dear one, I feel sure she knows they have souls.”

“I wonder,” Mr. Darling said thoughtfully, “I wonder.” It was an opportunity, his wife felt, for telling him about the boy. At first he pooh-poohed the story, but he became thoughtful when she showed him the shadow.

“It is nobody I know,” he said, examining it carefully, “but it does look a scoundrel.”

“We were still discussing it, you remember,” says Mr. Darling, “when Nana came in with Michael’s medicine. You will never carry the bottle in your mouth again, Nana, and it is all my fault.”

Strong man though he was, there is no doubt that he had behaved rather foolishly over the medicine. If he had a weakness, it was for thinking that all his life he had taken medicine boldly, and so now, when Michael dodged the spoon in Nana's mouth, he had said reprovingly, "Be a man, Michael."

"Won't; won't!" Michael cried naughtily. Mrs. Darling left the room to get a chocolate for him, and Mr. Darling thought this showed want of firmness.

"Mother, don't pamper him," he called after her. "Michael, when I was your age I took medicine without a murmur. I said, `Thank you, kind parents, for giving me bottles to make we well.'"

He really thought this was true, and Wendy, who was now in her night-gown, believed it also, and she said, to encourage Michael, "That medicine you sometimes take, father, is much nastier, isn't it?"

"Ever so much nastier," Mr. Darling said bravely, "and I would take it now as an example to you, Michael, if I hadn't lost the bottle."

He had not exactly lost it; he had climbed in the dead of night to the top of the wardrobe and hidden it there. What he did not know was that the faithful Liza had found it, and put it back on his wash-stand.

"I know where it is, father," Wendy cried, always glad to be of service. "I'll bring it," and she was off before he could stop her. Immediately his spirits sank in the strangest way.

"John," he said, shuddering, "it's most beastly stuff. It's that nasty, sticky, sweet kind."

"It will soon be over, father," John said cheerily, and then in rushed Wendy with the medicine in a glass.

"I have been as quick as I could," she panted.

"You have been wonderfully quick," her father retorted, with a vindictive politeness that was quite thrown away upon her. "Michael first," he said doggedly.

"Father first," said Michael, who was of a suspicious nature.

"I shall be sick, you know," Mr. Darling said threateningly.

"Come on, father," said John.

"Hold your tongue, John," his father rapped out.

Wendy was quite puzzled. "I thought you took it quite easily, father."

"That is not the point," he retorted. "The point is, that there is more in my glass than in Michael's spoon." His proud heart was nearly bursting. "And it isn't fair; I would say it though it were with my last breath; it isn't fair."

"Father, I am waiting," said Michael coldly.

"It's all very well to say you are waiting; so am I waiting."

"Father's a cowardly custard."

"So are you a cowardly custard."

"I'm not frightened."

"Neither am I frightened."

"Well, then, take it."

"Well, then, you take it."

Wendy had a splendid idea. "Why not both take it at the same time?"

"Certainly," said Mr. Darling. "Are you ready, Michael?"

Wendy gave the words, one, two, three, and Michael took his medicine, but Mr. Darling slipped his behind his back.

There was a yell of rage from Michael, and "O father!" Wendy exclaimed.

"What do you mean by 'O father'?" Mr. Darling demanded. "Stop that row, Michael. I meant to take mine, but I – I missed it."

It was dreadful the way all the three were looking at him, just as if they did not admire him. "Look here, all of you," he said entreatingly, as soon as Nana had gone into the bathroom, "I have just thought of a splendid joke. I shall pour my medicine into Nana's bowl, and she will drink it, thinking it is milk!"

It was the colour of milk; but the children did not have their father's sense of humour, and they looked at him reproachfully as he poured the medicine into Nana's bowl. "What fun!" he said doubtfully, and they did not dare expose him when Mrs. Darling and Nana returned.

"Nana, good dog," he said, patting her, "I have put a little milk into your bowl, Nana."

Nana wagged her tail, ran to the medicine, and began lapping it. Then she gave Mr. Darling such a look, not an angry look: she showed him the great red tear that makes us so sorry for noble dogs, and crept into her kennel.

Mr. Darling was frightfully ashamed of himself, but he would not give in. In a horrid silence Mrs. Darling smelt the bowl. "O George," she said, "it's your medicine!"

"It was only a joke," he roared, while she comforted her boys, and Wendy hugged Nana. "Much good," he said bitterly, "my wearing myself to the bone trying to be funny in this house."

And still Wendy hugged Nana. "That's right," he shouted. "Coddle her! Nobody coddles me. Oh dear no! I am only the breadwinner, why should I be coddled – why, why, why!"

"George," Mrs. Darling entreated him, "not so loud; the servants will hear you." Somehow they had got into the way of calling Liza the servants.

"Let them!" he answered recklessly. "Bring in the whole world. But I refuse to allow that dog to lord it in my nursery for an hour longer."

The children wept, and Nana ran to him beseechingly, but he waved her back. He felt he was a strong man again. "In vain, in vain," he cried; "the proper place for you is the yard, and there you go to be tied up this instant."

"George, George," Mrs. Darling whispered, "remember what I

told you about that boy."

Alas, he would not listen. He was determined to show who was master in that house, and when commands would not draw Nana from the kennel, he lured her out of it with honeyed words, and seizing her roughly, dragged her from the nursery. He was ashamed of himself, and yet he did it. It was all owing to his too affectionate nature, which craved for admiration. When he had tied her up in the back-yard, the wretched father went and sat in the passage, with his knuckles to his eyes.

In the meantime Mrs. Darling had put the children to bed in unwonted silence and lit their night-lights. They could hear Nana barking, and John whimpered, "It is because he is chaining her up in the yard," but Wendy was wiser.

"That is not Nana's unhappy bark," she said, little guessing what was about to happen; "that is her bark when she smells danger."

Danger!

"Are you sure, Wendy?"

"Oh, yes."

Mrs. Darling quivered and went to the window. It was securely fastened. She looked out, and the night was peppered with stars. They were crowding round the house, as if curious to see what was to take place there, but she did not notice this, nor that one or two of the smaller ones winked at her. Yet a nameless fear clutched at her heart and made her cry, "Oh, how I wish that I wasn't going to a party to-night!"

Even Michael, already half asleep, knew that she was perturbed, and he asked, "Can anything harm us, mother, after the night- lights are lit?"

"Nothing, precious," she said; "they are the eyes a mother leaves behind her to guard her children."

She went from bed to bed singing enchantments over them, and little Michael flung his arms round her. "Mother," he cried, "I'm glad of you." They were the last words she was to hear from him for a long time.

No. 27 was only a few yards distant, but there had been a slight fall of snow, and Father and Mother Darling picked their way over it deftly not to soil their shoes. They were already the only persons in the street, and all the stars were watching them. Stars are beautiful, but they may not take an active part in anything, they must just look on for ever. It is a punishment put on them for something they did so long ago that no star now knows what it was. So the older ones have become glassy-eyed and seldom speak (winking is the star language), but the little ones still wonder. They are not really friendly to Peter, who had a mischievous way of stealing up behind them and trying to blow them out; but they are so fond of fun that they were on his side to-night, and anxious to get the grown-ups out of the way. So as soon as the door of 27 closed on Mr. and Mrs. Darling there was a commotion in the firmament, and the smallest of all the stars in the Milky Way screamed out:

"Now, Peter!"

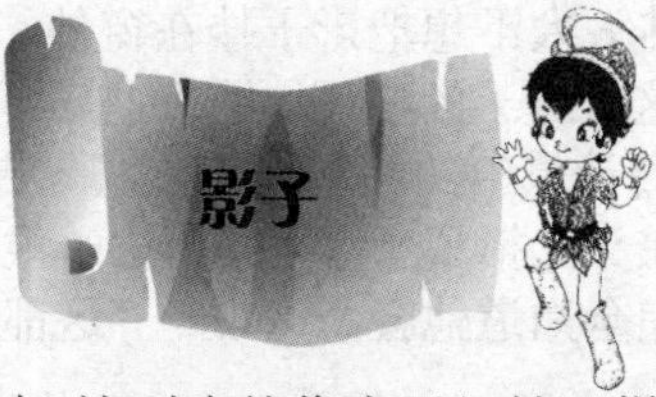

影子

达林太太尖叫了一声，这叫声就像应了门铃一样，房门打开了，娜娜冲了进来，她刚好散步回来。娜娜咆哮着跃向那个男孩，而他却轻盈地从窗口跳了出去。达林太太又尖叫了一声，不过这次是为那孩子担忧而叫，她以为这孩子摔死了，急忙跑到街上去寻找他的尸体，但是并没有找着。她抬头仰望天空，在这漆黑的夜里除了一点亮光，她什么也看不见，她还以为那是一颗流星呢。

当她回到育儿室，看见娜娜嘴里叼着什么东西，原来是那小男孩的影子。当他跳出窗子的时候，娜娜迅速地关上了窗户。不过动作太慢没能捉住他，可是他的影子还来不及跳出去，窗户砰的一声关上了，影子被扯了下来。

你也许会觉得达林太太肯定会仔细检查那个影子，不过它的确只是个非常普通的影子而已。

娜娜一定知道怎么妥当处置这个影子。她想把它挂在窗子外面，因为她觉得“彼得肯定会回来取走这影子的，就把它放在容易拿到而又不惊动孩子们的地方吧。”

但是，达林太太不想把影子挂在窗外，因为这看起来像是在晾衣服，会降低这所房子的格调。她想把影子给达林先生看看，不过达林先生正忙着计算给约翰和迈克尔买冬衣要花的钱；为了保持头脑清醒，他还在头上搭了条湿毛巾。这时候去打搅他似乎有点不太合适，况且她完全知道他会怎么说："这都是因为找了条狗来当保姆。"

达林太大决定把这影子卷成一团，小心地存放在抽屉里，等适当的时候再告诉她丈夫。我的天啊！

一个星期后机会真的来了。那是在一个令人永远无法忘怀的星期五，当然那天是星期五。

"星期五的时候我应该特别小心才对。"事后，她总是会对丈夫说这话，与此同时娜娜也在她的身边，握着她的手。

"不，不，"达林先生总是这么说，"所有事情都该由我负责，都是我乔治·达林干的。皆吾之过，皆吾之责任。"他曾受过古典文学的教育。

他们就这样坐着，夜夜回想着那个不幸的星期五，直到所有的细节都深深地烙进他们的脑子，就像劣质的钱币一样从另一面穿透过来。

"如果那天我没有接受二十七号会馆的晚宴邀请就好了。"达林太太说。

"如果那天我没有把我的药倒进娜娜的碗里就好了。"达林先生说。

"如果那天我假装爱喝那药水就好了。"娜娜的泪眼表达了她的意思。

"都怪我太爱参加舞会了，乔治。"

"都怪我那天的幽默感，亲爱的。"

"都怪我太爱计较了，亲爱的主人。"

于是他们当中的一个或几个便痛哭起来。娜娜心想："是啊，是啊，他们不该让一只狗当保姆。"达林先生一次次地用手帕给娜娜擦干眼泪。

"都是彼得·潘那个恶魔！"达林先生大声喊道，娜娜吠着与之呼应，可是达林太太从未责怪过彼得，因为她的右嘴角上有些什么东西不让她骂彼得。

他们坐在空荡荡的育儿室里，傻傻地回想着那个可怕的夜里所发生的事情的每一个微小细节。刚开始时，那天晚上就像其他无数个夜晚一样，非常平凡无奇，娜娜给迈克尔倒好了洗澡水，然后驮着他去洗澡。

“我不要睡觉，”迈克尔喊道，自以为这件事由他说了算，“我不睡，我不睡。娜娜，还没到六点呢。哎呀，我再也不爱你了，娜娜。我说了我不要洗澡，我不要洗嘛，我不要洗嘛！”

这时穿着白色晚礼服的达林太太走了进来。她很早就已经穿戴完毕，因为温迪非常喜欢看她穿晚礼服的样子，她脖子上戴着乔治送给她的项链，胳臂上戴着温迪的手镯——那是她向温迪借的，温迪也很愿意把她的手镯借给妈妈。

达林太太看见老大跟老二正在玩过家家，上演她自己和达林先生在温迪出生那天的情景。只听约翰在说：

“我很高兴地告诉你，达林太太，你当妈妈了。”那语调就好像达林先生真的在那个场合说过这句话似的。

温迪高兴地手舞足蹈起来，就像真正的达林太太肯定这么跳过似的。

接着约翰出生了，他的神情格外得意，他以为这是因为生了个男孩吧。这时，迈克尔洗完澡过来，也要求把他生下来，可是约翰蛮横地说，他们不想再生了。

迈克尔几乎快要哭出来了。“没人要我了，”他说，当然穿晚礼服的那位太太绝不会坐视不理。

“我要，”她说，“我多么想要第三个孩子啊。”

“要男孩还是女孩？”迈克尔问，他并没有太过期待。

“男孩。”

于是，他跳进妈妈的怀抱。现在回想起来，达林夫妇和娜娜都觉得，这不过是件小事；但如果想到这是迈克尔在育儿室的最后一夜，那就不算什么小事了。

他们继续回忆着。

“就在那时候，我像一阵旋风似的闯了进来，是不是？”达林先生自嘲道，当时他确实像一阵旋风。

也许他确实情有可原。那时他也正在为舞会穿衣打扮，一切都顺顺利利的，直到打领结的时候，他就卡在那儿了。这事儿说起来也确实让人讶异，达林先生虽然懂得股票和红利，却没办法摆平他的领结。有时候这玩意儿倒也是伏伏帖帖的屈从于他；但如果他能放下自己的自尊，戴上一个现成的领结，那这个家也会比现在好很多。

这次恰巧就碰上了这么个场合。达林先生手里捏着一条皱巴巴的混蛋小领结，急匆匆地冲进育儿室。

“哎呀，发生什么事儿了，亲爱的爸爸？”

“什么事！”他吼叫着，他确实是在狂吼。“这个领结，它系不上去。”他的语气变得非常讽刺，“在我的脖子上就系不上去！在床柱上就可以！是啊，我在床柱上已经成功二十次了，可是在我脖子上就是不行！哦，不要这样！求你饶了我吧！”

他觉得达林太太并没有特别在意他说的话，于是接着严厉地说道：“孩子他妈，我可警告你，除非这领结系在我的脖子上，要不然今晚我们就不去舞会了；如果我今晚没去参加晚宴，那我就再也不去上班了；如果我再也不去上班，你我就会饿死，我们的孩子就会流落街头。”

即便如此，达林太太还是十分镇定，“让我来试试吧，亲爱的。”她说。其实这正是达林先生跑来想让她做的事。达林太太用她那双灵巧的手给他系上了领带，与此同时孩子们都围在一旁，等待着他们的命运。就这么轻而易举地她就打好了领带，有些男人也许会因此而生气，不过达林先生天性就深明大义，对此并不在意。他随随便便对太太说了声谢谢，就平息了自己怒火，转眼之间，已经背着迈克尔在房里跳起舞来。

此刻，达林太太回想起那时的情景说道：“那时候我们玩得多带劲啊！”

“那是我们最后一次嬉闹了！”达林先生叹息着说。

“啊，乔治！你是否记得迈克尔某次突然问我：‘你是怎么认识我的，妈妈？’”

“我记得。”

“那时候他们真是可爱啊，对不对，乔治？”

“他们曾经是我们的，是我们的，可现在他们都不见了。”

那晚直到娜娜出现，他们才停止闹腾。非常不幸的是，达林先生撞在娜娜身上，裤子上粘满了狗毛。这不仅仅是一条新裤子，而且还是达林先生生平第一条带花边的裤子，因此他不得不咬着嘴唇，防止眼泪掉下来。当然，达林太太帮他刷干净了。可是，他又开始发牢骚，说用一只狗当保姆真是个错误。

“乔治，娜娜可是我们的宝贝。”

“没错，但有时候我会有点不自在，总觉得她把孩子们当小狗看待。”

“不会啊，亲爱的，我相信她知道他们是有灵魂的。”

“我怀疑，”达林先生深思熟虑后说道，“我很怀疑。”他的妻子觉得这是个机会，可以趁机把那小男孩的事告诉他。刚开始他对这个故事嗤之以鼻，但是当达林太太拿出影子给他看后，他就变得关切起来了。

“我不认识这个人啊，”他一边仔细端详着那个影子，一边说，“不过他看起来的确像个无赖。”

“你还记得吗，我们还在讨论的时候，”达林先生说，“娜娜带着迈克尔的药进来了。你以后再也不要用嘴去拿药瓶了，娜娜。这都是我的错啊。”

虽然他是个坚强的人，但在吃药这点上，他表现得的确非常愚蠢。如果他有什么弱点的话，那就是，他自以为他这一生吃起药来都很勇敢。因此，当迈克尔把头避开娜娜嘴里衔着的药匙时，他训斥道：“要像个男子汉，迈克尔。”

“我不要，我不要吃嘛。”迈克尔调皮地哭喊着。达林太太走出房间给他拿了块巧克力，达林先生觉得，这表现得还不够坚决。

“孩子他妈，不要太纵容他。”他在达林太太的后面喊道，“迈克尔，我像你这么大的时候，吃起药来可是一声不吭的，我会说：‘亲爱的爸爸妈妈，谢谢你们给我吃药，让我的病快点好转。’”

迈克尔信以为真，已经穿上睡衣的温迪也相信了这些话，为了鼓励迈克尔，她说："爸爸，你偶尔吃的那种药比这个还要难吃，是不是？"

"非常难吃，"达林先生勇敢地说，"如果我没有把那瓶药弄丢的话，迈克尔，我会立刻示范给你看。"

事实上，他并没有把药瓶子弄丢，只是在夜深人静的时候爬上衣橱，把它藏在那上面了。可他万万没想到，忠实的仆人莉莎找到了那只瓶子，又把它放回了盥洗台。

"我知道药瓶在哪里，爸爸，"温迪嚷嚷着，她总是乐意为别人效劳。"我去拿。"达林先生还没来得及阻止她，她就跑了出去。这时达林先生立马就莫名其妙地泄了气。

"约翰，"达林先生战战兢兢地说，"那玩意儿非常恶心，难吃死了，黏黏的，甜得要死。"

"很快就会没事的，爸爸。"约翰兴高采烈地说。这时，温迪拿着一杯药水，匆匆忙忙地跑了进来。

"我已经尽快地跑回来了。"她气喘吁吁地说。

"你真是出奇的快啊，"她爸爸恨恨地但又彬彬有礼地反驳道，"迈克尔，你先吃。"他固执地说。

"爸爸先吃。"迈克尔说，他生性就多疑。

"吃下去会不舒服的，你知道吗？"达林先生吓唬他说。

"快吃吧，爸爸。"约翰说。

"让我安静点，约翰。"他爸爸严厉地说道。

温迪感到非常困惑，"我还以为你会毫不费力地吃下去呢，爸爸。"

"这不是重点，"他反驳道，"重点是，我这杯子里的药比迈克尔匙子里的多很多。"他那颗饱含自尊的心几乎快要迸裂了。"这不公平，即便我只剩下最后一口气，我也要说，这不公平。"

"爸爸，我还等着你喝呢。"迈克尔冷冷地说道。

"你等着，你说得倒挺好，那我也等着。"

"爸爸是个胆小鬼。"

"那你也是个胆小鬼。"

“我才不怕。”

“我也不怕。”

“那好，喝下去。”

“那好，你喝。”

温迪想到一个绝妙的好方法：“为什么不两个一起喝呢？”

“当然可以，”达林先生说，“你准备好了吗，迈克尔？”

温迪数着，一，二，三，迈克尔喝下了他的药，可是达林先生却把药藏在他背后。

迈克尔愤怒地大叫着。温迪惊叫说：“噢，爸爸！”

“‘噢，爸爸’是什么意思？”达林先生质问道，“不许吵，迈克尔。我是想喝来着，可是我——我没喝着啊。”

三个孩子盯着达林先生，那种眼神真是可怕，就好像他们不再敬佩他似的。“你们都看这边，”当娜娜一走进浴室，达林先生就恳求他们说，“我刚刚想到一个很棒的鬼点子，我要把这杯药倒进娜娜的碗里，她会以为这是牛奶而把它喝掉的！”

药的颜色确实很像牛奶。不过孩子们并没有他们爸爸的那种幽默感，他们用责备的目光看着达林先生把药倒进娜娜的碗里。“多有意思啊。”达林先生含含糊糊地说。达林太太和娜娜回到房间以后，孩子们也不敢泄露秘密。

“娜娜，乖乖狗，”达林先生拍了拍她，说道，“我在你的碗里倒了一点牛奶，娜娜。”

娜娜摇着尾巴，跑了过去，舔了舔那碗药，然后给达林先生一个眼神，那眼神并不是愤怒，而是含着一滴又大又红的眼泪，这让我们为这条忠厚的狗感到难过。她爬进了狗窝。

达林先生感到非常羞愧，可是他并不想让步。在一阵令人害怕的沉默中，达林太太闻了闻那只碗。“噢，乔治，”她说，“这是你的药啊！”

正当达林太太安慰着两个男孩而温迪拥抱着娜娜时，达林先生大声喊叫道，“这只是个恶作剧而已。”“很好，”达林先生心酸地说，“我这样累死累活，还不是想让全家开心。”

温迪依旧抱着娜娜。“是啊，”达林先生叫喊着，“你们就宠着她吧！都没有人来爱我，一个都没有！我只不过是个养家糊口的人，为什么要有人来爱我呢！为什么，为什么，为什么！”

“乔治，”达林太太恳求他说，“别那么大声，佣人们会听到的。”不知为何，他们管莉莎叫佣人们，这已成了习惯。

“就让他们听见好了，”达林先生毫无顾忌地回答道，“让全世界的人都来听听吧。但是我不会再让那条狗在我的育儿室里作威作福了，一刻也不行。”

孩子们都哭了，娜娜跑到达林先生面前求情，可是他挥挥手让她走开。他觉得自己又是个坚强的男子汉了。“没有用的，一切都是徒劳，”他喊道，“院子比较适合你，到院子里去，我立马就把你拴起来。”

“乔治，乔治，”达林太太低声说道，“别忘了我跟你讲的关于那个男孩的事。”

唉，他听不进去了。他决定要看看谁才是这个家的主人。当他的命令无法将娜娜从狗窝里唤出来时，他就用甜言蜜语引诱她出来，然后粗暴地抓住她，把她拖出育儿室。他觉得挺惭愧的，但他还是这么做了。这一切都是因为他生性太重感情，渴望得到钦佩。当他把娜娜拴在后院之后，这个可怜的父亲就走到过道，坐在那里，用手掩住眼睛。

与此同时，达林太太在少有的寂静中哄着孩子们上床睡觉，点燃了夜灯。他们可以听到娜娜的吠声，约翰呜咽着说：“这都是因为爸爸把她拴在院子里。”可是温迪更聪明。

“那不是娜娜伤心时的吠声，”温迪说，并没有猜到将要发生什么事，“那是她闻到危险时的吠声。”

危险！

“你确定吗，温迪？”

“哦，当然。”

达林太太颤抖着走到窗前。窗户被死死地锁紧了。她看着屋外，夜空中繁星点点。这些星星全都聚集在这所房子周围，就像在好奇地想要看看那里将会发生什么事。但是她并没有注意到这些，也没有看到有一两颗小星星正对她使眼色。“唉，我多么希望今晚不用去参加舞会啊！”

即便是睡意朦胧的迈克尔也知道妈妈心有不安，他问：“妈妈，点着了夜灯，还有什么东西可以伤害到我们吗？”

“没有，宝贝，”她说，“夜灯是妈妈留下来守护孩子们的眼睛。”

达林太太走到每一张床前，给他们唱摇篮曲，小迈克尔张开双臂搂着她的脖子。“妈妈，”他叫道，“我爱你。”这是很长一段时间里她听到小迈克尔说的最后一句话。

二十七号公馆离他们家只有几步路，不过刚下了点小雪，为了不把鞋子弄脏，达林夫妇只好挑着路走。街上只剩下他们俩了，满天的繁星都注视着他们。星星很漂亮，可是它们无法参与任何事情，永远都只能做个旁观者。这是对它们的惩罚，因为很久以前它们做过错事。由于时间太过久远，如今已经没有一个星星知道到底是什么错事了。所以年长的星星们都变得目光呆滞，少言寡语（眨眼就是星星的语言），可是小星星们仍旧非常好奇。实际上它们对彼得并不是十分友好，因为他非常淘气，常常偷偷摸摸地走到它们背后，想要吹灭它们。但是它们太喜欢玩乐了，因此今晚都站在彼得这一边，恨不得把大人们都支开。所以当达林夫妇走进二十七号公馆，一关上门，天空就立刻骚动起来，银河里最小的那颗星星高声尖叫起来：

“开始啦，彼得！”

Chapter 3
第三章

Come Away, Come Away!

For a moment after Mr. and Mrs. Darling left the house the night-lights by the beds of the three children continued to burn clearly. They were awfully nice little night-lights, and one cannot help wishing that they could have kept awake to see Peter; but Wendy's light blinked and gave such a yawn that the other two yawned also, and before they could close their mouths all the three went out.

There was another light in the room now, a thousand times brighter than the night-lights, and in the time we have taken to say this, it had been in all the drawers in the nursery, looking for Peter's shadow, rummaged the wardrobe and turned every pocket inside out. It was not really a light; it made this light by flashing about so quickly, but when it came to rest for a second you saw it was a fairy, no longer than your hand, but still growing. It was a girl called Tinker Bell exquisitely gowned in a skeleton leaf, cut low and square, through which her figure could be seen to the best advantage. She was slightly inclined to *embonpoint*. (*plump hourglass figure*)

A moment after the fairy's entrance the window was blown open by the breathing of the little stars, and Peter dropped in. He had carried Tinker Bell part of the way, and his hand was still messy with the fairy dust.

"Tinker Bell," he called softly, after making sure that the children were asleep, "Tink, where are you?" She was in a jug for the moment, and liking it extremely; she had never been in a jug before.

"Oh, do come out of that jug, and tell me, do you know where they put my shadow?"

The loveliest tinkle as of golden bells answered him. It is the fairy language. You ordinary children can never hear it, but if you were to hear it you would know that you had heard it once before.

Tink said that the shadow was in the big box. She meant the chest of drawers, and Peter jumped at the drawers, scattering their contents to the floor with both hands, as kings toss ha'pence to the crowd. In a moment he had recovered his shadow, and in his delight he forgot that he had shut Tinker Bell up in the drawer.

If he thought at all, but I don't believe he ever thought, it was that he and his shadow, when brought near each other, would join like drops of water, and when they did not he was appalled. He tried to stick it on with soap from the bathroom, but that also failed. A shudder passed through Peter, and he sat on the floor and cried.

His sobs woke Wendy, and she sat up in bed. She was not alarmed to see a stranger crying on the nursery floor; she was only pleasantly interested.

"Boy," she said courteously, "why are you crying?"

Peter could be exceeding polite also, having learned the grand manner at fairy ceremonies, and he rose and bowed to her beautifully. She was much pleased, and bowed beautifully to him from the bed.

"What's your name?" he asked.

"Wendy Moira Angela Darling," she replied with some satisfaction. "What is your name?"

"Peter Pan."

She was already sure that he must be Peter, but it did seem a comparatively short name.

"Is that all?"

"Yes," he said rather sharply. He felt for the first time that it was a shortish name.

"I'm so sorry," said Wendy Moira Angela.

"It doesn't matter," Peter gulped.

She asked where he lived.

"Second to the right," said Peter, "and then straight on till morning."

"What a funny address!"

Peter had a sinking. For the first time he felt that perhaps it was a funny address.

"No, it isn't," he said.

"I mean," Wendy said nicely, remembering that she was hostess, "is that what they put on the letters?"

He wished she had not mentioned letters.

"Don't get any letters," he said contemptuously.

"But your mother gets letters?"

"Don't have a mother," he said. Not only had he no mother, but he had not the slightest desire to have one. He thought them very over-rated persons. Wendy, however, felt at once that she was in the presence of a tragedy.

"O Peter, no wonder you were crying," she said, and got out of bed and ran to him.

"I wasn't crying about mothers," he said rather indignantly. "I was crying because I can't get my shadow to stick on. Besides, I wasn't crying."

"It has come off?"

"Yes."

Then Wendy saw the shadow on the floor, looking so draggled, and she was frightfully sorry for Peter. "How awful!" she said, but she could not help smiling when she saw that he had been trying to stick it on with soap. How exactly like a boy!

Fortunately she knew at once what to do. "It must be sewn on," she said, just a little patronisingly.

"What's sewn?" he asked.

"You're dreadfully ignorant."

"No, I'm not."

But she was exulting in his ignorance. "I shall sew it on for you, my little man," she said, though he was tall as herself, and she got out her housewife (*sewing bag*), and sewed the shadow on to Peter's foot.

"I daresay it will hurt a little," she warned him.

"Oh, I shan't cry," said Peter, who was already of the opinion that he had never cried in his life. And he clenched his teeth and did not cry, and soon his shadow was behaving properly, though still a little creased.

"Perhaps I should have ironed it," Wendy said thoughtfully, but Peter, boylike, was indifferent to appearances, and he was now jumping about in the wildest glee. Alas, he had already forgotten that he owed his bliss to Wendy. He thought he had attached the shadow himself. "How clever I am!" he crowed rapturously, "oh, the cleverness of me!"

It is humiliating to have to confess that this conceit of Peter was one of his most fascinating qualities. To put it with brutal frankness, there never was a cockier boy.

But for the moment Wendy was shocked. "You conceit (*braggart*)," she exclaimed, with frightful sarcasm; "of course I did nothing!"

"You did a little," Peter said carelessly, and continued to dance.

"A little!" she replied with hauteur (*pride*). "if I am no use I can at least withdraw," and she sprang in the most dignified way into bed and covered her face with the blankets.

To induce her to look up he pretended to be going away, and when this failed he sat on the end of the bed and tapped her gently with his foot. "Wendy," he said, "don't withdraw. I can't help crowing, Wendy, when I'm pleased with myself." Still she would not look up, though she was listening eagerly. "Wendy," he continued, in a voice that no woman has ever yet been able to resist, "Wendy, one girl is more use than twenty boys."

Now Wendy was every inch a woman, though there were not very many inches, and she peeped out of the bed-clothes.

"Do you really think so, Peter?"

"Yes, I do."

"I think it's perfectly sweet of you," she declared, "and I'll get up again," and she sat with him on the side of the bed. She also said she would give him a kiss if he liked, but Peter did not know what she meant, and he held out his hand expectantly.

"Surely you know what a kiss is?" she asked, aghast.

"I shall know when you give it to me," he replied stiffly, and not to hurt his feeling she gave him a thimble.

"Now," said he, "shall I give you a kiss?" and she replied with a slight primness, "If you please." She made herself rather cheap by inclining her face toward him, but he merely dropped an acorn button into her hand, so she slowly returned her face to where it had been before, and said nicely that she would wear his kiss on the chain around her neck. It was lucky that she did put it on that chain, for it was afterwards to save her life.

When people in our set are introduced, it is customary for them to ask each other's age, and so Wendy, who always liked to do the correct thing, asked Peter how old he was. It was not really a happy question to ask him; it was like an examination paper that asks grammar, when what you want to be asked is Kings of England.

"I don't know," he replied uneasily, "but I am quite young." He really knew nothing about it, he had merely suspicions, but he said at a venture, "Wendy, I ran away the day I was born."

Wendy was quite surprised, but interested; and she indicated in the charming drawing-room manner, by a touch on her night-gown, that he could sit nearer her.

"It was because I heard father and mother," he explained in a low voice, "talking about what I was to be when I became a man." He was extraordinarily agitated now. "I don't want ever to be a man," he said with passion. "I want always to be a little boy and to have fun. So I ran away to Kensington Gardens and lived a long long time among the fairies."

She gave him a look of the most intense admiration, and he thought it was because he had run away, but it was really because he knew fairies. Wendy had lived such a home life that to know fairies struck her as quite delightful. She poured out questions about them, to his surprise, for they were rather a nuisance to him, getting in his way and so on, and indeed he sometimes had to give them a hiding (*spanking*). Still, he liked them on the whole, and he told her about the beginning of fairies.

"You see, Wendy, when the first baby laughed for the first time, its laugh broke into a thousand pieces, and they all went skipping about, and that was the beginning of fairies."

Tedious talk this, but being a stay-at-home she liked it.

"And so," he went on good-naturedly, "there ought to be one fairy for every boy and girl."

"Ought to be? Isn't there?"

"No. You see children know such a lot now, they soon don't believe in fairies, and every time a child says, `I don't believe in fairies,' there is a fairy somewhere that falls down dead."

Really, he thought they had now talked enough about fairies, and it struck him that Tinker Bell was keeping very quiet. "I can't think where she has gone to," he said, rising, and he called Tink by name. Wendy's heart went flutter with a sudden thrill.

"Peter," she cried, clutching him, "you don't mean to tell me that there is a fairy in this room!"

"She was here just now," he said a little impatiently. "You don't hear her, do you?" and they both listened.

"The only sound I hear," said Wendy, "is like a tinkle of bells."

"Well, that's Tink, that's the fairy language. I think I hear her too."

The sound come from the chest of drawers, and Peter made a merry face. No one could ever look quite so merry as Peter, and the loveliest of gurgles was his laugh. He had his first laugh still.

"Wendy," he whispered gleefully, "I do believe I shut her up in the drawer!"

He let poor Tink out of the drawer, and she flew about the nursery screaming with fury. "You shouldn't say such things," Peter retorted. "Of course I'm very sorry, but how could I know you were in the drawer?"

Wendy was not listening to him. "O Peter," she cried, "if she would only stand still and let me see her!"

"They hardly ever stand still," he said, but for one moment Wendy saw the romantic figure come to rest on the cuckoo clock. "O the lovely!" she cried, though Tink's face was still distorted with passion.

"Tink," said Peter amiably, "this lady says she wishes you were her fairy."

Tinker Bell answered insolently.

"What does she say, Peter?"

He had to translate. "She is not very polite. She says you are a great ugly girl, and that she is my fairy."

He tried to argue with Tink. "You know you can't be my fairy, Tink, because I am an gentleman and you are a lady."

To this Tink replied in these words, "You silly ass," and disappeared into the bathroom. "She is quite a common fairy," Peter explained apologetically, "she is called Tinker Bell because she mends the pots and kettles (*tinker = tin worker*)." (*Similar to "cinder" plus "elle" to get Cinderella*)

They were together in the armchair by this time, and Wendy plied him with more questions.

"If you don't live in Kensington Gardens now – "

"Sometimes I do still."

"But where do you live mostly now?"

"With the lost boys."

"Who are they?"

"They are the children who fall out of their perambulators when the nurse is looking the other way. If they are not claimed in seven days they are sent far away to the Neverland to defray expenses. I'm captain."

"What fun it must be!"

"Yes," said cunning Peter, "but we are rather lonely. You see we have no female companionship."

"Are none of the others girls?"

"Oh, no; girls, you know, are much too clever to fall out of their prams."

This flattered Wendy immensely. "I think," she said, "it is perfectly lovely the way you talk about girls; John there just despises us."

For reply Peter rose and kicked John out of bed, blankets and all;

one kick. This seemed to Wendy rather forward for a first meeting, and she told him with spirit that he was not captain in her house. However, John continued to sleep so placidly on the floor that she allowed him to remain there. “And I know you meant to be kind,” she said, relenting, “so you may give me a kiss.”

For the moment she had forgotten his ignorance about kisses. “I thought you would want it back,” he said a little bitterly, and offered to return her the thimble.

“Oh dear,” said the nice Wendy, “I don’t mean a kiss, I mean a thimble.”

“What’s that?”

“It’s like this.” She kissed him.

“Funny!” said Peter gravely. “Now shall I give you a thimble?”

“If you wish to,” said Wendy, keeping her head erect this time.

Peter thimbled her, and almost immediately she screeched. “What is it, Wendy?”

“It was exactly as if someone were pulling my hair.”

“That must have been Tink. I never knew her so naughty before.”

And indeed Tink was darting about again, using offensive language.

“She says she will do that to you, Wendy, every time I give you a thimble.”

“But why?”

“Why, Tink?”

Again Tink replied, “You silly ass.” Peter could not understand why, but Wendy understood, and she was just slightly disappointed when he admitted that he came to the nursery window not to see her but to listen to stories.

“You see, I don’t know any stories. None of the lost boys knows any stories.”

"How perfectly awful," Wendy said.

"Do you know," Peter asked "why swallows build in the eaves of houses? It is to listen to the stories. O Wendy, your mother was telling you such a lovely story."

"Which story was it?"

"About the prince who couldn't find the lady who wore the glass slipper."

"Peter," said Wendy excitedly, "that was Cinderella, and he found her, and they lived happily ever after."

Peter was so glad that he rose from the floor, where they had been sitting, and hurried to the window.

"Where are you going?" she cried with misgiving.

"To tell the other boys."

"Don't go, Peter," she entreated, "I know such lots of stories."

Those were her precise words, so there can be no denying that it was she who first tempted him.

He came back, and there was a greedy look in his eyes now which ought to have alarmed her, but did not.

"Oh, the stories I could tell to the boys!" she cried, and then Peter gripped her and began to draw her toward the window.

"Let me go!" she ordered him.

"Wendy, do come with me and tell the other boys."

Of course she was very pleased to be asked, but she said, "Oh dear, I can't. Think of mummy! Besides, I can't fly."

"I'll teach you."

"Oh, how lovely to fly."

"I'll teach you how to jump on the wind's back, and then away we go."

"Oo!" she exclaimed rapturously.

"Wendy, Wendy, when you are sleeping in your silly bed you

might be flying about with me saying funny things to the stars."

"Oo!"

"And, Wendy, there are mermaids."

"Mermaids! With tails?"

"Such long tails."

"Oh," cried Wendy, "to see a mermaid!"

He had become frightfully cunning. "Wendy," he said, "how we should all respect you."

She was wriggling her body in distress. It was quite as if she were trying to remain on the nursery floor.

But he had no pity for her.

"Wendy," he said, the sly one, "you could tuck us in at night."

"Oo!"

"None of us has ever been tucked in at night."

"Oo," and her arms went out to him.

"And you could darn our clothes, and make pockets for us. None of us has any pockets."

How could she resist. "Of course it's awfully fascinating!" she cried. "Peter, would you teach John and Michael to fly too?"

"If you like," he said indifferently, and she ran to John and Michael and shook them. "Wake up," she cried, "Peter Pan has come and he is to teach us to fly."

John rubbed his eyes. "Then I shall get up," he said. Of course he was on the floor already. "Hallo," he said, "I am up!"

Michael was up by this time also, looking as sharp as a knife with six blades and a saw, but Peter suddenly signed silence. Their faces assumed the awful craftiness of children listening for sounds from the grown-up world. All was as still as salt. Then everything was right. No, stop! Everything was wrong. Nana, who had been barking distressfully all the evening, was quiet now. It was her silence they had heard!

"Out with the light! Hide! Quick!" cried John, taking command for the only time throughout the whole adventure. And thus when Liza entered, holding Nana, the nursery seemed quite its old self, very dark, and you would have sworn you heard its three wicked inmates breathing angelically as they slept. They were really doing it artfully from behind the window curtains.

Liza was in a bad temper, for she was mixing the Christmas puddings in the kitchen, and had been drawn from them, with a raisin still on her cheek, by Nana's absurd suspicions. She thought the best way of getting a little quiet was to take Nana to the nursery for a moment, but in custody of course.

"There, you suspicious brute," she said, not sorry that Nana was in disgrace. "They are perfectly safe, aren't they? Every one of the little angels sound asleep in bed. Listen to their gentle breathing."

Here Michael, encouraged by his success, breathed so loudly that they were nearly detected. Nana knew that kind of breathing, and she tried to drag herself out of Liza's clutches.

But Liza was dense. "No more of it, Nana," she said sternly, pulling her out of the room. "I warn you if bark again I shall go straight for master and missus and bring them home from the party, and then, oh, won't master whip you, just."

She tied the unhappy dog up again, but do you think Nana ceased to bark? Bring master and missus home from the party? Why, that was just what she wanted. Do you think she cared whether she was whipped so long as her charges were safe? Unfortunately Liza returned to her puddings, and Nana, seeing that no help would come from her, strained and strained at the chain until at last she broke it. In another moment she had burst into the dining-room of 27 and flung up her paws to heaven, her most expressive way of making a communication. Mr. and Mrs. Darling knew at once that something terrible was happening in their nursery, and without a good-bye to their hostess they rushed into the street.

But it was now ten minutes since three scoundrels had been breathing behind the curtains, and Peter Pan can do a great deal in ten minutes.

We now return to the nursery.

"It's all right," John announced, emerging from his hiding-place. "I say, Peter, can you really fly?"

Instead of troubling to answer him Peter flew around the room, taking the mantelpiece on the way.

"How topping!" said John and Michael.

"How sweet!" cried Wendy.

"Yes, I'm sweet, oh, I am sweet!" said Peter, forgetting his manners again.

It looked delightfully easy, and they tried it first from the floor and then from the beds, but they always went down instead of up.

"I say, how do you do it?" asked John, rubbing his knee. He was quite a practical boy.

"You just think lovely wonderful thoughts," Peter explained, "and they lift you up in the air."

He showed them again.

"You're so nippy at it," John said, "couldn't you do it very slowly once?"

Peter did it both slowly and quickly. "I've got it now, Wendy!" cried John, but soon he found he had not. Not one of them could fly an inch, though even Michael was in words of two syllables, and Peter did not know A from Z.

Of course Peter had been trifling with them, for no one can fly unless the fairy dust has been blown on him. Fortunately, as we have mentioned, one of his hands was messy with it, and he blew some on each of them, with the most superb results.

"Now just wiggle your shoulders this way," he said, "and let go."

They were all on their beds, and gallant Michael let go first. He did not quite mean to let go, but he did it, and immediately he was borne across the room.

"I flewed!" he screamed while still in mid-air.

John let go and met Wendy near the bathroom.

"Oh, lovely!"

"Oh, ripping!"

"Look at me!"

"Look at me!"

"Look at me!"

They were not nearly so elegant as Peter, they could not help kicking a little, but their heads were bobbing against the ceiling, and there is almost nothing so delicious as that. Peter gave Wendy a hand at first, but had to desist, Tink was so indignant.

Up and down they went, and round and round. Heavenly was Wendy's word.

"I say," cried John, "why shouldn't we all go out!"

Of course it was to this that Peter had been luring them.

Michael was ready: he wanted to see how long it took him to do a billion miles. But Wendy hesitated.

"Mermaids!" said Peter again.

"Oo!"

"And there are pirates."

"Pirates," cried John, seizing his Sunday hat, "let us go at once!"

It was just at this moment that Mr. and Mrs. Darling hurried with Nana out of 27. They ran into the middle of the street to look up at the nursery window; and, yes, it was still shut, but the room was ablaze with light, and most heart-gripping sight of all, they could see in shadow on the curtain three little figures in night attire circling round and round, not on the floor but in the air.

Not three figures, four!

In a tremble they opened the street door. Mr. Darling would have rushed upstairs, but Mrs. Darling signed him to go softly. She even tried to make her heart go softly.

Will they reach the nursery in time? If so, how delightful for them, and we shall all breathe a sigh of relief, but there will be no story. On the other hand, if they are not in time, I solemnly promise that it will all come right in the end.

They would have reached the nursery in time had it not been that the little stars were watching them. Once again the stars blew the window open, and that smallest star of all called out:

"Cave, Peter!"

Then Peter knew that there was not a moment to lose. "Come," he cried imperiously, and soared out at once into the night, followed by John and Michael and Wendy.

Mr. and Mrs. Darling and Nana rushed into the nursery too late. The birds were flown.

走啦，走啦！

达林夫妇离开家门之后，那三个孩子床边的夜灯还一直明亮地照着。那是三盏非常精致的小夜灯，我们巴不得它们能一直醒着，这样就可以看见彼得了。但是温迪的灯眨了下眼睛，打了一个大大的哈欠，另外两盏夜灯也跟着打起了哈欠，还没等打完哈欠的嘴闭上，三盏灯就全都灭了。

此时房间里又出现了一个亮光，比夜灯还要亮一千倍。就在我们说到这儿的时候，那亮光已经翻遍了育儿室里所有的抽屉，寻找着彼得的影子，它在衣柜里乱翻一气，把每一件衣服的口袋都彻底翻了过来。其实它并不是什么亮光，只因为它飞得太快，看起来就一道亮光。可是当它停下来休息时，你会发现它是一个精灵，还没有手掌那么大，不过它还在长身体。她是一个叫叮叮铃的女精灵，身上裹着一片用干树叶做成的精致长袍，领口开得很低，呈四方形，恰到好处地展现了她的身段。她稍微有点丰满（有点像沙漏）。

精灵进来不久，窗户就被小星星们吹开了，彼得跳了进来。因为他带着叮叮铃走过一段路程，所以他的手上还沾着很多仙尘。

在他确定孩子们都睡着之后，就轻声地呼唤道："叮叮铃，你在哪儿？"此刻叮叮铃正在一只罐子里，她非常喜欢这地方，因为她从没有在罐子里呆过。

"唉，快从罐子里出来，告诉我，你知不知道他们把我的影子藏在哪儿啦？"

一个极其可爱的叮当声回答了他，那声音就像金铃一样清脆。这是精灵的语言，普通的小孩子是永远都听不到这种声音的；可是如果你听到过，那你就会知道，自己曾经听过一次。

叮叮铃说，影子在那只大箱子里，其实她指的是那只抽屉柜。彼得跳到抽屉跟前，两只手把里面的东西全都撒在地板上，就像国王向人群抛撒半便士的硬币一样。很快他就找到了自己的影子，他高兴极了，把叮叮铃被关在抽屉里的事都忘了。

如果他仔细想想——不过我相信他从来没有想过——当他和他的影子相互靠近的时候，就会像两滴水一样融合在一起。可是，他们并没有合在一起，这着实把他吓了一跳。他试着用浴室里的肥皂把影子粘上，但同样失败了。彼得浑身打了一个寒颤，坐在地板上哭了起来。

彼得的哭声把温迪给惊醒了，她坐了起来。当她看到一个陌生人坐在育儿室的地板上哭泣时，她并没有惊慌，只是觉得非常好奇。

“小男孩，”她亲切地说，“你为什么哭啊？”

彼得也非常有礼貌，因为他在精灵的庆典上学会了一些高贵的礼节。他站起来，非常绅士地向温迪鞠了一躬；温迪受宠若惊，也优雅地在床上回了一躬。

“你叫什么名字？”彼得问。

“温迪·莫伊拉·安琪拉·达林。”她颇为得意地回答道，“你叫什么名字？”

“彼得·潘。”

温迪已经肯定他就是彼得，不过，这名字还真是有点短。

“完了吗？”

“是啊。”彼得尖声回答她。他第一次觉得自己的名字很短。

“真可惜。”温迪·莫伊拉·安琪拉说。

“没关系。”彼得强忍着这口气。

温迪问他住在哪儿。

“第二个路口往右拐，”彼得说，“然后一直向前走，直到天亮。”

“这地址可真可笑！”

彼得有点失落。他第一次觉得这地名或许有点可笑。

“不，一点都不可笑。”他说。

“我的意思是说，”温迪想起自己是女主人，于是温柔地说：“难道他们在信封上就写这个地址吗？”

彼得宁愿她没提起信的事儿。

“我从来没收到过信。”他轻蔑地说。

“可是你妈妈也不收信吗？”

“我没有妈妈。”彼得说。他不但没有妈妈，而且压根儿就不想要什么妈妈。他觉得人们太看重这些妈妈们了。不过温迪立刻就想到，他肯定碰上什么悲惨的事情了。

“啊，彼得，难怪你会哭。”温迪说着跳下床跑到他面前。

“我又不是为了妈妈才哭的，”彼得颇为气愤地说道，“我是因为自己没法把影子粘上才哭的。再说，我也没在哭啊。”

“影子掉下来了吗？”

“是的。”

这时，温迪看到了地板上的影子，已经被拖得脏兮兮的，她为彼得感到非常难过。“真糟糕！”她说道。可是，当她看到彼得试着用肥皂粘影子时，又情不自禁地笑了起来，真是个不折不扣的小男孩啊。

幸亏她立刻就想到了办法。“一定要用针线缝上才行。”她带点小大人的口气说道。

“什么叫缝？”彼得问。

“你真是笨得要死啊。”

“不，我一点儿也不笨。”

不过，温迪就是喜欢他的傻样。虽然彼得和她一样高，但她还是说，“小家伙，我来帮你缝上吧。”她拿出自己的针线盒，把影子缝在彼得的脚上。

“我想会有点儿疼的。”她警告彼得说。

“啊，我不会哭的。”彼得说，他自以为他这辈子从来都没有哭过。他咬紧牙关，还真的没哭。很快，影子就缝补妥当了，不过还是有点皱褶。

“或许我应该把它熨一下。”温迪想了想说。可是，彼得跟别的男孩子一样，对外表一点儿都不在乎，此刻他正疯狂地笑着、跳

着。唉，他早已忘记，这快乐还得归功于温迪。他以为这影子是他自己粘上的。“我太聪明了，”他兴高采烈地大叫着，“啊，我多聪明啊！”

虽然这让人有点不好意思，但我们还是得承认，彼得的狂妄自大，正是他最惹人喜欢的地方。坦白讲，从没有见过像彼得这样骄傲的孩子。

不过，温迪顿时惊呆了。“你真是个自大狂，”她语带讽刺地尖叫着，“当然我也什么都没做！”

“你也是有点贡献的。”彼得一边毫不在乎地说着，一边继续跳舞。

“有点儿！”温迪傲慢地回敬他说，“就算我什么都没做，那我至少可以不理你吧。”她相当优雅地跳上床，用毯子蒙上脸。

彼得假装要离开的样子，想吸引温迪抬头，但并没有成功。于是他坐在床尾，用脚轻轻地踢她。“温迪，”他说，“别不理我呀，温迪，我只要一高兴，就会忍不住欢叫起来。”温迪仍旧没有抬头，尽管她非常热切地听着。“温迪，”彼得继续说道，那种语调没有哪个女孩子能抵抗得了，“温迪，我觉得一个女孩要比二十个男孩还管用。”

虽然温迪的身高不过几寸，但是她毕竟是个女孩子，因此还是忍不住从床单底下探出头来偷看。

“你真的这么想吗，彼得？”

“是啊，我真这么想。”

“觉得你实在是太可爱了，”温迪说，“我现在就起来。”她和彼得并排坐在床边。她还说，如果彼得愿意的话，她想给他一个吻；然而彼得并不知道她的意思，就满怀期待地伸出双手。

“你应该知道什么叫吻吧？”温迪惊讶地问道。

“把吻给我，我自然就知道了啊。”彼得固执地回答。为了不让他伤心，温迪就给了他一枚顶针。

彼得说：“那我可不可以也给你一个吻呢？”温迪面带拘谨地回答：“如果你愿意，那就请吧。”她迫不及待地把脸颊凑了过去。不过彼得只是把一粒橡子放在她的手上；于是温迪又慢慢地把脸缩

了回来，亲切地说，她要把他的吻拴在项链上，戴在脖子上。幸亏她真把橡子挂在了项链上，因为后来这东西救了她一命。

人们相互认识之后，总是会照例询问一下彼此的年龄。于是一向喜欢做对事的温迪就问彼得他几岁了。这个问题对他来说确实很不恰当，这就好像考试的时候，你希望试卷上考的是英国的国王，可是却考的是语法一样。

“我不知道，”彼得不安地回答说，“不过我还很小啊。”对此他的确一无所知，不过是猜想自己很小，可是他胡乱地说：“温迪，在我出生的那天就跑出来了。”

温迪感到非常惊讶，可是又觉得挺有意思的。于是她极其礼貌地碰了碰睡衣，暗示彼得可以坐近一些。

“因为我听见父母在谈论，”彼得轻声地解释道，“我将来长大以后要做一个什么样的人。”说到这里，他变得激动起来。“我永远都不想长大，”他激动地说，“我心快乐。于是我就逃到了肯辛顿公园，和精灵们在一起住了很久很久。”

温迪好不羡慕地看了他一眼，彼得以为她是在羡慕自己离家出走，其实是羡慕他认识精灵。温迪一天到晚窝在家里，在她看来，能认识精灵一定有趣至极。她问了一大堆关于精灵的问题，这让彼得感到很惊讶，因为对他来说，精灵们令人生厌，老是碍手碍脚等等。事实上，有时候他甚至得避开她们。不过，大体上说来，他还是喜欢她们的。他还跟温迪说起了精灵们的由来。

“你知道吗，温迪，当第一个婴儿第一次放声大笑的时候，那个笑声就裂开变成了成千上万个微笑，这些笑到处蹦来蹦去，那就是精灵们的起源。”

当然这话相当单调乏味，但是对于不爱出门的温迪来说，她很喜欢这个故事。

“所以，”彼得继续好脾气地说道，“每个男孩和女孩都应该有个精灵。”

“应该？真的吗？”

“不，你知道现在的孩子们懂得太多，很快他们就不再相信精灵。每次一有小孩子说‘我不相信精灵了’，就会有一个精灵在某个地方掉下来死掉了。”

其实此刻彼得觉得关于精灵的话题已经谈论得够多了，而且他忽然想起来叮叮铃一直没吭声。“不知道她去哪儿了。”彼得说着站起身来，叫着叮叮铃的名字，温迪的心突然兴奋得猛跳起来。

“彼得，”她紧紧抓着他，叫道，“你不会是想告诉我说这房间里有精灵吧！”

“刚才她还在这里呢，”彼得有点不耐烦地说道，“你听不到她的声音吧？”他们俩安静地听着。

温迪说：“我只听见叮叮当当的铃声。”

“没错，那就是叮叮铃，那是精灵的语言。我好像也听到了。”

声音是从抽屉柜里传出来的，彼得脸上乐开了花。没人可以像彼得那样拥有如此灿烂的笑容，最可爱的就是他那咯咯的笑声。他还保留着他那第一声笑。

“温迪，”彼得开心地轻声说道，“我想我肯定把她关在抽屉里了！”

他把可怜的叮叮铃从抽屉里放了出来，叮叮铃一边在育儿室里到处乱飞，一边还怒气冲冲地尖叫着：“你不该把那些事儿说出来。”彼得反驳道，“我真的很抱歉，可是我又怎么会知道你在抽屉里面呢？”

温迪并没有注意他说的话。“啊，彼得，”她叫道，“如果她能停下来让我看看她，那该有多棒啊！”

“她们精灵几乎从来不曾消停过。”彼得说。可是，有一刹那温迪看见那个神奇的小精灵停在一座布谷鸟钟上。“哦，真可爱啊！”她喊道，尽管叮叮铃的脸因为生气而依旧扭曲着。

“叮叮铃，”彼得亲切地说，“这位小姐说，她希望你来当她的精灵。”

叮叮铃非常傲慢无礼地回答了一声。

“她说了些什么，彼得？”温迪问。

彼得不得不当起翻译来：“她非常没礼貌。她说你是个十分丑陋的女孩，还说她是我的精灵。”

他跟叮叮铃争论：“叮叮铃，你知道你不能当我的精灵，因为我是一个男人，而你是一个女人。”

对于这话叮叮铃是这么回应的：“你这个愚蠢的家伙。”说完就飞进浴室里消失不见了。“她不过是个相当普通的精灵，”彼得怀有歉意地解释说，“之所以叫她叮叮铃，是因为她专门修理锅壶之类的东西。”

这时他们俩一起坐在同一把扶手椅上，温迪又缠着彼得问了很多问题。

“你现在是不是不住在肯辛顿公园了？”

“有时还是会住在那儿。”

“那你现在通常住在哪儿？”

“跟丢失的男孩们住在一起。”

“他们都是谁啊？”

“他们是在保姆不注意，看向别的地方时，从婴儿车里掉出来的小孩子。如果七天之内没人来认领的话，他们就会被送到遥远的梦幻岛，以节省开支，而我就是队长。”

“那一定很好玩！”

“对啊，”狡猾的彼得说，“不过我们非常孤单。你知道都没有女孩子陪我们。”

“孩子里面没女孩子吗？”

“唉，没有；你知道，女孩子都太聪明，根本不会从婴儿车里掉出来。”

这马屁拍得温迪心里美滋滋的。“我觉得，”她说，“你讲得太好了。那边那个约翰，他只会瞧不起我们女孩子。”

听到这里，彼得站了起来，一脚把约翰连人带毯踹下了床。温迪觉得，第一次见面就这样，未免太过鲁莽了，她厉声地对彼得说，他不是这房间里的队长。不过约翰仍旧在地板上安安稳稳地睡着，温迪也就由着他睡在地上。“我知道你是好意，”温迪有些后悔地说道，“你可以给我一个吻。”

此时温迪已经忘记彼得不知道什么是吻。“我就知道，你会把它要回去的。”彼得略带伤心地说着，拿出顶针想要还给她。

“唉，天啊！”善良的温迪说道，“我指的是吻，不是顶针。”

“什么是顶针？”

“就像这样。”温迪亲了他一下。

“真有意思！”彼得庄重地说，“那我现在可不可以给你一个顶针呢？”

“如果你想的话，当然可以。”温迪说，这一次她把头直起来了。

彼得给了她一个吻，几乎就在同时，她尖叫了一声。

“怎么了，温迪？”

“好像有人揪了一把我的头发。”

“那一定是叮叮铃，不过她以前从不这么淘气的。”

果然是叮叮铃在他们周围飞来飞去，嘴里还不停地说着令人气愤的话。

“温迪，她说只要我给你一个顶针，她就这么捉弄你一次。”

“可是为什么呢？”

“为什么，叮叮铃？”

叮叮铃再次回答道：“你这个笨蛋。”彼得还是不知道叮叮铃为什么这么做，可是温迪已经明白了。当彼得承认自己到育儿室窗口并不是看温迪，而是来听故事的时候，温迪感到有一点失望。

“你知道，我没听过什么故事。那些走丢的孩子没一个会讲故事的。”

“那真是糟糕透了。”温迪说。

“你知道燕子为什么会在屋檐下筑巢吗？”彼得问，“就是为了听故事。对了，温迪，那天你妈妈给你讲的那个故事真好听啊。”

“哪个故事？”

“说的是一个王子找不到那个穿玻璃鞋的姑娘。”

“彼得，”温迪兴奋地说，“那是灰姑娘，最后王子找到她了，他们永远幸福甜蜜地生活在一起。”

彼得听后高兴极了，从坐着的地板上跳了起来，急忙跑到窗口。

“你要去哪儿？”温迪疑惑地大声问道。

“去告诉其他男孩儿。”

“别走，彼得，”温迪央求道，“我还知道很多很多故事呢。”

她的的确确就是这么说的，因此，无可否认是她先勾引彼得的。

彼得走了回来，眼睛中闪烁着贪婪的目光，这目光本应该让温迪感到惊恐的，但她却一点儿也不害怕。

“啊，我可以讲很多故事给那些孩子们听！”温迪喊道。此时彼得一把抓住了她，想把她往窗口那边拉去。

“放开我！”温迪命令道。

“温迪，跟我走吧，去讲故事给那些孩子们听。”

温迪收到这个邀请自然感到非常高兴，可是她说：“哎呀，我不能去啊，我得替妈妈想想！况且，我又不会飞。”

“我可以教你。”

“啊，会飞是多么有趣啊。”

“我教你如何跳上风的背，然后我们就可以飞走了。”

“啊！”温迪欣喜若狂地呼喊着。

“温迪啊温迪，你何必要躺在那张无聊的床上睡觉呢，你可以跟我一块儿飞翔，跟星星们聊一聊有趣的事啊。”

“啊。”

“而且，温迪，那里还有美人鱼哦。”

“美人鱼？长着尾巴的那种吗？”

“那尾巴可长了。”

“啊，”温迪叫了起来，“看美人鱼喽！”

彼得变得极其狡猾，“温迪，”他说，“我们都会非常敬重你的。”

温迪苦恼地扭了扭身子，就好像在努力让自己留在育儿室的地板上一样。

可是彼得一点儿也不可怜她。

“温迪，”这个狡猾的家伙说，“到了晚上睡觉时候，你可以帮我们捂被子。”

“啊!”

“从没有人在晚上给我们捂过被子。”

“哎呀。”温迪伸出两手抱着他。

“你还可以给我们补衣服、缝口袋,我们的衣服都没有口袋。”

温迪怎么可能抗拒得了这种诱惑呢。“这一定非常有趣!”她喊道,“彼得,你能不能也教约翰和迈克尔飞呢?”

“只要你喜欢就行,”彼得毫不在意地说;于是温迪跑到约翰和迈克尔床前,把他们摇醒。“快起来,”她喊道,“彼得·潘来了,他要教我们飞。”

约翰揉了揉眼睛,说:“那我这就起来。”其实他早已经躺在地上了。“你好,”他说,“我起来了!”

这时候迈克尔也起来了,他精神抖擞,就像一把带六刃一锯的刀,不过彼得暗示他们安静一点。他们的脸上装出孩子般的充满敬畏的神情,仔细听着成人世界的声音。一切都显得非常平静。不,等一等!所有的事情都有些不正常,娜娜一整晚都在痛苦地吠着,可这时候却安静了下来,他们听不到娜娜的声音。

“把灯吹灭!藏起来!快!”约翰喊道。在整个冒险过程中,这是他惟一一次发号施令。因此,当莉莎牵着娜娜进来的时候,育儿室又恢复了原样,一片漆黑。你甚至可以发誓说,你听得见三个淘气的小主人睡觉时发出的天使般的呼吸声。其实,这声音是他们躲在窗帘后面巧妙地装出来的。

莉莎脸上还沾着一颗葡萄干,她非常生气,因为她正在厨房里做圣诞布丁,娜娜荒谬的猜疑让她不得不丢下布丁。她想,要想得到那一点点清静,最好带着娜娜去育儿室看看,不过当然是在她的看管之下才行。

“好了,你这个多疑的畜牲,”她说,一点都不替娜娜的失宠感到遗憾,“他们都很安全,不是吗?三个小天使都躺在床上睡得正香呢,听听他们轻柔的呼吸声吧。”

这时迈克尔受到自己成功的鼓舞,便更加大声地呼吸起来,害得他们差点儿被识破。娜娜认得出那种呼吸声,她想方设法要挣脱莉莎。

可是莉莎反应很迟钝。“不要再闹了，娜娜，”她一边严厉地呵斥着，一边把娜娜拽出了房间。“我警告你，如果你再叫，我立马就把先生太太从舞会上给请回来，那时候，哈哈，主人不拿鞭子抽你才怪。”

她把这只不幸的狗又拴了起来。可是，你真的觉得娜娜会怕么？把先生太太从舞会上请回家？这正是她求之不得的。只要她照看的孩子平安无事，你觉得她会在乎自己挨鞭子吗？不幸的是，莉莎又回去做她的布丁了。既然不能从她那儿得到什么帮助，娜娜就拼了命地拉扯锁链，到最后终于把锁链挣断了。转眼间的功夫，她就闯进了二十七号公馆的餐厅，举起她的两只爪子在空中猛挥。这是她最明白易懂的表达方式了。达林夫妇立即明白了，他家的育儿室里发生了一些可怕的事儿。还没来得及跟女主人告别，他们就冲进了街道。

但是此刻距离三个小坏蛋藏在窗帘后面假装呼吸，已经有十分钟了，在这十分钟的时间里，彼得·潘可以做很多事。

我们回过头来继续讲育儿室里的事。

“没事儿了，”约翰从藏身的地方走出来宣布道，“我说彼得，你真会飞吗？”

彼得并没有费口舌去回答他，而是绕着房间飞了起来，半路上还拿起了壁炉架。

“真棒！”约翰和迈克尔说。

“好帅啊！”温迪喊道。

“是啊，我多帅啊，我真是帅呆了！”彼得说着，又开始得意忘形起来。

看起来飞行好像很容易，他们先是在地板上尝试，接着又在床上试，但是一直都在往下掉，并没有升起来。

“说，你是怎么飞起来的？”约翰揉了揉他的膝盖，问道。他是个挺讲实干的男孩。

“只要想些奇妙有趣的念头，”彼得解释道，“它们就会把你升到空中。”

彼得又给他们表演了一次。

“你做得太快了，”约翰说，“能不能慢慢地再做一次？”

彼得就把快的慢的都做了一次。“我学会了，温迪！”约翰叫道，可是很快他就发现自己并没有学会。他们之中，没有一个能飞上一寸远的；尽管在识字方面，连迈克尔都能认两个音节的单字，彼得却连二十六个字母都不认得。

当然，彼得是在跟他们开玩笑，因为只有身上沾了仙尘，他们才能飞起来。前面已经说过，彼得的有一只手沾满了仙尘，他往每个人身上吹了一点，果真产生了奇妙的作用。

“现在，像我这样扭动你们的肩膀，”彼得说，“起飞！”

他们三个都站在床上，勇敢的迈克尔第一个起飞。其实他并没打算要起飞，但就这么一扭动，他就立刻飞过了房间。

“我会飞了！”他在半空中就尖叫了起来。

约翰也飞起来了，在浴室附近遇到了温迪。

“啊，真有意思！”

“啊，太棒啦！”

“快看我！”

“快看我！”

“瞧我的！”

他们都没有彼得飞得那么优雅，双腿还会不自觉地蹬几下，不过他们的脑袋已经可以碰到天花板了，没有什么能比这个更美妙的了。刚开始彼得还会伸手帮温迪一把，不过又不得不立即缩回来，因为叮叮铃已经非常愤怒了。

他们一上一下、一圈又一圈地飞着，照温迪所说，就像在天堂一样。

“我说，”约翰嚷道，“我们为什么不飞到外面去呢！”

这正是彼得想引诱他们做的事。

迈克尔已经准备好了，他想看看，飞十亿里路需要花多少时间，而温迪却还在犹豫。

“去看美人鱼啊！”彼得再一次说道。

“啊！”

“那里还有海盗呢。”

“海盗，”约翰喊着，一把抓起他的帽子，“立刻出发吧。”

就在这时候，达林夫妇带着娜娜冲出了二十七号公馆。他们来到街中央，抬头看着育儿室的窗户。还好，窗户还紧紧地关着，可是房间里却灯火通明。最让人心惊胆战的是，他们看见窗帘上有三个穿着睡衣的小身影转来转去，不是在地上，而是在半空中。

不是三个，是四个。

他们颤抖着推开临街的大门。达林先生本想健步冲上楼去，不过达林太太示意他放轻脚步，她甚至努力让自己的心跳得轻些。

他们会及时赶到育儿室吗？如果赶上了，他们该多高兴啊，我们也可以松一口气；但那样的话，就没故事可讲了。但是，即使他们没赶上，我也可以向大家郑重承诺，最终故事结局还是会大团圆。

如果没有那些星星监视着他们，他们就可以及时赶到育儿室了。星星们又一次吹开了窗户，其中最小的那颗星星大声喊道：

“快跑，彼得！”

彼得知道，没有时间可以浪费了。“走。”他专制地命令道，然后立刻飞进了夜空，约翰、迈克尔和温迪也紧随其后飞了出去。

达林夫妇和娜娜冲进育儿室的时候已经太迟了，鸟儿们已经飞走了。

Chapter 4
第四章

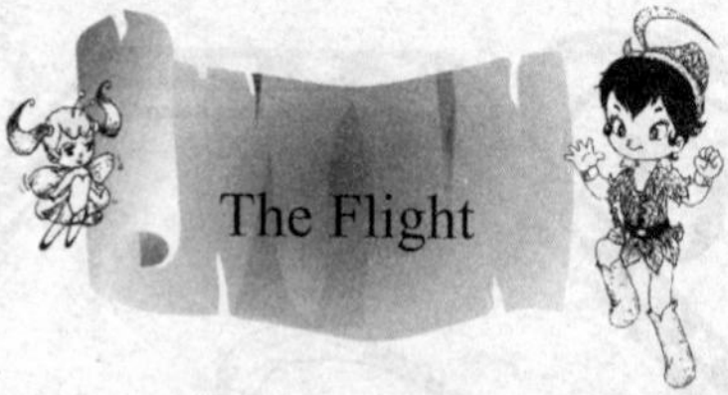

The Flight

"Second to the right, and straight on till morning."

That, Peter had told Wendy, was the way to the Neverland; but even birds, carrying maps and consulting them at windy corners, could not have sighted it with these instructions. Peter, you see, just said anything that came into his head.

At first his companions trusted him implicitly, and so great were the delights of flying that they wasted time circling round church spires or any other tall objects on the way that took their fancy.

John and Michael raced, Michael getting a start.

They recalled with contempt that not so long ago they had thought themselves fine fellows for being able to fly round a room.

Not long ago. But how long ago? They were flying over the sea before this thought began to disturb Wendy seriously. John thought it was their second sea and their third night.

Sometimes it was dark and sometimes light, and now they were very cold and again too warm. Did they really feel hungry at times, or were they merely pretending, because Peter had such a jolly new way of feeding them? His way was to pursue birds who had food in their mouths suitable for humans and snatch it from them; then the birds would follow and snatch it back; and they would all go chasing each other gaily for miles, parting at last with mutual expressions of good-will. But Wendy noticed with gentle concern that Peter did not seem to know that this was rather an odd way of getting your bread and butter, nor even that there are other ways.

Certainly they did not pretend to be sleepy, they were sleepy; and that was a danger, for the moment they popped off, down they fell. The awful thing was that Peter thought this funny.

"There he goes again!" he would cry gleefully, as Michael suddenly dropped like a stone.

"Save him, save him!" cried Wendy, looking with horror at the cruel sea far below. Eventually Peter would dive through the air, and catch Michael just before he could strike the sea, and it was lovely the way he did it; but he always waited till the last moment, and you felt it was his cleverness that interested him and not the saving of human life. Also he was fond of variety, and the sport that engrossed him one moment would suddenly cease to engage him, so there was always the possibility that the next time you fell he would let you go.

He could sleep in the air without falling, by merely lying on his back and floating, but this was, partly at least, because he was so light that if you got behind him and blew he went faster.

"Do be more polite to him," Wendy whispered to John, when they were playing "Follow my Leader."

"Then tell him to stop showing off," said John.

When playing Follow my Leader, Peter would fly close to the water and touch each shark's tail in passing, just as in the street you may run your finger along an iron railing. They could not follow him in this with much success, so perhaps it was rather like showing off, especially as he kept looking behind to see how many tails they missed.

"You must be nice to him," Wendy impressed on her brothers. "What could we do if he were to leave us!"

"We could go back," Michael said.

"How could we ever find our way back without him?"

"Well, then, we could go on," said John.

"That is the awful thing, John. We should have to go on, for we don't know how to stop."

This was true, Peter had forgotten to show them how to stop.

John said that if the worst came to the worst, all they had to do was to go straight on, for the world was round, and so in time they must come back to their own window.

"And who is to get food for us, John?"

"I nipped a bit out of that eagle's mouth pretty neatly, Wendy."

"After the twentieth try," Wendy reminded him. "And even though we became good a picking up food, see how we bump against clouds and things if he is not near to give us a hand."

Indeed they were constantly bumping. They could now fly strongly, though they still kicked far too much; but if they saw a cloud in front of them, the more they tried to avoid it, the more certainly did they bump into it. If Nana had been with them, she would have had a bandage round Michael's forehead by this time.

Peter was not with them for the moment, and they felt rather lonely up there by themselves. He could go so much faster than they that he would suddenly shoot out of sight, to have some adventure in which they had no share. He would come down laughing over something fearfully funny he had been saying to a star, but he had already forgotten what it was, or he would come up with mermaid scales still sticking to him, and yet not be able to say for certain what had been happening. It was really rather irritating to children who had never seen a mermaid.

"And if he forgets them so quickly," Wendy argued, "how can we expect that he will go on remembering us?"

Indeed, sometimes when he returned he did not remember them, at least not well. Wendy was sure of it. She saw recognition come into his eyes as he was about to pass them the time of day and go on; once even she had to call him by name.

"I'm Wendy," she said agitatedly.

He was very sorry. "I say, Wendy," he whispered to her, "always if you see me forgetting you, just keep on saying `I'm Wendy,' and then I'll remember."

Of course this was rather unsatisfactory. However, to make amends he showed them how to lie out flat on a strong wind that was going their way, and this was such a pleasant change that they tried it several times and found that they could sleep thus with security. Indeed they would have slept longer, but Peter tired quickly of sleeping, and soon he would cry in his captain voice, "We get off here." So with occasional tiffs, but on the whole rollicking, they drew near the Neverland; for after many moons they did reach it, and, what is more, they had been going pretty straight all the time, not perhaps so much owing to the guidance of Peter or Tink as because the island was looking for them. It is only thus that any one may sight those magic shores.

"There it is," said Peter calmly.

"Where, where?"

"Where all the arrows are pointing."

Indeed a million golden arrows were pointing it out to the children, all directed by their friend the sun, who wanted them to be sure of their way before leaving them for the night.

Wendy and John and Michael stood on tip-toe in the air to get their first sight of the island. Strange to say, they all recognized it at once, and until fear fell upon them they hailed it, not as something long dreamt of and seen at last, but as a familiar friend to whom they were returning home for the holidays.

"John, there's the lagoon!"

"Wendy, look at the turtles burying their eggs in the sand."

"I say, John, I see your flamingo with the broken leg!"

"Look, Michael, there's your cave!"

"John, what's that in the brushwood?"

"It's a wolf with her whelps. Wendy, I do believe that's your little whelp!"

"There's my boat, John, with her sides stove in!"

"No, it isn't. Why, we burned your boat."

"That's her, at any rate. I say, John, I see the smoke of the redskin camp!"

"Where? Show me, and I'll tell you by the way smoke curls whether they are on the war-path."

"There, just across the Mysterious River."

"I see now. Yes, they are on the war-path right enough."

Peter was a little annoyed with them for knowing so much, but if he wanted to lord it over them his triumph was at hand, for have I not told you that anon fear fell upon them?

It came as the arrows went, leaving the island in gloom.

In the old days at home the Neverland had always begun to look a little dark and threatening by bedtime. Then unexplored patches arose in it and spread, black shadows moved about in them, the roar of the beasts of prey was quite different now, and above all, you lost the certainty that you would win. You were quite glad that the night-lights were on. You even liked Nana to say that this was just the mantelpiece over here, and that the Neverland was all make-believe.

Of course the Neverland had been make-believe in those days, but it was real now, and there were no night-lights, and it was getting darker every moment, and where was Nana?

They had been flying apart, but they huddled close to Peter now. His careless manner had gone at last, his eyes were sparkling, and a tingle went through them every time they touched his body. They were now over the fearsome island, flying so low that sometimes a tree grazed their feet. Nothing horrid was visible in the air, yet their progress had become slow and laboured, exactly as if they were pushing their way through hostile forces. Sometimes they hung in the air until Peter had beaten on it with his fists.

"They don't want us to land," he explained.

"Who are they?" Wendy whispered, shuddering.

But he could not or would not say. Tinker Bell had been asleep on his shoulder, but now he wakened her and sent her on in front.

Sometimes he poised himself in the air, listening intently, with his hand to his ear, and again he would stare down with eyes so bright that they seemed to bore two holes to earth. Having done these things, he went on again.

His courage was almost appalling. "Would you like an adventure now," he said casually to John, "or would you like to have your tea first?"

Wendy said "tea first" quickly, and Michael pressed her hand in gratitude, but the braver John hesitated.

"What kind of adventure?" he asked cautiously.

"There's a pirate asleep in the pampas just beneath us," Peter told him. "If you like, we'll go down and kill him."

"I don't see him," John said after a long pause.

"I do."

"Suppose," John said, a little huskily, "he were to wake up."

Peter spoke indignantly. "You don't think I would kill him while he was sleeping! I would wake him first, and then kill him. That's the way I always do."

"I say! Do you kill many?"

"Tons."

John said "How ripping," but decided to have tea first. He asked if there were many pirates on the island just now, and Peter said he had never known so many.

"Who is captain now?"

"Hook," answered Peter, and his face became very stern as he said that hated word.

"Jas. Hook?"

"Ay."

Then indeed Michael began to cry, and even John could speak in gulps only, for they knew Hook's reputation.

"He was Blackbeard's bo'sun," John whispered huskily. "He is the worst of them all. He is the only man of whom Barbecue was afraid."

"That's him," said Peter.

"What is he like? Is he big?"

"He is not so big as he was."

"How do you mean?"

"I cut off a bit of him."

"You!"

"Yes, me," said Peter sharply.

"I wasn't meaning to be disrespectful."

"Oh, all right."

"But, I say, what bit?"

"His right hand."

"Then he can't fight now?"

"Oh, can't he just!"

"Left-hander?"

"He has an iron hook instead of a right hand, and he claws with it."

"Claws!"

"I say, John," said Peter.

"Yes."

"Say, 'Ay, ay, sir.'"

"Ay, ay, sir."

"There is one thing," Peter continued, "that every boy who serves under me has to promise, and so must you."

John paled.

"It is this, if we meet Hook in open fight, you must leave him to me."

"I promise," John said loyally.

For the moment they were feeling less eerie, because Tink was flying with them, and in her light they could distinguish each other. Unfortunately she could not fly so slowly as they, and so she had to go round and round them in a circle in which they moved as in a halo. Wendy quite liked it, until Peter pointed out the drawbacks.

"She tells me," he said, "that the pirates sighted us before the darkness came, and got Long Tom out."

"The big gun?"

"Yes. And of course they must see her light, and if they guess we are near it they are sure to let fly."

"Wendy!"

"John!"

"Michael!"

"Tell her to go away at once, Peter," the three cried simultaneously, but he refused.

"She thinks we have lost the way," he replied stiffly, "and she is rather frightened. You don't think I would send her away all by herself when she is frightened!"

For a moment the circle of light was broken, and something gave Peter a loving little pinch.

"Then tell her," Wendy begged, "to put out her light."

"She can't put it out. That is about the only thing fairies can't do. It just goes out of itself when she falls asleep, same as the stars."

"Then tell her to sleep at once," John almost ordered.

"She can't sleep except when she's sleepy. It is the only other thing fairies can't do."

"Seems to me," growled John, "these are the only two things worth doing."

Here he got a pinch, but not a loving one.

"If only one of us had a pocket," Peter said, "we could carry her in it." However, they had set off in such a hurry that there was not a pocket between the four of them.

He had a happy idea. John's hat!

Tink agreed to travel by hat if it was carried in the hand. John carried it, though she had hoped to be carried by Peter. Presently Wendy took the hat, because John said it struck against his knee as he flew; and this, as we shall see, led to mischief, for Tinker Bell hated to be under an obligation to Wendy.

In the black topper the light was completely hidden, and they flew on in silence. It was the stillest silence they had ever known, broken once by a distant lapping, which Peter explained was the wild beasts drinking at the ford, and again by a rasping sound that might have been the branches of trees rubbing together, but he said it was the redskins sharpening their knives.

Even these noises ceased. To Michael the loneliness was dreadful. "If only something would make a sound!" he cried.

As if in answer to his request, the air was rent by the most tremendous crash he had ever heard. The pirates had fired Long Tom at them.

The roar of it echoed through the mountains, and the echoes seemed to cry savagely, "Where are they, where are they, where are they?"

Thus sharply did the terrified three learn the difference between an island of make-believe and the same island come true.

When at last the heavens were steady again, John and Michael found themselves alone in the darkness. John was treading the air mechanically, and Michael without knowing how to float was floating.

"Are you shot?" John whispered tremulously.

"I haven't tried (myself out) yet," Michael whispered back.

We know now that no one had been hit. Peter, however, had been carried by the wind of the shot far out to sea, while Wendy was blown upwards with no companion but Tinker Bell.

It would have been well for Wendy if at that moment she had dropped the hat.

I don't know whether the idea came suddenly to Tink, or whether she had planned it on the way, but she at once popped out of the hat and began to lure Wendy to her destruction.

Tink was not all bad; or, rather, she was all bad just now, but, on the other hand, sometimes she was all good. Fairies have to be one thing or the other, because being so small they unfortunately have room for one feeling only at a time. They are, however, allowed to change, only it must be a complete change. At present she was full of jealousy of Wendy. What she said in her lovely tinkle Wendy could not of course understand, and I believe some of it was bad words, but it sounded kind, and she flew back and forward, plainly meaning "Follow me, and all will be well."

What else could poor Wendy do? She called to Peter and John and Michael, and got only mocking echoes in reply. She did not yet know that Tink hated her with the fierce hatred of a very woman. And so, bewildered, and now staggering in her flight, she followed Tink to her doo.

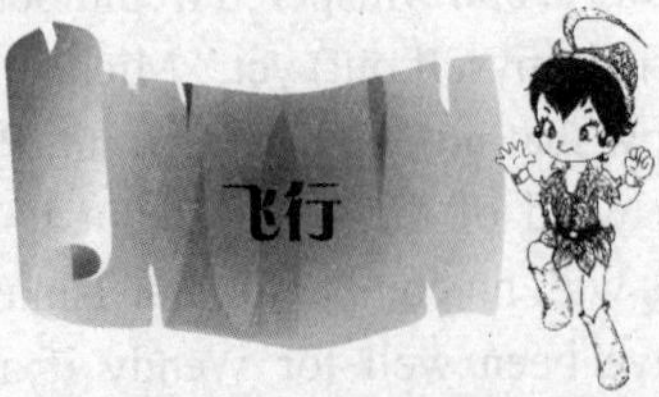

“第二个路口往右拐，然后一直向前走，直到天亮。”

这是彼得之前告诉温迪去梦幻岛的路，但即便是天上的鸟儿带着地图，按照上面每一个风角，按照每个指示也无法找到这个地方。你知道，彼得只是想到什么就随口说出来而已。

刚开始时，他的同伴们还对他深信不疑，而且飞行的乐趣如此美妙，以至于他们浪费了不少时间绕着礼拜堂的塔尖，或是绕着沿途中其他有趣的高耸的东西飞行。

约翰和迈克尔比赛谁飞得快，结果迈克尔领先。

不久前他们只不过能绕着房间飞就觉得自己非常了不起了，现在想想还真有点可笑。

不久前，但到底是多久之前呢？当他们飞跃一片大海之后，这个问题就开始让温迪心神不宁了。约翰以为这是他们飞过的第二片大海和第三个夜晚。

有时候天很黑，有时候天又很亮；有时候很冷，有时候又太热。也不知道有时候他们是真的饿了，还是假装饿了。因为彼得用一种非常有趣的方法给他们觅食——追逐那些嘴里叼着人能吃的东西的鸟类，从它们那里抢夺食物。然后那些鸟儿就会追上来，又把食物夺回去。他们就这样开开心心地相互追逐了好几里地；最后在相互表示友好之后告别对方。但是，善解人意的温迪发现，彼得似乎不知道这种觅食的方法有多怪异，也不知道还有其他觅食的办法。

当然他们不可能装出困倦的样子，他们是真的困了。在空中睡觉是很危险的，因为只要一打盹，就会掉下去。更可怕的是，彼得居然觉得这挺有意思的。

迈克尔突然像块石头似的往下掉时，彼得居然高兴地大喊道：“他又掉下去了！”

“救他，快救救他！”温迪呼喊道，惊恐地望着下面那片汹涌的大海。最后，在迈克尔就要掉进大海的一刹那，彼得从空中俯冲下来，一把抓住迈克尔。他这身手真是漂亮极了；不过他总要等到关键时刻才出手相救，你会觉得，他想要的只是卖弄他敏捷的身手，而不是为了救人。而且他的喜好变幻无常，这一阵他会全神贯注于某种乐趣，但过会儿他又会突然对此失去兴趣；因此下一次你往下掉时，他很有可能就不理你了。

彼得可以在空中睡觉而不往下掉，他只需仰卧着就能漂浮在半空中。这是因为他身子太轻了，如果你在他身后吹一口气，他就会漂得更快。

当他们在玩起“学头头”的游戏时，温迪低声对约翰耳语道：“对他礼貌点。”

“那你跟他说让他别再炫耀了。”约翰说。

原来在玩“学头头”的时候，彼得贴着水面飞行，与此同时，又顺便摸了摸每条鲨鱼的尾巴，就像你走在街上时，用手指滑过一根根铁栏杆一样。这一招他们是做不来的，因此，彼得像是在炫耀一样，特别是当他时不时回过头来张望，看看他们到底有多少条鲨鱼尾巴没摸到时。

“你们一定得对他好点儿，”温迪再三叮嘱弟弟们说，“如果他丢下我们不管了，那我们该怎么办啊？”

“我们可以回家啊。”迈克尔说。

“没有他，我们怎么找到回去的路呢？”

“那我们就继续往前飞。”约翰说。

“其实这才是最糟的，约翰。我们不得不一直往前飞，因为我们根本不知道怎么停下来。”

这倒是没错，彼得忘记告诉他们该怎样停下来了。

约翰说，如果这最最倒霉的事情真的发生了，他们只要一直往前飞就行，反正地球是圆的，总有一天他们会飞到自家的窗前。

“那谁给我们找吃的，约翰？”

“我可以干净利落地从老鹰嘴里夺一小块食物来，温迪。”

“那是你尝试了二十次之后才成功的，”温迪提醒他说，“就算我们顺利地找到食物，没有彼得在身边照应，我们就会撞上云彩或是其他什么的。”

确实不错，他们老是撞到东西。现在他们可以飞得稳稳当当了，尽管两腿还是蹬踢很多次；但是当看到前面有云朵时，他们越是想躲开它，就越是要撞上去。如果娜娜跟着他们，这时候她一定会在迈克尔的头上缠一条绷带。

这会儿彼得没和他们在一起，他们也觉得在天空中挺寂寞的。彼得可比他们飞得快多了，可以突然消失在眼前，来点冒险什么的，这可没他们的份。他会因为想起和某颗星星说过的有趣笑话而狂笑着俯冲下来；可是他已经忘记这笑话讲的是什么了。有时他又会从海里飞上来，身上还沾着美人鱼的鳞片，可是他又说不上来究竟发生了什么事。这对那些从没见过美人鱼的孩子们来说，确实让人气愤。

“如果他能那么快就把这些事忘记，”温迪说，“那我们怎么能指望他会一直记着我们呢？”

是啊，有时候他回来时真的不认识他们了，至少是认不大清了。温迪确信了这一点，白天在彼得正要超过他们时，她看到他眼里流露出辨认的神情。有一次，她甚至不得不喊出自己的名字才让他认出来。

“我是温迪。”她焦急地说。

彼得感到非常抱歉。“我说，温迪，”他对温迪轻声说道，“如果你发现我把你忘了，你只需一直说‘我是温迪’，我就会想起来了。”

当然，这事儿让他们觉得有点不满。不过，作为补偿，彼得教他们如何平躺在一阵与他们同向的狂风上。这变化着实让人兴奋，试了几次之后，他们发现这样就能安安稳稳地睡觉了。其实他们很想多睡一会儿，无奈彼得很快就不想睡了，立马用队长式的口吻喊道：“我们要在这儿着陆了。”这一路上尽管偶尔有些小争吵，可总的说来还是欢快的，他们终于快到梦幻岛了。经历了那么多个月，他们真的飞到了，自始自终他们都是笔直地向前飞行，这倒不完全是因为有彼得或是叮叮铃的带领，而是因为那些岛正期盼着他们的到来。只有这样，人们才能看见那些神奇的海岸。

“就在那儿。”彼得平静地说道。

“哪里，在哪里？”

“所有金箭所指着的地方。”

真的有一百万支金箭为孩子们指出了岛所在的位置。那些金箭都是他们的好朋友太阳照射出来的。在黑夜来临之前，太阳要让孩子们认清道路。

温迪、约翰还有迈克尔在空中踮着脚尖，想要看看这小岛。说来奇怪，他们都一下子就认出它来了；在还没害怕之前，他们冲它打起了招呼。他们觉得那岛并不像是梦想已久而终于见到的东西，而像是放假回家遇见的老朋友。

“约翰，那边有礁湖。”

“温迪，快看那些往沙堆里埋蛋的海龟。”

“约翰，我看见你那只断脚的火烈鸟了。”

“看，迈克尔，那是你的洞穴。”

“约翰，那灌木丛里是什么？”

“是一只狼，还有它的小狼崽。温迪，我肯定那就是你的小狼。”

“那是我的小船，约翰，船舷都破了。”

“不对，那不是你的船。我们早就把你的船烧掉了。”

“不管怎样，那就是我的船。约翰，我看见从印第安人帐篷里冒出来的烟了。”

“在哪儿？指给我看看，我可以告诉你，看这些烟怎么弯曲就能知道他们是不是要打仗了。”

“在那儿，刚好穿越了那条神秘河。”

“我看见了，没错，他们正准备出兵打仗呢。”

他们懂得太多了，这让彼得有点恼火。但是，如果他想在他们面前逞威风，那是唾手可得，因为，我前面不是已经说过，不久之后他们就会害怕起来了吗？

当金箭的消失使整个岛陷入黑暗的时候，恐惧也随之降临了。

以前在家的时候，每到睡觉时间，梦幻岛就开始变得黑暗吓人。岛上出现了一些未知的荒凉地带，慢慢扩张开来，黑影穿梭其中，野兽的吼声听起来也和从前大不一样了；最重要的是你失去了胜利的信心。当夜灯亮起的时候，你会非常开心。你甚至很愿意听娜娜说，那不过是壁炉罢了，梦幻岛只是他们的想像而已。

在家的时候，梦幻岛当然是想像出来的。但此时此刻它是真实的，这里没有夜灯，天也慢慢地越来越黑了，娜娜又在哪儿呢？

他们本来是散开飞的，现在却都紧紧挨在彼得身边。彼得那漠不关心的神态终于不见了，他的眼里闪烁着光芒。每次碰到彼得的身体，他们就会浑身颤抖。此刻他们正在那个恐怖岛屿的上空，飞得很低很低，以至于他们的脚会时常擦过树梢。天空中看不见什么阴森恐怖的东西，可是，他们却飞得越来越慢，越来越谨慎，就好像要防备什么敌人似的。有时他们还会停在半空中，等彼得用拳头敲打一番之后，才继续前进。

“他们不想让我们着陆。”彼得解释说。

“他们是谁？”温迪颤抖着小声说道。

可是彼得说不上来，或者是他不愿意说。叮叮铃已经在他肩上睡着了，不过又被他叫醒了，让她在前面飞。

有时候彼得会停在空中，把手放在耳边，专注地听着；然后又往下看，那目光亮得就好像要把地面钻两个洞似的。之后，他又接着向前飞去。

彼得的胆量真是惊人。“现在你是想先去冒险呢，”他漫不经心地对约翰说道，“还是想先吃茶点？”

温迪立即回答说“先吃茶点”，迈克尔感激地握了握她的手，可是，较为勇敢的约翰犹豫了。

“是什么样的冒险？”他慎重地问道。

“就在我们下面的这片草原上，睡着一个海盗，”彼得对他说，“如果你愿意，我们这就下去杀掉他。”

“我看不到他啊。”顿了半晌之后，约翰说。

“我看得到。”

约翰有点沙哑地说:“如果他醒了怎么办？”

彼得愤慨地说：“你以为我会趁他睡觉的时候杀死他吗！我要先把他叫醒，然后杀了他。我一直都是这么做的。”

“我说，你杀过很多人吗？”

“成吨成吨的。”

约翰说：“真厉害。”不过他还是决定先吃茶点。他问彼得现在这个岛上是不是有很多海盗。彼得说他从没见过有这么多海盗。

“现在谁是船长？”

“胡克。”彼得回答说，说到这个可憎的名字，他的脸都变得严肃起来。

“詹姆斯·胡克？”

“是。”

迈克尔一听，真的哭了起来，就连约翰也吓得说话直咽口水，因为他们早已听说了胡克的恶名。

“他是个黑胡子船长，”约翰沙哑地轻声说道，“是这群海盗里边最凶恶的一个，没有人不怕他的。”

“就是他。”彼得说。

“他长什么样？个子高大吗？”

“没有以前那么魁梧了。”

“这话什么意思？”

“我从他身上砍下了一块肉。”

“你？”

“对，就是我。”彼得厉声说道。

“我并没有冒犯的意思。”

“哦，没关系。”

“话说回来，你砍掉他哪了？”

“他的右手。”

“那他现在不能打架了吗？”

“还是照样能打啊！”

“用左手吗？”

“他用一只铁钩子代替右手，用铁钩子来抓人。”

“抓？”

“我说，约翰。”彼得说。

“怎么？”

“要说‘是，是，先生。’”

“是，是，先生。”

“有一件事得告诉你，”彼得继续说着，“凡是在我手下做事的孩子都必须对我发誓，所以你也一样。”

约翰吓得脸色苍白。

“这事儿就是：如果我们和胡克公开交战，那你一定要把他交给我来对付。”

“我保证。”约翰忠诚地说。

这时候他们已经不觉得那么害怕了，因为有叮叮铃跟着他们一起飞，在她亮光的照射下，他们可以看见彼此。但不幸的是，她没办法飞得和他们一样慢，因此她就得一圈一圈地绕着他们飞，他们就像是在光圈里行走一样。温迪很喜欢亮光，可是后来彼得指出了亮光的危害。

“叮叮铃告诉我，”彼得说，“在天黑之前海盗就发现了我们，他们已经把‘长汤姆’拖出来了。”

“是大炮吗？”

“没错。他们肯定看得见叮叮铃的亮光，如果他们猜到我们就在亮光的附近，一定会攻击我们的。”

“温迪！”

“约翰！”

“迈克尔！”

“快叫叮叮铃走开，彼得。”三个人异口同声地喊道，但是被彼得拒绝了。

“她以为我们迷路了，”彼得固执地回答道，“她吓坏了。你觉得我会在她害怕的时候把她赶走吗？”

忽然那一圈亮光灭了，有什么东西亲昵地捏了彼得一把。

“那你就告诉她，”温迪恳求道，“让她把光熄灭了。”

“可她没办法熄灭。那大概是精灵们惟一做不到的事情了。

等她睡着的时候亮光自然就熄灭，跟星星一样。”

“那就让她马上睡觉。”约翰几乎是在命令他。

“除非是她困了，否则她是睡不着的。这大概又是一件精灵们做不到的事了。”

“依我看，”约翰埋怨道，“也只有这两件事才值得做。”

话音刚落，他就被拧了一下，但不是亲昵的。

“如果我们谁有一个口袋就好了，”彼得说，“那就可以把她放在口袋里。”不过，他们出发时太过匆忙，四个人连一个口袋都没有。

彼得想出一个妙计：约翰的帽子。

叮叮铃同意呆在帽子里，只要这帽子拿在手里就行。帽子由约翰拿着，尽管叮叮铃希望让彼得来拿。这会儿，温迪接过了帽子，因为约翰说，在他飞的时候，帽子一直碰到他的膝盖。这样一来，可就有好戏看了，因为叮叮铃才不想领温迪的情。

亮光完全被黑帽子遮盖着，孩子们继续静悄悄地向前飞。这是他们这一生中经历过的最为安静的沉寂了。偶尔从远处传来舔食的声音，彼得说，那是野兽在河边喝水；后来又听到一种沙沙声，大概是树枝在风中相互摩擦吧，可是彼得说，那是印第安人在磨刀。

现在，就连这些声音也停止了。对迈克尔来说，这寂静太可怕了。“如果有点声音就好了！”他喊道。

刚一说完，空中就爆发了一声他从未听过的巨响，就像在回答他的请求似的。是海盗们向他们开炮了。

炮声在山谷中回荡着，那回声似乎在凶猛地嘶喊：“他们在哪儿？他们在哪儿？他们在哪儿？”

三个恐惧的孩子这才突然意识到，真实的岛和想像中的岛是多么不同。

天空终于再次平静了下来，此时约翰和迈克尔发现，黑暗之中只剩下他们两个。约翰机械地踩着空气，原本不知道如何漂浮的迈克尔竟也会漂浮了。

“你被击中了吗？”约翰畏惧地低声问道。

“我还不知道呢。”迈克尔轻声回答。

现在我们知道没有人被炮击中。但是，彼得被炮弹引起的狂风远远地吹到了海上，温迪被吹到了高空之中，只有叮叮铃在她身旁。

如果那时候温迪把帽子扔掉就好了。

不知道叮叮铃是突然想到，还是在路上早已盘算好，她立刻从帽子里钻出来，引诱温迪走向死亡。

叮叮铃并非十恶不赦，或者说，她只是在这一刻心肠恶毒。另有时她又会变得心地善良。精灵们不是这样就是那样，因为她们身体太小，以至于在同一时间，她们体内只能容下一种感情。她们可以改变自己的感情，然而，要改就得彻底改。此刻叮叮铃心里充满了对温迪的嫉妒。她说出的那种可爱的叮叮声，温迪肯定是听不懂的，不过我相信有些话一定很难听，虽然声音听起来很亲切。她来来回回地飞着，很明显是在告诉温迪，“跟我来，一切都会没事的”。

可怜的温迪还能怎么做呢？她呼喊着彼得、约翰还有迈克尔，听到的只是嘲笑自己的回声。至今她还不知道叮叮铃就像一个女人一样狠毒地嫉恨着她。她不知所措，晃晃悠悠地飞着，跟着叮叮铃走向死亡。

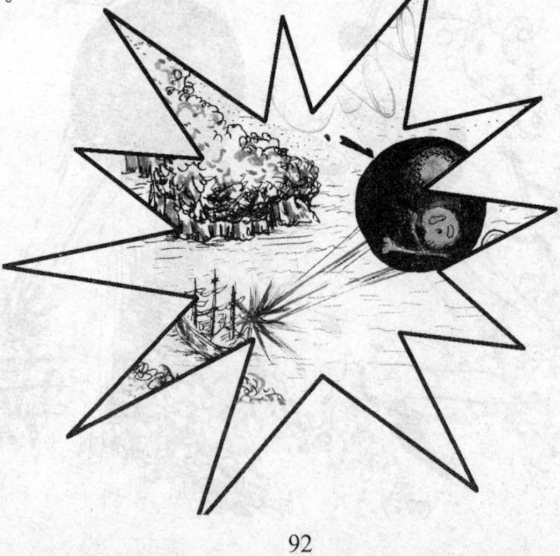

Chapter 5
第五章

The Island Come True

Feeling that Peter was on his way back, the Neverland had again woke into life. We ought to use the pluperfect and say wakened, but woke is better and was always used by Peter.

In his absence things are usually quiet on the island. The fairies take an hour longer in the morning, the beasts attend to their young, the redskins feed heavily for six days and nights, and when pirates and lost boys meet they merely bite their thumbs at each other. But with the coming of Peter, who hates lethargy, they are under way again: if you put your ear to the ground now, you would hear the whole island seething with life.

On this evening the chief forces of the island were disposed as follows. The lost boys were out looking for Peter, the pirates were out looking for the lost boys, the redskins were out looking for the pirates, and the beasts were out looking for the redskins. They were going round and round the island, but they did not meet because all were going at the same rate.

All wanted blood except the boys, who liked it as a rule, but to-night were out to greet their captain. The boys on the island vary, of course, in numbers, according as they get killed and so on; and when they seem to be growing up, which is against the rules, Peter thins them out; but at this time there were six of them, counting the twins as two. Let us pretend to lie here among the sugar-cane and watch them as they steal by in single file, each with his hand on his dagger.

They are forbidden by Peter to look in the least like him, and they wear the skins of the bears slain by themselves, in which they are so round and furry that when they fall they roll. They have therefore become very sure-footed.

The first to pass is Tootles, not the least brave but the most unfortunate of all that gallant band. He had been in fewer adventures than any of them, because the big things constantly happened just when he had stepped round the corner; all would be quiet, he would take the opportunity of going off to gather a few sticks for firewood, and then when he returned the others would be sweeping up the blood. This ill-luck had given a gentle melancholy to his countenance, but instead of souring his nature had sweetened it, so that he was quite the humblest of the boys. Poor kind Tootles, there is danger in the air for you to-night. Take care lest an adventure is now offered you, which, if accepted, will plunge you in deepest woe. Tootles, the fairy Tink, who is bent on mischief this night is looking for a tool (for doing her mischief), and she thinks you are the most easily tricked of the boys. 'Ware Tinker Bell'

Would that he could hear us, but we are not really on the island, and he passes by, biting his knuckles.

Next comes Nibs, the gay and debonair, followed by Slightly, who cuts whistles out of the trees and dances ecstatically to his own tunes. Slightly is the most conceited of the boys. He thinks he remembers the days before he was lost, with their manners and customs, and this has given his nose an offensive tilt. Curly is fourth; he is a pickle, (a person who gets in pickles-predicaments) and so often has he had to deliver up his person when Peter said sternly, "Stand forth the one who did this thing," that now at the command he stands forth automatically whether he has done it or not. Last come the Twins, who cannot be described because we should be sure to be describing the wrong one. Peter never quite knew what twins were, and his band were not allowed to know anything he did not know, so these two were always vague about themselves, and did their best to give satisfaction by keeping close together in an apologetic sort of way.

The boys vanish in the gloom, and after a pause, but not a long pause, for things go briskly on the island, come the pirates on their track. We hear them before they are seen, and it is always the same dreadful song:

> "Avast belay, yo ho, heave to,
> A-pirating we go,
> And if we're parted by a shot
> We're sure to meet below!"

A more villainous-looking lot never hung in a row on Execution dock. Here, a little in advance, ever and again with his head to the ground listening, his great arms bare, pieces of eight in his ears as ornaments, is the handsome Italian Cecco, who cut his name in letters of blood on the back of the governor of the prison at Gao. That gigantic black behind him has had many names since he dropped the one with which dusky mothers still terrify their children on the banks of the Guadjo-mo. Here is Bill Jukes, every inch of him tattooed, the same Bill Jukes who got six dozen on the walrus from Flint before he would drop the bag of moidores (Portuguese gold pieces); and Cookson, said to be Black Murphy's brother (but this was never proved), and Gentleman Starkey, once an usher in a public school and still dainty in his ways of killing; and Skylights (Morgan's Skylights); and the Irish bo'sun Smee, an oddly genial man who stabbed, so to speak, without offence, and was the only Non-conformist in Hook's crew; and Noodler, whose hands were fixed on backwards; and Robt. Mullins and Alf Mason and many another ruffian long known and feared on the Spanish Main.

In the midst of them, the blackest and largest in that dark setting, reclined James Hook, or as he wrote himself, Jas. Hook, of whom it is said he was the only man that the Sea-Cook feared. He lay at his ease in a rough chariot drawn and propelled by his men, and instead of a right hand he had the iron hook with which ever and anon he encouraged them to increase their pace. As dogs this terrible man treated and addressed them, and as dogs they obeyed him. In person he was cadaverous (dead looking) and blackavized (dark faced), and his hair was dressed in long curls, which at a little distance looked like black candles, and gave a singularly threatening expression to his handsome countenance. His eyes were of the blue of the forget-me-not, and of a profound melancholy, save when he was plunging his hook into you, at which time two red spots appeared in them and lit them up horribly. In manner, something of the grand seigneur still clung to him, so that he even ripped you up with an air, and I have been told that he was a raconteur (storyteller) of repute. He was never more sinister than when he was most polite, which is probably the truest test of breeding; and the elegance of his diction, even when he was swearing, no less than the distinction of his demeanour, showed him one of a different cast from his crew. A man of indomitable courage, it was said that the only thing he shied at was the sight of his own blood, which was thick and of an unusual colour. In dress he somewhat aped the attire associated with the name of Charles II, having heard it said in some earlier period of his career that he bore a strange resemblance to the ill-fated Stuarts; and in his mouth he had a holder of his own contrivance which enabled him to smoke two cigars at once. But undoubtedly the grimmest part of him was his iron claw.

Let us now kill a pirate, to show Hook's method. Skylights will do. As they pass, Skylights lurches clumsily against him, ruffling his lace collar; the hook shoots forth, there is a tearing sound and one screech, then the body is kicked aside, and the pirates pass on. He has not even taken the cigars from his mouth.

Such is the terrible man against whom Peter Pan is pitted. Which will win?

On the trail of the pirates, stealing noiselessly down the war-path, which is not visible to inexperienced eyes, come the redskins, every one of them with his eyes peeled. They carry tomahawks and knives, and their naked bodies gleam with paint and oil. Strung around them are scalps, of boys as well as of pirates, for these are the Piccaninny tribe, and not to be confused with the softer-hearted Delawares or the Hurons. In the van, on all fours, is Great Big Little Panther, a brave of so many scalps that in his present position they somewhat impede his progress. Bringing up the rear, the place of greatest danger, comes Tiger Lily, proudly erect, a princess in her own right. She is the most beautiful of dusky Dianas (Diana = goddess of the woods) and the belle of the Piccaninnies, coquettish (flirting), cold and amorous (loving) by turns; there is not a brave who would not have the wayward thing to wife, but she staves off the altar with a hatchet. Observe how they pass over fallen twigs without making the slightest noise. The only sound to be heard is their somewhat heavy breathing. The fact is that they are all a little fat just now after the heavy gorging, but in time they will work this off. For the moment, however, it constitutes their chief danger.

The redskins disappear as they have come like shadows, and soon their place is taken by the beasts, a great and motley procession: lions, tigers, bears, and the innumerable smaller savage things that flee from them, for every kind of beast, and, more particularly, all the man-eaters, live cheek by jowl on the favoured island. Their tongues are hanging out, they are hungry to-night.

When they have passed, comes the last figure of all, a gigantic crocodile. We shall see for whom she is looking presently.

The crocodile passes, but soon the boys appear again, for the procession must continue indefinitely until one of the parties stops or changes its pace. Then quickly they will be on top of each other.

All are keeping a sharp look-out in front, but none suspects that the danger may be creeping up from behind. This shows how real the island was.

The first to fall out of the moving circle was the boys. They flung themselves down on the sward (turf), close to their underground home.

“I do wish Peter would come back,” every one of them said nervously, though in height and still more in breadth they were all larger than their captain.

“I am the only one who is not afraid of the pirates,” Slightly said, in the tone that prevented his being a general favourite; but perhaps some distant sound disturbed him, for he added hastily, “but I wish he would come back, and tell us whether he has heard anything more about Cinderella.”

They talked of Cinderella, and Tootles was confident that his mother must have been very like her.

It was only in Peter’s absence that they could speak of mothers, the subject being forbidden by him as silly.

“All I remember about my mother,” Nibs told them, “is that she often said to my father, `Oh, how I wish I had a cheque-book of my own!’ I don’t know what a cheque-book is, but I should just love to give my mother one.”

While they talked they heard a distant sound. You or I, not being wild things of the woods, would have heard nothing, but they heard it, and it was the grim song:

"Yo ho, yo ho, the pirate life,
The flag o' skull and bones,
A merry hour, a hempen rope,
And hey for Davy Jones."

At once the lost boys – but where are they? They are no longer there. Rabbits could not have disappeared more quickly.

I will tell you where they are. With the exception of Nibs, who has darted away to reconnoitre (look around), they are already in their home under the ground, a very delightful residence of which we shall see a good deal presently. But how have they reached it? for there is no entrance to be seen, not so much as a large stone, which if rolled away, would disclose the mouth of a cave. Look closely, however, and you may note that there are here seven large trees, each with a hole in its hollow trunk as large as a boy. These are the seven entrances to the home under the ground, for which Hook has been searching in vain these many moons. Will he find it tonight?

As the pirates advanced, the quick eye of Starkey sighted Nibs disappearing through the wood, and at once his pistol flashed out. But an iron claw gripped his shoulder.

"Captain, let go!" he cried, writhing.

Now for the first time we hear the voice of Hook. It was a black voice. "Put back that pistol first," it said threateningly.

"It was one of those boys you hate. I could have shot him dead."

"Ay, and the sound would have brought Tiger Lily's redskins upon us. Do you want to lose your scalp?"

"Shall I after him, Captain," asked pathetic Smee, "and tickle him with Johnny Corkscrew?" Smee had pleasant names for everything, and his cutlass was Johnny Corkscrew, because he wiggled it in the wound. One could mention many lovable traits in Smee. For instance, after killing, it was his spectacles he wiped instead of his weapon.

"Johnny's a silent fellow," he reminded Hook.

"Not now, Smee," Hook said darkly. "He is only one, and I want to mischief all the seven. Scatter and look for them."

The pirates disappeared among the trees, and in a moment their Captain and Smee were alone. Hook heaved a heavy sigh, and I know not why it was, perhaps it was because of the soft beauty of the evening, but there came over him a desire to confide to his faithful bo'sun the story of his life. He spoke long and earnestly, but what it was all about Smee, who was rather stupid, did not know in the least.

Anon (later) he caught the word Peter.

"Most of all," Hook was saying passionately, "I want their captain, Peter Pan. 'Twas he cut off my arm." He brandished the hook threateningly. "I've waited long to shake his hand with this. Oh, I'll tear him!"

"And yet," said Smee, "I have often heard you say that hook was worth a score of hands, for combing the hair and other homely uses."

"Ay," the captain answered, "if I was a mother I would pray to have my children born with this instead of that," and he cast a look of pride upon his iron hand and one of scorn upon the other. Then again he frowned.

"Peter flung my arm," he said, wincing, "to a crocodile that happened to be passing by."

"I have often," said Smee, "noticed your strange dread of crocodiles."

"Not of crocodiles," Hook corrected him, "but of that one crocodile." He lowered his voice. "It liked my arm so much, Smee, that it has followed me ever since, from sea to sea and from land to land, licking its lips for the rest of me."

"In a way," said Smee, "it's sort of a compliment."

"I want no such compliments," Hook barked petulantly. "I want Peter Pan, who first gave the brute its taste for me."

He sat down on a large mushroom, and now there was a quiver in his voice. "Smee," he said huskily, "that crocodile would have had me before this, but by a lucky chance it swallowed a clock which goes tick tick inside it, and so before it can reach me I hear the tick and bolt." He laughed, but in a hollow way.

"Some day," said Smee, "the clock will run down, and then he'll get you."

Hook wetted his dry lips. "Ay," he said, "that's the fear that haunts me."

Since sitting down he had felt curiously warm. "Smee," he said, "this seat is hot." He jumped up. "Odds bobs, hammer and tongs I'm burning."

They examined the mushroom, which was of a size and solidity unknown on the mainland; they tried to pull it up, and it came away at once in their hands, for it had no root. Stranger still, smoke began at once to ascend. The pirates looked at each other. "A chimney!" they both exclaimed.

They had indeed discovered the chimney of the home under the ground. It was the custom of the boys to stop it with a mushroom when enemies were in the neighbourhood.

Not only smoke came out of it. There came also children's voices, for so safe did the boys feel in their hiding-place that they were gaily chattering. The pirates listened grimly, and then replaced the mushroom. They looked around them and noted the holes in the seven trees.

"Did you hear them say Peter Pan's from home?" Smee whispered, fidgeting with Johnny Corkscrew.

Hook nodded. He stood for a long time lost in thought, and at last a curdling smile lit up his swarthy face. Smee had been waiting for it. "Unrip your plan, captain," he cried eagerly.

"To return to the ship," Hook replied slowly through his teeth, "and cook a large rich cake of a jolly thickness with green sugar on it. There can be but one room below, for there is but one chimney. The silly moles had not the sense to see that they did not need a door apiece. That shows they have no mother. We will leave the cake on the shore of the Mermaids' Lagoon. These boys are always swimming about there, playing with the mermaids. They will find the cake and they will gobble it up, because, having no mother, they don't know how dangerous 'tis to eat rich damp cake." He burst into laughter, not hollow laughter now, but honest laughter. "Aha, they will die!"

Smee had listened with growing admiration.

"It's the wickedest, prettiest policy ever I heard of!" he cried, and in their exultation they danced and sang:

"Avast, belay, when I appear,
By fear they're overtook,
Nought's left upon your bones when you
Have shaken claws with Hook."

They began the verse, but they never finished it, for another sound broke in and stilled them. There was at first such a tiny sound that a leaf might have fallen on it and smothered it, but as it came nearer it was more distinct.

Tick tick tick tick!

Hook stood shuddering, one foot in the air.

"The crocodile!" he gasped, and bounded away, followed by his bo'sun.

It was indeed the crocodile. It had passed the redskins, who were now on the trail of the other pirates. It oozed on after Hook.

Once more the boys emerged into the open; but the dangers of the night were not yet over, for presently Nibs rushed breathless into their midst, pursued by a pack of wolves. The tongues of the pursuers were hanging out; the baying of them was horrible.

"Save me, save me!" cried Nibs, falling on the ground.

"But what can we do, what can we do?"

It was a high compliment to Peter that at that dire moment their thoughts turned to him.

"What would Peter do?" they cried simultaneously.

Almost in the same breath they cried, "Peter would look at them through his legs."

And then, "Let us do what Peter would do."

It is quite the most successful way of defying wolves, and as one boy they bent and looked through their legs. The next moment is the long one, but victory came quickly, for as the boys advanced upon them in the terrible attitude, the wolves dropped their tails and fled.

Now Nibs rose from the ground, and the others thought that his staring eyes still saw the wolves. But it was not wolves he saw.

"I have seen a wonderfuller thing," he cried, as they gathered round him eagerly. "A great white bird. It is flying this way."

"What kind of a bird, do you think?"

"I don't know," Nibs said, awestruck, "but it looks so weary, and as it flies it moans, 'Poor Wendy,'"

"Poor Wendy?"

"I remember," said Slightly instantly, "there are birds called Wendies."

"See, it comes!" cried Curly, pointing to Wendy in the heavens.

Wendy was now almost overhead, and they could hear her

plaintive cry. But more distinct came the shrill voice of Tinker Bell. The jealous fairy had now cast off all disguise of friendship, and was darting at her victim from every direction, pinching savagely each time she touched.

"Hullo, Tink," cried the wondering boys.

Tink's reply rang out: "Peter wants you to shoot the Wendy."

It was not in their nature to question when Peter ordered. "Let us do what Peter wishes!" cried the simple boys. "Quick, bows and arrows!"

All but Tootles popped down their trees. He had a bow and arrow with him, and Tink noted it, and rubbed her little hands.

"Quick, Tootles, quick," she screamed. "Peter will be so pleased."

Tootles excitedly fitted the arrow to his bow. "Out of the way, Tink," he shouted, and then he fired, and Wendy fluttered to the ground with an arrow in her breast.

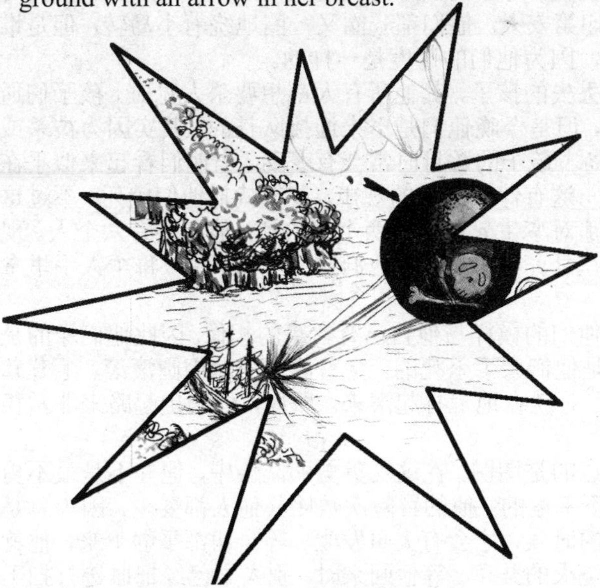

来到了真正的岛

梦幻岛察觉到彼得已经在回来的途中，便苏醒过来，重新焕发出生机。我们应该说它已经被唤醒了，但是说“苏醒”更好，而且彼得也常常这么说。

彼得不在的时候，岛上通常会非常清静。早上精灵们偷懒会多睡一小时，野兽们照看着自己的幼崽，印第安人们大吃大喝了整整六天六夜，当海盗和遗失的孩子们相遇时，他们只是咬着大拇指，相互看着对方。可是讨厌死气沉沉的彼得一回来，他们又全都活跃起来。如果此时你把耳朵贴在地上，你就会听到整个岛都在沸腾。

这天晚上，岛上的中坚力量在进行着下面这些活动：丢失的孩子们出来寻找彼得，海盗们出来寻找遗失的孩子，印第安人寻找海盗，野兽寻找印第安人。他们都一圈又一圈地绕着小岛转，但是谁也没有追上谁，因为他们的速度是一样的。

除了那些丢失的孩子，其他所有人都想要杀人见血。孩子们通常都爱看流血，但是今晚他们是出来迎接队长的。其实因为被杀或是其他原因，岛上孩子的数目时常会有变动。当他们看起来似乎在长大的时候——这有悖于岛上的规矩，彼得就把他们饿死。不过这个时候如果把那对孪生兄弟算为两个人的话，他们共有六个人。现在假设我们趴在甘蔗林里，偷看他们排成一列纵队，每个人手里拿着匕首。

彼得禁止他们的模样与他自己有丝毫的相像。因此他们穿的是熊皮，那熊还是他们亲手杀死的。穿着熊皮的他们圆滚滚、毛茸茸的，如果跌倒了，就在地上打起滚来。所以，他们走起路来非常稳健。

第一个经过的是图图。在这支英勇的队伍中，他并不是最不勇敢的，而是最不幸运的。他的冒险次数比其他人都要少，因为总是等他走过拐角的时候，才会有大事发生。等一切都平静下来，他就趁机走开找点烧火的柴草。等他回来时，别人早已经把血迹打扫干净了。这种霉运使得他总是面带忧郁；但是他的性格并没有因此变坏，反而变得更可爱了，因此他是这些孩子中最谦虚的一个。可怜又善良的图图，今晚有危险在等着你啊。千万要当心，否则冒险的事儿就要落在你头上了。如果你接受这个冒险，你就会陷入最为沉痛的悲哀之中。图图，今天晚上精灵叮叮铃一心想捣乱，正在找人当杀人工具呢，她认为你是这些孩子当中最容易上当的一个。要提防叮叮铃啊！

但愿图图能听见我们的话，不过我们并不在岛上，他咬着手指头走了过去。

第二个走过来的是尼布斯，活泼且温文尔雅，后面跟着斯莱特利，他把树枝削成哨子，和着自己吹的曲子跳起舞来。斯莱特利是这些孩子中最自以为是的一个，他总认为自己还记得走失前的事，还有那些礼节与习俗，所以他的鼻子总向上翘着，让人讨厌。第四个是卷毛，他是个顽皮的孩子。每当彼得厉声说“这是谁干的，站出来”时，他总是不得不站出来。因此现在一听到这个命令，他就自动站出来，也不管自己有没有做过。走在最后的是一对孪生兄弟，我们无法形容他们，因为我们肯定会把他们两个搞错。彼得从不知道什么叫双胞胎，而且只要是他不知道的事，他的队员也不许知道。所以，这对双胞胎自己也是糊里糊涂的，他们不得不惭愧地靠在一起，努力让别人感到满意。

孩子们消失在黑暗之中，一段时间过后，并不是很长时间，因为岛上的事都发生得非常快，一群海盗跟踪而来。我们在看到他们以前，就听到了他们的歌声，而且他们总是唱着那首骇人的歌：

系上缆绳，唷嗬，抛锚停船，
我们去抢劫！
即使炮弹将我们打散，
我们注定会在深深的海底重逢！

即便在绞架上也从未见过如此凶神恶煞的一群海盗。稍稍走在前头的是帅气的意大利人切科，他时不时地把头贴在地上听着什么。两条强壮的胳膊赤裸着，耳朵上挂着两枚西班牙古银币作为装饰。在加奥的监狱里，他曾用刀在监狱长的背上刻下他自己的名字。走在切科后面的是一名彪悍的黑人，在加若木河沿岸，那些坏心肠的母亲仍用他的名字来吓唬孩子们。自从他抛弃这个名字之后，他又用了很多名字。这位叫比尔·鸠克斯，浑身上下都刺满了文身，就是那个在海象号船上被弗林特砍了七十二刀才丢下金币袋的那个比尔·鸠克斯。还有库克森，据说是黑墨菲的弟弟（不过这点从未被证实过）。还有绅士斯塔奇，他曾是一所公立学校的助教，现在杀起人来依旧是文质彬彬的。还有“天窗”（摩根的“天窗”）。还有爱尔兰水手长斯密，他是个非常和气的人，可以说就算他捅人家一刀，也不会得罪人家；在胡克的海盗群体里边，他是惟一一个不信国教的人。还有努得勒，他的手总是放在背后。还有罗伯特·木林斯和阿尔夫·梅森，以及其他许多在西班牙的国土上臭名昭著，人人畏惧的恶棍。

在他们这群恶贯满盈的海盗之中，最邪恶、最粗暴的当然要数詹姆斯·胡克了。他自己把名字写成詹·胡克，据说，他是惟一一个能让海上库克害怕的人。胡克安逸地躺在一辆简陋的战车上，由他的手下推着向前走。胡克没有右手，而是装了一只铁钩来代替。他时不时地挥动着铁钩，催促他的手下加快点速度。这个可憎的家伙像狗一样看待他们、使唤他们，而他们也像狗一样顺从他。关于相貌，他的脸色铁青，头发长而卷曲，远远看去活像一支支黑蜡烛，他那俊俏的五官显现出一种异乎寻常的凶狠神情。除了他用铁钩向你捅来，他眼睛里会出现两点如同熊熊火焰的红光的时候，他的眼睛像勿忘我花一样蓝，眼神中透露着一种深邃的忧郁。至于行为举止，他身上还残留着某种贵族的气派，因此他那种跋扈的气势也能将你撕成碎片。我还听说他以前出了名地会讲故事。他最温文儒雅的时候，也正是他最阴险狠毒的时候，这也许就是他具有贵族血统的最确凿证据吧。即便在他下诅咒时，那高雅的措辞也正如他显赫的举止一样，显示了他和他的水手们的阶层差异。胡克这个人性格不屈不挠、无所畏惧。据说，惟一让他惧怕的就是看到自己的血。他的血很浓，颜色与众不同。说到穿着，他有点儿在模仿查理二世。因为在他年轻的时候他听别人说自己长得很像那位倒霉的斯图亚特国王。他的嘴里叼着一根他自己发明的烟斗，那烟斗可以让他同时吸两支雪茄。他身上最令人生畏的无疑就是那只铁爪了。

现在让我们拿一个海盗做示范，看看胡克是怎么杀人的，就拿天窗来说吧。在海盗们行进的时候，天窗步履蹒跚、笨手笨脚地凑到了胡克跟前，摸了摸他那镶边的衣领。胡克的铁钩伸了出来，只听见嘶的一声，接着就是一声惨叫，随后天窗的尸体被踢到了一边，海盗们继续前进。胡克甚至都没把雪茄从嘴里拿下来。

彼得·潘要面对的就是这样一个可怕的人。谁会赢呢？

紧跟在海盗后面，悄无声息地行走的便是印第安人。对于缺乏经验的眼睛来说，这条小径是很难被觉察到的，他们个个都把眼睛睁得大大的。手持战斧和匕首，赤裸的身体上涂满了油彩，闪闪发亮。身上挂着成串的战利品，有小孩的，也有海盗的。因为这些印第安人属于野蛮部落，和那些心肠较好的印第安人族群大不相同。冲在最前方匍匐前进的是伟大的小豹子，他是一名骁将，身上挂满了战利品，在爬行时，这些东西多少有些阻碍他的前行。走在最后处于最危险位置的便是骄傲地站立着的虎莲公主，她生来就是位公主。她是黑人女将中最漂亮的一个，也是部落里的大美人。她时而妖艳，时而冷酷，时而多情。没有哪一个勇士不想娶这位变化无常的公主为妻的，但是所有的求婚者都被她那把短斧挡在了门外。让我们看看他们是如何穿过掉在地上的枝叶而不发出声响的。惟一能听到的就是他们粗重的喘息声，这是因为他们在大快朵颐之后，肚子有些鼓起，不过，慢慢地食物就会消化了。可是，目前来说，这是他们主要的危险。

印第安人来无影去无踪，很快，他们的位置就被野兽取代了，杂七杂八的一大群：狮子、老虎、熊，还有在前面躲避他们的无数小动物。各种各样的兽类，特别是所有的食人兽，都在这个得天独厚的岛上杂处并存。它们的舌头都伸了出来，今晚它们都饿了。

野兽过去之后，最后一个角色出场了，一条巨大的鳄鱼，待会儿我们就会知道它到底是在找谁了。

鳄鱼爬过去了，但是没过多久孩子们又出现了。因为队列必须无休止地进行下去，直到某一队停下来，或是改变前进的速度。然后他们很快就会相互厮杀开来。

所有人都在密切注视着前方，可是谁都没有察觉到，危险可能从背后偷袭过来。从这儿可以看出，这个岛是多么真实。

最先停止绕圈的就是那些孩子们。他们全都躺在离他们地下的家很近的那片草地上。

“真希望彼得能回来啊。”每个人都不安地说道，尽管他们的身高体型都超过了他们的队长。

“我是惟一一个不怕海盗的人。”斯莱特利说，那腔调使他不被大家喜爱。不过大概是远处的声响惊动了他，他又慌忙加了一句，“不过我也希望彼得能回来，给我们讲讲关于灰姑娘的新故事。”

孩子们谈起了灰姑娘。图图确信他妈妈以前一定很像灰姑娘。

只有当彼得不在的时候，他们才会提起自己的妈妈，因为彼得觉得这个话题很无聊，于是禁止大家谈论。

“我能记起关于我妈妈的事情，”尼布斯对他们说，“就是，她总是对我爸爸说，‘啊，真希望我能有自己的支票本。’虽然我不知道支票本是什么东西，但是我很想给我妈妈弄一个来。”

正聊着天时，他们听到远处传来了什么声音。你我都不是林中的生物，当然是听不到的，但是他们听见了，就是那首可怕的歌：

唷嗬，唷嗬，海盗的生活
骷髅和白骨做成的旗帜，
一阵欢乐，一根绳索，
你好，大卫琼斯。

刹那间，那些丢失的孩子们——可他们都在哪儿？他们已经不在那里了。连兔子都没办法像他们这样溜得那么快。

我告诉你们他们在哪里，除了尼布斯飞快地跑去侦察敌情之外，其他人全都已经回到了地下的家中，那真是个非常有趣的住处，等一下我就会详细介绍的。可他们是怎么进去的呢？因为根本看不见一个入口，连块大石头也没有；如果有一块大石头，搬开之后就会露出洞口。不过你再仔细看看，就会发现那儿有七棵大树，每个空心的树干下面都有一个洞，洞口有孩子的身体那么大。这就是地下屋的七个入口，这几个月以来，胡克一直都没能找到这些入口。今晚他能找到吗？

随着海盗的逼近，斯密眼明手快，发现尼布斯消失在树林中，他立刻掏出手枪，可是一只铁钩紧紧抓住了他的肩膀。

“船长，放开我。”他挣扎着叫道。

此刻我们第一次听到了胡克的声音，那是个邪恶的声音。“先把枪放回去。”那声音威胁道。

“那孩子不正是你的宿敌吗？我本来可以打死他的。”

“是啊，不过枪声会把虎莲公主的印第安人引过来。你是不是不想要你的脑袋了？”

“那我可以去追他吗，船长？”可怜的斯密问，“我可以用我的约翰钻挠他痒痒吗？”斯密给每件东西起了个很好听的名字，他的短刀就叫约翰钻，因为他喜欢拿刀在伤口处旋转。斯密身上还有很多可爱的特征。譬如说杀人之后，他总是擦一擦他的眼镜，而不是擦他的武器。

“强尼是个非常安静的伙伴。”他提醒道。

“现在还不行，斯密。”胡克秘密地说道，“他只不过才一个人，我想要的是把他们七个全部干掉。大家分头去找。”

海盗们在树林里消失了，很快就只剩下船长和斯密两个人。胡克沉重地叹了口气。我并不知道他为什么叹气，也许是因为这温柔美好的夜色吧。不过他忽然心生一念，想把自己一生的故事全讲给他忠诚的水手听。他真诚地讲了很久，然而愚蠢的斯密完全不知道他在说什么。

之后斯密听到了彼得这个名字。

胡克愤恨地说，“我最想要抓的就是他们的队长彼得·潘。就是他砍掉了我的手臂。”他凶狠地挥舞着那只铁钩。“我等了那么长时间，就是想要拿这铁钩跟他握个手。噢，我要把他撕成碎片。”

“可是，”斯密说，“我常听您说，这钩子能顶二十只手，而且还能梳头，做别的家务事儿。”

“是啊，”船长回答说，“如果我是个母亲，我一定祈求我的孩子生下来就有这铁钩，而不是那只手。”他得意地看了一眼他那只铁腕，又轻蔑地瞥了一眼另一只手。接着，他又皱起了眉头。

他畏畏缩缩地说：“彼得把我的手臂扔给了一条碰巧路过的鳄鱼。”

斯密说：“我常看到你对鳄鱼有一种莫名的恐惧。”

“我不是怕所有的鳄鱼，”胡克纠正说，“唯独怕那一条鳄鱼。”他压低了嗓音说。“那条鳄鱼很喜欢吃我的手臂，斯密。从那时开始，它就一直跟着我，穿山过海地跟着我，舔着它的舌头，想吃我身体的其他部位。”

“从某种程度上来说，”斯密说，“这也是一种赞美。”

“我才不要这种赞美，”胡克任性地咆哮道，“我要的是彼得·潘，是他先让那畜生尝到了我的滋味。”

胡克坐在一只大蘑菇上，此时他的声音有些颤抖。“斯密，”他沙哑地说道，“其实那条鳄鱼早该把我吃掉的，幸亏它吞下了一只钟，在它肚子里滴答滴答作响；因此在它抓到我之前，我就听到了滴答声，然后撒腿就跑。”他大笑起来，不过那是一种干笑。

“可是总有一天，”斯密说，“那钟会停下来不走的，到时候鳄鱼就会抓住你了。”

胡克舐舐他干涩的嘴唇。“是啊，”他说，“我怕的就是这个。”

他坐下来之后，就觉得出奇的热。“斯密，”他说，“这个座位是热的。”他跳了起来。“不得了啦，不得了啦，我快要被烧焦了！”

他们仔细检查了这只蘑菇，一个从未在大陆上见过的既大又硬的蘑菇。他们试图把它拔起来，没想到一下子就拔了起来，原来这蘑菇没有根。更奇怪的是，地上立刻冒出了一股烟。两个海盗相互对视，“是一个烟囱！”他们异口同声地惊叫道。

他们真的发现了地下屋的烟囱。当敌人在附近的时候，孩子们就用蘑菇把烟囱盖上，这是他们的习惯。

烟囱里不光冒出烟来，还传出了孩子们的声音。因为他们都觉得藏在这个地方十分安全，所以大家都快活地聊着天。海盗阴森地听了一会，然后把蘑菇放回原位。他们四下搜寻了一番，发现了七棵树上的洞穴。

“您有没有听见他们说彼得·潘不在家？”斯密一边轻声地说，一边摆弄着他那只约翰钻。

胡克点了点头，站在那儿思索了半天，最后他那黝黑的脸上浮现出一丝冷笑。斯密已经整装待发。“说出您的计划吧，船长。”斯密急切地说道。

“回船上去，”胡克慢慢地从牙缝里挤出几个字来，“做一个多料的大蛋糕，奶油要厚，还要淋上青糖。那下面应该只有一间屋子，因为只有一个烟囱。这些愚蠢的‘鼹鼠’们竟然不知道他们只需要一个出口就够了，可见他们真的没有妈妈教育。我们把蛋糕放在美人鱼的礁湖边上，那些小孩儿经常在那里游泳，和美人鱼嬉闹。他们会发现这个蛋糕，然后狼吞虎咽地把它吃掉。因为他们没有妈妈教育，他们不知道吃多料潮湿的蛋糕有多么危险。”他突然笑了起来，这次不是干笑，是开怀大笑。“哈哈，他们死定了。”

斯密越听越佩服。

“这是我听说过的最歹毒、最完美的计策了。”斯密叫道。两人得意忘形地又跳又唱：

停船系绳，我来了，
他们吓得魂飞魄散；
只要跟胡克的铁钩一握手，
就会皮开肉绽只剩骨头。

他们开始唱起这首歌来，不过并没能把它唱完，因为另一个声音忽然响起，打断了他们的歌声。起初，那声音很小，树叶掉下来的声音都能将它湮没，但是随着它越靠越近，声音也就越来越清晰。

滴答，滴答，滴答，滴答……

胡克战战兢兢地站着，一只脚悬在空中。

“是鳄鱼。”他气喘吁吁地大叫一声，撒腿就跑，身后紧跟着他的水手。

真的是那只鳄鱼，它已经超过了在追踪海盗的印第安人。而此时印第安人正在追踪其他海盗。鳄鱼慢悠悠地跟在胡克身后。

孩子们再次回到了地面上，可是，黑夜的危险并没有结束，因为很快尼布斯就气喘吁吁地跑到他们中间，后面跟着一群恶狼，各个吐着舌头，发出可怕的嚎叫声。

“救救我，快救救我！”尼布斯呼喊着，跌倒在地上。

“可我们要怎么做，我们该怎么做？”

在这可怕的时刻，他们都想到了彼得，这应该是对彼得的最高赞誉了。

“如果彼得在，他会怎么做？”他们不约而同地喊道。

他们几乎异口同声地说：“彼得会从两腿中间看着它们。”

然后，“那我们就照彼得的做吧。”

那真是一种对付狼群最有效的办法了，他们全都弯下腰，从两腿中间往后看。接下来的时间显得有些漫长，可是胜利来得很快，因为孩子们用这种可怕的姿势向狼逼进时，那群狼全都夹着尾巴逃走了。

尼布斯从地上爬了起来，依旧目不转睛地盯着，其他孩子以为他还在看那些狼，可是他看的并不是狼。

“我看见一个更奇怪的东西，”他喊道，其他孩子都急切地团团围过来，“有一只很大的白鸟正朝这边飞过来。”

“什么鸟？”

“我不知道，”尼布斯充满敬畏地说，“但是它看起来很疲倦，一边飞还在一边呻吟‘可怜的温迪’。”

“可怜的温迪？”

“我想起来了，”斯莱特利马上说道，“有一种鸟就叫温迪。”

“看，它飞过来了。”卷毛指着空中的温迪喊道。

温迪现在差不多已经飞到他们头顶上了，孩子们可以听到她哀伤的声音。可是听得更为清楚的是叮叮铃的尖叫声。这个心怀嫉妒的精灵，此刻已经抛弃了一切友好的伪装，从四面八方对温迪进行攻击，每每撞到她的身体时，就狠狠地拧她一把。

“喂，叮叮铃。”那些满脸疑惑的孩子们喊道。

叮叮铃回答说：“彼得要你们射死这个温迪。”

只要彼得有令，他们从不怀疑。“只要是彼得的吩咐，我们就遵命。”这些单纯的孩子嚷嚷着。“快，准备弓箭。”

除了图图，所有人都钻进了他们的树洞。图图随身携带着弓箭，叮叮铃发现了，搓了搓她的小手。

“快，图图，快射她！”叮叮铃大声叫道，“彼得会很开心的。”

图图激动地张弓搭箭。“别挡着，叮叮铃。”他大喊道，接着箭就射了出去，温迪摇摇晃晃地倒到地上，胸口插着一支箭。

Chapter 6
第六章

The Little House

Foolish Tootles was standing like a conqueror over Wendy's body when the other boys sprang, armed, from their trees.

"You are too late," he cried proudly, "I have shot the Wendy. Peter will be so pleased with me."

Overhead Tinker Bell shouted "Silly ass!" and darted into hiding. The others did not hear her.

They had crowded round Wendy, and as they looked a terrible silence fell upon the wood. If Wendy's heart had been beating they would all have heard it.

Slightly was the first to speak. "This is no bird," he said in a scared voice. "I think this must be a lady."

"A lady?" said Tootles, and fell a-trembling.

"And we have killed her," Nibs said hoarsely.

They all whipped off their caps.

"Now I see," Curly said: "Peter was bringing her to us." He threw himself sorrowfully on the ground.

"A lady to take care of us at last," said one of the twins, "and you have killed her!"

They were sorry for him, but sorrier for themselves, and when he took a step nearer them they turned from him.

Tootles' face was very white, but there was a dignity about him now that had never been there before.

"I did it," he said, reflecting. "When ladies used to come to me in dreams, I said, 'Pretty mother, pretty mother.' But when at last she really came, I shot her."

He moved slowly away.

"Don't go," they called in pity.

"I must," he answered, shaking; "I am so afraid of Peter."

It was at this tragic moment that they heard a sound which made the heart of every one of them rise to his mouth. They heard Peter crow.

"Peter!" they cried, for it was always thus that he signalled his return.

"Hide her," they whispered, and gathered hastily around Wendy. But Tootles stood aloof.

Again came that ringing crow, and Peter dropped in front of them. "Greetings, boys," he cried, and mechanically they saluted, and then again was silence.

He frowned.

"I am back," he said hotly, "why do you not cheer?"

They opened their mouths, but the cheers would not come. He overlooked it in his haste to tell the glorious tidings.

"Great news, boys," he cried, "I have brought at last a mother for you all."

Still no sound, except a little thud from Tootles as he dropped on his knees.

"Have you not seen her?" asked Peter, becoming troubled. "She flew this way."

"Ah me!" once voice said, and another said, "Oh, mournful day."

Tootles rose. "Peter," he said quietly, "I will show her to you," and when the others would still have hidden her he said, "Back, twins, let Peter see."

So they all stood back, and let him see, and after he had looked for a little time he did not know what to do next.

"She is dead," he said uncomfortably. "Perhaps she is frightened at being dead."

He thought of hopping off in a comic sort of way till he was out of sight of her, and then never going near the spot any more. They would all have been glad to follow if he had done this.

But there was the arrow. He took it from her heart and faced his band.

"Whose arrow?" he demanded sternly.

"Mine, Peter," said Tootles on his knees.

"Oh, dastard hand," Peter said, and he raised the arrow to use it as a dagger.

Tootles did not flinch. He bared his breast. "Strike, Peter," he said firmly, "strike true."

Twice did Peter raise the arrow, and twice did his hand fall. "I cannot strike," he said with awe, "there is something stays my hand."

All looked at him in wonder, save Nibs, who fortunately looked at Wendy.

"It is she," he cried, "the Wendy lady, see, her arm!"

Wonderful to relate, Wendy had raised her arm. Nibs bent over her and listened reverently. "I think she said, 'Poor Tootles,'" he whispered.

"She lives," Peter said briefly.

Slightly cried instantly, "The Wendy lady lives."

Then Peter knelt beside her and found his button. You remember she had put it on a chain that she wore round her neck.

"See," he said, "the arrow struck against this. It is the kiss I gave her. It has saved her life."

"I remember kisses," Slightly interposed quickly, "let me see it. Ay, that's a kiss."

Peter did not hear him. He was begging Wendy to get better quickly, so that he could show her the mermaids. Of course she could not answer yet, being still in a frightful faint; but from overhead came a wailing note.

"Listen to Tink," said Curly, "she is crying because the Wendy lives."

Then they had to tell Peter of Tink's crime, and almost never had they seen him look so stern.

"Listen, Tinker Bell," he cried, "I am your friend no more. Begone from me for ever."

She flew on to his shoulder and pleaded, but he brushed her off. Not until Wendy again raised her arm did he relent sufficiently to say, "Well, not for ever, but for a whole week."

Do you think Tinker Bell was grateful to Wendy for raising her arm? Oh dear no, never wanted to pinch her so much. Fairies indeed are strange, and Peter, who understood them best, often cuffed (slapped) them.

But what to do with Wendy in her present delicate state of health?

"Let us carry her down into the house," Curly suggested.

"Ay," said Slightly, "that is what one does with ladies."

"No, no," Peter said, "you must not touch her. It would not be sufficiently respectful."

"That," said Slightly, "is what I was thinking."

"But if she lies there," Tootles said, "she will die."

"Ay, she will die," Slightly admitted, "but there is no way out."

"Yes, there is," cried Peter. "Let us build a little house round her."

They were all delighted. "Quick," he ordered them, "bring me each of you the best of what we have. Gut our house. Be sharp."

In a moment they were as busy as tailors the night before a wedding. They skurried this way and that, down for bedding, up for firewood, and while they were at it, who should appear but John and Michael. As they dragged along the ground they fell asleep standing, stopped, woke up, moved another step and slept again.

"John, John," Michael would cry, "wake up! Where is Nana, John, and mother?"

And then John would rub his eyes and mutter, "It is true, we did fly."

You may be sure they were very relieved to find Peter.

"Hullo, Peter," they said.

"Hullo," replied Peter amicably, though he had quite forgotten them. He was very busy at the moment measuring Wendy with his feet to see how large a house she would need. Of course he meant to leave room for chairs and a table. John and Michael watched him.

"Is Wendy asleep?" they asked.

"Yes."

"John," Michael proposed, "let us wake her and get her to make supper for us," but as he said it some of the other boys rushed on carrying branches for the building of the house. "Look at them!" he cried.

"Curly," said Peter in his most captainy voice, "see that these boys help in the building of the house."

"Ay, ay, sir."

"Build a house?" exclaimed John.

"For the Wendy," said Curly.

"For Wendy?" John said, aghast. "Why, she is only a girl!"

"That," explained Curly, "is why we are her servants."

"You? Wendy's servants!"

"Yes," said Peter, "and you also. Away with them."

The astounded brothers were dragged away to hack and hew and carry. "Chairs and a fender (fireplace) first," Peter ordered. "Then we shall build a house round them."

"Ay," said Slightly, "that is how a house is built; it all comes back to me."

Peter thought of everything. "Slightly," he cried, "fetch a doctor."

"Ay, ay," said Slightly at once, and disappeared, scratching his head. But he knew Peter must be obeyed, and he returned in a moment, wearing John's hat and looking solemn.

"Please, sir," said Peter, going to him, "are you a doctor?"

The difference between him and the other boys at such a time was that they knew it was make-believe, while to him make-believe and true were exactly the same thing. This sometimes troubled them, as when they had to make-believe that they had had their dinners.

If they broke down in their make-believe he rapped them on the knuckles.

"Yes, my little man," Slightly anxiously replied, who had chapped knuckles.

"Please, sir," Peter explained, "a lady lies very ill."

She was lying at their feet, but Slightly had the sense not to see her.

"Tut, tut, tut," he said, "where does she lie?"

"In yonder glade."

"I will put a glass thing in her mouth," said Slightly, and he made-believe to do it, while Peter waited. It was an anxious moment when the glass thing was withdrawn.

"How is she?" inquired Peter.

"Tut, tut, tut," said Slightly, "this has cured her."

"I am glad!" Peter cried.

"I will call again in the evening," Slightly said; "give her beef tea out of a cup with a spout to it"; but after he had returned the hat to John he blew big breaths, which was his habit on escaping from a difficulty.

In the meantime the wood had been alive with the sound of axes; almost everything needed for a cosy dwelling already lay at Wendy's feet.

"If only we knew," said one, "the kind of house she likes best."

"Peter," shouted another, "she is moving in her sleep."

"Her mouth opens," cried a third, looking respectfully into it. "Oh, lovely!"

"Perhaps she is going to sing in her sleep," said Peter. "Wendy, sing the kind of house you would like to have."

Immediately, without opening her eyes, Wendy began to sing:

"I wish I had a pretty house,
The littlest ever seen,
With funny little red walls
And roof of mossy green."

They gurgled with joy at this, for by the greatest good luck the branches they had brought were sticky with red sap, and all the ground was carpeted with moss. As they rattled up the little house they broke into song themselves:

"We've built the little walls and roof
And made a lovely door,
So tell us, mother Wendy,
What are you wanting more?"

To this she answered greedily:

"Oh, really next I think I'll have
Gay windows all about,
With roses peeping in, you know,
And babies peeping out."

With a blow of their fists they made windows, and large yellow leaves were the blinds. But roses – ?

"Roses!" cried Peter sternly.

Quickly they made-believe to grow the loveliest roses up the walls.

Babies?

To prevent Peter ordering babies they hurried into song again:

"We've made the roses peeping out,
The babes are at the door,
We cannot make ourselves, you know,
'cos we've been made before."

Peter, seeing this to be a good idea, at once pretended that it was his own. The house was quite beautiful, and no doubt Wendy was very cosy within, though, of course, they could no longer see her. Peter strode up and down, ordering finishing touches. Nothing escaped his eagle eyes. Just when it seemed absolutely finished:

"There's no knocker on the door," he said.

They were very ashamed, but Tootles gave the sole of his shoe, and it made an excellent knocker.

Absolutely finished now, they thought.

Not of bit of it. "There's no chimney," Peter said; "we must have a chimney."

"It certainly does need a chimney," said John importantly. This gave Peter an idea. He snatched the hat off John's head, knocked out the bottom (top), and put the hat on the roof. The little house was so pleased to have such a capital chimney that, as if to say thank you, smoke immediately began to come out of the hat.

Now really and truly it was finished. Nothing remained to do but to knock.

"All look your best," Peter warned them; "first impressions are awfully important."

He was glad no one asked him what first impressions are; they were all too busy looking their best.

He knocked politely, and now the wood was as still as the children, not a sound to be heard except from Tinker Bell, who was watching from a branch and openly sneering.

What the boys were wondering was, would any one answer the knock? If a lady, what would she be like?

The door opened and a lady came out. It was Wendy. They all whipped off their hats.

She looked properly surprised, and this was just how they had hoped she would look.

"Where am I?" she said.

Of course Slightly was the first to get his word in. "Wendy lady," he said rapidly, "for you we built this house."

"Oh, say you're pleased," cried Nibs.

"Lovely, darling house," Wendy said, and they were the very words they had hoped she would say.

"And we are your children," cried the twins.

Then all went on their knees, and holding out their arms cried, "O Wendy lady, be our mother."

"Ought I?" Wendy said, all shining. "Of course it's frightfully fascinating, but you see I am only a little girl. I have no real experience."

"That doesn't matter," said Peter, as if he were the only person present who knew all about it, though he was really the one who knew least. "What we need is just a nice motherly person."

"Oh dear!" Wendy said, "you see, I feel that is exactly what I am."

"It is, it is," they all cried; "we saw it at once."

"Very well," she said, "I will do my best. Come inside at once, you naughty children; I am sure your feet are damp. And before I put you to bed I have just time to finish the story of Cinderella."

In they went; I don't know how there was room for them, but you can squeeze very tight in the Neverland. And that was the first of the many joyous evenings they had with Wendy. By and by she tucked them up in the great bed in the home under the trees, but she herself slept that night in the little house, and Peter kept watch outside with drawn sword, for the pirates could be heard carousing far away and the wolves were on the prowl. The little house looked so cosy and safe in the darkness, with a bright light showing through its blinds, and the chimney smoking beautifully, and Peter standing on guard. After a time he fell asleep, and some unsteady fairies had to climb over him on their way home from an orgy. Any of the other boys obstructing the fairy path at night they would have mischiefed, but they just tweaked Peter's nose and passed on.

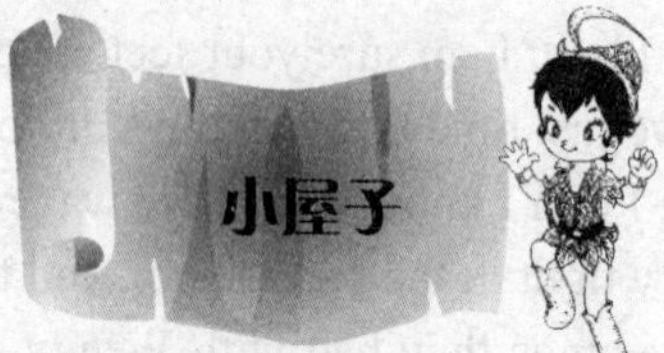

小屋子

当其他孩子手拿武器从树洞里跳出来的时候，愚蠢的图图像个胜利者似的站立在温迪的尸体旁边。

“你们来晚了，”他骄傲地喊道，“我已经把温迪射死了，彼得一定会喜欢死我的。”

头顶上的叮叮铃大喊了一声“笨蛋”就急忙逃走，躲了起来，其他人都没有听见她在说什么。

他们围在温迪的周围，盯着她看，林中笼罩着一种可怕的寂静。如果温迪的心还会跳，他们一定能听得到。

斯莱特利第一个开口说话了。“这不是鸟，”他惊恐地说道，“我想这肯定是一位小姐。”

“小姐？”图图说，心里打了阵寒颤。

“可是我们已经把她杀死了。”尼布斯沙哑地说道。

他们都摘下了帽子。

“现在我明白了，”卷毛说，“是彼得把她带过来的。”说完便悲痛地倒在地上。

“终于有一位小姐来照料我们了，”双胞胎中的一个说道，“可是你却把她杀了。”

他们替图图感到愧疚，更为自己感到难过，图图靠近他们时，他们都转过身去不理他。

此时图图的脸色惨白，可是他的脸上却浮现出一种前所未有的尊严。

“是我干的，”他反省地说道，“以前每当小姐们来到我梦里时，我总是说，‘漂亮妈妈，漂亮妈妈。’可是，这次她真的来了，而我却把她射死了。”

说完之后他慢慢地走开了。

“别走。”其他人同情地说道。

“我非走不可，”图图颤抖地回答说，“我非常害怕彼得。”

就在这悲伤的时刻，他们听到了一个声音，这让他们的心都提到了嗓子眼里，因为那正是彼得的叫喊声。

“彼得！”他们大喊道，因为彼得每次回来都要发出这样的信号。

“快把她藏起来。”他们耳语着，匆匆忙忙地把温迪围了起来。只有图图孤零零地站在一边。

这时又传来一阵响亮的叫喊声，彼得落在了他们面前。“你们好啊，孩子们！”他喊道，孩子们按照惯例向他行了个礼，接着又是一阵沉默。

彼得皱了皱眉头。

“我回来了，”他激动地说，“你们为什么不欢呼啊？”

他们都张开了嘴，却没有发出欢呼声。彼得并没有注意到这些，而是忙着要告诉他们特大喜讯。

“好消息，孩子们，”他喊道，“我终于给你们带来了一位妈妈。”

依旧是一片沉默，只听图图扑通一声跪倒在地上。

“你们没有见到她吗？”彼得有点不安地问道，“她朝这边飞过来了啊。”

“唉，”一个声音叹息着，另一个声音说，“唉，真是令人悲伤啊。”

图图站了起来。“彼得，”他平静地说道，“你来看看她吧。”其他孩子还想遮掩，图图说，“退后，双胞胎兄弟，让彼得看看。”

于是，他们都往后退了退，给彼得看。彼得观望了一会儿之后，也不知道接下来该怎么办。

“她死了，”彼得心神不宁地说，“也许她是因为受到惊吓而死的吧。”

彼得想要跳着滑稽的步子离开这里，直到看不见她，然后再也不回这个地方。如果他真这么做了，孩子们也会乐意跟着他走的。

可是有支箭很明显地插在那儿。他把箭从温迪的心上拔了下来，看着自己的队伍。

“这是谁的箭？”他严厉地询问道。

“是我的，彼得。”图图跪在地上说。

“啊，你这个懦夫！”彼得说着，举起那支箭，把它当成一把刀想要刺去。

图图没有丝毫畏缩，袒开胸膛。“刺吧，彼得，”他坚定地说，“用力刺过来吧。”

彼得两次举起箭，但两次都放下了。“我没办法刺，”他惊慌地说道，“好像有什么东西拉住了我的手。”

所有人都惊讶地望着他，尼布斯除外，他碰巧正盯着温迪看。

“是她，”尼布斯叫道，“是温迪小姐，快看，她的手臂。”

说来奇怪，温迪真的举起手臂。尼布斯弯下身去，恭敬地听着她说话。

“我想她好像是在说‘可怜的图图’。”他轻声地说道。

“她还活着。”彼得简短地说。

斯莱特利立刻叫道：“温迪小姐还活着。”

彼得跪在她的身旁，发现了他那颗橡子。你还记得吧，温迪曾把它穿在项链上，挂在自己脖子上。

“快看，”他说，“箭刚好射中了这东西，这是我送给温迪的一个吻，是它救了温迪的命。”

“我记得吻的样子，”斯莱特利立刻插嘴说，“让我看看，没错，那是一个吻。”

彼得没有听到斯莱特利在说什么，他只是祈祷温迪可以快点康复，好让自己带她去看美人鱼。当然，温迪还没办法说话，因为她仍在极度昏迷当中。此时却从头上传来了一阵嚎啕的哭声。

“听，是叮叮铃，”卷毛说，“因为温迪还活着，她就哭了。”

于是孩子们不得不告诉彼得叮叮铃所犯的罪行，他们从没见过彼得脸上如此严峻的神情。

“听着，叮叮铃，”他喊道，“我再也不是你的朋友了，走吧，永远离开我。”

叮叮铃停在他的肩上，向他求情，但是被彼得摔开了。直到温迪再一次举起她的手臂，他才十分宽厚地说："好吧，那就不要永远，一个星期好了。"

你觉得叮叮铃会因为温迪举起手而感激她吗？绝对不会，她反而更想狠狠地拧她一把。精灵们确实都很奇怪，彼得最了解她们，因而时常用手打她们。可是现在温迪身体那么虚弱，该怎么办呢？

"我们把她抬进屋里去吧。"卷毛建议说。

"没错，"斯莱特利说，"就应该这么对待一位小姐。"

"不行，不行，"彼得说，"你们不能碰她，那太不礼貌了。"

"我刚才就是这么想的。"斯莱特利说。

"但是如果让她就这么躺在这儿，"图图说，"她会死的。"

"是啊，她会死的，"斯莱特利承认，"但是还有什么别的办法吗？"

"有办法了，"彼得喊道，"我们围着她盖一座小房子吧。"

他们都非常高兴。"快，"彼得命令道，"把你们最好的东西都给我拿出来。把家里所有的东西都搬出来，快点。"

顿时他们就像婚礼前夕的裁缝一样忙碌起来。他们东奔西跑，回家取被褥、出门找木柴。正当大家忙作一团的时候，约翰和迈克尔来了。他们拖着脚步走过来，站着就睡着了；停住脚步，就醒过来；再走一步，又睡着了。

"约翰，约翰，"迈克尔喊道，"快醒醒，娜娜在哪儿，约翰？还有妈妈呢？"

接着约翰揉揉眼睛，嘀咕着："是真的，我们会飞了。"

你可以想像他们俩再见到彼得时有多欣慰。

“你好，彼得。”他们说。

“你们好。”彼得友善地回答道，尽管他已经完全把他们俩给忘了。此时彼得正忙着用脚测量温迪的身高，看看她需要多大的房子。当然，他还留出了放桌椅的地方。约翰和迈克尔在一旁望着他。

“温迪睡着了吗？”他们问。

“是的。”

“约翰，”迈克尔提议说，“我们把她叫醒，让她给我们做晚饭吧。”在这说话的间隙里，他发现很多孩子抱着造房子用的树枝跑了过来。“快看他们！”迈克尔喊道。

“卷毛，”彼得操着队长的腔调说，“让这两个人去帮忙造房子。”

“是，是，队长……”

“造房子？”约翰惊呼道。

“给温迪的。”卷毛说。

“给温迪？”约翰惊讶地说，“为什么？她不过是个女孩子。”

“就是因为这样，”卷毛解释说，“所以我们都是她的仆人。”

“你们？温迪的仆人！”

“没错，”彼得说，“你们也是，把他们带走。”

这对惊讶的兄弟被人拉去砍树运木头了。“先做椅子和壁炉，”彼得命令道，“然后再围着它们造屋子。”

“没错，”斯莱特利说，“房子就是这么造的，我全都记起来了。”

彼得想得很周全。“斯莱特利，”他喊道，“去请个医生来。”

“是，是。”斯莱特利立刻回答，然后挠着头皮离开了。他知道彼得的命令必须服从。很快他就戴着约翰的帽子回来了，神情很严肃。

“请问，先生，”彼得走上前去说道，“你是医生吗？”

在这种情况下，彼得和其他孩子不同的地方就是，他们知道这是假扮的，而对他来说，真的假的都是一回事儿。有时候这个问题常常让他们感到很为难，比如说，他们不得不假装自己已经吃过晚饭了。如果他们露了馅，彼得就会敲他们的骨头。

“是的，小伙子。”斯莱特利战战兢兢地回答说，因为他有些骨头已经被敲裂了。

“那就拜托您了，医生。”彼得解释说，“有位小姐病得很重。”

病人就躺在他们的脚旁，可是，斯莱特利却假装没看到她。

“啧，啧，啧，”他说，“病人躺在哪儿呢？”

“在那边的草地上。”

“我要把一个玻璃棒放进她嘴里。”斯莱特利说，并假装这么做着，彼得则守在一旁。当斯莱特利把玻璃棒从嘴里拿出来的时候，那真叫人担心啊。

“她怎么样？”彼得问。

“啧，啧，”斯莱特利说，“这东西已经把她治好了。”

“太好了。”彼得说。

“晚上我还会再来的，”斯莱特利说，“用一个带嘴的杯子喂她喝点牛肉汤。”但是当他把帽子还给约翰时，他深深地呼了口气，这是他逃过难关时的一种习惯性表现。

与此同时，树林里传来一阵阵斧头声。造一座舒适的房子所需要的材料几乎都已经堆放在温迪的脚边了。

一个孩子说：“如果我们知道她喜欢什么样的房子就好了。”

“彼得，”另一个孩子喊道，“她睡着的时候动弹了一下。”

“她张开嘴巴了，”第三个孩子说着，恭恭敬敬地往她的嘴巴看了看，“啊，好可爱。”

“也许她在梦里想唱歌，”彼得说，“温迪，把你喜欢的房子唱出来吧。”

温迪连眼睛都没有睁开，就立刻唱了起来：

我想要一间漂亮的房子，
从未见过的小巧的房子，
四面都是可爱的小红墙，
屋顶铺满绿油油的苔草。

孩子们听了，都咯咯笑了起来，他们的运气真是好极了，那些砍来的树枝刚好都黏着红色液汁，而地上都长满了青苔。他们造起房子的时候，自己也唱起歌来：

我们造好小红墙和屋顶，
还有一扇很可爱的小门，
温迪妈妈，请告诉我们，
你还要什么？

对于这个问题，温迪回答得有些贪婪：

我要四周都有明亮的窗户，

玫瑰花儿往里窥探，
小小婴儿向外张望。

他们一挥拳头，就造起了窗户，黄色的大叶子当窗帘，可是玫瑰花呢？

“玫瑰花！”彼得厉声喊道。

很快他们就假装沿着墙壁栽上了可爱的玫瑰花。

婴儿呢？

为了防止彼得要婴儿，他们赶紧唱道：

我们已经让玫瑰向外张望，
婴儿已经等在门外，
你知道我们已经做过婴儿，
所以现在不能再当了。

彼得觉得这主意不错，就立刻假装这是他出的主意。房子非常漂亮，毫无疑问，温迪住在里面一定非常舒服，虽然他们已经看不见她了。彼得在房子外面走来走去，安排最后的工作。任何东西都无法逃过他那双鹰眼。正当房子似乎完全竣工时——

“门上还没有门环呢。”彼得说。

孩子们感到很羞愧，不过图图拿起他的鞋底，做出了一个绝妙的门环。

他们想，现在应该完了吧。

还差得远呢。“没有烟囱，”彼得说，“一定要有烟囱。”

“当然要有烟囱啦。”约翰煞有介事地说道。这倒让彼得想到了一个好主意，他一把抓过约翰头上的帽子，在帽顶上挖个洞，然后把帽子扣在屋顶上。有这么一个绝妙的烟囱，小房子似乎非常高兴，一缕青烟立刻从帽子里冉冉升起，就像是在表达谢意。

现在真的完工了。所有事情都已经做完，就只剩下敲门了。

“都把自己打扮得体面些，”彼得警告他们说，“第一印象是十分重要的。”

他很庆幸没有人问他什么是第一印象，因为他们都忙着打扮去了。

彼得很有礼貌地敲了敲门。此刻树林和孩子们一样寂静，除了

叮叮铃发出的声音之外，听不到一点声响；她正坐在树枝上看着他们，毫不掩饰地嘲笑着。

孩子们好奇的是会有人开门吗？如果是位小姐，她会是什么样子呢？

门开了，一位小姐走了出来，那人正是温迪，孩子们都摘下帽子。她看起来有些惊讶，这正是他们希望看到的表情。

“我这是在哪儿？”她问。

第一个回答的当然就是斯莱特利。“温迪小姐，”他迅速地抢话道，“我们为你造了这间房子。”

“你喜欢吗？”尼布斯问道。

“多可爱的房子啊。”温迪说，这正是他们希望听到的话。

“我们是你的孩子。”双胞胎兄弟说道。

之后他们全都跪下来，张开双臂叫道：“啊，温迪小姐，请你做我们的妈妈吧。”

“我可以吗？”温迪笑容满面地说，“这一定非常有意思，但你们都看见了，我只是一个小女孩，没有一点儿经验呀。”

“那不要紧。”彼得说，好像这里就只有

他一人懂得这些事情。其实，他是懂得最少的。“我们需要的，只是一位像妈妈一样温柔的人。”

“哎呀！”温迪说，“你们瞧，我觉得我就是这样一个人。”

“没错，没错，”他们全都喊道，“我们一下子就看出来了。”

“那就好，”温迪说，“我一定会尽力当个好妈妈的。快进来吧，你们这些淘气的小家伙；我想你们的脚一定都湿了吧。在我安顿你们上床睡觉之前，应该还有时间讲完灰姑娘的故事吧。”

孩子们进去了。我不知道为什么这房子可以容得下那么多人。不过在梦幻岛，人是可以挤得紧紧的。这是他们与温迪一起度过的第一个快乐夜晚，他们还会度过很多个这样的夜晚。不久之后，温迪把他们安顿在地下屋的大床上。那一晚她自己却睡在小屋里。彼得手拿着出鞘的刀，在屋外边守着，因为海盗们还在远处寻欢作乐，狼群也在四处徘徊觅食。在黑暗中，这座小屋显得如此舒适安全，窗帘后透出亮光；烟囱里冒出缕缕轻烟，还有彼得在外面站岗。过了一会儿，彼得睡着了。一些纵酒狂欢之后回家的精灵们摇摇晃晃的，不得不从他身上爬过去。如果是其他孩子挡住了精灵们的夜归路，他们一定会恶作剧一番；不过，对于彼得，他们只会捏一捏他的鼻子，然后走过去。

Chapter 7
第七章

The Home Under the Ground

One of the first things Peter did next day was to measure Wendy and John and Michael for hollow trees. Hook, you remember, had sneered at the boys for thinking they needed a tree apiece, but this was ignorance, for unless your tree fitted you it was difficult to go up and down, and no two of the boys were quite the same size. Once you fitted, you drew in (let out) your breath at the top, and down you went at exactly the right speed, while to ascend you drew in and let out alternately, and so wriggled up. Of course, when you have mastered the action you are able to do these things without thinking of them, and nothing can be more graceful.

But you simply must fit, and Peter measures you for your tree as carefully as for a suit of clothes: the only difference being that the clothes are made to fit you, while you have to be made to fit the tree. Usually it is done quite easily, as by your wearing too many garments or too few, but if you are bumpy in awkward places or the only available tree is an odd shape, Peter does some things to you, and after that you fit. Once you fit, great care must be taken to go on fitting, and this, as Wendy was to discover to her delight, keeps a whole family in perfect condition.

Wendy and Michael fitted their trees at the first try, but John had to be altered a little.

After a few days' practice they could go up and down as gaily as buckets in a well. And how ardently they grew to love their home under the ground; especially Wendy! It consisted of one large room, as all houses should do, with a floor in which you could dig (for worms) if you wanted to go fishing, and in this floor grew stout mushrooms of a charming colour, which were used as stools. A Never tree tried hard to grow in the centre of the room, but every morning they sawed the trunk through, level with the floor. By tea-time it was always about two feet high, and then they put a door on top of it, the whole thus becoming a table; as soon as they cleared away, they sawed off the trunk again, and thus there was more room to play. There was an enormous fireplace which was in almost any part of the room where you cared to light it, and across this Wendy stretched strings, made of fibre, from which she suspended her washing. The bed was tilted against the wall by day, and let down at 6:30, when it filled nearly half the room; and all the boys slept in it, except Michael, lying like sardines in a tin. There was a strict rule against turning round until one gave the signal, when all turned at once. Michael should have used it also, but Wendy would have (desired) a baby, and he was the littlest, and you know what women are, and the short and long of it is that he was hung up in a basket.

It was rough and simple, and not unlike what baby bears would have made of an underground house in the same circumstances. But there was one recess in the wall, no larger than a bird-cage, which was the private apartment of Tinker Bell. It could be shut off from the rest of the house by a tiny curtain, which Tink, who was most fastidious (particular), always kept drawn when dressing or undressing. No woman, however large, could have had a more exquisite boudoir (dressing room) and bed-chamber combined. The couch, as she always called it, was a genuine Queen Mab, with club legs; and she varied the bedspreads according to what fruit- blossom was in season. Her mirror was a Puss-in-Boots, of which there are now only three, unchipped, known to fairy dealers; the washstand was Pie-crust and reversible, the chest of drawers an authentic Charming the Sixth, and the carpet and rugs the best (the early) period of Margery and Robin. There was a chandelier from Tiddlywinks for the look of the thing, but of course she lit the residence herself. Tink was very contemptuous of the rest of the house, as indeed was perhaps inevitable, and her chamber, though beautiful, looked rather conceited, having the appearance of a nose permanently turned up.

I suppose it was all especially entrancing to Wendy, because those rampageous boys of hers gave her so much to do. Really there were whole weeks when, except perhaps with a stocking in the evening, she was never above ground. The cooking, I can tell you, kept her nose to the pot, and even if there was nothing in it, even if there was no pot, she had to keep watching that it came aboil just the same. You never exactly knew whether there would be a real meal or just a make-believe, it all depended upon Peter's whim: he could eat, really eat, if it was part of a game, but he could not stodge (cram down the food) just to feel stodgy (stuffed with food), which is what most children like better than anything else; the next best thing being to talk about it. Make-believe was so real to him that during a meal of it you could see him getting rounder. Of course it was trying, but you simply had to follow his lead, and if you could prove to him that you were getting loose for your tree he let you stodge.

Wendy's favourite time for sewing and darning was after they had all gone to bed. Then, as she expressed it, she had a breathing time for herself; and she occupied it in making new things for them, and putting double pieces on the knees, for they were all most frightfully hard on their knees.

When she sat down to a basketful of their stockings, every heel with a hole in it, she would fling up her arms and exclaim, "Oh dear, I am sure I sometimes think spinsters are to be envied!"

Her face beamed when she exclaimed this.

You remember about her pet wolf. Well, it very soon discovered that she had come to the island and it found her out, and they just ran into each other's arms. After that it followed her about everywhere.

As time wore on did she think much about the beloved parents she had left behind her? This is a difficult question, because it is quite impossible to say how time does wear on in the Neverland, where it is calculated by moons and suns, and there are ever so many more of them than on the mainland. But I am afraid that Wendy did not really worry about her father and mother; she was absolutely confident that they would always keep the window open for her to fly back by, and this gave her complete ease of mind. What did disturb her at times was that John remembered his parents vaguely only, as people he had once known, while Michael was quite willing to believe that she was really his mother. These things scared her a little, and nobly anxious to do her duty, she tried to fix the old life in their minds by setting them examination papers on it, as like as possible to the ones she used to do at school. The other boys thought this awfully interesting, and insisted on joining, and they made slates for themselves, and sat round the table, writing and thinking hard about the questions she had written on another slate and passed round. They were the most ordinary questions – "What was the colour of Mother's eyes? Which was taller, Father or Mother? Was Mother blonde or brunette? Answer all three questions if possible." "(A) Write an essay of not less than 40 words on How I spent my last Holidays, or The Characters of Father and Mother compared. Only one of these to be attempted." Or "(1) Describe Mother's laugh; (2) Describe Father's laugh; (3) Describe Mother's Party Dress; (4) Describe the Kennel and its Inmate."

They were just everyday questions like these, and when you could not answer them you were told to make a cross; and it was really dreadful what a number of crosses even John made. Of course the only boy who replied to every question was Slightly, and no one could have been more hopeful of coming out first, but his answers were perfectly ridiculous, and he really came out last: a melancholy thing.

Peter did not compete. For one thing he despised all mothers except Wendy, and for another he was the only boy on the island who could neither write nor spell; not the smallest word. He was above all that sort of thing.

By the way, the questions were all written in the past tense. What was the colour of Mother's eyes, and so on. Wendy, you see, had been forgetting, too.

Adventures, of course, as we shall see, were of daily occurrence; but about this time Peter invented, with Wendy's help, a new game that fascinated him enormously, until he suddenly had no more interest in it, which, as you have been told, was what always happened with his games. It consisted in pretending not to have adventures, in doing the sort of thing John and Michael had been doing all their lives, sitting on stools flinging balls in the air, pushing each other, going out for walks and coming back without having killed so much as a grizzly. To see Peter doing nothing on a stool was a great sight; he could not help looking solemn at such times, to sit still seemed to him such a comic thing to do. He boasted that he had gone walking for the good of his health. For several suns these were the most novel of all adventures to him; and John and Michael had to pretend to be delighted also; otherwise he would have treated them severely.

He often went out alone, and when he came back you were never absolutely certain whether he had had an adventure or not. He might have forgotten it so completely that he said nothing about it; and then when you went out you found the body; and, on the other hand, he might say a great deal about it, and yet you could not find the body. Sometimes he came home with his head bandaged, and then Wendy cooed over him and bathed it in lukewarm water, while he told a dazzling tale. But she was never quite sure, you know. There were, however, many adventures which she knew to be true because she was in them herself, and there were still more that were at least partly true, for the other boys were in them and said they were wholly true. To describe them all would require a book as large as an English-Latin, Latin-English Dictionary, and the most we can do is to give one as a specimen of an average hour on the island. The difficulty is which one to choose. Should we take the brush with the redskins at Slightly Gulch? It was a sanguinary (cheerful) affair, and especially interesting as showing one of Peter's peculiarities, which was that in the middle of a fight he would suddenly change sides. At the Gulch, when victory was still in the balance, sometimes leaning this way and sometimes that, he called out, "I'm redskin to-day; what are you, Tootles?" And Tootles answered, "Redskin; what are you, Nibs?" and Nibs said, "Redskin; what are you Twin?" and so on; and they were all redskins; and of course this would have ended the fight had not the real redskins fascinated by Peter's methods, agreed to be lost boys for that once, and so at it they all went again, more fiercely than ever.

The extraordinary upshot of this adventure was – but we have not decided yet that this is the adventure we are to narrate. Perhaps a better one would be the night attack by the redskins on the house under the ground, when several of them stuck in the hollow trees and had to be pulled out like corks. Or we might tell how Peter saved Tiger Lily's life in the Mermaids' Lagoon, and so made her his ally.

Or we could tell of that cake the pirates cooked so that the boys might eat it and perish; and how they placed it in one cunning spot after another; but always Wendy snatched it from the hands of her children, so that in time it lost its succulence, and became as hard as a stone, and was used as a missile, and Hook fell over it in the dark.

Or suppose we tell of the birds that were Peter's friends, particularly of the Never bird that built in a tree overhanging the lagoon, and how the nest fell into the water, and still the bird sat on her eggs, and Peter gave orders that she was not to be disturbed. That is a pretty story, and the end shows how grateful a bird can be; but if we tell it we must also tell the whole adventure of the lagoon, which would of course be telling two adventures rather than just one. A shorter adventure, and quite as exciting, was Tinker Bell's attempt, with the help of some street fairies, to have the sleeping Wendy conveyed on a great floating leaf to the mainland. Fortunately the leaf gave way and Wendy woke, thinking it was bath-time, and swam back. Or again, we might choose Peter's defiance of the lions, when he drew a circle round him on the ground with an arrow and dared them to cross it; and though he waited for hours, with the other boys and Wendy looking on breathlessly from trees, not one of them dared to accept his challenge.

Which of these adventures shall we choose? The best way will be to toss for it.

I have tossed, and the lagoon has won. This almost makes one wish that the gulch or the cake or Tink's leaf had won. Of course I could do it again, and make it best out of three; however, perhaps fairest to stick to the lagoon.

地下的家

第二天，彼得做的第一件事就是给温迪、约翰和迈克尔量体形，给他们找合适的空心树。你应该还记得，胡克曾经因为这些孩子每个人都有一棵空心树而嘲笑他们；其实，胡克才无知。因为，除非那棵树适合你的体形，要不然上上下下是很困难的；而孩子的身材都各不相同。如果树洞大小合适，只要你在上面吸一口气，就能不紧不慢地往下滑；等上来时，你只要一呼一吸，就能扭动着爬上来了。当然，等你掌握这套动作之后，就能不假思索地自由上下了，而且没有什么姿态能比这个更优美。

不过，体形和树洞得完全合适才行，因此彼得在量体形时，就像量一身衣服一样仔细。惟一不同的是，衣服是按照你的身材做的；而现在必须是你去适应树洞的大小。通常这种事情是很容易办到的，你可以通过多穿或少穿衣服来解决；但是，如果你身上的某些笨拙部位太过臃肿，或者那棵惟一可用的树长得奇形怪状，彼得就得在你身上动动手脚，然后就合适了。一旦合适之后，就得格外小心地保持这种合适的体形。正因为这样，后来温迪高兴地发现，全家人都维持着良好的身体状况。

温迪和迈克尔第一次尝试就适合那棵树了，不过约翰还得要更换几棵。

练习几天之后，他们就能像井里的水桶一样上下自如了。渐渐地他们都疯狂地爱上了这个地下屋，特别是温迪。跟所有的家一样，这里也有一间大厅；这大厅的地面，如果你想要钓鱼，就可以挖一个坑出来钓；地上还长着五颜六色的大蘑菇，可以当凳子坐。有一棵永无树顽强地生长在大厅的中间，不过每天早晨，孩子们都会把树干锯得跟地面一样平齐。等到下午吃茶点时，它又长到两英尺高了，于是他们就在树干上放上一块门板，就这样树干变成了一张大桌子；等他们吃完茶点，再把树干锯掉，于是，屋子里又有宽敞的地方可以玩耍了。屋里有一个极其庞大的壁炉，几乎在这房子的各个角落，你想要在哪儿生火都可以。温迪在炉前系了很多用须根搓成的绳子，可以用来晾晒洗过的衣物。白天的时候床铺就斜靠在墙边，到了晚上六点半时就放下来，这时候，床铺几乎占据了半个屋子。除迈克尔之外，所有的孩子都睡在这张床上，像罐头里的沙丁鱼一样，一个挨着一个地躺着。翻身是有严格规定的，由一个人发号施令，大家一起翻身。迈克尔本来也应该睡在床上，不过温迪需要一个婴儿，而且他最小，你应该知道女人们的心思；结果，迈克尔就被放在篮子里，挂了起来。

这个家很简陋，如果熊宝宝能找到这种地方，它也能把房间布置得跟这里差不多。只不过这墙上有一个小壁龛，跟鸟笼差不多大，那是叮叮铃的闺房。一幅小小的门帘把她同外面相隔开来。叮叮铃是个细心的精灵，不管是穿衣还是脱衣，她都要把门帘拉上。没有哪个女人能拥有这样一间卧室与起居室相结合的精致闺房，不管那人有多大。她的卧榻——她总是这么称呼她的床，是真正女王式的，有三叶草形的床脚。随着不同季节的果树开花，床罩也随之更换。她的镜子是穿长筒靴的猫用的那种镜子，据精灵界的商贩所知，如今这世上只剩下三面这种还没有打碎的镜子。洗脸盆是馅饼皮式的，可以翻转过来；抽屉柜是货真价实的六世时代的迷人古董，地毯是马杰里和罗宾鼎盛时期(早期)的物品。一盏用亮片装饰的大吊灯，只不过是挂在那儿装点门面的；当然，她用自己发出的光就可以照亮她的房间。叮叮铃很瞧不起这个家中的其他部分，这也难怪，尽管她的房间非常漂亮，可看起来却如此自以为是，趾高气扬。

我想，对温迪来说，这一切一定会令她神魂颠倒，因为她那些吵闹的孩子可真让她忙得够呛。确实，除了有些晚上来到上面补个袜子之外，整整几个星期，她都没有到过地面上。说到做饭，可以这样告诉你：她的鼻子就一直没能离开那口锅，即使那锅里什么都没有，又或是根本就没有那口锅，她还是得照样看着它冒烟。不过你永远都无法确切地知道他们到底是真在吃饭还是假装在吃饭，这都取决于彼得的一时兴致。如果把吃饭当成是游戏的一部分，他就能吃，而且是真吃；但是，他不会为了填饱肚子而去吃，可大多数孩子都喜欢这么做。其次就是谈论吃的。对于彼得来说，假装吃饭也非常真实，在他假装吃饭的时候，你可以看到他的肚子真的变得圆鼓鼓起来。当然，假装吃饱是件折磨人的事；可是，你又不得不完全照彼得的样子做。如果你能向他证明，树洞对你来说变得太大了，他就会让你饱餐一顿。

等他们全都上床睡觉之后，就是温迪缝补衣物的好时光了。据她所说，只有在这个时候，她才有喘息的机会。她利用这段时间来给他们做新衣服，还在膝盖部位缝上两层，因为他们的裤子差不多都在膝盖那儿磨损得厉害。

温迪坐下来看着一满筐的袜子，每一双后跟都有一个洞。这时候，她会伸一伸胳膊，惊呼道："哎呀，有时候我还真羡慕那些没结婚的小姑娘。"

在她叹息时，她的脸上却洋溢着灿烂的笑容。

你们还记得她那只可爱的小野狼吧。没错，它很快就发现温迪来到了这个岛上，而且找到了她，他们彼此拥抱起来。从那之后，它就形影不离地跟着温迪。

随着时光的消逝，难道温迪不会日益想念远离她的亲爱的父母吗？这是个很难回答的问题，因为谁也说不清楚，在这梦幻岛里到底过了多少时间，在这里，时间是按月亮和太阳计算的；而岛上的太阳和月亮要比在大陆的多很多。我恐怕温迪并不会非常想念她的父母，她绝对相信他们一定会时刻开着窗户，等着她飞回去，因此，她觉得非常安心。有时候让她感到有点不安的是，约翰只是模模糊糊地记得他的父母，他们就像是他曾经认识的人；而迈克尔倒很乐意相信，温迪真的就是他妈妈。这些事都让她有点害怕，于是她义无反顾地承担起姐姐的责任。她用考试的方法，就像她过去在学校里做的试卷一样，试着唤起他们心中对往昔的记忆。其他孩子都觉得这非常有趣，执意要参加考试。他们还给自己准备了石板，温迪用另一块石板写下问题，然后让他们传看。他们则围坐在桌旁，努力地思考着去回答这些非常普通的问题。"妈妈的眼睛是什么颜色的？爸爸妈妈谁比较高？妈妈的头发是浅色还是深色？可能的话，

三道题都必须回答。”“写一篇不少于四十个字的文章，以‘我是如何度过上次假期’，或‘比较爸爸妈妈的性格’为主题。任选一题回答。”“一．描写妈妈的笑；二．描写爸爸的笑；三．描写妈妈的礼服；四．描写狗窝和里面的小狗。”

每天问的问题大致就是这样，如果你答不上来，就打一个×。约翰打的×多得吓死人。当然每道题目都回答的只有斯莱特利了，没有人像他那样热衷于第一个交卷的了；可是他的答案也非常可笑，因此实际上他总是倒数第一名，多么悲哀啊。

彼得没有参加考试。首先，因为除了温迪之外，他瞧不起所有做妈妈的人；其次，他是岛上惟一一个不会读书写字的孩子，就连最短的单字都不会。他才不屑做这种事。

顺便提一下，所有的问题都是用过去时态写的。过去妈妈的眼睛是什么颜色的，等等。你看，就连温迪也有点忘记了。

冒险的事自然是天天都会发生，下面我们就会讲到。但是这几天，彼得在温迪的帮助下，发明了一种新的游戏，这令他着了迷，但有一天又忽然对它失去了兴趣。前面已经讲到过，他的游戏向来都是这种结果。这个游戏的内容是，假装没有冒险，做约翰和迈克尔过去常做的那些事：坐在小凳子上，向空中丢球，相互推挤，出去散步，回来时连一只灰熊都没有打死。看彼得无所事事坐在小凳子上的样子，那真叫有意思呢；在他看来，坐着不动是一件非常滑稽可笑的事，而此时他却要摆出一副一本正经的模样。他还自夸说，为了自己的身体健康，他出去散了一会儿步。一连几天，对他来说，这些就是所有冒险中最新奇的事了；约翰和迈克尔不得不装出很高兴的样子，否则，彼得就会对他们不客气。

彼得常常独自一个人外出。他回来时，谁也不能确定他到底有没有做过什么冒险的事情。也许是他把事情忘得一干二净了，所以就什么都没说；可等你出去的时候，你就会看到一具被杀的尸体。而有时候他又会大谈特谈他的冒险；可你却找不到那具尸体。有时候他回到家，头上会绑着绷带；温迪就过去安慰他，用温水给他洗伤口。此时，他就会讲起一段惊心动魄的故事。不过，你知道，对于彼得的故事，温迪从来都不会完全相信。可是她知道有许多冒险故事是真的，因为她自己也参与其中；还有更多的故事，她知道至少有部分是真的，因为其他孩子参与了，证实彼得说的全都是真的。如果把这些冒险故事全都记叙一番，那就要写成一本像英语拉丁语、拉丁语英语双解词典那么厚的书了，我们最多只能举一个例子，看看这岛上的一小时是怎样度过的。可难就难在到底该举哪一个例子。要不我们就讲一讲在斯莱特利谷和印第安人的那场小冲突吧。这是一场血淋淋的战争，特别有趣的是，它表现了彼得的一个特点，那就是，在战斗过程中，他会突然转变阵营。在山谷里，当胜利看似时而倾向这一方、时而又倾向那一方时，彼得会大喊："今天我是印第安人。你是什么，图图？"图图说："印第安人。你是什么，尼布斯？"尼布斯说："印第安人。你们是什么，双胞胎？"等等。于是他们都成了印第安人。战争可能会因此而结束，不过那些真正的印第安人会被彼得的做法所迷惑，也就暂时同意这一次变成丢失的孩子，然后继续战斗，而且比刚才打得更勇猛。

这次冒险活动非同寻常的结局就是——但是，我们还没有决定是不是要讲这个冒险故事呢。也许印第安人夜袭地下屋的故事更有趣些。那一次，有好几个印第安人被卡在树洞里，不得不像软木塞似的被拔出来。或许我们可以讲一讲，在美人鱼的礁湖上，彼得是如何救了虎莲公主的命，从而双方结盟的故事。

或许我们还可以讲一讲海盗们做的那只大蛋糕，孩子们可能会吃了它而死去；讲一讲海盗们是如何一次又一次地把它放在巧妙的地方，而温迪却总是把它从孩子们的手中夺走；因此到最后，那蛋糕就变干了，硬得像块石头一样，可以用来当飞弹。胡克就是在一天夜里被它打中，摔了一跤。

要不我们可以讲一讲彼得的那些鸟类朋友，特别是那只永无鸟。它的巢筑在礁湖上面的一棵树上。讲一讲巢是怎么落入水中，可那鸟却还在孵着蛋，彼得下令不许去打扰它。这是个很美的故事，它的结局显示了鸟类是多么知恩图报。可是，如果要讲这个故事，我们就必须讲到在礁湖里发生的整个冒险故事，很显然这样就得讲两个故事，而不是一个。还有一个较短的冒险故事，不过也同样令人激动：那就是叮叮铃在一些流浪精灵的帮助下，企图把睡着了的温迪放在一大片树叶上，让她漂回大陆。幸好树叶被淹没了，温迪惊醒了过来，她以为自己在洗澡，就游了回来。或者我们还可以选彼得挑战狮群的故事来讲一讲。他用箭在地上围着自己画了一个圈，挑衅狮子们跨进圈子；他等了好几个钟头，其他孩子和温迪都屏住呼吸在树上观望着，可是没有一只狮子敢接受他的挑战。

我们应该选哪一个冒险故事呢？最好的办法就是掷钱币来决定。

我掷过了，礁湖的故事获胜。这样有人就会希望得胜的是山谷，或是蛋糕，或是叮叮铃的大树叶。当然，我可以再掷一次，三次决定胜负；不过，或许直接讲礁湖的故事才是最公平的方法。

Chapter 8
第八章

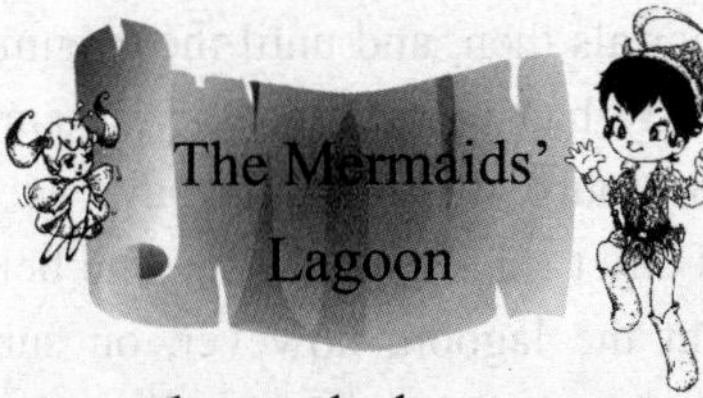

If you shut your eyes and are a lucky one, you may see at times a shapeless pool of lovely pale colours suspended in the darkness; then if you squeeze your eyes tighter, the pool begins to take shape, and the colours become so vivid that with another squeeze they must go on fire. But just before they go on fire you see the lagoon. This is the nearest you ever get to it on the mainland, just one heavenly moment; if there could be two moments you might see the surf and hear the mermaids singing.

The children often spent long summer days on this lagoon, swimming or floating most of the time, playing the mermaid games in the water, and so forth. You must not think from this that the mermaids were on friendly terms with them: on the contrary, it was among Wendy's lasting regrets that all the time she was on the island she never had a civil word from one of them. When she stole softly to the edge of the lagoon she might see them by the score, especially on Marooners' Rock, where they loved to bask, combing out their hair in a lazy way that quite irritated her; or she might even swim, on tiptoe as it were, to within a yard of them, but then they saw her and dived, probably splashing her with their tails, not by accident, but intentionally.

They treated all the boys in the same way, except of course Peter, who chatted with them on Marooners' Rock by the hour, and sat on their tails when they got cheeky. He gave Wendy one of their combs.

The most haunting time at which to see them is at the turn of the moon, when they utter strange wailing cries; but the lagoon is dangerous for mortals then, and until the evening of which we have now to tell, Wendy had never seen the lagoon by moonlight, less from fear, for of course Peter would have accompanied her, than because she had strict rules about every one being in bed by seven. She was often at the lagoon, however, on sunny days after rain, when the mermaids come up in extraordinary numbers to play with their bubbles. The bubbles of many colours made in rainbow water they treat as balls, hitting them gaily from one to another with their tails, and trying to keep them in the rainbow till they burst. The goals are at each end of the rainbow, and the keepers only are allowed to use their hands. Sometimes a dozen of these games will be going on in the lagoon at a time, and it is quite a pretty sight.

But the moment the children tried to join in they had to play by themselves, for the mermaids immediately disappeared. Nevertheless we have proof that they secretly watched the interlopers, and were not above taking an idea from them; for John introduced a new way of hitting the bubble, with the head instead of the hand, and the mermaids adopted it. This is the one mark that John has left on the Neverland.

It must also have been rather pretty to see the children resting on a rock for half an hour after their mid-day meal. Wendy insisted on their doing this, and it had to be a real rest even though the meal was make-believe. So they lay there in the sun, and their bodies glistened in it, while she sat beside them and looked important.

It was one such day, and they were all on Marooners' Rock. The rock was not much larger than their great bed, but of course they all knew how not to take up much room, and they were dozing, or at least lying with their eyes shut, and pinching occasionally when they thought Wendy was not looking. She was very busy, stitching.

While she stitched a change came to the lagoon. Little shivers ran over it, and the sun went away and shadows stole across the water, turning it cold. Wendy could no longer see to thread her needle, and when she looked up, the lagoon that had always hitherto been such a laughing place seemed formidable and unfriendly.

It was not, she knew, that night had come, but something as dark as night had come. No, worse than that. It had not come, but it had sent that shiver through the sea to say that it was coming. What was it?

There crowded upon her all the stories she had been told of Marooners' Rock, so called because evil captains put sailors on it and leave them there to drown. They drown when the tide rises, for then it is submerged.

Of course she should have roused the children at once; not merely because of the unknown that was stalking toward them, but because it was no longer good for them to sleep on a rock grown chilly. But she was a young mother and she did not know this; she thought you simply must stick to your rule about half an hour after the mid-day meal. So, though fear was upon her, and she longed to hear male voices, she would not waken them. Even when she heard the sound of muffled oars, though her heart was in her mouth, she did not waken them. She stood over them to let them have their sleep out. Was it not brave of Wendy?

It was well for those boys then that there was one among them who could sniff danger even in his sleep. Peter sprang erect, as wide awake at once as a dog, and with one warning cry he roused the others.

He stood motionless, one hand to his ear.

"Pirates!" he cried. The others came closer to him. A strange smile was playing about his face, and Wendy saw it and shuddered. While that smile was on his face no one dared address him; all they could do was to stand ready to obey. The order came sharp and incisive.

"Dive!"

There was a gleam of legs, and instantly the lagoon seemed deserted. Marooners' Rock stood alone in the forbidding waters as if it were itself marooned.

The boat drew nearer. It was the pirate dinghy, with three figures in her, Smee and Starkey, and the third a captive, no other than Tiger Lily. Her hands and ankles were tied, and she knew what was to be her fate. She was to be left on the rock to perish, an end to one of her race more terrible than death by fire or torture, for is it not written in the book of the tribe that there is no path through water to the happy hunting-ground? Yet her face was impassive; she was the daughter of a chief, she must die as a chief's daughter, it is enough.

They had caught her boarding the pirate ship with a knife in her mouth. No watch was kept on the ship, it being Hook's boast that the wind of his name guarded the ship for a mile around. Now her fate would help to guard it also. One more wail would go the round in that wind by night.

In the gloom that they brought with them the two pirates did not see the rock till they crashed into it.

"Luff, you lubber," cried an Irish voice that was Smee's; "here's the rock. Now, then, what we have to do is to hoist the redskin on to it and leave her here to drown."

It was the work of one brutal moment to land the beautiful girl on the rock; she was too proud to offer a vain resistance.

Quite near the rock, but out of sight, two heads were bobbing up and down, Peter's and Wendy's. Wendy was crying, for it was the first tragedy she had seen. Peter had seen many tragedies, but he had forgotten them all. He was less sorry than Wendy for Tiger Lily: it was two against one that angered him, and he meant to save her. An easy way would have been to wait until the pirates had gone, but he was never one to choose the easy way.

There was almost nothing he could not do, and he now imitated the voice of Hook.

"Ahoy there, you lubbers!" he called. It was a marvellous imitation.

"The captain!" said the pirates, staring at each other in surprise.

"He must be swimming out to us," Starkey said, when they had looked for him in vain.

"We are putting the redskin on the rock," Smee called out.

"Set her free," came the astonishing answer.

"Free!"

"Yes, cut her bonds and let her go."

"But, captain – "

"At once, d'ye hear," cried Peter, "or I'll plunge my hook in you."

"This is queer!" Smee gasped.

"Better do what the captain orders," said Starkey nervously.

"Ay, ay." Smee said, and he cut Tiger Lily's cords. At once like an eel she slid between Starkey's legs into the water.

Of course Wendy was very elated over Peter's cleverness; but she knew that he would be elated also and very likely crow and thus betray himself, so at once her hand went out to cover his mouth. But it was stayed even in the act, for "Boat ahoy!" rang over the lagoon in Hook's voice, and this time it was not Peter who had spoken.

Peter may have been about to crow, but his face puckered in a whistle of surprise instead.

"Boat ahoy!" again came the voice.

Now Wendy understood. The real Hook was also in the water.

He was swimming to the boat, and as his men showed a light to guide him he had soon reached them. In the light of the lantern Wendy saw his hook grip the boat's side; she saw his evil swarthy face as he rose dripping from the water, and, quaking, she would have liked to swim away, but Peter would not budge. He was tingling with life and also top-heavy with conceit. "Am I not a wonder, oh, I am a wonder!" he whispered to her, and though she thought so also, she was really glad for the sake of his reputation that no one heard him except herself.

He signed to her to listen.

The two pirates were very curious to know what had brought their captain to them, but he sat with his head on his hook in a position of profound melancholy.

"Captain, is all well?" they asked timidly, but he answered with a hollow moan.

"He sighs," said Smee.

"He sighs again," said Starkey.

"And yet a third time he sighs," said Smee.

Then at last he spoke passionately.

"The game's up," he cried, "those boys have found a mother."

Affrighted though she was, Wendy swelled with pride.

"O evil day!" cried Starkey.

"What's a mother?" asked the ignorant Smee.

Wendy was so shocked that she exclaimed. "He doesn't know!" and always after this she felt that if you could have a pet pirate Smee would be her one.

Peter pulled her beneath the water, for Hook had started up, crying, "What was that?"

"I heard nothing," said Starkey, raising the lantern over the waters, and as the pirates looked they saw a strange sight. It was the nest I have told you of, floating on the lagoon, and the Never bird was sitting on it.

"See," said Hook in answer to Smee's question, "that is a mother. What a lesson! The nest must have fallen into the water, but would the mother desert her eggs? No."

There was a break in his voice, as if for a moment he recalled innocent days when – but he brushed away this weakness with his hook.

Smee, much impressed, gazed at the bird as the nest was borne past, but the more suspicious Starkey said, "If she is a mother, perhaps she is hanging about here to help Peter."

Hook winced. "Ay," he said, "that is the fear that haunts me."

He was roused from this dejection by Smee's eager voice.

"Captain," said Smee, "could we not kidnap these boys' mother and make her our mother?"

"It is a princely scheme," cried Hook, and at once it took practical shape in his great brain. "We will seize the children and carry them to the boat: the boys we will make walk the plank, and Wendy shall be our mother."

Again Wendy forgot herself.

"Never!" she cried, and bobbed.

"What was that?"

But they could see nothing. They thought it must have been a leaf in the wind. "Do you agree, my bullies?" asked Hook.

"There is my hand on it," they both said.

"And there is my hook. Swear."

They all swore. By this time they were on the rock, and suddenly Hook remembered Tiger Lily.

"Where is the redskin?" he demanded abruptly.

He had a playful humour at moments, and they thought this was one of the moments.

"That is all right, captain," Smee answered complacently; "we let her go."

"Let her go!" cried Hook.

"'Twas your own orders," the bo'sun faltered.

"You called over the water to us to let her go," said Starkey.

"Brimstone and gall," thundered Hook, "what cozening (cheating) is going on here!" His face had gone black with rage, but he saw that they believed their words, and he was startled. "Lads," he said, shaking a little, "I gave no such order."

"It is passing queer," Smee said, and they all fidgeted uncomfortably. Hook raised his voice, but there was a quiver in it.

"Spirit that haunts this dark lagoon to-night," he cried, "dost hear me?"

Of course Peter should have kept quiet, but of course he did not. He immediately answered in Hook's voice:

"Odds, bobs, hammer and tongs, I hear you."

In that supreme moment Hook did not blanch, even at the gills, but Smee and Starkey clung to each other in terror.

"Who are you, stranger? Speak!" Hook demanded.

"I am James Hook," replied the voice, "captain of the Jolly Roger."

"You are not; you are not," Hook cried hoarsely.

"Brimstone and gall," the voice retorted, "say that again, and I'll cast anchor in you."

Hook tried a more ingratiating manner. "If you are Hook," he said almost humbly, "come tell me, who am I?"

"A codfish," replied the voice, "only a codfish."

"A codfish!" Hook echoed blankly, and it was then, but not till then, that his proud spirit broke. He saw his men draw back from him.

"Have we been captained all this time by a codfish!" they muttered. "It is lowering to our pride."

They were his dogs snapping at him, but, tragic figure though he had become, he scarcely heeded them. Against such fearful evidence it was not their belief in him that he needed, it was his own. He felt his ego slipping from him. "Don't desert me, bully," he whispered hoarsely to it.

In his dark nature there was a touch of the feminine, as in all the great pirates, and it sometimes gave him intuitions. Suddenly he tried the guessing game.

"Hook," he called, "have you another voice?"

Now Peter could never resist a game, and he answered blithely in his own voice, "I have."

"And another name?"

"Ay, ay."

"Vegetable?" asked Hook.

"No."

"Mineral?"

"No."

"Animal?"

"Yes."

"Man?"

"No!" This answer rang out scornfully.

"Boy?"

"Yes."

"Ordinary boy?"

"No!"

"Wonderful boy?"

To Wendy's pain the answer that rang out this time was "Yes."

"Are you in England?"

"No."

"Are you here?"

"Yes."

Hook was completely puzzled. "You ask him some questions," he said to the others, wiping his damp brow.

Smee reflected. "I can't think of a thing," he said regretfully.

"Can't guess, can't guess!" crowed Peter. "Do you give it up?"

Of course in his pride he was carrying the game too far, and the miscreants (villains) saw their chance.

"Yes, yes," they answered eagerly.

"Well, then," he cried, "I am Peter Pan."

Pan!

In a moment Hook was himself again, and Smee and Starkey were his faithful henchmen.

"Now we have him," Hook shouted. "Into the water, Smee. Starkey, mind the boat. Take him dead or alive!"

He leaped as he spoke, and simultaneously came the gay voice of Peter.

"Are you ready, boys?"

"Ay, ay," from various parts of the lagoon.

"Then lam into the pirates."

The fight was short and sharp. First to draw blood was John, who gallantly climbed into the boat and held Starkey. There was fierce struggle, in which the cutlass was torn from the pirate's grasp. He wriggled overboard and John leapt after him. The dinghy drifted away.

Here and there a head bobbed up in the water, and there was a flash of steel followed by a cry or a whoop. In the confusion some struck at their own side. The corkscrew of Smee got Tootles in the fourth rib, but he was himself pinked (nicked) in turn by Curly.

Farther from the rock Starkey was pressing Slightly and the twins hard.

Where all this time was Peter? He was seeking bigger game.

The others were all brave boys, and they must not be blamed for backing from the pirate captain. His iron claw made a circle of dead water round him, from which they fled like affrighted fishes.

But there was one who did not fear him: there was one prepared to enter that circle.

Strangely, it was not in the water that they met. Hook rose to the rock to breathe, and at the same moment Peter scaled it on the opposite side. The rock was slippery as a ball, and they had to crawl rather than climb. Neither knew that the other was coming. Each feeling for a grip met the other's arm: in surprise they raised their heads; their faces were almost touching; so they met.

Some of the greatest heroes have confessed that just before they fell to (began combat) they had a sinking (feeling in the stomach). Had it been so with Peter at that moment I would admit it. After all, he was the only man that the Sea-Cook had feared. But Peter had no sinking, he had one feeling only, gladness; and he gnashed his pretty teeth with joy. Quick as thought he snatched a knife from Hook's belt and was about to drive it home, when he saw that he was higher up the rock that his foe. It would not have been fighting fair. He gave the pirate a hand to help him up.

It was then that Hook bit him.

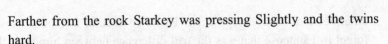

Not the pain of this but its unfairness was what dazed Peter. It made him quite helpless. He could only stare, horrified. Every child is affected thus the first time he is treated unfairly. All he thinks he has a right to when he comes to you to be yours is fairness. After you have been unfair to him he will love you again, but will never afterwards be quite the same boy. No one ever gets over the first unfairness; no one except Peter. He often met it, but he always forgot it. I suppose that was the real difference between him and all the rest.

So when he met it now it was like the first time; and he could just stare, helpless. Twice the iron hand clawed him.

A few moments afterwards the other boys saw Hook in the water striking wildly for the ship; no elation on the pestilent face now, only white fear, for the crocodile was in dogged pursuit of him. On ordinary occasions the boys would have swum alongside cheering; but now they were uneasy, for they had lost both Peter and Wendy, and were scouring the lagoon for them, calling them by name. They found the dinghy and went home in it, shouting "Peter, Wendy" as they went, but no answer came save mocking laughter from the mermaids. "They must be swimming back or flying," the boys concluded. They were not very anxious, because they had such faith in Peter. They chuckled, boylike, because they would be late for bed; and it was all mother Wendy's fault!

When their voices died away there came cold silence over the lagoon, and then a feeble cry.

"Help, help!"

Two small figures were beating against the rock; the girl had fainted and lay on the boy's arm. With a last effort Peter pulled her up the rock and then lay down beside her. Even as he also fainted he saw that the water was rising. He knew that they would soon be drowned, but he could do no more.

As they lay side by side a mermaid caught Wendy by the feet, and began pulling her softly into the water. Peter, feeling her slip from him, woke with a start, and was just in time to draw her back. But he had to tell her the truth.

"We are on the rock, Wendy," he said, "but it is growing smaller.

Soon the water will be over it."

She did not understand even now.

"We must go," she said, almost brightly.

"Yes," he answered faintly.

"Shall we swim or fly, Peter?"

He had to tell her.

"Do you think you could swim or fly as far as the island, Wendy, without my help?"

She had to admit that she was too tired.

He moaned.

"What is it?" she asked, anxious about him at once.

"I can't help you, Wendy. Hook wounded me. I can neither fly nor swim."

"Do you mean we shall both be drowned?"

"Look how the water is rising."

They put their hands over their eyes to shut out the sight. They thought they would soon be no more. As they sat thus something brushed against Peter as light as a kiss, and stayed there, as if saying timidly, "Can I be of any use?"

It was the tail of a kite, which Michael had made some days before. It had torn itself out of his hand and floated away.

"Michael's kite," Peter said without interest, but next moment he had seized the tail, and was pulling the kite toward him.

"It lifted Michael off the ground," he cried; "why should it not carry you?"

"Both of us!"

"It can't lift two; Michael and Curly tried."

"Let us draw lots," Wendy said bravely.

"And you a lady; never." Already he had tied the tail round her. She clung to him; she refused to go without him; but with a

"Good-bye, Wendy," he pushed her from the rock; and in a few minutes she was borne out of his sight. Peter was alone on the lagoon.

The rock was very small now; soon it would be submerged. Pale rays of light tiptoed across the waters; and by and by there was to be heard a sound at once the most musical and the most melancholy in the world: the mermaids calling to the moon.

Peter was not quite like other boys; but he was afraid at last. A tremor ran through him, like a shudder passing over the sea; but on the sea one shudder follows another till there are hundreds of them, and Peter felt just the one. Next moment he was standing erect on the rock again, with that smile on his face and a drum beating within him. It was saying, "To die will be an awfully big adventure."

人鱼的礁湖

有时候如果你闭上双眼，且运气够好的话，你会看到一汪没有形状的湖水悬浮在黑暗之中，湖水的颜色灰白，非常可爱。然后，如果你把眼睛闭紧一点，湖水就开始现出形状，颜色也变得更加鲜明；如果再闭得紧些，它们就开始燃烧起来。但就在燃烧之前，你可以看见那个礁湖。这就是你在大陆上能看到礁湖的最近景象了，不过就只有这迷人的一瞬间，如果能有两瞬间的功夫，也许你还能看到海浪，听到美人鱼的歌声。

孩子们常常在礁湖上消磨漫长的夏日，他们大部分时间都在游泳，或浮水，在水里玩着美人鱼的游戏，等等。你可不要因此就认为，美人鱼和他们的交情甚好；恰恰相反，温迪在岛上的这段时间里，始终没有听到美人鱼们对她说过一句客气话，这是温迪心中一个永远的遗憾。当她蹑手蹑脚地来到湖边的时候，她也许可以看到成群的美人鱼，特别是在流囚岩上，她们喜欢在那儿晒太阳，慵懒地梳理她们的长发。这些情景让温迪心里直痒痒。她甚至可以像踮着脚走路那样，悄悄游到离她们一码远的地方。不过这时美人鱼发现了她，都纷纷潜入水中，可能还会用尾巴溅她一身水，这并非无意，而是故意的。

美人鱼们也是如此对待男孩子们的，当然除了彼得之外。他可以和美人鱼们坐在流囚岩上长谈，玩到兴起之时，还会骑上她们的尾巴。后来彼得送了温迪一把她们的梳子。

想要看美人鱼，最令人无法忘怀的时间就是在月亮初升的时候。那时，她们会发出怪异的哀号声。不过，那时候礁湖对人类来说非常危险，在我们将要说到的那个夜晚之前，温迪从没见过月光下的礁湖。倒不是她害怕，因为彼得肯定会陪伴在她左右，而是因为，她有严格规定，只要一到七点，每个人都必须上床睡觉。不过在雨过天晴之后，温迪时常会来礁湖，那时候，成群的美人鱼会浮

上水面，玩起水泡。美人鱼们把用彩虹中的水汽做成的五颜六色的水泡当作球，用尾巴欢快地传来传去，试着把它们传进彩虹，直到破碎为止。球门就在彩虹的两端，只有守门员才可以用手接球。有时候，礁湖里会有十几场比赛同时展开，场面蔚为壮观。

但是，孩子们刚想加入到她们的游戏之中，美人鱼们就立刻钻进水里消失不见了，孩子们又不得不自己玩起来。然而，我们有证据证明她们在暗中注视着这帮不速之客，而且也很乐意从孩子们那儿学个好点子。因为约翰发明了一种新方法，用头顶水泡而不是用手打，美人鱼们也采用了这种方法。这是约翰留在梦幻岛的一个盛名。

午饭之后，孩子们会躺在岩石上休息半小时，这场景也非常漂亮。温迪坚决要求他们这么做，即便午饭是假装的，午休也必须得是真的。所以他们全都躺在阳光下，身体被太阳晒得闪闪发亮，温迪则坐在他们旁边，看上去神气十足。

有一天，他们全都躺在流囚岩上。这岩石并不比他们的床大多少，不过，他们当然都知道如何可以少占些地方。他们打着盹，至少是闭着眼睛躺在那儿，趁温迪不注意时，偶尔相互捏一下。温迪则忙着做她的针线活。

正当她缝缝补补的时候，礁湖上起了变化。湖面微微地颤抖了一会，太阳躲了起来，阴影随即笼罩了整个湖面，湖水也变冷了。温迪也没有办法看清针线了。她抬头一看，迄今为止一直充满欢笑的瞧湖，此时已经变得令人生畏、不敢亲近。

她知道，并不是黑夜降临了，而是某种跟夜一样黑暗的东西来了。不，比夜更黑暗。虽然那东西还没有到，可是，它已经从海上送来了一阵颤抖，预示着它的到来。这是什么东西呢？

这时温迪忽然想起了所有她听说过的关于流囚岩的故事。之所以叫它流囚岩，是因为邪恶的船长把水手们丢在这里，让他们活活淹死。当海水涨潮的时候，岩石被会被淹没，水手们就会被淹死。

当然，她应该立即唤醒孩子们；不仅因为这股莫名的危险正在逼近他们，而且睡在一块渐渐变冷的岩石上，对他们的身体也不好。然而，她只是一位年轻的母亲，根本不懂这个道理。她觉得，你必须严格遵守午饭后休息半小时的规矩。因此，虽然她非常害怕，渴望听到男孩子们的声音，她也不愿把他们叫醒。甚至当她听到一阵压抑的桨声的时候，尽管她的心已经跳到了嗓子眼里，但她仍旧没有叫醒他们。温迪站在他们身边，让他们睡足半小时。难道她还不勇敢吗？

幸亏这些男孩当中，有一个人即使睡着了，也能用鼻子闻到危险。彼得纵身跳了起来，像狗一样，立刻清醒了，他发出一声警告，唤醒了其他孩子。

他一动不动地站着，一只手放在耳朵上仔细听着。

“是海盗！”彼得叫道。其他孩子都紧紧围在他身边。一丝怪异的笑容浮现在他的脸上，温迪看了不禁战栗起来。当他脸上露出那种笑容的时候，没人敢跟他说话，他们只能站着随时准备听从他的指挥。 彼得的命令下得又快又干脆。

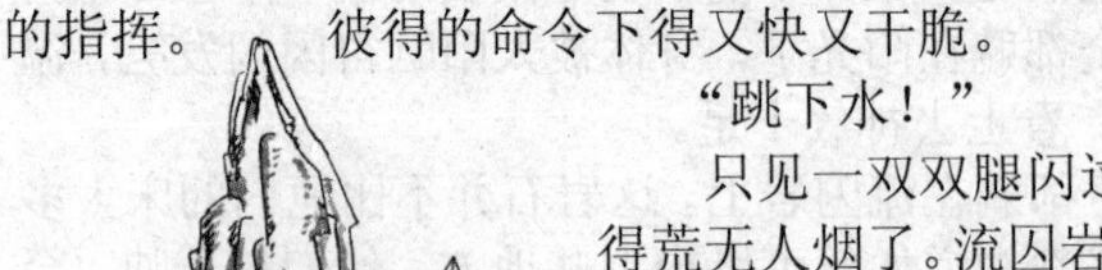

“跳下水！”

只见一双双腿闪过，顷刻间礁湖就变得荒无人烟了。流囚岩孤零零地屹立在汹涌的湖 水之中，仿佛是它自己被流放到那儿一样。

船慢慢靠近了，是海盗的船，上面有三个人——斯密，斯塔奇，第三个是俘虏，不是别人，正是虎莲公主。她的手脚都被绑着，她知道自己的命运会是如何。她将被扔到流囚岩上 等死。在她那个部落的人看来，这种结局要比用火烧或严刑拷打还要可怕。因为，在部落里的经书上，清清楚楚地写着，通过水路是无法到达那幸福的梦想领域的。但是她的表情依旧从容不迫，她是酋长的女儿，死也要死得像个酋长的女儿，这就够了。

正当虎莲嘴里咬着一把刀登上海盗船的时候，海盗们将她抓住了。船上无人看守，因为胡克总是夸口说，方圆一英里凭他的盛名足以守护他的船了。现在，虎莲的命运也能是看守他的船了。在这夜里，又将有一声哀号随风飘散在这空中。

在自己带来的这片黑暗中，两个海盗根本无法看清礁石，直到撞上之后才察觉到。

“快转舵，你这傻子。”一个爱尔兰口音喊道，那是斯密的声音，“这就是那块石头。现在我们只要把这印第安人拾起来丢到石头上，让她淹死就完事儿了。”

把这样一位漂亮的公主丢到岩石上，这还真是件残酷的事。可是，高傲的虎莲并没有作无谓的反抗。

在离岩石不远，人看不见的地方，有两个脑袋在水里忽隐忽现，那是彼得和温迪。温迪哭了，因为这是她看到的第一个惨剧。彼得看过很多惨剧，可是他全都给忘了。彼得并没有像温迪那样，为虎莲感到遗憾。令他愤怒的是，居然两个人对付一个；因此，他决定要救虎莲。最容易的方法就是等海盗走后再去救她，可是彼得向来不是一个挑简单方法做事的人。

几乎没有他办不到的事情，于是，他模仿起胡克的声音。

“喂，那边的，你们这些笨蛋。”彼得喊道，这声音模仿得像极了。

“是船长。”两个海盗诧异地看着对方，说道。

“他肯定正往这边游过来呢。”两人寻找胡克未果之后，斯塔奇说。

“我们正要把印第安人扔到石头上。”斯密大声喊道。

“放了她。”这回答让人惊讶。

“放了她？”

“是的，割断绳索，放她走。”

“可是，船长——”

“立刻放了她，听见没有？”彼得喊道，“否则我就把我这铁钩插进你们心里。”

“这真是奇怪。”斯密急促地说道。

“还是照船长的命令去做吧。”斯塔奇不安地说。

“没错，没错。”斯密说着就割断了虎莲的绳索。虎莲像条泥鳅似的，立刻从斯塔奇的两腿之间溜进了水里。

看到彼得如此聪明，温迪自然觉得非常高兴；可是她知道，彼得自己也一定非常高兴，很可能会欢叫起来，从而暴露了自己。因此她立刻伸手去捂住他的嘴。手快伸到的时候却停住了，“喂，那边的小船！”湖面上传来胡克的声音，而这次并不是彼得说的。

彼得也许正想要叫喊，可是他却皱起了脸，吹出一声惊恐的口哨。

“喂，那边的小船！”又是这个声音。

此刻温迪明白了，真正的胡克也来到了这湖上。

胡克正朝着小船游过去，他的部下提着灯笼给他引路，因此很快他就游到了他们身边。借着灯笼的亮光，温迪看到他的铁钩钩住了船舷；当胡克湿淋淋地从水中爬上去的时候，温迪看见了他那张凶狠的黑脸，她哆嗦了一下，恨不得立刻游开这个地方；可是彼得不肯走，他蠢蠢欲动，被狂妄冲昏了头脑。“我不是个奇才吗，啊，我是个奇才！”彼得轻声地对温迪说；虽然温迪也这么认为，但是为了他的声誉，她还是真心希望，除了自己之外，没有第二个人听到他这番话。

彼得对她做了个手势，示意她仔细听着。

这两个海盗很想知道是什么风把船长吹到这儿来了。不过，胡克只是坐在那儿，用铁钩托着头，露出一副非常忧郁的神情。

“船长，没出什么事儿吧？”他们胆怯地问道。可是，胡克只是深深地叹了口气。

“他叹气了。”斯密说。

“又叹气了。”斯塔奇说。

“第三次叹气了。”斯密说。

最后，胡克暴躁地说话了。

“我们的计策失败了，”他叫道，“那些男孩找到了一个妈妈。”

虽然温迪有些害怕，但心里却充满了自豪感。

“啊，真糟糕。”斯塔奇喊道。

“什么是妈妈？”无知的斯密问道。

温迪颇感震惊，大声叫道：“他居然不知道什么是妈妈！”而从此之后，她一直觉得，如果想要收养小海盗的话，斯密就是最佳人选。

彼得一把将温迪拖进水里，因为胡克忽然站起来惊叫了一声：“什么声音？”

“我什么都没听到啊。”斯塔奇一边说着一边举起灯笼照了照湖面。正当海盗们四处张望时，他们看到了一个奇怪的场景，就是前面提到过的那只鸟巢飘浮在湖面上，那只永无鸟则卧在巢里。

“看，”胡克回答斯密的问题说，“那就是个妈妈。多好的一堂课啊！鸟巢一定是掉进水里了，但是鸟妈妈会舍弃她的蛋吗？不会。”

忽然胡克顿了一下，仿佛一时想起了那些天真无邪的日子——可是他用铁钩挥去了这个软弱的念头。

深受感动的斯密凝视着那只鸟，看着那鸟巢慢慢漂走；可是，多疑的斯塔奇却说：“如果她是个妈妈，那她在这里漂来漂去，也许是为了帮助彼得。”

胡克畏缩了。“是啊，”他说，“我担心的正是这个。”

斯密热切的声音，把胡克从沮丧中唤醒过来。

“船长，”斯密说，“为什么我们不把孩子们的妈妈抓来当我们的妈妈呢？”

“这计划真是太棒了。”胡克喊道，脑海里立刻就浮现出具体的方案，“我们可以抓住那些孩子，带他们上船，然后让他们走跳板淹死，这样温迪就变成我们的妈妈了。”

温迪再次忘记了自己的处境。

“绝不！”她喊道，头在水中晃动了一下。

“什么声音？”

但是海盗们什么都看不见，他们认为那只是风吹树叶的声音。

“你们同意这个计划吗，伙计们？”胡克问。

“我举手赞成。”他们俩同时回答说。

“我举钩赞成，现在宣誓。”

宣誓后他们都站在岩石上，胡克忽然想起了虎莲。

“那个印第安人呢？”他突然问道。

胡克时常会开个玩笑，要点幽默，他们以为他在说笑。

“没问题，船长。”斯密沾沾自喜地回答说，“我们把她放了。”

“把她放了！”胡克大叫道。

“那是您的命令啊。”水手头支支吾吾地说。

“您在水里的时候，命令我们把她放了。”斯塔奇说。

“气死我了，”胡克暴跳如雷地喊道，“这是怎么回事？”他气得脸色发黑，但是，他看到手下那么肯定自己所说的话，就不禁诧异起来。

“伙计们，”他微微颤抖地说道，“我从没下过这种命令啊。”

“这可就奇怪了。”斯密说。所有人都坐立不安起来。胡克提高了嗓音，不过这声音之中夹杂着一丝颤抖。

“今晚在这湖上游荡的孤魂野鬼们，”他喊道，“你们都听见了吗？”

彼得本该保持沉默的，但这不符合他的个性。他立刻模仿胡克的声音回答：

“该死的，叫那么大声，我听到了。”

在这个节骨眼上，胡克的脸色并没有吓得惨白，倒是斯密和斯塔奇俩早已吓得抱作一团。

“说！你到底是谁？”胡克问。

“我是詹姆斯·胡克，”那声音回答说，“海盗船的船长。”

“你不是，你不是。”胡克嘶哑地叫嚷着。

“该死的，”那声音反驳道，“你再说一次，我就在你身上抛锚。”

胡克试着用逢迎的方式跟他对话。“如果你是胡克，”他几乎是低声下气地说道，“那你告诉我，我又是谁？”

“一条鳕鱼，”那声音回答说，“只不过是一条鳕鱼。”

“一条鳕鱼！”胡克茫然地重复着，他过去那副骄傲的神情在这一刻破裂了，他看见自己的部下往身后退了退。

“难道至自始至终我们都拥戴一条鳕鱼作船长吗？”他们咕哝着，“这可真是丢脸啊。”

他们都是胡克的走狗，现在反倒咬了他一口。不过，虽然胡克伤心欲绝，但是他根本没有注意到他们。要反驳一个如此可怕的证词，他需要的并不是他们对他的信任，而是他自己对自己的信任。他觉得，自己的灵魂正慢慢离他而去。“不要抛弃我，伙计。”他嘶哑地轻声唤道。

跟所有大海盗都一样，胡克那凶悍的天性里，也残留着一些女性的娇柔，有时候也会因此而得到一些直觉。忽然他试起了猜谜游戏。

“胡克，”他问，“你还有其他声音吗？”

此时，彼得根本无法抵抗游戏的诱惑。于是他用自己的声音欢快地回答说：“有啊。”

“有其他名字吗？”

“有啊，有啊。”

“是蔬菜？”胡克问。

“不是。”

“是矿物？”

“不是。”

“是动物？

“是。”

“是男人？”

“不是！”这问题回答得颇为轻蔑。

“是男孩？”

“对了。”

“普通男孩？

“不是！”

“奇妙的男孩？”

令温迪苦恼的是，彼得这次的回答是“没错”。

“你住在英国吗？”

“没有。”

“你住在这里？”

“对。”

胡克完全被闹糊涂了。“你们两个也问他几个问题。”他一边对另外两个人说，一边擦擦他那汗湿的前额。

斯密思考了一下。“我想不出什么问题。”他抱歉地说道。

“猜不出啦，猜不出啦，”彼得欢快地叫道，“你们认输了吧？”

彼得的骄傲让恶棍们看到了机会。

“是的，是的。”他们急切地回答道。

“那好吧，我来告诉你们，”他叫道，“我是彼得·潘！”

是彼得·潘！

刹那间，胡克又恢复了凶恶的原形，斯密和斯塔奇又成了他忠实的部下。

“我们终于找到他啦。”胡克大声呼喊道，“斯密，下水。斯塔奇，看着船。不管是死是活，都要给我把他抓上来。”

胡克边说边跳下了水，与此同时，湖面上也响起彼得那快活的声音。

“准备好了吗？孩子们？”

“好啦，好啦。”声音从礁湖的四面八方传过来。

“那么，向海盗进攻吧。”

战斗很短，却很激烈。第一个让敌人流血的是约翰，他勇敢地爬上小船，抓住了斯塔奇。在激烈的争斗中，斯塔奇手中的弯刀落了下来，人也挣扎着掉进了水里，约翰跟着他跳了下去，小船就漂走了。

湖面上不时地冒出一个个脑袋，刀光一闪，跟着便是一声惨叫，或是一声呐喊。在混战之中，大家都分不清敌我了。斯密的开瓶钻捅到了图图的第四根肋骨，接着斯密又被卷毛刺伤。离岩石较远的地方，斯塔奇正紧紧追赶着斯莱特利和双胞胎兄弟。

这个时候的彼得又在哪儿呢？他在寻找更大的猎物。

其他孩子都非常勇敢，他们避开海盗船长是无可指责的。胡克的铁钩把他的周围变成了死亡地带，孩子们就像受惊的鱼一样急忙逃开。

但是还有一个不怕胡克的人打算闯进这个地带。

说也奇怪，彼得和胡克从没有在水里相遇过。胡克爬上岩石喘了口气，同一时刻，彼得也从岩石对面爬了上来。这岩石就像球一样非常光滑，他们没办法攀缘，只能慢慢地匍匐着爬上去。两个人都不知道对方也在往上爬。两个人都在摸索着一块能抓紧的地方，不料竟摸到了对方的手。他们惊讶得抬起头来，两个人的脸几乎挨在了一起。他们就这样相遇了。

一些伟大的英雄都承认，在他们交手之前，心里也难免会有些不安。如果那时候彼得也是如此，我也不会替他掩饰。毕竟他的对手胡克是惟一一个能令海上库克畏惧的人。可是彼得并没有感到不安，他心里只有一种感觉：兴奋。他欢快地咬紧了他那口漂亮的牙齿。转念之间，他已经拔出了胡克皮带上的刀，正准备插入胡克的身体时，他突然发现自己所站的岩石比敌人的高，这样的战斗是不公平的。于是，他伸出手把那海盗拉了上来。

就在这时，胡克咬了他一口。

彼得感到一阵晕眩，并不是因为疼痛，而是因为不公平。这让他变得不知所措，只是惊恐地瞪着胡克。每个孩子在他第一次遇到不公平的待遇时，都会受到影响。当他跟你坦诚相见的时候，他心里所想的只是他有权利受到公平的待遇。如果你对他不公平，他还是会爱你，但是从此之后他就不再是以前的那个孩子了。谁也忘不了第一次受到的不公平，彼得除外。他经常遭遇到不公平的事情，不过总是忘记。我想这就是他和别人真正不同的地方吧。

所以，此时彼得遇到了不公平，就像他第一次遇到那样，只能无助地凝视着。胡克的铁钩已经抓了他两次。

没过多久，其他孩子就看见胡克在水里疯狂地挣扎着游向小船。这时，他那讨人厌的脸上已经没有得意洋洋的神情，只剩下惨白的惊恐，原来那只鳄鱼正穷追不舍地跟在他后面。如果是在平时，孩子们会一边在旁游泳，一边欢呼；但现在他们心里都忐忑不安的，因为彼得和温迪两个人都失踪了。于是纷纷下水四处寻找他们，呼唤他们。孩子们找到了那只小船，坐了上去，一边划着船回家，一边大喊着："彼得，温迪。"但是除了美人鱼的嘲笑之外，没有任何声音。"他们肯定已经游回去了，要不然就是飞回去了。”孩子们推断说。他们并没有非常着急，因为他们对彼得有信心。他们像孩子似的咯咯笑着，因为，今晚他们可以晚点睡觉了，这全都是温迪妈妈的错。

当孩子们的笑声渐渐平息之后，湖面上笼罩着一片冷清的寂静，之后传来一声微弱的叫声。

“救命啊，救命啊！”

两个瘦小的身躯朝着岩石游去，女孩已经晕过去，躺在男孩的手臂上。彼得使出最后一点力气，把温迪推上岩石；然后，躺倒在她身边。昏迷中，他看到湖水正在上涨。他知道他们很快就会被淹死，可是却无能为力。

当他们并排躺在岩石上时，一条美人鱼抓住温迪的脚，轻轻地将她拖入水中。彼得感觉到她正在往下滑，猛地惊醒过来，恰好及时把她拉回来。现在，他不得不把事情告诉温迪了。

“我们在岩石上，温迪，”他说，“可是这石头越来越小了，很快湖水就会把它淹没。”

尽管如此，温迪还是听不懂。

“我们该走了。”她似乎相当清醒地说道。

“是啊。”彼得无精打采地回答说。

“彼得，我们是游回去还是飞回去？”

彼得只得告诉她：

“温迪，如果没有我的帮助，你觉得你能游泳或飞到那么远的岛上去吗？”

温迪不得不承认自己太累了。

彼得呻吟了一声。

“你怎么了？”温迪问道，立刻担心起彼得来。

“我没办法帮你，温迪。胡克把我打伤了，现在我既不会飞，也不会游泳。”

“你是说，我们两个都会淹死吗？”

“你看，这湖水涨得多快啊。”

他们用手捂住眼睛，不敢去看眼前的情景，他们心想自己很快就要没命了。就在他们这样坐着的时候，有个东西像吻似的轻轻从彼得身上拂过，然后就停在那儿不动了，仿佛在羞怯地说：“我能派上什么用场吗？”

那是一只风筝的尾巴，这风筝是迈克尔几天前刚做出来的。有一天它挣脱了迈克尔的手，飞走了。

“是迈克尔的风筝。”彼得毫无兴趣地说，可是话音未落，他突然抓住这尾巴，把风筝拉到身边。

“既然这风筝可以把迈克尔从地上拉起来，”他喊道，“那它应该也能把你带走吧？”

“把我们两个都带走！”

“两个带不动的，迈克尔和卷毛试过了。”

“那我们抽签吧。”温迪勇敢地说道。

“你是个女孩子，我不能这么做。”正说着彼得已经把风筝的尾巴系在了她身上。温迪紧紧地抱住彼得，彼得不走她就不走。可是，随着一声“再见，温迪”，彼得就把她推下了岩石。几分钟功夫，她就消失在眼前了。彼得则独自一人留在礁石上。

此时的岩石已经变得非常小了，很快就会被完全淹没。灰白的月光偷偷地袭上湖面，不久之后，就立刻响起了这世上最悦耳动听、最凄凉悲伤的曲调：人鱼唱月。

虽然彼得和其他孩子有所不同，可是，最后他也害怕了。他浑身一阵颤抖，就像海面上掠过的波涛；不过，波涛一个接着一个，直到形成惊涛骇浪；而彼得只感觉到一阵颤抖。转眼间，他又笔直地站在岩石上，脸上露出他特有的微笑，心像小鼓似的敲打着，像是在说：“死亡是一次最大的冒险。”

Chapter 9
第九章

The Never Bird

The last sounds Peter heard before he was quite alone were the mermaids retiring one by one to their bedchambers under the sea. He was too far away to hear their doors shut; but every door in the coral caves where they live rings a tiny bell when it opens or closes (as in all the nicest houses on the mainland), and he heard the bells.

Steadily the waters rose till they were nibbling at his feet; and to pass the time until they made their final gulp, he watched the only thing on the lagoon. He thought it was a piece of floating paper, perhaps part of the kite, and wondered idly how long it would take to drift ashore.

Presently he noticed as an odd thing that it was undoubtedly out upon the lagoon with some definite purpose, for it was fighting the tide, and sometimes winning; and when it won, Peter, always sympathetic to the weaker side, could not help clapping; it was such a gallant piece of paper.

It was not really a piece of paper; it was the Never bird, making desperate efforts to reach Peter on the nest. By working her wings, in a way she had learned since the nest fell into the water, she was able to some extent to guide her strange craft, but by the time Peter recognised her she was very exhausted. She had come to save him, to give him her nest, though there were eggs in it. I rather wonder at the bird, for though he had been nice to her, he had also sometimes tormented her. I can suppose only that, like Mrs. Darling and the rest of them, she was melted because he had all his first teeth.

She called out to him what she had come for, and he called out to her what she was doing there; but of course neither of them understood the other's language. In fanciful stories people can talk to the birds freely, and I wish for the moment I could pretend that this were such a story, and say that Peter replied intelligently to the Never bird; but truth is best, and I want to tell you only what really happened. Well, not only could they not understand each other, but they forgot their manners.

"I – want – you – to – get – into – the – nest," the bird called, speaking as slowly and distinctly as possible, "and – then – you – can – drift – ashore, but – I – am – too – - tired – to – bring – it – any – nearer – so – you – must – try – to – swim – to – it."

"What are you quacking about?" Peter answered. "Why don't you let the nest drift as usual?"

"I – want – you – " the bird said, and repeated it all over.

Then Peter tried slow and distinct.

"What – are – you – quacking – about?" and so on.

The Never bird became irritated; they have very short tempers.

"You dunderheaded little jay," she screamed, "Why don't you do as I tell you?"

Peter felt that she was calling him names, and at a venture he retorted hotly:

"So are you!"

Then rather curiously they both snapped out the same remark:

"Shut up!"

"Shut up!"

Nevertheless the bird was determined to save him if she could, and by one last mighty effort she propelled the nest against the rock. Then up she flew; deserting her eggs, so as to make her meaning clear.

Then at last he understood, and clutched the nest and waved his thanks to the bird as she fluttered overhead. It was not to receive his thanks, however, that she hung there in the sky; it was not even to watch him get into the nest; it was to see what he did with her eggs.

There were two large white eggs, and Peter lifted them up and reflected. The bird covered her face with her wings, so as not to see the last of them; but she could not help peeping between the feathers.

I forget whether I have told you that there was a stave on the rock, driven into it by some buccaneers of long ago to mark the site of buried treasure. The children had discovered the glittering hoard, and when in a mischievous mood used to fling showers of moidores, diamonds, pearls and pieces of eight to the gulls, who pounced upon them for food, and then flew away, raging at the scurvy trick that had been played upon them. The stave was still there, and on it Starkey had hung his hat, a deep tarpaulin, watertight, with a broad brim. Peter put the eggs into this hat and set it on the lagoon. It floated beautifully.

The Never bird saw at once what he was up to, and screamed her admiration of him; and, alas, Peter crowed his agreement with her. Then he got into the nest, reared the stave in it as a mast, and hung up his shirt for a sail. At the same moment the bird fluttered down upon the hat and once more sat snugly on her eggs. She drifted in one direction, and he was borne off in another, both cheering.

Of course when Peter landed he beached his barque (small ship, actually the Never Bird's nest in this particular case in point) in a place where the bird would easily find it; but the hat was such a great success that she abandoned the nest. It drifted about till it went to pieces, and often Starkey came to the shore of the lagoon, and with many bitter feelings watched the bird sitting on his hat. As we shall not see her again, it may be worth mentioning here that all Never birds now build in that shape of nest, with a broad brim on which the youngsters take an airing.

Great were the rejoicings when Peter reached the home under the ground almost as soon as Wendy, who had been carried hither and thither by the kite. Every boy had adventures to tell; but perhaps the biggest adventure of all was that they were several hours late for bed. This so inflated them that they did various dodgy things to get staying up still longer, such as demanding bandages; but Wendy, though glorying in having them all home again safe and sound, was scandalised by the lateness of the hour, and cried, "To bed, to bed," in a voice that had to be obeyed. Next day, however, she was awfully tender, and gave out bandages to every one, and they played till bed-time at limping about and carrying their arms in slings.

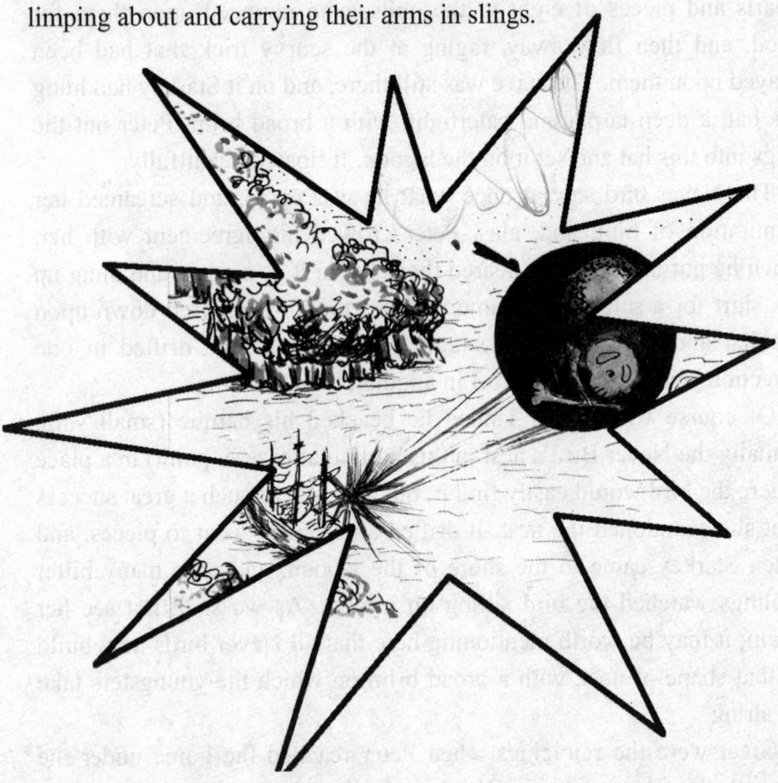

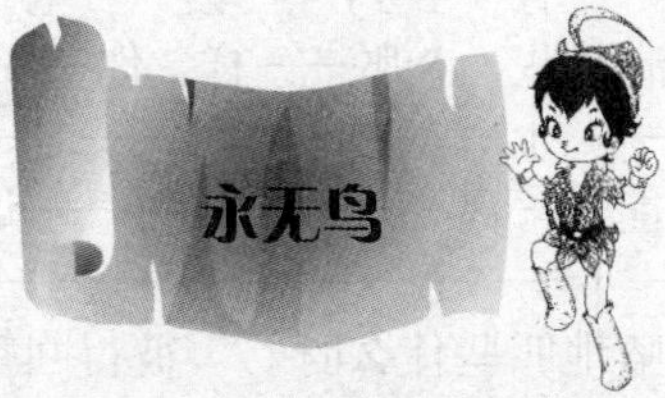

永无鸟

礁湖上只剩下彼得一个人了，他听到的最后声音，是美人鱼一个接一个回到海底睡房时发出的声响。他离得太远了，听不到关门的声音。不过，她们居住的珊瑚窟的每扇门上都有一个小铃，开门关门时总会叮当作响（就像英国本土最讲究的房子那样），这铃声被彼得听到了。

海水渐渐涨上来了，一小口一小口地吞噬着彼得的脚。在海水把自己整个吞没以前，他凝视着漂游在礁湖上的惟一一样东西来消磨时间。彼得想，那大概是一张漂浮着的纸片，或许是风筝上的一部分。他闲得无聊，估算着那东西还要多长时间才能漂到岸边。

忽然，彼得发现这东西有点异乎寻常——它一定是带着某种目的到湖上来的，因为，它正在逆浪而行，有时还战胜了海浪。每次它胜利时，总是同情弱者的彼得就忍不住为它鼓掌。好勇敢的一张纸片。

其实，那不是一张纸片，那是永无鸟。她正坐在巢上拼命向彼得划过来。自打鸟巢落水之后，她就学会了用翅膀划水，现在居然也能勉强行驶她那只奇异的小船了。不过，在彼得认出她时，她已经非常疲乏了。她是来救彼得的，尽管巢里还有鸟蛋，她还是要把巢让给彼得。我还不能完全理解这只鸟的举动，因为，虽然彼得待她好，可有时也折磨她。我只能猜想，这鸟大概也像达林太太之类的人一样，一看到彼得的满口乳牙，就心软了吧。

那鸟向彼得大声喊着，解释她来的目的，彼得也大声询问大鸟在那儿干什么。当然他们都听不懂对方的话。在神话里，人可以和鸟自由交谈。我也希望这是个神话故事，这样彼得就可以和永无鸟自由地谈话了。但最好还是实话实说，实际上是，他们不仅语言不通，而且连礼貌都忘记了。

“我——要——你——到——巢——里——来，”那鸟叫道，尽量叫得慢些，清楚些，“那——样，你——就——可——以——漂——到——岸——上——去……可——是——我——太——累——了，不——能——离——你——再——近——了，你——得——想——法——自——己——游——过——来。”

“你叽叽喳喳地叫些什么呀？”彼得回答说，“你为什么不让你的巢像平常一样漂着呢？”

“我——要——你——”永无鸟说，又重复了一遍刚才的话。

接着，彼得也又慢又清楚地说：

“你——叽——叽——喳——喳——地——叫——些——什——么——呀？”等等。

永无鸟烦躁起来了，这种鸟的脾气是很急的。

“你这个呆头呆脑、啰里啰嗦的小傻瓜，”她尖声叫道，“你为什么不照我的话去做？”

彼得觉出了她是在骂自己，于是气冲冲地回敬了一句：

“你才是呢！”

然后他们竟奇怪地互相对骂起同一句话来：

“闭嘴！”

“闭嘴！”

不过，这鸟决心尽力救彼得，她作了最后一次的努力，终于把巢划到了岩石边。然后她为了让彼得明白她的意思，就飞了起来，丢下了她的卵。

彼得终于明白了，他抓住了鸟巢，向空中飞着的鸟挥手致谢。永无鸟在空中飞来飞去，并不是为了领受他的谢意，也不是要看他怎样爬进巢里，她是想看看彼得怎样对待她的卵。

鸟巢里有两只白色的大鸟蛋，彼得把它们捧了起来，心里盘算着。那鸟用翅膀捂住了脸，不敢看她的卵的下场，可还是忍不住从羽毛缝里窥望。

我不记得是否告诉过你们，岩石上有一块木板，是很久以前海盗钉在那儿的，用来标志藏宝的位置。孩子们发现了这堆闪闪发光的宝藏，有时淘气劲儿上来，就抓起一把把的金币、钻石、珍珠之类的抛向海鸥；海鸥以为是食物，扑过来啄食，当它们发现这是卑鄙的恶作剧时就生气得飞走了。那块木板还在，斯塔奇把他的帽子挂在了上面了，那是一顶宽边的、高高的防水油布帽。彼得把卵放在帽子里，再把帽子放在水上，它就平平稳 稳地漂起来了。

永无鸟立刻看清了彼得的妙计，高声欢叫，向他表示钦佩，彼得也应声欢呼起来。然后他跨进巢去，把木板竖起来当桅杆，又把自己的衬衣挂在上面做帆。这时，永无鸟也落到帽子上，又安安逸逸地孵起卵来。鸟向这边漂来，彼得向那边漂去，皆大欢喜。

彼得上岸以后，自然是把他搭乘过的“小船”放在一个永无鸟容易发现的地方，可是，帽子太可心了，鸟宁愿放弃她的巢。这个巢就漂来漂去，直到最后完全散架。后来，斯塔奇每次来到湖上，总看见那鸟孵在他的帽子上，便恼怒不已。由于我们以后不再见到永无鸟了，所以在这里值得一提的是，现在所有的永无鸟都把巢筑成这个帽子的样子，有一道宽边，小鸟可以在上面溜达散心。

彼得回到地下的家时，温迪也刚好被风筝东飘西荡地带回家。大家全都兴高采烈，每个孩子都有一段冒险故事可讲，可是最大的冒险或许就是他们已经迟睡了好几个小时。这件事使他们非常得意，以至于又磨磨蹭蹭地找包扎伤口之类的理由，好再多耗些时候再上床。温迪呢，虽然看到他们一个个平平安安地回了家，满心欢喜，可是时间实在晚得不像话了，于是她用那令人不得不服从的语调喊道：“全都给我上床去！”不过到了第二天，温迪又变得异常温柔了，她把绷带还给孩子们，于是他们有的跛着脚，有的吊着胳臂，一直玩到上床睡觉。

Chapter 10
第十章

The Happy Home

One important result of the brush (with the pirates) on the lagoon was that it made the redskins their friends. Peter had saved Tiger Lily from a dreadful fate, and now there was nothing she and her braves would not do for him. All night they sat above, keeping watch over the home under the ground and awaiting the big attack by the pirates which obviously could not be much longer delayed. Even by day they hung about, smoking the pipe of peace, and looking almost as if they wanted tit-bits to eat.

They called Peter the Great White Father, prostrating themselves (lying down) before him; and he liked this tremendously, so that it was not really good for him.

"The great white father," he would say to them in a very lordly manner, as they grovelled at his feet, "is glad to see the Piccaninny warriors protecting his wigwam from the pirates."

"Me Tiger Lily," that lovely creature would reply. "Peter Pan save me, me his velly nice friend. Me no let pirates hurt him."

She was far too pretty to cringe in this way, but Peter thought it his due, and he would answer condescendingly, "It is good. Peter Pan has spoken."

Always when he said, "Peter Pan has spoken," it meant that they must now shut up, and they accepted it humbly in that spirit; but they were by no means so respectful to the other boys, whom they looked upon as just ordinary braves. They said "How-do?" to them, and things like that; and what annoyed the boys was that Peter seemed to think this all right.

Secretly Wendy sympathised with them a little, but she was far too loyal a housewife to listen to any complaints against father. "Father knows best," she always said, whatever her private opinion must be. Her private opinion was that the redskins should not call her a squaw.

We have now reached the evening that was to be known among them as the Night of Nights, because of its adventures and their upshot. The day, as if quietly gathering its forces, had been almost uneventful, and now the redskins in their blankets were at their posts above, while, below, the children were having their evening meal; all except Peter, who had gone out to get the time. The way you got the time on the island was to find the crocodile, and then stay near him till the clock struck.

The meal happened to be a make-believe tea, and they sat around the board, guzzling in their greed; and really, what with their chatter and recriminations, the noise, as Wendy said, was positively deafening. To be sure, she did not mind noise, but she simply would not have them grabbing things, and then excusing themselves by saying that Tootles had pushed their elbow. There was a fixed rule that they must never hit back at meals, but should refer the matter of dispute to Wendy by raising the right arm politely and saying, "I complain of so-and-so;" but what usually happened was that they forgot to do this or did it too much.

"Silence," cried Wendy when for the twentieth time she had told them that they were not all to speak at once. "Is your mug empty, Slightly darling?"

"Not quite empty, mummy," Slightly said, after looking into an imaginary mug.

"He hasn't even begun to drink his milk," Nibs interposed.

This was telling, and Slightly seized his chance.

"I complain of Nibs," he cried promptly.

John, however, had held up his hand first.

"Well, John?"

"May I sit in Peter's chair, as he is not here?"

"Sit in father's chair, John!" Wendy was scandalised. "Certainly not."

"He is not really our father," John answered. "He didn't even know how a father does till I showed him."

This was grumbling. "We complain of John," cried the twins.

Tootles held up his hand. He was so much the humblest of them, indeed he was the only humble one, that Wendy was specially gentle with him.

"I don't suppose," Tootles said diffidently (bashfully or timidly), "that I could be father."

"No, Tootles."

Once Tootles began, which was not very often, he had a silly way of going on.

"As I can't be father," he said heavily, "I don't suppose, Michael, you would let me be baby?"

"No, I won't," Michael rapped out. He was already in his basket.

"As I can't be baby," Tootles said, getting heavier and heavier and heavier, "do you think I could be a twin?"

"No, indeed," replied the twins; "it's awfully difficult to be a twin."

"As I can't be anything important," said Tootles, "would any of you like to see me do a trick?"

"No," they all replied.

Then at last he stopped. "I hadn't really any hope," he said.

The hateful telling broke out again.

"Slightly is coughing on the table."

"The twins began with cheese-cakes."

"Curly is taking both butter and honey."

"Nibs is speaking with his mouth full."

"I complain of the twins."

"I complain of Curly."

"I complain of Nibs."

"Oh dear, oh dear," cried Wendy, "I'm sure I sometimes think that spinsters are to be envied."

She told them to clear away, and sat down to her work-basket, a heavy load of stockings and every knee with a hole in it as usual.

"Wendy," remonstrated Michael, "I'm too big for a cradle."

"I must have somebody in a cradle," she said almost tartly, "and you are the littlest. A cradle is such a nice homely thing to have about a house."

While she sewed they played around her; such a group of happy faces and dancing limbs lit up by that romantic fire. It had become a very familiar scene, this, in the home under the ground, but we are looking on it for the last time.

There was a step above, and Wendy, you may be sure, was the first to recognize it.

"Children, I hear your father's step. He likes you to meet him at the door."

Above, the redskins crouched before Peter.

"Watch well, braves. I have spoken."

And then, as so often before, the gay children dragged him from his tree. As so often before, but never again.

He had brought nuts for the boys as well as the correct time for Wendy.

"Peter, you just spoil them, you know," Wendy simpered (exaggerated a smile).

"Ah, old lady," said Peter, hanging up his gun.

"It was me told him mothers are called old lady," Michael whispered to Curly.

"I complain of Michael," said Curly instantly.

The first twin came to Peter. "Father, we want to dance."

"Dance away, my little man," said Peter, who was in high good humour.

"But we want you to dance."

Peter was really the best dancer among them, but he pretended to be scandalised.

"Me! My old bones would rattle!"

"And mummy too."

"What," cried Wendy, "the mother of such an armful, dance!"

"But on a Saturday night," Slightly insinuated.

It was not really Saturday night, at least it may have been, for they had long lost count of the days; but always if they wanted to do anything special they said this was Saturday night, and then they did it.

"Of course it is Saturday night, Peter," Wendy said, relenting.

"People of our figure, Wendy!"

"But it is only among our own progeny (children)."

"True, true."

So they were told they could dance, but they must put on their nighties first.

"Ah, old lady," Peter said aside to Wendy, warming himself by the fire and looking down at her as she sat turning a heel, "there is nothing more pleasant of an evening for you and me when the day's toil is over than to rest by the fire with the little ones near by."

"It is sweet, Peter, isn't it?" Wendy said, frightfully gratified. "Peter, I think Curly has your nose."

"Michael takes after you."

She went to him and put her hand on his shoulder.

"Dear Peter," she said, "with such a large family, of course, I have now passed my best, but you don't want to (ex)change me, do you?"

"No, Wendy."

Certainly he did not want a change, but he looked at her uncomfortably, blinking, you know, like one not sure whether he was awake or asleep.

"Peter, what is it?"

"I was just thinking," he said, a little scared. "It is only make-believe, isn't it, that I am their father?"

"Oh yes," Wendy said primly (formally and properly).

"You see," he continued apologetically, "it would make me seem so old to be their real father."

"But they are ours, Peter, yours and mine."

"But not really, Wendy?" he asked anxiously.

"Not if you don't wish it," she replied; and she distinctly heard his sigh of relief. "Peter," she asked, trying to speak firmly, "what are your exact feelings to me?"

"Those of a devoted son, Wendy."

"I thought so," she said, and went and sat by herself at the extreme end of the room.

"You are so queer," he said, frankly puzzled, "and Tiger Lily is just the same. There is something she wants to be to me, but she says it is not my mother."

"No, indeed, it is not," Wendy replied with frightful emphasis. Now we know why she was prejudiced against the redskins.

"Then what is it?"

"It isn't for a lady to tell."

"Oh, very well," Peter said, a little nettled. "Perhaps Tinker Bell will tell me."

"Oh yes, Tinker Bell will tell you," Wendy retorted scornfully. "She is an abandoned little creature."

Here Tink, who was in her bedroom, eavesdropping, squeaked out something impudent.

"She says she glories in being abandoned," Peter interpreted.

He had a sudden idea. "Perhaps Tink wants to be my mother?"

"You silly ass!" cried Tinker Bell in a passion.

She had said it so often that Wendy needed no translation.

"I almost agree with her," Wendy snapped. Fancy Wendy snapping! But she had been much tried, and she little knew what was to happen before the night was out. If she had known she would not have snapped.

None of them knew. Perhaps it was best not to know. Their ignorance gave them one more glad hour; and as it was to be their last hour on the island, let us rejoice that there were sixty glad minutes in it. They sang and danced in their night-gowns. Such a deliciously creepy song it was, in which they pretended to be frightened at their own shadows, little witting that so soon shadows would close in upon them, from whom they would shrink in real fear. So uproariously gay was the dance, and how they buffeted each other on the bed and out of it! It was a pillow fight rather than a dance, and when it was finished, the pillows insisted on one bout more, like partners who know that they may never meet again. The stories they told, before it was time for Wendy's good-night story! Even Slightly tried to tell a story that night, but the beginning was so fearfully dull that it appalled not only the others but himself, and he said happily:

"Yes, it is a dull beginning. I say, let us pretend that it is the end."

And then at last they all got into bed for Wendy's story, the story they loved best, the story Peter hated. Usually when she began to tell this story he left the room or put his hands over his ears; and possibly if he had done either of those things this time they might all still be on the island. But to-night he remained on his stool; and we shall see what happened.

快乐家庭

这次礁湖交锋的一个重大成果，就是和印第安人交上了朋友。彼得把虎莲从可怕的厄运中救了出来。现在，她和她的勇士们无不乐于全力以赴地帮助彼得。海盗们的进攻显然已经近在眼前，勇士们就整夜坐在地面上，守卫着地下的家，防备着海盗们的大举进攻。即使在白天，印第安人也在附近一带巡游，悠闲地吸着烟斗，好像在等着有人给送来什么精美的小吃。

印第安人管彼得叫伟大的白人父亲，匍匐在他面前。彼得很喜欢，但这对他并没什么好处。

当印第安人拜倒在他脚下时，彼得就威严地对他们说："伟大的白人父亲很乐意看到你们这些小红战士保卫他的小屋，抵抗海盗。"

"我虎莲，"那个可爱的人儿说，"是彼得·潘救的，我是他的好朋友，我决不让海盗伤害他。"

虎莲太漂亮了，不该这样卑躬屈膝，可是彼得认为他受之无愧："彼得·潘说了，这很好。"

每次他说"彼得·潘说了"，意思就是叫印第安人闭嘴，他们也就心领神会地从命了。但是，他们对其他的孩子可不这么恭敬，只把他们看成普通的勇士，只对他们说声"你好！"之类的话。彼得似乎认为这是理所当然的，这让孩子们觉得气恼。

私下里，温迪有点同情那些孩子们，但她是一个非常忠实贤惠的主妇，对于抱怨父亲的话，一概不听。无论她个人看法如何，她总是说"父亲不会错的"。她觉得印第安人不该叫她"女人"。

这一天终于到了，他们称这一天叫"夜中之夜"，因为这一夜的冒险及其结局特别重要。白天平静无事，像是在养精蓄锐。此刻，印第安人在上面裹着毯子站岗。孩子们在地下吃晚饭；只有彼得不在，他出去打听时间去了。在岛上，要打听时间就得去找那条鳄鱼，一直在它旁边等着听它肚里的钟报时。

这顿饭是一顿假想的茶点，孩子们围坐在桌边，狼吞虎咽地大嚼，聊天斗嘴，按温迪的话说简直是震耳欲聋。当然，温迪并不怎么在乎吵闹，但她不能允许他们一边抢东西吃，一边接口说图图撞了自己的胳臂。他们有一条吃饭的规矩，就是不能还手打人，而应该礼貌地举起右手，向温迪报告："我控告某某人。"可是实际上，他们不是根本忘记了这条规矩，就是做得太过火了。

"不要吵，"温迪喊道，她已经第二十次告诉他们不要一起讲话了。"你的葫芦杯空了吗，斯莱特利宝贝？"

"还不大空，妈妈。"斯莱特利望了一眼假想的杯子，然后说。

"他连牛奶都还没喝呢。"尼布斯插嘴说。

他这是告状，斯莱特利抓住了这个机会。

"我控告尼布斯。"他立即喊道。

不过，约翰先举起了手。

"什么事，约翰？"

"彼得不在，我可不可以坐他的椅子？"

"坐父亲的椅子，约翰！"温迪认为这简直不成体统，"当然不可以。"

"他并不真是我们的父亲，"约翰回答，"他甚至都不知道怎么做父亲，还是我教他的呢。"

他这是抱怨。"我们控告约翰。"双胞胎喊道。

图图举起了手。他是孩子们当中最谦逊的一个，说实在的，他也是惟一一个谦逊的孩子，所以温迪对他特别温和。

"我估摸着，"图图犹犹豫豫地说，"我是当不了父亲的。"

"不行，图图。"

图图很少开口，可是他一旦开口，就会傻里傻气地说个没完。

"既然我当不了父亲，"他心情沉重地说，"我猜，迈克尔，你也不会让我去当婴儿吧？"

"不，我不让。"迈克尔生气地叫起来。他早已经钻到摇篮里了。

"既然我当不了婴孩，"图图说，心情越发沉重了，"你们觉得我能当一个双胞胎吗？"

"不，当然不能，"双胞胎回答说，"当双胞胎太难了。"

"既然我什么重要角色也当不了，"图图说，"你们有谁愿意看我表演一套把戏？"

"不。"大家都回答。

他只得住口了。"我真的没救了。"他说。

烦人的告状又开始了。

"斯莱特利在饭桌上咳嗽。"

"双胞胎先吃了奶酪蛋糕。"

"卷毛吃了黄油还吃蜂蜜。"

"尼布斯满嘴吃的还说话。"

"我控告双胞胎。"

"我控告卷毛。"

"我控告尼布斯。"

"天哪，天哪，"温迪喊道，"我有时觉得没孩子也是件好事。"

她吩咐孩子们收拾饭桌，之后便坐下做起针线来。针线筐里堆满了长袜子，每只袜子的膝盖上都毫不例外地有一个洞。

"温迪，"迈克尔抗议说，"摇篮太小了，我睡不下。"

"总得有一个人睡摇篮，"温迪几乎是声色俱厉地说，"你是最小的一个，而且摇篮是一个屋子里最可爱、最有家庭味儿的东西。"

温迪补着袜子，孩子们在她身边玩耍。一个个的脸蛋都笑盈盈的，手舞足蹈地挥动着小胳臂小腿，浪漫的炉火把他们照得闪闪发亮。这种景象在地下的家里是常见的，但对我们来说，这是最后一次见到了。

上面有脚步声。第一个听出来的，当然是温迪。

"孩子们，我听到你们父亲的脚步声了，他喜欢你们到门口去迎接他。"

上面，印第安人向彼得鞠躬致意。

"好好看守，勇士们，我说了。"

然后，欢天喜地的孩子们像从前那样拽着他下了树洞。这样的事以前是常有的，但今后再也不会有了。

彼得给孩子们带来了坚果，给温迪带来了准确的时间。

“你知道吗，彼得？你把他们惯坏了。”温迪傻呵呵地笑着说。

“是啊，老太婆。”彼得边说边把枪挂起来。

“是我告诉他的，要叫妈妈老太婆。”迈克尔悄悄地对卷毛说。

“我控告迈克尔。”卷毛马上提出。

双胞胎中的老大走到彼得跟前说：“父亲，我们想跳舞。”

“那就跳吧，小家伙。”彼得说，他兴致很高。

“可是我们想让你也跳。”

彼得其实是他们当中跳得最好的一个，但他假装一副吃惊的样子说：

“我嘛！我这把老骨头都要嘎嘎作响啦！”

“妈妈也要跳。”

“什么！”温迪喊，“都一大群孩子了，还跳舞！”

“可这是礼拜六晚上啊！”斯莱特利讨好地说。

其实那不是礼拜六晚上，不过也许是，因为他们早就把日期给忘了。但是．如果他们想做点什么特别的事，就总是说，这是礼拜六晚上，然后就开始行动了。

“当然这是礼拜六晚上，彼得。”温迪说，她有点回心转意了。

“像我们这样的人……温迪。”

“但现在只是跟孩子们一起呀。”

“当然，当然。”

于是孩子们可以跳舞了，不过得先穿上睡衣。

“哎，老太婆。”彼得悄悄地招呼温迪。他正在炉前取暖，一边低头看着温迪坐在那里补一只袜子的后跟，“一天的劳累之后，咱们坐在炉前歇着，小家伙在旁边玩闹，这样的晚上真是再愉快不过了。”

“真甜蜜啊，彼得，是不是？”温迪心满意足地说，“彼得，我觉得卷毛的鼻子像你。”

“迈克尔像你。”

温迪走到彼得跟前，两手搭在他肩上。

“亲爱的彼得，”温迪说，“养育了这么一大家子，我也不再年轻了，你不会把我扔下再找一个吧？”

“不会的，温迪。”

彼得当然不喜欢变来变去，可是他不安地望着温迪，眨巴着眼睛，那样子也说不清他究竟是醒着，还是睡着了。

“彼得，怎么回事？”

“我在想，”彼得带着一丝恐慌说，“我是他们的父亲，这只是假装的，是不是？”

“是啊。”温迪严肃地说。

“你瞧，”彼得有点抱歉似的接着说，“要做他们真正的父亲，我就会显得很老。”

“可他们是咱们的，彼得，是咱们俩的。”

“但不是真的对吧，温迪？”彼得焦急地问。

“你要是不愿意，就不是真的。”温迪回答说，她清楚地听到了彼得放心地叹了一口气。“彼得，”她尽量镇定地说，“你对我究竟是什么感觉？”

“就像一个孝顺的儿子一样，温迪。”

“我早就料到了。”温迪说，走到屋里最远的一头，独自坐下。

“你真怪，”彼得坦白地表示他的迷惑，“虎莲也是这样。她想要做我的什么，可她又说不是做我的母亲。”

“哼！当然不是。”温迪重重地说。现在我们明白她为什么对印第安人没有好感了。

“那她想做我的什么？”

“这可不是一位小姐该说的话。”

“那好吧，”彼得有点带刺儿地说，“也许叮叮铃会告诉我的。”

“那当然，叮叮铃会告诉你的。”温迪轻蔑地顶了他一句，“那个放荡的小东西。”

叮叮铃正在她的卧房里偷听，尖声嚷出了一句无礼的话。

“她说她以放荡为荣。”彼得翻译道。

彼得忽然想到：“也许叮叮铃愿意做我的母亲吧？”

“你这个笨货！”叮叮铃怒气冲冲地喊道。

这句话她说了那么多次，温迪都不用翻译也能听懂了。

“我差不多也同意。”温迪生气地说。想想看，温迪居然也会这么说话，可见她已经受够了。她绝没想到这个晚上会发生什么事。要是她早知道的话，她绝不会发火的。

他们谁也不知道，也许不知道更好。他们的懵懵懂懂让他们能再享受一小时的快乐。由于这是他们在岛上的最后一小时，大家就都尽情享受这六十分钟吧。他们穿着睡衣又唱又跳，唱着一支美妙歌，在歌中他们假装害怕自己的影子，一点儿都不知道，阴影很快就会笼罩他们，让他们陷入真正的恐惧。他们的舞跳得那么欢快热闹，还在床上床下互相打闹。比起跳舞来，那更像是一场枕头战；打完之后，那些枕头硬要再打一阵，就像一帮知道永不会再见的伙伴一样。在温迪讲安睡的故事以前，他们讲了多少故事啊！就连斯莱特利那晚也想讲一个故事，可是一开头，就讲得那么沉闷乏味，连他自己也讲不下去了。于是他沮丧地说：

“是啊，这个开头很没意思。我说，就把它当结尾吧。”

最后，他们都上了床听温迪的故事，这故事是他们最爱听的，却是彼得最不喜欢的。平时温迪一开始讲这个故事，彼得不是离开这屋子，就是用手捂住耳朵；这一次，要是他也这样做了，他们或许还会留在岛上。可是今晚，彼得仍旧坐在他的小凳子上。让我们看看将来会发生什么事。

Chapter 11
第十一章

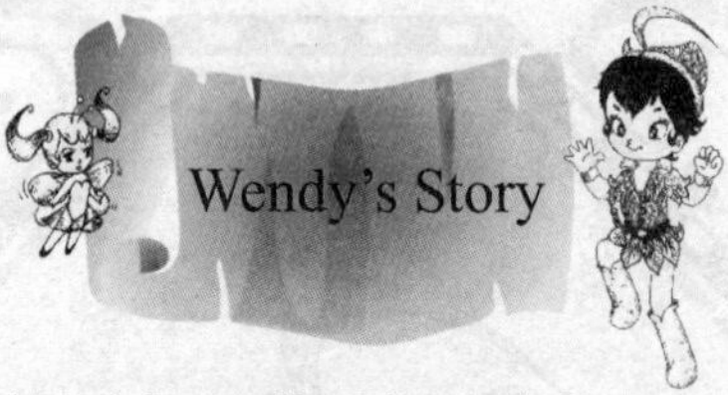

Wendy's Story

"Listen, then," said Wendy, settling down to her story, with Michael at her feet and seven boys in the bed. "There was once a gentleman – "

"I had rather he had been a lady," Curly said.

"I wish he had been a white rat," said Nibs.

"Quiet," their mother admonished (cautioned) them. "There was a lady also, and – "

"Oh, mummy," cried the first twin, "you mean that there is a lady also, don't you? She is not dead, is she?"

"Oh, no."

"I am awfully glad she isn't dead," said Tootles. "Are you glad, John?"

"Of course I am."

"Are you glad, Nibs?"

"Rather."

"Are you glad, Twins?"

"We are glad."

"Oh dear," sighed Wendy.

"Little less noise there," Peter called out, determined that she should have fair play, however beastly a story it might be in his opinion.

"The gentleman's name," Wendy continued, "was Mr. Darling, and her name was Mrs. Darling."

"I knew them," John said, to annoy the others.

"I think I knew them," said Michael rather doubtfully.

"They were married, you know," explained Wendy, "and what do you think they had?"

"White rats," cried Nibs, inspired.

"No."

"It's awfully puzzling," said Tootles, who knew the story by heart.

"Quiet, Tootles. They had three descendants."

"What is descendants?"

"Well, you are one, Twin."

"Did you hear that, John? I am a descendant."

"Descendants are only children," said John.

"Oh dear, oh dear," sighed Wendy. "Now these three children had a faithful nurse called Nana; but Mr. Darling was angry with her and chained her up in the yard, and so all the children flew away."

"It's an awfully good story," said Nibs.

"They flew away," Wendy continued, "to the Neverland, where the lost children are."

"I just thought they did," Curly broke in excitedly. "I don't know how it is, but I just thought they did!"

"O Wendy," cried Tootles, "was one of the lost children called Tootles?"

"Yes, he was."

"I am in a story. Hurrah, I am in a story, Nibs."

"Hush. Now I want you to consider the feelings of the unhappy parents with all their children flown away."

"Oo!" they all moaned, though they were not really considering the feelings of the unhappy parents one jot.

"Think of the empty beds!"

"Oo!"

"It's awfully sad," the first twin said cheerfully.

"I don't see how it can have a happy ending," said the second twin. "Do you, Nibs?"

"I'm frightfully anxious."

"If you knew how great is a mother's love," Wendy told them triumphantly, "you would have no fear." She had now come to the part that Peter hated.

"I do like a mother's love," said Tootles, hitting Nibs with a pillow. "Do you like a mother's love, Nibs?"

"I do just," said Nibs, hitting back.

"You see," Wendy said complacently, "our heroine knew that the mother would always leave the window open for her children to fly back by; so they stayed away for years and had a lovely time."

"Did they ever go back?"

"Let us now," said Wendy, bracing herself up for her finest effort, "take a peep into the future"; and they all gave themselves the twist that makes peeps into the future easier. "Years have rolled by, and who is this elegant lady of uncertain age alighting at London Station?"

"O Wendy, who is she?" cried Nibs, every bit as excited as if he didn't know.

"Can it be – yes – no – it is – the fair Wendy!"

"Oh!"

"And who are the two noble portly figures accompanying her, now grown to man's estate? Can they be John and Michael? They are!"

"Oh!"

"'See, dear brothers,'"says Wendy pointing upwards, "'there is the window still standing open. Ah, now we are rewarded for our sublime faith in a mother's love.' So up they flew to their mummy and daddy, and pen cannot describe the happy scene, over which we draw a veil."

That was the story, and they were as pleased with it as the fair narrator herself. Everything just as it should be, you see. Off we skip like the most heartless things in the world, which is what children are, but so attractive; and we have an entirely selfish time, and then when we have need of special attention we nobly return for it, confident that we shall be rewarded instead of smacked.

So great indeed was their faith in a mother's love that they felt they could afford to be callous for a bit longer.

But there was one there who knew better, and when Wendy finished he uttered a hollow groan.

"What is it, Peter?" she cried, running to him, thinking he was ill. She felt him solicitously, lower down than his chest. "Where is it, Peter?"

"It isn't that kind of pain," Peter replied darkly.

"Then what kind is it?"

"Wendy, you are wrong about mothers."

They all gathered round him in affright, so alarming was his agitation; and with a fine candour he told them what he had hitherto concealed.

"Long ago," he said, "I thought like you that my mother would always keep the window open for me, so I stayed away for moons and moons and moons, and then flew back; but the window was barred, for mother had forgotten all about me, and there was another little boy sleeping in my bed."

I am not sure that this was true, but Peter thought it was true; and it scared them.

"Are you sure mothers are like that?"

"Yes."

So this was the truth about mothers. The toads!

Still it is best to be careful; and no one knows so quickly as a child when he should give in. "Wendy, let us go home," cried John and Michael together.

"Yes," she said, clutching them.

"Not to-night?" asked the lost boys bewildered. They knew in what they called their hearts that one can get on quite well without a mother, and that it is only the mothers who think you can't.

"At once," Wendy replied resolutely, for the horrible thought had come to her: "Perhaps mother is in half mourning by this time."

This dread made her forgetful of what must be Peter's feelings, and she said to him rather sharply, "Peter, will you make the necessary arrangements?"

"If you wish it," he replied, as coolly as if she had asked him to pass the nuts.

Not so much as a sorry-to-lose-you between them! If she did not mind the parting, he was going to show her, was Peter, that neither did he.

But of course he cared very much; and he was so full of wrath against grown-ups, who, as usual, were spoiling everything, that as soon as he got inside his tree he breathed intentionally quick short breaths at the rate of about five to a second. He did this because there is a saying in the Neverland that, every time you breathe, a grown-up dies; and Peter was killing them off vindictively as fast as possible.

Then having given the necessary instructions to the redskins he returned to the home, where an unworthy scene had been enacted in his absence. Panic-stricken at the thought of losing Wendy the lost boys had advanced upon her threateningly.

"It will be worse than before she came," they cried.

"We shan't let her go."

"Let's keep her prisoner."

"Ay, chain her up."

In her extremity an instinct told her to which of them to turn.

"Tootles," she cried, "I appeal to you."

Was it not strange? She appealed to Tootles, quite the silliest one.

Grandly, however, did Tootles respond. For that one moment he dropped his silliness and spoke with dignity.

"I am just Tootles," he said, "and nobody minds me. But the first who does not behave to Wendy like an English gentleman I will blood him severely."

He drew back his hanger; and for that instant his sun was at noon. The others held back uneasily. Then Peter returned, and they saw at once that they would get no support from him. He would keep no girl in the Neverland against her will.

"Wendy," he said, striding up and down, "I have asked the redskins to guide you through the wood, as flying tires you so."

"Thank you, Peter."

"Then," he continued, in the short sharp voice of one accustomed to be obeyed, "Tinker Bell will take you across the sea. Wake her, Nibs."

Nibs had to knock twice before he got an answer, though Tink had really been sitting up in bed listening for some time.

"Who are you? How dare you? Go away," she cried.

"You are to get up, Tink," Nibs called, "and take Wendy on a journey."

Of course Tink had been delighted to hear that Wendy was going; but she was jolly well determined not to be her courier, and she said so in still more offensive language. Then she pretended to be asleep again.

"She says she won't!" Nibs exclaimed, aghast at such insubordination, whereupon Peter went sternly toward the young lady's chamber.

"Tink," he rapped out, "if you don't get up and dress at once I will open the curtains, and then we shall all see you in your negligée (nightgown)."

This made her leap to the floor. "Who said I wasn't getting up?" she cried.

In the meantime the boys were gazing very forlornly at Wendy, now equipped with John and Michael for the journey. By this time they were dejected, not merely because they were about to lose her, but also because they felt that she was going off to something nice to which they had not been invited. Novelty was beckoning to them as usual.

Crediting them with a nobler feeling Wendy melted.

"Dear ones," she said, "if you will all come with me I feel almost sure I can get my father and mother to adopt you."

The invitation was meant specially for Peter, but each of the boys was thinking exclusively of himself, and at once they jumped with joy.

"But won't they think us rather a handful?" Nibs asked in the middle of his jump.

"Oh no," said Wendy, rapidly thinking it out, "it will only mean having a few beds in the drawing-room; they can be hidden behind the screens on first Thursdays."

"Peter, can we go?" they all cried imploringly. They took it for granted that if they went he would go also, but really they scarcely cared. Thus children are ever ready, when novelty knocks, to desert their dearest ones.

"All right," Peter replied with a bitter smile, and immediately they rushed to get their things.

"And now, Peter," Wendy said, thinking she had put everything right, "I am going to give you your medicine before you go." She loved to give them medicine, and undoubtedly gave them too much. Of course it was only water, but it was out of a bottle, and she always shook the bottle and counted the drops, which gave it a certain medicinal quality. On this occasion, however, she did not give Peter his draught (portion), for just as she had prepared it, she saw a look on his face that made her heart sink.

"Get your things, Peter," she cried, shaking.

"No," he answered, pretending indifference, "I am not going with you, Wendy."

"Yes, Peter."

"No."

To show that her departure would leave him unmoved, he skipped up and down the room, playing gaily on his heartless pipes. She had to run about after him, though it was rather undignified.

"To find your mother," she coaxed.

Now, if Peter had ever quite had a mother, he no longer missed her. He could do very well without one. He had thought them out, and remembered only their bad points.

"No, no," he told Wendy decisively; "perhaps she would say I was old, and I just want always to be a little boy and to have fun."

"But, Peter – "

"No."

And so the others had to be told.

"Peter isn't coming."

Peter not coming! They gazed blankly at him, their sticks over their backs, and on each stick a bundle. Their first thought was that if Peter was not going he had probably changed his mind about letting them go.

But he was far too proud for that. "If you find your mothers," he said darkly, "I hope you will like them."

The awful cynicism of this made an uncomfortable impression, and most of them began to look rather doubtful. After all, their faces said, were they not noodles to want to go?

"Now then," cried Peter, "no fuss, no blubbering; good-bye,

Wendy"; and he held out his hand cheerily, quite as if they must really go now, for he had something important to do.

She had to take his hand, and there was no indication that he would prefer a thimble.

"You will remember about changing your flannels, Peter?" she said, lingering over him. She was always so particular about their flannels.

"Yes."

"And you will take your medicine?"

"Yes."

That seemed to be everything, and an awkward pause followed. Peter, however, was not the kind that breaks down before other people. "Are you ready, Tinker Bell?" he called out.

"Ay! Ay!"

"Then lead the way."

Tink darted up the nearest tree; but no one followed her, for it was at this moment that the pirates made their dreadful attack upon the redskins. Above, where all had been so still, the air was rent with shrieks and the clash of steel. Below, there was dead silence. Mouths opened and remained open. Wendy fell on her knees, but her arms were extended toward Peter. All arms were extended to him, as if suddenly blown in his direction; they were beseeching him mutely not to desert them. As for Peter, he seized his sword, the same he thought he had slain Barbecue with, and the lust of battle was in his eye.

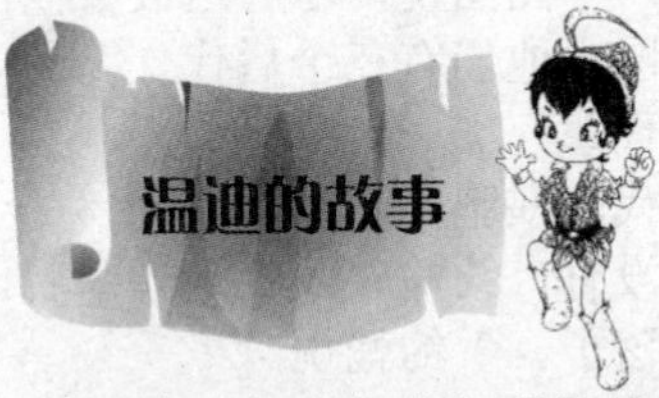

“好吧，听着，”温迪说，坐下来准备讲她的故事了。迈克尔坐在她脚边，七个孩子坐在床上。“从前有一位先生……”

“我倒宁愿是位太太。”卷毛说。

“我希望是只白老鼠。”尼布斯说。

“安静，”母亲警告他们，“还有一位太太，而且……”

“啊，妈妈，”双胞胎的老大说，“你是说还有一位太太，是不是？她没有死，是不是？”

“没有。”

“她没有死，我高兴极了，”图图说，“你高兴吗，约翰？”

“我当然高兴。”

“你高兴吗，尼布斯？”

“很高兴。”

“你们高兴吗，双胞胎？”

“我们也高兴。”

“唉，天哪。”温迪叹了口气。

“别吵！”彼得大声说。他觉得不管这故事怎么无聊，也应该让温迪讲完才算公道。

“这位先生姓达林，”温迪接着说，“女士呢，就叫达林太太。”

“我认识他们。”约翰为了让别的孩子难过而说道。

“我想我也认识他们。”迈克尔有点迟疑地说。

“他们结了婚，你们知道吧？”温迪解释说，“你们知道他们有了什么？”

“白老鼠。”尼布斯灵机一动说。

“不是。”

“真难猜呀。”图图说，尽管这故事他已能背得出。

“安静，图图。他们有三个后代。”

“什么叫后代？”

“你就是后代，双胞胎。”

“你听见了没有，约翰？我就是一个后代。”

“后代就是孩子。”约翰说。

“啊，天哪，天哪，”温迪叹气说，“好吧，这三个孩子有位忠实的保姆，名叫娜娜；可是达林先生生她的气，把她拴在院子里，然后三个孩子就全部飞走了。”

“这故事真好。”尼布斯说。

“他们飞到了梦幻岛，”温迪接着说，“那里住着许多丢失的小孩……”

“我就知道他们是在那儿，”卷毛兴奋地插嘴说，“不知怎么的，反正我就觉得他们是在那儿。”

“啊，温迪，”图图喊道，“遗失的孩子里，是不是有一个叫图图的？”

“是的。”

“我在故事里啦，哈哈，我在故事里啦，尼布斯。”

“别闹了。现在你们好好想想，孩子们都飞走了，不幸的父母们的心情会怎样呢？”

“唉！”他们全都哀叹起来，虽然他们半点也不关心那对不幸的父母的心情。

“想想那些空床！”

“哎。”

“真惨哪。”双胞胎的老大开心地说。

“我看这故事不会有什么好结果。”双胞胎的老二说，“你说呢，尼布斯？”

“我很担心。”

“要是你们知道母爱有多伟大，”温迪得意地告诉他们，“你们就不会害怕了。”现在讲到了彼得最讨厌的那部分了。

“我喜欢母爱。”图图边说边用枕头砸尼布斯，“你喜欢母爱吗？尼布斯？”

“我可喜欢呐。”尼布斯边反击边说道。

“你们看，”温迪愉快地说，“我们故事里的女主角知道，那位母亲肯定总是开着窗子，好让她的孩子们飞回来。而孩子们却在外面一呆许多年，玩个痛快。”

“他们回过家没有？”

“现在，”温迪说，鼓起勇气做最后的努力，“让我们来瞅瞅后来发生了什么事吧。”于是大家都扭动了一下，这样可以更容易看到将来。“很多年以后，一位不知年龄的漂亮小姐在伦敦车站下了火车，她是谁呢？”

“啊，温迪，她是谁？”尼布斯喊道，浑身上下都兴奋起来，就像他真的不知道似的。

“会不会是——是——不是——正是——美丽的温迪啊！”

“啊！”

“陪着她一道的那两个仪表堂堂的男子汉又是谁？会不会是约翰和迈克尔呢？正是他们！”

“啊！”

“‘你们瞧，亲爱的弟弟，’温迪指着上面说，‘那扇窗子还开着呐。因为我们对母爱的崇高信念，现在我们终于得到回报了。’于是，他们就飞起来了，飞到了妈妈和爸爸的身边。那重逢的快乐场面，不是笔墨所能描写的，我们就不去细说了。”

这个故事就是这样的，听的人和讲的人一样高兴。这故事讲得合情合理，是吧？我们有时会像那些没心肝的东西——孩子们那样，说走就走，不过这些孩子们也怪逗人喜爱的。走了之后，我们会自私地在外面玩个痛快；当我们需要别人关心时，就又大大方方地回去，而且很有把握地知道自己不但不会受惩罚，还会得到奖赏。

对母爱的深信不疑让他们觉得在外面多流连些时候也没关系。

可是，这儿有一个人比他们懂得更多，温迪讲完后，他重重地呻吟了一下。

"怎么回事，彼得？"温迪喊着跑到彼得身边，以为他病了。她关切地抚摸着他的胸口。"你哪儿疼，彼得？"

"不是那种疼。"彼得忧伤地回答道。

"那是什么样的疼？"

"温迪，你对母亲的看法不对。"

彼得这出人意料的话这么吓人，孩子们全都慌乱不安地围拢过来。于是，彼得一五一十地说出了他一直深藏在心里的话。

"很久以前，"彼得说，"我也和你们一样，相信我的母亲会永远开着窗子等我；所以，我在外面玩了一个月又一个月才飞回去，可是窗子已经锁上了，因为母亲已经把我全忘了，有另一个小男孩睡在了我的床上。"

我不敢说这是真的，但彼得认为是真的，这可把孩子们吓坏了。

"你能肯定母亲们就是这样吗？"

"是的。"

这么说，母亲们原来是这样，真可怕！

不过，还是小心些好，只有小孩子最清楚什么时候该适可而止。

"温迪，我们回家吧。"约翰和迈克尔一齐喊道。

"好吧。"温迪搂着他们说。

"该不会是今晚吧？"那些走失的孩子们迷惑不解地问。在他们所谓的心里，他们知道自己没有母亲也可以过得蛮好，只有母亲们才以为孩子们没有母亲就没法生活。

"马上就走。"温迪果断地说。因为一个可怕的念头忽然浮现在她的脑海里："说不定母亲这时已经开始哀悼我们了。"

这种恐惧使她忽略了彼得的心情，她猛地对彼得说："彼得，请你做必要的准备，好吗？"

"遵命，"彼得冷冷地回答，那神情就像温迪请他递个干果来似的。

温迪连一句惜别的话也没说！要是温迪不在乎分手，那么，他也要让她瞧瞧，他彼得也不在乎。

不过，当然他是非常在乎的；他对那些大人有一肚子的怨气，那些大人老是把一切都搞糟。所以，每次他钻进树洞，他就故意急促地呼吸，大约每秒钟呼吸五次之多。他这样做是因为在梦幻岛有个说法，你每呼吸一次，就会有一个大人死去。所以彼得就心存报复地想让他们死得越多越好。

彼得向印第安人做了必要交代之后，就回到了地下的家。在他离开的当儿，家里竟发生了不像话的事情。那些遗失的孩子们害怕温迪离开他们，竟威胁起她来。

“事情会比她来以前更糟。”他们嚷道。

“我们不让她走。”

“我们把她关起来吧。”

“对，把她锁起来。”

在危急的时候温迪灵机一动，想到了应该向谁求助。

“图图．”她喊道，“我向你申诉。”

怪不怪？她竟向图图申诉，图图可是最笨的一个。

然而，图图的反应却出人意料的严正。那一刻，他不再愚笨，回答中饱含尊严。

“我不过是图图，”他说，“谁也不拿我当回事。可是只要有人对温迪的态度不像个英国绅士，我就要叫他流血流个痛快。”

说着，他拔出了刀。这一刻，他气势咄咄逼人。别的孩子不安地退了下去。这时彼得回来了，他们立刻就看出来，从彼得那儿是得不到支持的。他是不肯违背一个女孩的意愿，强留她在梦幻岛的。

“温迪，”彼得一边说一边在房里踱来踱去，“我已经吩咐印第安人护送你们走出树林，你们飞出去太累了。”

“谢谢你，彼得。”

“然后，”彼得又用那种令人服从的短促尖锐的声音说，“叮叮铃带着你们过海。叫醒她，尼布斯。”

尼布斯敲了两次门才听到叮叮铃来应门。但其实她早已坐在床上，偷听了多时。

“你是什么人？你怎么敢这样？滚开！”她嚷道。

“你该起床啦，叮叮铃。”尼布斯喊道：“该带温迪出远门了。”

当然，叮叮铃听说温迪要走了非常高兴；可是她下定决心，决不给温迪领路；于是她说了更难听的话，随后就假装又睡着了。

“她说她不起来给温迪领路。”尼布斯大声叫道。彼得对她这样的公然抗命很是吃惊，于是严肃地向那位女郎的寝室走去。

“叮叮铃，”他大喊一声，“要是你不马上起床穿衣，我就要拉开门帘了，那我们就全都看见你穿睡袍的样子了。”

她一下子跳到了地上，喊道：“谁说我不起来？”

这时，孩子们都伤心地呆望着温迪，觉得自己好像被遗弃了。温迪、约翰和迈克尔已经收拾停当，准备上路。这时，孩子们心情沮丧，不单是因为他们就要失去温迪；而且是因为，他们觉得有什么好事在等着温迪，可是没他们的份儿。他们一贯是喜欢新鲜事的。

温迪以为他们这时怀着一种高尚的感情，她不由得心软了。

“亲爱的孩子们，”她说，“要是你们都和我一道回去，我几乎可以肯定，我父亲和母亲会把你们都收养下来的。”

这个邀请原是特别对彼得说的，可是，每个孩子都觉得是对自己说的，就都立刻快活得跳了起来。

“可是他们会不会嫌我们人太多？”尼布斯一边跳着一边问道。

“啊，不会的，”温迪说，很快地合计出来，“只要在客厅里加几张床就行了。头几个礼拜四，可以把床藏在屏风后面。”

“彼得，我们可以去吗？”孩子们一齐恳求。他们想当然地认为要是他们都去了，彼得也一定会去；不过他们其实并不怎么在乎彼得去不去。孩子们总是这样，只要有新奇的事临头，他们就宁愿扔下最亲爱的人。

“好吧。”彼得苦笑着说，孩子们立刻跑去收拾自己的东西了。

“现在，彼得，”温迪说，心想她一切都安排妥了，“在走之前，我要给你们吃药。”她喜欢给他们药吃，而且肯定会多给。当然啦，那只不过是清水，不过，水是从一只葫芦瓶里倒出来的。温迪总是摇晃着葫芦瓶，数着滴数，好像这就把水变成了药。但是，这一回她没有给彼得吃，因为她刚要给他吃的时候，忽然看到彼得脸上的神情，不由得心头一沉。

“去收拾你的东西，彼得。”温迪颤抖着喊道。

“不，”彼得回答，装作若无其事的样子，“我不跟你们去，温迪。”

“你应该跟我们一起走，彼得！”

“不。”

为了表示对温迪离去的无动于衷，彼得在房里溜达，美滋滋地吹着他那支没心没肺的笛子。温迪只得追着他跑，虽然那样子不大体面。

“去找你的母亲吧。”温迪怂恿他说。

就算彼得真有一个母亲，他也已经不再惦记她了。没有母亲，他也能过得挺好；他早就把她们看透了，现在能想起的只有她们的坏处。

“不！不！”彼得斩钉截铁地告诉温迪，“也许母亲会说，我已经长大了；可我只愿意永远做个小男孩，永远玩下去。”

“可是，彼得……”

“不。”

这消息必须得告诉其他人。

“彼得不打算走。”

彼得不走！孩子们呆呆地望着他。他们每人肩上扛着一根木棍，木棍的一头，挂着一个包袱。他们的头一个念头是，要是彼得不去，他或许会改变主意，也不让他们去。

但是彼得太高傲了，不屑于这样做。“要是你们找到了母亲，”他阴沉地说，“但愿你们会喜欢她们。”

这句带有很重的讥讽意味的话，让孩子们感到很不自在，多数人都露出疑惑的神色。他们的脸色似乎是在说，到头来，要是去的话．会不会是傻瓜呢？

“好啦，”彼得喊道，“别心烦，别哭鼻子，再见吧，温迪。”他痛痛快快地伸出手，就像他们真的就要走了似的，因为他还有重要的事要做。

温迪只得握了握他的手，因为彼得没有表示他想要一只“顶针”。

“别忘了换你的法兰绒衣裳，彼得！”温迪说，恋恋不舍地望着他，她对他们的法兰绒衣裳总是非常在意的。

“好。”

“还要记得吃药，知道吗？”

“知道了。”

好像该说的都说了，跟着是一阵别扭的沉默。但是彼得不是那种在人面前痛哭流涕的人。“叮叮铃，你准备好了吗？”他大声喊道。

“好了，好了，”

“那就带路吧。”

叮叮铃飞上了最近一棵树，可是没人跟上去。因为正在这时候，海盗们对印第安人发起了一场可怕的进攻。地面上本来悄无声息；现在，空气中震荡着一片呐喊声和兵器撞击声。地下是死一般的寂静。一张张嘴张大了，僵持着。温迪跪了下来，双臂伸向彼得。所有的手臂都伸向彼得，像是突然被一阵风刮了过去；孩子们无声地请求彼得，求他不要抛下他们。彼得呢，他一把抓起了他的剑，就是那把他以为用来杀死了巴比克的剑，眼睛里闪耀着渴望作战的光芒。

Chapter 12
第十二章

The Children Are Carried Off

The pirate attack had been a complete surprise: a sure proof that the unscrupulous Hook had conducted it improperly, for to surprise redskins fairly is beyond the wit of the white man.

By all the unwritten laws of savage warfare it is always the redskin who attacks, and with the wiliness of his race he does it just before the dawn, at which time he knows the courage of the whites to be at its lowest ebb. The white men have in the meantime made a rude stockade on the summit of yonder undulating ground, at the foot of which a stream runs, for it is destruction to be too far from water. There they await the onslaught, the inexperienced ones clutching their revolvers and treading on twigs, but the old hands sleeping tranquilly until just before the dawn. Through the long black night the savage scouts wriggle, snake-like, among the grass without stirring a blade. The brushwood closes behind them, as silently as sand into which a mole has dived. Not a sound is to be heard, save when they give vent to a wonderful imitation of the lonely call of the coyote. The cry is answered by other braves; and some of them do it even better than the coyotes, who are not very good at it. So the chill hours wear on, and the long suspense is horribly trying to the paleface who has to live through it for the first time; but to the trained hand those ghastly calls and still ghastlier silences are but an intimation of how the night is marching.

That this was the usual procedure was so well known to Hook that in disregarding it he cannot be excused on the plea of ignorance.

The Piccaninnies, on their part, trusted implicitly to his honour, and their whole action of the night stands out in marked contrast to his. They left nothing undone that was consistent with the reputation of their tribe.

With that alertness of the senses which is at once the marvel and despair of civilised peoples, they knew that the pirates were on the island from the moment one of them trod on a dry stick; and in an incredibly short space of time the coyote cries began. Every foot of ground between the spot where Hook had landed his forces and the home under the trees was stealthily examined by braves wearing their mocassins with the heels in front. They found only one hillock with a stream at its base, so that Hook had no choice; here he must establish himself and wait for just before the dawn. Everything being thus mapped out with almost diabolical cunning, the main body of the redskins folded their blankets around them, and in the phlegmatic manner that is to them, the pearl of manhood squatted above the children's home, awaiting the cold moment when they should deal pale death.

Here dreaming, though wide-awake, of the exquisite tortures to which they were to put him at break of day, those confiding savages were found by the treacherous Hook. From the accounts afterwards supplied by such of the scouts as escaped the carnage, he does not seem even to have paused at the rising ground, though it is certain that in that grey light he must have seen it: no thought of waiting to be attacked appears from first to last to have visited his subtle mind; he would not even hold off till the night was nearly spent; on he pounded with no policy but to fall to (get into combat). What could the bewildered scouts do, masters as they were of every war-like artifice save this one, but trot helplessly after him, exposing themselves fatally to view, while they gave pathetic utterance to the coyote cry.

Around the brave Tiger Lily were a dozen of her stoutest warriors, and they suddenly saw the perfidious pirates bearing down upon them. Fell from their eyes then the film through which they had looked at victory. No more would they torture at the stake. For them the happy hunting-grounds was now. They knew it; but as their father's sons they acquitted themselves. Even then they had time to gather in a phalanx (dense formation) that would have been hard to break had they risen quickly, but this they were forbidden to do by the traditions of their race. It is written that the noble savage must never express surprise in the presence of the white. Thus terrible as the sudden appearance of the pirates must have been to them, they remained stationary for a moment not a muscle moving; as if the foe had come by invitation. Then, indeed, the tradition gallantly upheld, they seized their weapons, and the air was torn with the war-cry; but it was now too late.

It is no part of ours to describe what was a massacre rather than a fight. Thus perished many of the flower of the Piccaninny tribe. Not all unavenged did they die, for with Lean Wolf fell Alf Mason, to disturb the Spanish Main no more, and among others who bit the dust were Geo. Scourie, Chas. Turley, and the Alsatian Foggerty. Turley fell to the tomahawk of the terrible Panther, who ultimately cut a way through the pirates with Tiger Lily and a small remnant of the tribe.

To what extent Hook is to blame for his tactics on this occasion is for the historian to decide. Had he waited on the rising ground till the proper hour he and his men would probably have been butchered; and in judging him it is only fair to take this into account. What he should perhaps have done was to acquaint his opponents that he proposed to follow a new method. On the other hand, this, as destroying the element of surprise, would have made his strategy of no avail, so that the whole question is beset with difficulties. One cannot at least withhold a reluctant admiration for the wit that had conceived so bold a scheme, and the fell genius with which it was carried out.

What were his own feelings about himself at that triumphant moment? Fain would his dogs have known, as breathing heavily and wiping their cutlasses, they gathered at a discreet distance from his hook, and squinted through their ferret eyes at this extraordinary man.

Elation must have been in his heart, but his face did not reflect it: ever a dark and solitary enigma, he stood aloof from his followers in spirit as in substance.

The night's work was not yet over, for it was not the redskins he had come out to destroy; they were but the bees to be smoked, so that he should get at the honey. It was Pan he wanted, Pan and Wendy and their band, but chiefly Pan.

Peter was such a small boy that one tends to wonder at the man's hatred of him. True he had flung Hook's arm to the crocodile, but even this and the increased insecurity of life to which it led, owing to the crocodile's pertinacity, hardly account for a vindictiveness so relentless and malignant. The truth is that there was a something about Peter which goaded the pirate captain to frenzy. It was not his courage, it was not his engaging appearance, it was not – . There is no beating about the bush, for we know quite well what it was, and have got to tell. It was Peter's cockiness.

This had got on Hook's nerves; it made his iron claw twitch, and at night it disturbed him like an insect. While Peter lived, the tortured man felt that he was a lion in a cage into which a sparrow had come.

The question now was how to get down the trees, or how to get his dogs down? He ran his greedy eyes over them, searching for the thinnest ones. They wriggled uncomfortably, for they knew he would not scruple to ram them down with poles.

In the meantime, what of the boys? We have seen them at the first clang of the weapons, turned as it were into stone figures, open-mouthed, all appealing with outstretched arms to Peter; and we return to them as their mouths close, and their arms fall to their sides. The pandemonium above has ceased almost as suddenly as it arose, passed like a fierce gust of wind; but they know that in the passing it has determined their fate.

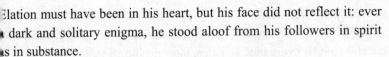

Which side had won?

The pirates, listening avidly at the mouths of the trees, heard the question put by every boy, and alas, they also heard Peter's answer.

"If the redskins have won," he said, "they will beat the tom- tom; it is always their sign of victory."

Now Smee had found the tom-tom, and was at that moment sitting on it. "You will never hear the tom-tom again," he muttered, but inaudibly of course, for strict silence had been enjoined . To his amazement Hook signed him to beat the tom-tom, and slowly there came to Smee an understanding of the dreadful wickedness of the order Never, probably, had this simple man admired Hook so much.

Twice Smee beat upon the instrument, and then stopped to listen gleefully.

"The tom-tom," the miscreants heard Peter cry; "an Indian victory!"

The doomed children answered with a cheer that was music to the black hearts above, and almost immediately they repeated their good-byes to Peter. This puzzled the pirates, but all their other feelings were swallowed by a base delight that the enemy were about to come up the trees. They smirked at each other and rubbed their hands. Rapidly and silently Hook gave his orders: one man to each tree, and the others to arrange themselves in a line two yards apart.

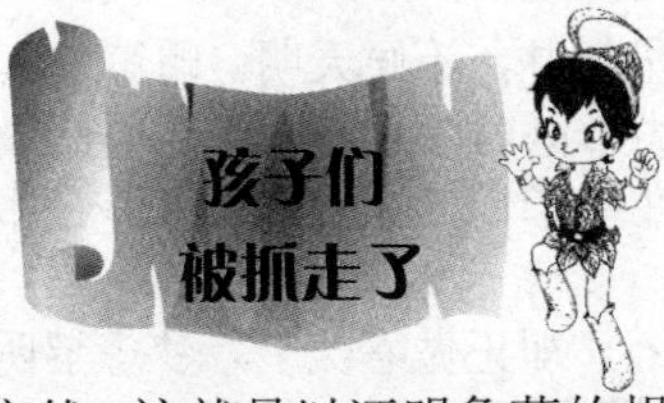

海盗的袭击过于突然，这就足以证明鲁莽的胡克指挥不当。因为要想出其不意地袭击印第安人，白人还不够聪明。

按照半开化民族的不成文法，首先发起攻击的总是印第安人。印第安人是很狡黠的，他们总是在拂晓前出击；因为他们知道，这是白人士气最低落的时候。与此同时，白人也在那片起伏不平的山地的最高处筑起了一道简陋的栅栏；在山脚下还有一条小河流过，因为若离水太远人就活不下去了。他们就在那儿等待着袭击。这些没有经验的人紧握着手枪，踏着枯枝来回走动；老手们却安逸地一觉睡到天亮。在黑魆魆的漫漫长夜里，印第安人的侦察兵在草丛里像蛇一样匍匐潜行，连一根草叶都不碰乱；那片小树林在他们身后无声地合拢，就像鼹鼠寂静无声地钻进沙地一样。一点声响都听不到，除了他们偶尔学着草原狼，惟妙惟肖地发出一声凄凉的嗥叫。这声嗥叫又得到其他人的呼应，有的人甚至叫得比那不擅长嗥叫的草原狼更好。寒夜就这样渐渐地挨过，长时间的担惊受怕对于那些初次上阵的白人来说，真是特别难熬的；可是，在那些有经验的老手看来，那些阴森可怖的嗥叫声，以及更加阴森可怖的寂静无声，只不过暗示着黑夜是如何在行进罢了。

这种情况，胡克原是一清二楚的；如果他忽略了，我们就不能把它看作是因为他的无知而原谅他。

印第安人呢，他们完全相信胡克是信守自己的准则的，他们在这夜的行动，正和胡克的行动相反。他们部落所擅长的那些事，他们都一一完成了。他们灵敏的感觉使文明人既惊羡又害怕，只要一个海盗踩响了一根干树枝，他们立刻就知道海盗们已经来到了岛上。眨眼间草原狼的嗥叫声就开始了，从胡克的队伍登陆的海岸，到大树下的地下之家，每一寸地面都被他们穿着鹿皮鞋暗地里勘察过了。他们发现只有一座土丘，山脚下有一条小河；所以胡克别无选择，只能在这里暂驻，等候天明。印第安人十分狡猾地把一切布置停当之后，主力部队就裹起毯子，以他们最引以为豪的男子汉的镇静态度，守候在孩子们的家上面，等待着那个决一死战的严峻时刻。

他们虽然醒着，却正做着美梦，梦想黎明时能抓到胡克，并严刑拷打他。却不料他们反被奸诈的胡克发现了。据一位从这次屠杀中逃出来的印第安侦察兵说，尽管在灰蒙蒙的夜光里胡克肯定看到了那座土丘，但他根本就没停留。他心里始终没有打算等着印第安人来攻击，他连等待黑夜过去都等不及了。他的策略不是别的，正是立刻动手。这些被搞迷糊的印第安侦察兵原是精通多种战术的，却冷不防他这一手，只得无可奈何地被胡克牵着鼻子跑。当他们发出一声草原狼的哀号时，终于不幸地暴露了自己。

勇敢的虎莲身边聚集了十二名最勇猛强悍的武士，他们突然发现诡计多端的海盗正向他们袭来。胜利的美梦一下子从眼前消逝了。要想酷刑收拾胡克是办不到了。面对幸福的猎场，他们很明白，必须表现出自己是印第安人的后代。假如他们很快地聚拢，列成密集的阵式，那仍会是很难攻破的；但是印第安种族的传统禁止他们这样做。他们有一条成文的守则：凡是高贵的印第安人，在白人面前决不可表现得惊慌失措。尽管海盗的突然出现使他们惊骇，他们却仍巍然屹立，连一条肌肉都纹丝不动，就好像敌人是应邀来做客似的。这样英勇地遵从了传统之后，他们才拿起武器，发出了震天的喊杀声，可是已经太晚了。

这分明不是什么战斗，而是一场大屠杀，我们不去细说了。印第安部落的许多优秀战士就这样被杀害了。不过他们也没有白白死去，瘦狼和阿尔夫·梅森一起送了命，后者再也不能侵扰西班牙海岸了；还有乔治·斯库利、查理·托利和阿尔塞人福格蒂等人也一命呜呼。托利死在可怕的豹子的斧头下，豹子和虎莲以及少数残余部队，最后终于杀出一条血路，逃了出去。

在这次战斗中，胡克的战略有多少可以指责的地方，还是等历史学家去裁决吧。假若他呆在土丘上等待正当的时刻再交手，他和他的部下说不定全都被宰了。要公正地评判他，就必须把这一点考虑进去才公道。也许他应该预先通知对手，称他要采取新的策略。不过如果那样，就不能做到出其不意、攻其不备，因此他的战略计划也就会落空了。所以这个问题是很难下结论的。不过，他的智慧能构想出这样一个大胆的计划，他狠毒的天才能实现这个计划，尽管我们并不心甘情愿，也得佩服他。

胡克的手下人恨不能知道他在那个胜利时刻的想法如何。他们气喘吁吁地擦着刀，远远地躲开他的那只铁钩，偷偷地斜睨着这个奇特的怪人。胡克心里一定是洋洋自得，不过他脸上一点都没显露出来。在精神上和实际接触中，他总是与部下保持距离，他永远是个阴暗孤独的谜一样的人物。

不过，这一夜的工作还没有结束。胡克出来并不是为了杀印第安人，印第安人只不过是用烟熏走的蜜蜂，他要取的是蜜。他的目标是彼得·潘，还有温迪以及那帮孩子，但主要是彼得·潘。

彼得是那么小的一个小男孩，这就叫人琢磨不透，为什么胡克那么恨他。不错，他曾把胡克的一条胳臂扔给了鳄鱼；然而，正是因为鳄鱼的穷追不舍才使胡克的生命安全越发没有保证。不过，这也很难说明，胡克的报复心为什么这样残酷无情，凶狠毒辣。事实是，彼得身上有某种气质，让这位海盗船长暴怒如狂。不是彼得的勇敢，不是他那逗人喜爱的模样，不是……我们用不着乱猜了，因为我们都很清楚那是什么，也必须说出来。那就是彼得趾高气扬的傲气。

正是这个，刺激着胡克的神经，恨得他的铁钩直打颤；夜里，它像一只虫子，扰得他不能安睡。只要彼得活着，这个受折磨的人就觉得自己像是一头被关在笼子里的狮子，不断地被一只麻雀骚扰着。

现在的问题是，怎样钻进树洞，或者说，怎样把他的喽罗们塞进树洞。他抬起那贪婪的双眼扫视着他们，想找一个最瘦小的人。那些喽罗们局促不安地扭动着身子，因为他们知道，他是不惜用棍子把他们捅下去的。

这时，孩子们又怎样了呢？在兵刀声乍起时，我们看到他们一动不动像石雕一样，张着嘴，伸出手臂向彼得恳求。现在回头来看，只见他们闭上了嘴，垂下了手臂。头顶上的喧嚣声戛然停止了，像初起时一样来得突然，像是一阵狂风吹过似的。但他们知道，狂风过处，已经决定了他们的命运。

哪一方得胜了呢？

海盗们爬在树洞口屏息潜听，听到每个孩子提出的问题，不幸的是，也听到了彼得的回答。

“要是印第安人得胜，”彼得说，“他们一定会敲起战鼓；那是他们胜利的讯号。”

那只战鼓斯密已经找到了，这会儿他正坐在鼓上。“你们再也甭想听到鼓声了。”斯密低声嘲笑着说，声音低得谁也听不见．因为胡克严令不许出声。使他惊讶万分的是，胡克冲他打了个手势，叫他击鼓。斯密这才慢慢地领悟到，这个命令是多么阴险毒辣。这个头脑简单的人，或许从来没有像现在这样敬佩过胡克。

斯密敲了两遍鼓，心花怒放地静听反应。

“咚咚的鼓声，”海盗们听见彼得喊道，“印第安人胜利了！”

不幸的孩子们报以一声欢呼，在上面的黑心狼听来，这简直是美妙的音乐。接着，他们一连声地向彼得告别。海盗们听了莫名其妙，不过，他们所有的情绪都被卑鄙的欢喜盖过了，因为敌人就要从树洞里爬上来了。他们奸笑着，摩拳擦掌。胡克迅速、悄悄地下令：一人守一个树洞，其余的人排成一行，隔两码站一个人。

Chapter 13
第十三章

Do You Believe in Fairies?

The more quickly this horror is disposed of the better. The first to emerge from his tree was Curly. He rose out of it into the arms of Cecco, who flung him to Smee, who flung him to Starkey, who flung him to Bill Jukes, who flung him to Noodler, and so he was tossed from one to another till he fell at the feet of the black pirate. All the boys were plucked from their trees in this ruthless manner; and several of them were in the air at a time, like bales of goods flung from hand to hand.

A different treatment was accorded to Wendy, who came last. With ironical politeness Hook raised his hat to her, and, offering her his arm, escorted her to the spot where the others were being gagged. He did it with such an air, he was so frightfully DISTINGUE , that she was too fascinated to cry out. She was only a little girl.

Perhaps it is tell-tale to divulge that for a moment Hook entranced her, and we tell on her only because her slip led to strange results. Had she haughtily unhanded him (and we should have loved to write it of her), she would have been hurled through the air like the others, and then Hook would probably not have been present at the tying of the children; and had he not been at the tying he would not have discovered Slightly's secret, and without the secret he could not presently have made his foul attempt on Peter's life.

They were tied to prevent their flying away, doubled up with their knees close to their ears; and for this job the black pirate had cut a rope into nine equal pieces. All went well until Slightly's turn came, when he was found to be like those irritating parcels that use up all the string in going round and leave no tags with which to tie a knot. The pirates kicked him in their rage, just as you kick the parcel (though in fairness you should kick the string); and strange to say it was Hook who told them to belay their violence. His lip was curled with malicious triumph. While his dogs were merely sweating because every time they tried to pack the unhappy lad tight in one part he bulged out in another, Hook's master mind had gone far beneath Slightly's surface, probing not for effects but for causes; and his exultation showed that he had found them. Slightly, white to the gills, knew that Hook had surprised his secret, which was this, that no boy so blown out could use a tree wherein an average man need stick. Poor Slightly, most wretched of all the children now, for he was in a panic about Peter, bitterly regretted what he had done. Madly addicted to the drinking of water when he was hot, he had swelled in consequence to his present girth, and instead of reducing himself to fit his tree he had, unknown to the others, whittled his tree to make it fit him.

Sufficient of this Hook guessed to persuade him that Peter at last lay at his mercy, but no word of the dark design that now formed in the subterranean caverns of his mind crossed his lips; he merely signed that the captives were to be conveyed to the ship, and that he would be alone.

How to convey them? Hunched up in their ropes they might indeed be rolled down hill like barrels, but most of the way lay through a morass. Again Hook's genius surmounted difficulties. He indicated that the little house must be used as a conveyance. The children were flung into it, four stout pirates raised it on their shoulders, the others fell in behind, and singing the hateful pirate chorus the strange procession set off through the wood. I don't know whether any of the children were crying; if so, the singing drowned the sound; but as the little house disappeared in the forest, a brave though tiny jet of smoke issued from its chimney as if defying Hook.

Hook saw it, and it did Peter a bad service. It dried up any trickle of pity for him that may have remained in the pirate's infuriated breast.

The first thing he did on finding himself alone in the fast falling night was to tiptoe to Slightly's tree, and make sure that it provided him with a passage. Then for long he remained brooding; his hat of ill omen on the sward, so that any gentle breeze which had arisen might play refreshingly through his hair. Dark as were his thoughts his blue eyes were as soft as the periwinkle. Intently he listened for any sound from the nether world, but all was as silent below as above; the house under the ground seemed to be but one more empty tenement in the void. Was that boy asleep, or did he stand waiting at the foot of Slightly's tree, with his dagger in his hand?

There was no way of knowing, save by going down. Hook let his cloak slip softly to the ground, and then biting his lips till a lewd blood stood on them, he stepped into the tree. He was a brave man, but for a moment he had to stop there and wipe his brow, which was dripping like a candle. Then silently he let himself go into the unknown.

He arrived unmolested at the foot of the shaft, and stood still again, biting at his breath, which had almost left him. As his eyes became accustomed to the dim light various objects in the home under the trees took shape; but the only one on which his greedy gaze rested, long sought for and found at last, was the great bed. On the bed lay Peter fast asleep.

Unaware of the tragedy being enacted above, Peter had continued, for a little time after the children left, to play gaily on his pipes: no doubt rather a forlorn attempt to prove to himself that he did not care.

Then he decided not to take his medicine, so as to grieve Wendy. Then he lay down on the bed outside the coverlet, to vex her still more; for she had always tucked them inside it, because you never know that you may not grow chilly at the turn of the night. Then he nearly cried; but it struck him how indignant she would be if he laughed instead; so he laughed a haughty laugh and fell asleep in the middle of it.

Sometimes, though not often, he had dreams, and they were more painful than the dreams of other boys. For hours he could not be separated from these dreams, though he wailed piteously in them. They had to do, I think, with the riddle of his existence. At such times it had been Wendy's custom to take him out of bed and sit with him on her lap, soothing him in dear ways of her own invention, and when he grew calmer to put him back to bed before he quite woke up, so that he should not know of the indignity to which she had subjected him. But on this occasion he had fallen at once into a dreamless sleep. One arm dropped over the edge of the bed, one leg was arched, and the unfinished part of his laugh was stranded on his mouth, which was open, showing the little pearls.

Thus defenceless Hook found him. He stood silent at the foot of the tree looking across the chamber at his enemy. Did no feeling of compassion disturb his sombre breast? The man was not wholly evil; he loved flowers (I have been told) and sweet music (he was himself no mean performer on the harpsichord); and, let it be frankly admitted, the idyllic nature of the scene stirred him profoundly. Mastered by his better self he would have returned reluctantly up the tree, but for one thing.

What stayed him was Peter's impertinent appearance as he slept. The open mouth, the drooping arm, the arched knee: they were such a personification of cockiness as, taken together, will never again, one may hope, be presented to eyes so sensitive to their offensiveness. They steeled Hook's heart. If his rage had broken him into a hundred pieces every one of them would have disregarded the incident, and leapt at the sleeper.

Though a light from the one lamp shone dimly on the bed, Hook stood in darkness himself, and at the first stealthy step forward he discovered an obstacle, the door of Slightly's tree. It did not entirely fill the aperture, and he had been looking over it. Feeling for the catch, he found to his fury that it was low down, beyond his reach. To his disordered brain it seemed then that the irritating quality in Peter's face and figure visibly increased, and he rattled the door and flung himself against it. Was his enemy to escape him after all?

But what was that? The red in his eye had caught sight of Peter's medicine standing on a ledge within easy reach. He fathomed what it was straightaway, and immediately knew that the sleeper was in his power.

Lest he should be taken alive, Hook always carried about his person a dreadful drug, blended by himself of all the death- dealing rings that had come into his possession. These he had boiled down into a yellow liquid quite unknown to science, which was probably the most virulent poison in existence.

Five drops of this he now added to Peter's cup. His hand shook, but it was in exultation rather than in shame. As he did it he avoided glancing at the sleeper, but not lest pity should unnerve him; merely to avoid spilling. Then one long gloating look he cast upon his victim, and turning, wormed his way with difficulty up the tree. As he emerged at the top he looked the very spirit of evil breaking from its hole. Donning his hat at its most rakish angle, he wound his cloak around him, holding one end in front as if to conceal his person from the night, of which it was the blackest part, and muttering strangely to himself, stole away through the trees.

Peter slept on. The light guttered and went out, leaving the tenement in darkness; but still he slept. It must have been not less than ten o'clock by the crocodile, when he suddenly sat up in his bed, wakened by he knew not what. It was a soft cautious tapping on the door of his tree.

Soft and cautious, but in that stillness it was sinister. Peter felt for his dagger till his hand gripped it. Then he spoke.

"Who is that?"

For long there was no answer: then again the knock.

"Who are you?"

No answer.

He was thrilled, and he loved being thrilled. In two strides he reached the door. Unlike Slightly's door, it filled the aperture, so that he could not see beyond it, nor could the one knocking see him.

"I won't open unless you speak," Peter cried.

Then at last the visitor spoke, in a lovely bell-like voice.

"Let me in, Peter."

It was Tink, and quickly he unbarred to her. She flew in excitedly, her face flushed and her dress stained with mud.

"What is it?"

"Oh, you could never guess!" she cried, and offered him three guesses. "Out with it!" he shouted, and in one ungrammatical sentence, as long as the ribbons that conjurers pull from their mouths, she told of the capture of Wendy and the boys.

Peter's heart bobbed up and down as he listened. Wendy bound, and on the pirate ship; she who loved everything to be just so!

"I'll rescue her!" he cried, leaping at his weapons. As he leapt he thought of something he could do to please her. He could take his medicine.

His hand closed on the fatal draught.

"No!" shrieked Tinker Bell, who had heard Hook mutter about his deed as he sped through the forest.

"Why not?"

"It is poisoned."

"Poisoned? Who could have poisoned it?"

"Hook."

"Don't be silly. How could Hook have got down here?"

Alas, Tinker Bell could not explain this, for even she did not know the dark secret of Slightly's tree. Nevertheless Hook's words had left no room for doubt. The cup was poisoned.

"Besides," said Peter, quite believing himself "I never fell asleep."

He raised the cup. No time for words now; time for deeds; and with one of her lightning movements Tink got between his lips and the draught, and drained it to the dregs.

"Why, Tink, how dare you drink my medicine?"

But she did not answer. Already she was reeling in the air.

"What is the matter with you?" cried Peter, suddenly afraid.

"It was poisoned, Peter," she told him softly; "and now I am going to be dead."

"O Tink, did you drink it to save me?"

"Yes."

"But why, Tink?"

Her wings would scarcely carry her now, but in reply she alighted on his shoulder and gave his nose a loving bite. She whispered in his ear "You silly ass," and then, tottering to her chamber, lay down on the bed.

His head almost filled the fourth wall of her little room as he knelt near her in distress. Every moment her light was growing fainter; and he knew that if it went out she would be no more. She liked his tears so much that she put out her beautiful finger and let them run over it.

Her voice was so low that at first he could not make out what she said. Then he made it out. She was saying that she thought she could get well again if children believed in fairies.

Peter flung out his arms. There were no children there, and it was night time; but he addressed all who might be dreaming of the Neverland, and who were therefore nearer to him than you think: boys and girls in their nighties, and naked papooses in their baskets hung from trees.

"Do you believe?" he cried.

Tink sat up in bed almost briskly to listen to her fate.

She fancied she heard answers in the affirmative, and then again she wasn't sure.

"What do you think?" she asked Peter.

"If you believe," he shouted to them, "clap your hands; don't let Tink die."

Many clapped.

Some didn't.

A few beasts hissed.

The clapping stopped suddenly; as if countless mothers had rushed to their nurseries to see what on earth was happening; but already Tink was saved. First her voice grew strong, then she popped out of bed, then she was flashing through the room more merry and impudent than ever. She never thought of thanking those who believed, but she would have like to get at the ones who had hissed.

"And now to rescue Wendy!"

The moon was riding in a cloudy heaven when Peter rose from his tree, begirt with weapons and wearing little else, to set out upon his perilous quest. It was not such a night as he would have chosen. He had hoped to fly, keeping not far from the ground so that nothing unwonted should escape his eyes; but in that fitful light to have flown low would have meant trailing his shadow through the trees, thus disturbing birds and acquainting a watchful foe that he was astir.

He regretted now that he had given the birds of the island such strange names that they are very wild and difficult of approach.

There was no other course but to press forward in redskin fashion, at which happily he was an adept But in what direction, for he could not be sure that the children had been taken to the ship? A light fall of snow had obliterated all footmarks; and a deathly silence pervaded the island, as if for a space Nature stood still in horror of the recent carnage. He had taught the children something of the forest lore that he had himself learned from Tiger Lily and Tinker Bell, and knew that in their dire hour they were not likely to forget it. Slightly, if he had an opportunity, would blaze the trees, for instance, Curly would drop seeds, and Wendy would leave her handkerchief at some important place. The morning was needed to search for such guidance, and he could not wait. The upper world had called him, but would give no help.

The crocodile passed him, but not another living thing, not a sound, not a movement; and yet he knew well that sudden death might be at the next tree, or stalking him from behind.

He swore this terrible oath: "Hook or me this time."

Now he crawled forward like a snake; and again, erect, he darted across a space on which the moonlight played, one finger on his lip and his dagger at the ready. He was frightfully happy

这段恐怖故事，越快讲完越好。头一个钻出树洞的是卷毛，他一出来，立刻就落到了切科的手里；切科把他扔给了斯密，斯密把他扔给了斯塔奇，斯塔奇把他扔给了比尔·鸠克斯，比尔·鸠克斯又把他扔给了努得勒。就这样，他被他们一个接一个扔过去，最后被扔到了那个黑海盗的脚下。所有的孩子都被这样残忍地从树洞里拽了出来；有几个孩子有时候被抛到半空中，像传递一包包的货物一样。

最后一个出来的是温迪，她受到的待遇略有不同。胡克嘲弄地装作彬彬有礼的样子，向她脱帽致意，还用胳臂挽着她，把她搀扶到孩子们被囚禁的地方。胡克的风度是那样高贵，温迪像着了迷似的，竟没有哭喊出来。她只不过是个小女孩呀。

要说温迪这一刻被胡克迷住了，似乎是贬低了她；但我们提到这一点，是因为温迪的失误引起了意想不到的后果。要是她高傲地拒绝挽着胡克的手臂（我们当然愿意这样来写她），她就会像别的孩子一样被抛在空中，那么胡克也许就不会看到孩子们被捆绑的样子；假如他当时不在场，也就不会发现斯莱特利的秘密；假如没有发现这个秘密，他就不会去卑鄙地图谋彼得的性命。

为了防止孩子们逃跑飞走，海盗们把他们都捆了起来，膝盖贴近耳朵捆成一团。黑海盗把一根绳子割成相等的九段，其他孩子全都顺顺当当地捆好了，最后轮到捆斯莱特利时，却发现他像一个恼人的包裹一样，捆了一道一道，所有的绳子都用完了，剩下的绳头却不够打结。海盗们恼怒之下就踢他，就像踢一只包裹一样（说句公道话，应该踢绳子）。说也奇怪，胡克叫他们停止暴行。胡克的嘴唇翘起来了，露出恶毒的得意神气。他的部下在捆绑这个不幸的孩子时，每次要捆紧他的这一部分，另一部分就胀出来，累得他们汗如雨下。可是精明的胡克看透了斯莱特利的把戏，他发现的不是结果，而是原因。他那副洋洋得意的样子说明他已经发现了那个秘密。斯莱特利的脸发白了，他知道胡克已经发现了：一个胀得这么大的孩子能钻得进的树洞，一个普通大人不用棍子捅也一定能钻进去。可怜的斯莱持利，他现在是所有孩子们中最不幸的一个了；因为他为彼得担惊受怕，深深地懊悔他所做的事。原来，有一次他热极了，拼命喝水，把肚子胀得像现在这样大；他没有缩小自己的身体去适应他的树洞，而是悄悄地削大了树洞来迁就他胀大的身体。

这就够了，胡克相信彼得现在终于落进了他的手心。不过他阴暗的脑子里形成的这个计谋，一个字也没有从他嘴里吐露出来；他只作了个手势，命令把俘虏押上船去，他要独自留下。

怎样押送呢？他们被绳子捆成一团，原是可以像木桶一样滚下山坡的，但是途中要经过一些沼地。又是胡克的天才克服了困难。他指示，可以利用那间小屋子作为运输工具。孩子们被扔进了小屋子，四个强壮的海盗把它扛在肩上，其余的海盗跟在后面，唱起那支可恶的海盗歌。这支奇怪的队伍出发了，穿过了树林。我不知道孩子们是否有人在哭，即使有，那哭声也给歌声淹没了。可是，当小屋在树林里渐渐隐去时，从它的烟囱里升起了一缕细细的但是又勇敢的青烟，仿佛在向胡克挑战。

胡克看见了，这对彼得很不利。因为，即使这海盗心里还有一丝恻隐之心，这时也消失得一干二净了。

黑夜很快地降临，现在只剩下胡克独自一人了。他所做的第一件事，就是蹑手蹑脚地走到斯莱特利的那棵树跟前，想弄清楚他是不是能从那里钻进去。他思索了好半晌，把他那顶不吉利的帽子放在草地上，好让吹来的一股清风轻抚他的头发。他的心虽黑，他的蓝眼睛却像长春花一样柔和。他屏息静听地下的动静，可是下面也和上面一样寂静无声。地下的屋子像是一座空无一人的荒宅。那孩子是睡着了吗？还是站在斯莱特利的树根下，手里拿着刀在等他？

除非亲身去探个究竟，否则没有人会知道。胡克把他的外套轻轻地脱下放在地上，紧紧地咬着嘴唇，直咬得流出了污血。他踏进了树洞。他是个勇敢的人，可是，一时竟不得不停下来擦额上的汗，他的汗像蜡烛油一样直淌。然后，他悄悄地下到这个陌生的世界。

他平安地来到了树洞底下，又一动不动地站在那儿，几乎喘不过气来了。等到他的眼睛逐渐习惯了黑暗，才一件件看清楚树下屋里的东西。可是他贪婪的眼睛，只注视着一件东西，那是他找了很久才终于找到的，就是那张大床。床上躺着熟睡的彼得。

彼得一点也不知道上面发生的惨事。孩子们离开后，他继续欢快地吹了一阵笛子。当然，他只是在凄惶中故意这样做，为的是证明他一点也不在乎。然后，他决定不吃药，为的是让温迪伤心。他躺在床上故意不盖被子，好叫温迪更加烦恼，因为温迪总是把被子给他们盖得严严实实的，怕的是他们半夜里会着凉。然后彼得几乎要哭出来。可是他忽然又想到，要是他笑，温迪没准会更生气呢！于是他狂傲地大笑，笑着笑着就睡着了。

彼得有时会做梦。虽然他并不经常做梦，可是他的梦比别的孩子的更叫人难受。他在梦里常会痛哭，一连几个小时都摆脱不了噩梦的纠缠。他的梦，我猜想大概是和他那来历不明的身世有关。每到这种时候，温迪总是把他从床上扶起来，让他坐在自己膝上，用她自己发明的种种亲昵的方法抚慰他；等他稍稍平静下来，不等他醒又把他放回床上，为的是不让他知道有损他尊严的那些做法。可是这一回，彼得睡得很熟，一点梦都没做；一只胳臂耷拉在床沿下，一条腿拱了起来；嘴角上还残留着一点笑意，嘴张着，露出两排珍珠般的小牙。

彼得就在这样毫无防御的状态下被胡克发现了。胡克不声不响地站在树洞底下，隔着房间远远望着他的敌人。胡克那阴暗的心里，难道没有激起一丝同情吗？这个人并不是坏到家了：他爱花（我听说），爱美妙的音乐（他自己弹竖琴弹得不坏）。我们得坦白地承认，眼前这幅动人的景象深深地感动了他。要是他的善良一面占了上风，他也许会勉勉强强地走回树上去，可是有个东西把他留了下来。

让胡克留下的是彼得那倨傲不恭的睡态——嘴张着，胳臂耷拉着，膝盖拱着。这些姿态看起来十分盛气凌人，在胡克那敏感的眼睛看来，再也不会有比这更气人的了。这使得胡克又硬起了心肠。要是他的怒火把他爆裂成几百块碎片，那么每一片都会不顾一切地飞向那个熟睡的孩子。

一盏微弱的灯照在床上，胡克站在黑暗中。他刚偷偷地向前迈了一步，就遇到了障碍，那是斯莱特利的树洞的门。门和洞口并不完全吻合，所以胡克是从门上面朝里看的。他伸手去摸门闩，发现门闩很低，够不着。在他那纷乱的头脑里，彼得的姿态和面孔似乎越发可恶了。他使劲摇晃着门，用身子去撞门。他的敌人究竟能不能逃出他的毒手呢？

那是什么？胡克发红的眼睛瞅见了彼得的药杯，正摆在他伸手就能拿到的架子上。他一下子就明白了那是什么，知道这个熟睡的孩子已经落进了他的手心。

胡克生怕自己被人活捉了去，他总是随身带着一瓶可怕的毒药，那是他用找到的各种致命的毒草炮制成的。他把这些毒草熬成一种黄色的液体，科学家都没有见识过，这大概是世界上最毒的一种毒药了。

胡克在彼得的药杯里滴了五滴这种毒药。他的手不住地颤抖，那是因为狂喜，而不是因为羞愧。胡克滴药时，一眼也不去看彼得，不是因为怕心软下不了手，只是怕药洒了。然后，他久久地幸灾乐祸地凝望了他的受害者一眼，转身艰难地蠕动着爬上树去。胡克从树顶上钻出来时，那样子真像恶魔出了魔窟。他流里流气地歪戴着帽子，撕破他的外套披在身上，只在前面抓住一个角儿像是要把整个人藏起来不让黑夜看见。其实，他才是黑夜里最黑暗的一件东西。他喃喃地自言自语，咕哝着些奇怪的话，穿过树林溜走了。

彼得还在睡。灯火跳了一下，熄灭了，屋里一片黑暗，可他还是睡得很好。鳄鱼肚里的钟一定不止十点钟了，也不知道被什么惊醒了，彼得突然从床上坐起来。那是他的那棵树上，轻轻的、有礼貌的叩门声。

虽然声音很轻，很有礼貌，可是在寂静的深夜里，也是够瘆人的。彼得伸手去摸刀，他握住了刀，然后问道：

“谁？”

半晌没有回答，然后又是敲门声。

“你是谁？”

没有回答。

彼得毛骨悚然，但这正是他最喜欢的刺激。他两步跨到门前。这门不像斯莱特利的门，它和树洞严丝合缝，所以他看不到外面，敲门的人也看不到他。

“你不开口，我就不开门。”彼得喊道。

来人终于开口了，发出了小铃铛似的可爱的声音。

“让我进去，彼得。”

那是叮叮铃，彼得马上打开门闩让她进来。她飞了进来，神情激动，脸色通红，衣服上沾满了泥。

“怎么回事？”

“啊，你怎么也猜不到的！”她喊道。她让彼得猜三次。“快说！”彼得大声喊道。于是，叮叮铃用一句不合语法的长句子，长得像魔术师从嘴里抽出来的带子一样，说出了温迪和孩子们被俘的经过。

彼得一面听，一面心突突地跳。温迪被绑了，被抓到了海盗船上。她充满了爱心，却落得如此下场！

“我要去救她。”彼得跳了起来，去拿武器。他跳起来的时候，想起了一件可以让温迪高兴的事——他可以吃药。

他的手伸向那只致命的药杯。

“别喝！”叮叮铃尖声叫道，她听到了胡克匆匆穿过树林时，自言自语地嘟哝着他做过的事。

“为什么？”

“药里有毒。”

“有毒？谁能来下毒？”

“胡克。”

“别说傻话。胡克怎么能到这里来？”

咳！这一点叮叮铃也没法解释，因为就连她也不知道斯莱特利的树的秘密。不过，胡克的话是无可怀疑的，药杯里的确下了毒。

“况且，”彼得自信心十足地说，“我压根儿就没睡着。”

彼得举起了杯子。说话已经来不及了，只有立即行动。叮叮铃像闪电一般，迅速地蹿到彼得的嘴唇和杯子之间，一口喝干了杯中的药。

“怎么，叮叮铃？你怎么敢喝我的药？”

叮叮铃没有回答。她已经摇摇晃晃地在空中旋转了。

“你怎么啦？”彼得喊，他有点害怕了。

“药里有毒，彼得，”叮叮铃轻声对他说，“现在我要死啦。”

“啊，叮叮铃，你喝毒药是为了救我吗？”

“是的。”

“可是为什么呀，叮叮铃？”

叮叮铃的翅膀已经托不起她了，为了回答，她落到了彼得的肩上，在他的下巴上亲热地咬了一口，在他耳边悄悄地说：“你这个笨蛋。”然后她摇摇晃晃地回到她的寝室，躺倒在床上。

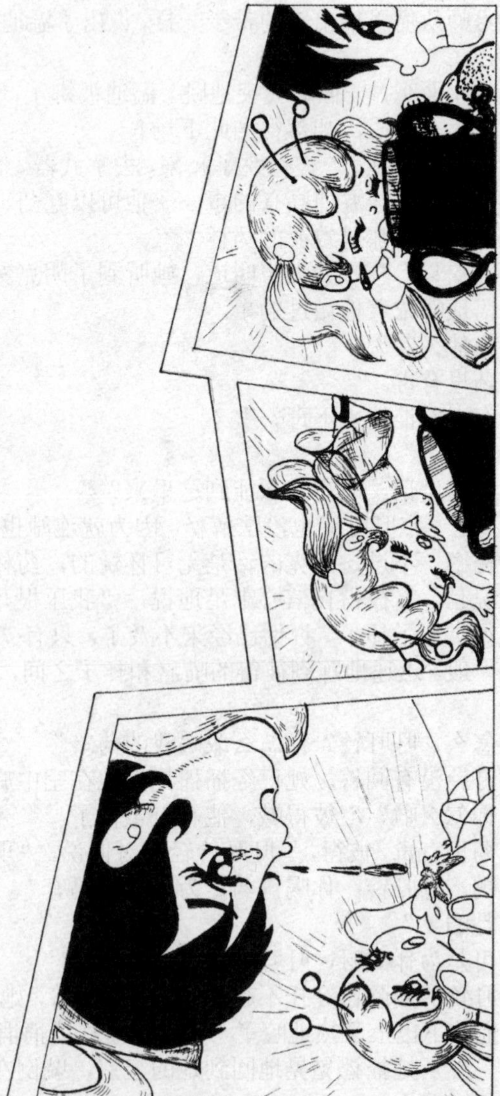

彼得悲哀地跪在她身边，他的头几乎塞满了整个小屋子。叮叮铃的亮光越来越暗了。彼得知道，要是这亮光熄灭了，叮叮铃就不复存在了。叮叮铃喜欢彼得的眼泪，她伸出美丽的手指，让眼泪在她手指上滚过。

叮叮铃的声音很微弱，起初，彼得几乎听不清她说些什么。后来，他听懂了。她在说，要是小孩儿们相信有仙子，她还会好起来的。

彼得伸出了双臂。可是眼前没有孩子，而且现在是深夜。不过，他是对所有梦到了梦幻岛的孩子们说话——穿着睡衣的男孩和女孩们，还有光着身子、睡在悬挂在树上的篮子里的印第安小娃娃，他们其实离彼得都很近，不像你所想的那么远。

“你们信不信有仙人？”他大声喊道。

叮叮铃一下子从床上坐了起来，几乎屏住气，静听她的命运。

她觉着她仿佛听到了肯定的回答，可又说不准。

“你是怎么想？”叮叮铃问彼得。

“要是你们相信，”彼得冲着孩子们大喊，“就拍手，别让叮叮铃死去。”

很多孩子拍了手。

有些孩子没拍手。

有少数几个没心肝的小畜牲发出了嘘声。

拍手声突然停止了，好像有数不清的母亲们奔进了育儿室，看看到底发生了什么事。不过叮叮铃已经得救了，先是她的声音变得洪亮了，随后她一阵风似的跳下了床。跟着，她就满屋子乱飞，比以往任何时候都来得欢快和起劲。她绝没有想到要感谢那些拍手的孩子，却一心想着要去对付那些发出嘘声的小东西。

“现在该去救温迪了。”

彼得钻出树洞时，月亮正在云天里行走。他全副武装，却没有多穿衣裳，就这样踏上了冒险的征途。他并不想挑这样一个夜晚去冒险。他本想低低地飞，离地面很近，这样所有异乎寻常的事就都逃不过他的眼睛了。但是，在时明时暗的月光下飞得很低，就会把他的影子投在树上，惊动了鸟，警觉的敌人就会发现他已经出动。

彼得现在后悔他不该给岛上的鸟起了些奇怪的名字，那让它们变得很野，很难接近。

现在没有别的办法，只有学着印第安人的样子，贴着地面爬，幸好他已经习惯了。可是朝什么方向爬呢？因为他还不能断定，孩子们是不是被带到了船上。一场小雪掩盖了所有的脚印，岛上笼罩着死一般的寂静，仿佛一时间大自然也被刚才发生的大屠杀吓呆了。彼得曾经从虎莲和叮叮铃那儿学过一些山林知识，并传授给了孩子们；他相信，碰到危急关头，他们是不会忘记的。例如，如果有机会，斯莱特利会在树上刻上标记，卷毛会在地上撒下树种；温迪会在紧要的地方扔下她的手帕。可是要找到这些目标，需要等到天明，彼得却不能再等了。上面的世界在召唤他，却不给他一点帮助。

除了从彼得身边爬过去的鳄鱼，此外再也没有别的活物了；没有一点声音，没有一丝动静。彼得很清楚，死亡也许就等在前面一棵树下，或者会从身后扑上来。

彼得立下了这样一句可怕的誓言：“胡克，这次不是你死就是我亡！”

现在，彼得像蛇一样向前爬着，时而又站起来，飞快地跑过一片月光照亮了的空地。他一个手指头按着嘴唇，一手握刀做好准备，兴奋得不得了。

Chapter 14
第十四章

The Pirate Ship

One green light squinting over Kidd's Creek, which is near the mouth of the pirate river, marked where the brig, the JOLLY ROGER, lay, low in the water; a rakish-looking craft foul to the hull, every beam in her detestable, like ground strewn with mangled feathers. She was the cannibal of the seas, and scarce needed that watchful eye, for she floated immune in the horror of her name.

She was wrapped in the blanket of night, through which no sound from her could have reached the shore. There was little sound, and none agreeable save the whir of the ship's sewing machine at which Smee sat, ever industrious and obliging, the essence of the commonplace, pathetic Smee. I know not why he was so infinitely pathetic, unless it were because he was so pathetically unaware of it; but even strong men had to turn hastily from looking at him, and more than once on summer evenings he had touched the fount of Hook's tears and made it flow. Of this, as of almost everything else, Smee was quite unconscious.

A few of the pirates leant over the bulwarks, drinking in the miasma of the night; others sprawled by barrels over games of dice and cards; and the exhausted four who had carried the little house lay prone on the deck, where even in their sleep they rolled skillfully to this side or that out of Hook's reach, lest he should claw them mechanically in passing.

Hook trod the deck in thought. O man unfathomable. It was his hour of triumph. Peter had been removed for ever from his path, and all the other boys were in the brig, about to walk the plank. It was his grimmest deed since the days when he had brought Barbecue to heel; and knowing as we do how vain a tabernacle is man, could we be surprised had he now paced the deck unsteadily, bellied out by the winds of his success?

But there was no elation in his gait, which kept pace with the action of his sombre mind. Hook was profoundly dejected.

He was often thus when communing with himself on board ship in the quietude of the night. It was because he was so terribly alone. This inscrutable man never felt more alone than when surrounded by his dogs. They were socially inferior to him.

Hook was not his true name. To reveal who he really was would even at this date set the country in a blaze; but as those who read between the lines must already have guessed, he had been at a famous public school; and its traditions still clung to him like garments, with which indeed they are largely concerned. Thus it was offensive to him even now to board a ship in the same dress in which he grappled her, and he still adhered in his walk to the school's distinguished slouch. But above all he retained the passion for good form.

Good form! However much he may have degenerated, he still knew that this is all that really matters.

From far within him he heard a creaking as of rusty portals, and through them came a stern tap-tap-tap, like hammering in the night when one cannot sleep. "Have you been good form to-day?" was their eternal question.

"Fame, fame, that glittering bauble, it is mine!" he cried.

"Is it quite good form to be distinguished at anything?" the tap-tap from his school replied.

"I am the only man whom Barbecue feared," he urged, "and Flint feared Barbecue."

"Barbecue, Flint – what house?" came the cutting retort.

Most disquieting reflection of all, was it not bad form to think about good form?

His vitals were tortured by this problem. It was a claw within him sharper than the iron one; and as it tore him, the perspiration dripped down his tallow countenance and streaked his doublet. Ofttimes he drew his sleeve across his face, but there was no damming that trickle.

Ah, envy not Hook.

There came to him a presentiment of his early dissolution. It was as if Peter's terrible oath had boarded the ship. Hook felt a gloomy desire to make his dying speech, lest presently there should be no time for it.

"Better for Hook," he cried, "if he had had less ambition!" It was in his darkest hours only that he referred to himself in the third person.

"No little children to love me!"

Strange that he should think of this, which had never troubled him before; perhaps the sewing machine brought it to his mind. For long he muttered to himself, staring at Smee, who was hemming placidly, under the conviction that all children feared him.

Feared him! Feared Smee! There was not a child on board the brig that night who did not already love him. He had said horrid things to them and hit them with the palm of his hand, because he could not hit with his fist, but they had only clung to him the more. Michael had tried on his spectacles.

To tell poor Smee that they thought him lovable! Hook itched to do it, but it seemed too brutal. Instead, he revolved this mystery in his mind: why do they find Smee lovable? He pursued the problem like the sleuth-hound that he was. If Smee was lovable, what was it that made him so? A terrible answer suddenly presented itself – "Good form?"

Had the bo'sun good form without knowing it, which is the best form of all?

He remembered that you have to prove you don't know you have it before you are eligible for Pop.

With a cry of rage he raised his iron hand over Smee's head; but he did not tear. What arrested him was this reflection:

"To claw a man because he is good form, what would that be?"

"Bad form!"

The unhappy Hook was as impotent as he was damp, and he fell forward like a cut flower.

His dogs thinking him out of the way for a time, discipline instantly relaxed; and they broke into a bacchanalian dance, which brought him to his feet at once, all traces of human weakness gone, as if a bucket of water had passed over him.

"Quiet, you scugs," he cried, "or I'll cast anchor in you"; and at once the din was hushed. "Are all the children chained, so that they cannot fly away?"

"Ay, ay."

"Then hoist them up."

The wretched prisoners were dragged from the hold, all except Wendy, and ranged in line in front of him. For a time he seemed unconscious of their presence. He lolled at his ease, humming, not unmelodiously, snatches of a rude song, and fingering a pack of cards. Ever and anon the light from his cigar gave a touch of colour to his face.

"Now then, bullies," he said briskly, "six of you walk the plank tonight, but I have room for two cabin boys. Which of you is it to be?"

"Don't irritate him unnecessarily," had been Wendy's instructions in the hold; so Tootles stepped forward politely. Tootles hated the idea of signing under such a man, but an instinct told him that it would be prudent to lay the responsibility on an absent person; and though a somewhat silly boy, he knew that mothers alone are always willing to be the buffer. All children know this about mothers, and despise them for it, but make constant use of it.

So Tootles explained prudently, "You see, sir, I don't think my mother would like me to be a pirate. Would your mother like you to be a pirate, Slightly?"

He winked at Slightly, who said mournfully, "I don't think so," as if he wished things had been otherwise. "Would your mother like you to be a pirate, Twin?"

"I don't think so," said the first twin, as clever as the others. "Nibs, would – "

"Stow this gab," roared Hook, and the spokesmen were dragged back. "You, boy," he said, addressing John, "you look as if you had a little pluck in you. Didst never want to be a pirate, my hearty?"

Now John had sometimes experienced this hankering at maths. prep.; and he was struck by Hook's picking him out.

"I once thought of calling myself Red-handed Jack," he said diffidently.

"And a good name too. We'll call you that here, bully, if you join."

"What do you think, Michael?" asked John.

"What would you call me if I join?" Michael demanded.

"Blackbeard Joe."

Michael was naturally impressed. "What do you think, John?" He wanted John to decide, and John wanted him to decide.

"Shall we still be respectful subjects of the King?" John inquired.

Through Hook's teeth came the answer: "You would have to swear, 'Down with the King.'"

Perhaps John had not behaved very well so far, but he shone out now.

"Then I refuse," he cried, banging the barrel in front of Hook.

"And I refuse," cried Michael.

"Rule Britannia!" squeaked Curly.

The infuriated pirates buffeted them in the mouth; and Hook roared out, "That seals your doom. Bring up their mother. Get the plank ready."

They were only boys, and they went white as they saw Jukes and Cecco preparing the fatal plank. But they tried to look brave when Wendy was brought up.

No words of mine can tell you how Wendy despised those pirates. To the boys there was at least some glamour in the pirate calling; but all that she saw was that the ship had not been tidied for years. There was not a porthole on the grimy glass of which you might not have written with your finger "Dirty pig"; and she had already written it on several. But as the boys gathered round her she had no thought, of course, save for them.

"So, my beauty," said Hook, as if he spoke in syrup, "you are to see your children walk the plank."

Fine gentlemen though he was, the intensity of his communings had soiled his ruff, and suddenly he knew that she was gazing at it. With a hasty gesture he tried to hide it, but he was too late.

"Are they to die?" asked Wendy, with a look of such frightful contempt that he nearly fainted.

"They are," he snarled. "Silence all," he called gloatingly, "for a mother's last words to her children."

At this moment Wendy was grand. “These are my last words, dear boys,” she said firmly. “I feel that I have a message to you from your real mothers, and it is this: ‘We hope our sons will die like English gentlemen.’”

Even the pirates were awed, and Tootles cried out hysterically, “I am going to do what my mother hopes. What are you to do, Nibs?”

“What my mother hopes. What are you to do, Twin?”

“What my mother hopes. John, what are – ”

But Hook had found his voice again.

“Tie her up!” he shouted.

It was Smee who tied her to the mast. “See here, honey,” he whispered, “I’ll save you if you promise to be my mother.”

But not even for Smee would she make such a promise. “I would almost rather have no children at all,” she said disdainfully .

It is sad to know that not a boy was looking at her as Smee tied her to the mast; the eyes of all were on the plank: that last little walk they were about to take. They were no longer able to hope that they would walk it manfully, for the capacity to think had gone from them; they could stare and shiver only.

Hook smiled on them with his teeth closed, and took a step toward Wendy. His intention was to turn her face so that she should see they boys walking the plank one by one. But he never reached her, he never heard the cry of anguish he hoped to wring from her. He heard something else instead.

It was the terrible tick-tick of the crocodile.

They all heard it – pirates, boys, Wendy; and immediately every head was blown in one direction; not to the water whence the sound proceeded, but toward Hook. All knew that what was about to happen concerned him alone, and that from being actors they were suddenly become spectators.

Very frightful was it to see the change that came over him. It was as if he had been clipped at every joint. He fell in a little heap.

The sound came steadily nearer; and in advance of it came this ghastly thought, "The crocodile is about to board the ship!"

Even the iron claw hung inactive; as if knowing that it was no intrinsic part of what the attacking force wanted. Left so fearfully alone, any other man would have lain with his eyes shut where he fell: but the gigantic brain of Hook was still working, and under its guidance he crawled on the knees along the deck as far from the sound as he could go. The pirates respectfully cleared a passage for him, and it was only when he brought up against the bulwarks that he spoke.

"Hide me!" he cried hoarsely.

They gathered round him, all eyes averted from the thing that was coming aboard. They had no thought of fighting it. It was Fate.

Only when Hook was hidden from them did curiosity loosen the limbs of the boys so that they could rush to the ship's side to see the crocodile climbing it. Then they got the strangest surprise of the Night of Nights; for it was no crocodile that was coming to their aid. It was Peter.

He signed to them not to give vent to any cry of admiration that might rouse suspicion. Then he went on ticking.

海盗船

一盏绿幽幽的桅灯，斜睨着海盗河口附近的基德山涧。那艘双桅帆船——快乐的罗杰号就停在那儿。这艘看起来穷凶极恶的船，从上到下没有一处不是污秽透顶，每一根龙骨都透着肃杀之气，像尸横遍野的地面一样可憎。这是海上的吃人生番，凭着那它恐怖的恶名，即使没有那只警觉的眼睛般的桅灯，也能豪无阻拦地横行海上。

这艘船被夜幕笼罩着，一点声音也传不到岸上。船上本来也没有多少声响，除了斯密正在用的那架缝纫机发出的哒哒转动声外，再听不到什么动听的声音了。平凡、可怜的斯密，永远是勤勤恳恳，乐于为人效劳的。我不知道他为什么这样可怜，也许正是因为他自己不觉得自己可怜的缘故吧。即使是那些强硬的汉子，也不忍多看他一眼。在夏天的夜晚，他竟不止一次触动了胡克的神经，使他热泪盈眶。而斯密对这件事浑然不觉，就像他对所有别的事一样。

有几个海盗靠在船舷边深深地吸着夜雾；其余的海盗都趴在木桶旁掷骰子，玩纸牌；那四个抬小屋的海盗则精疲力竭地趴在甲板上睡着了。即便在睡梦中，他们也灵活地滚过来滚过去，以免胡克经过他们身边时不小心挠伤了他们。

胡克在甲板上踱来踱去，沉思着。这个深奥莫测的人呐，他大获全胜的时刻来了。彼得已经被除掉了，再也不能挡他的道；别的孩子全都被捉到了船上，等着走跳板。自从他制伏了巴比克以来，这算是他最辉煌的一次战绩了。我们都知道，人是多么的虚荣，如果他现在在甲板上大摇大摆地踱着方步，由于胜利而趾高气扬，那也不足为怪。

但是，他的步子里丝毫显不出得意来，反而和他阴暗的心情相对应。胡克的情绪十分低落。

每当夜深人静，胡克在船上自思自忖时，他总是这样郁闷。这是因为，他感到极端孤独。这个捉摸不透的人，越是被下属围绕着，就越感到孤独。他们的社会地位比他低得太多了。

胡克不是他的真名。要是把他的真实身份揭露出来，就算在今天，也会轰动全国。但是，读书细心的人一定早已猜到，胡克曾经上过一所著名的中学，学校的风气至今还像衣服一样紧紧跟随着他。不过说实在的，风气也多半和衣着有关。所以，甚至到如今，如果他还穿着俘获这只船时所穿的衣裳上船，他也会感到厌恶。他走起路来，还保持着学校里那种气度不凡的慵懒神情。不过最重要的是，他仍保持着良好的风度。

良好的风度，不管他怎么堕落，他也知道这是真正至关重要的。

从他内心深处，他隐约听到了一种轧轧声，仿佛打开了一扇生锈的门；门外传来森严的哒哒声，就像一个人夜里睡不着觉时听到的敲锤声。“你今天保持良好的风度了吗？”那声音永远在问他。

“名声，名声，那个闪闪发光的玩意儿，是属于我的。”他喊道。

“在一切事情上都要出人头地，这能说是良好的风度吗？”来自学校的那个哒哒声这样反问。

“巴比克就怕我一个人，”胡克辩白说，“弗林特呢，他还怕巴比克。”

“巴比克，弗林特，他们是什么家庭出身？”那声音尖厉地反驳。

最令人不安的反省是：一心想要保持良好的风度，这不就是一种恶劣的风度吗？

这个问题搅得胡克五内俱焚，就像他内心的一只爪，比他的铁爪还要锋利。那只爪撕裂着他的心，汗从他油乎乎的脸上淌了下来，在他的衣裳上留下道道汗渍。他不时用袖子擦脸，可还是止不住那汗珠。

咳，不要羡慕胡克。

胡克忽然预感到自己要早死，好像彼得的那句可怕的诅咒已经登上了船。胡克突然悲哀地想到：他得说几句临终遗言，不然过一会儿就来不及说了。

“胡克啊，”他喊道，“要是他野心再小一点就好了。”只有在他心情最阴郁的时候，他才用第三人称称呼自己。

“没有一个小孩爱我。”

说也奇怪，他居然想到了这一点，这是他以前从来没有想到过的。也许是那架缝纫机让他想到的。他喃喃自语了很久，呆呆地望着斯密，斯密正在静静地缝衣边，自以为所有的孩子都怕他。

怕他！怕斯密！那一夜，船上的孩子没有一个不爱他。斯密给他们讲了一些骇人的事，还用手掌打过他们，因为他不能用拳头打他们。可越是这样，孩子们就越是缠住他不放，迈克尔还试着戴他的眼镜。

告诉可怜的斯密吧，说孩子们爱他！胡克恨不得这样做，可是这似乎太残忍了。胡克决定把这个秘密藏在心里。孩子们为什么觉得斯密可爱呢？胡克像警犬一样，对这个问题穷追不舍。斯密要是可爱，又可爱在哪里呢？一个可怕的回答突然冒出来了：“是良好的风度！”

这个水手头是不是有着顶好的风度，可又毫不自觉？这一点不恰恰是顶好的风度吗？

胡克记起来了：要加入波普俱乐部，你得先证明你不知道自己有良好的风度。

胡克狂怒地大吼一声，把铁爪举到了斯密头上，可是并没有伤害他，一个念头止住了他的手：

“因为一个人有好风度而去抓他，那算什么呢？”

“那是恶劣的风度！”

不幸的胡克，一下子变得有气无力，像一朵被折断的花一样垂下了头。

他的喽罗们以为他现在不会管着他们了，立刻就松懈下来，狂醉般地跳起舞来。这使得胡克顿时振作起来，像一桶冷水浇到了头上，把所有软弱的表现都一扫而光。

“安静点，你们这些浑蛋，”他嚷道，“要不，我要钩你们了。”喧闹声立刻止住了。“孩子们都用链子锁起来了没有？别让他们跑掉了。”

“是喽，是喽。”

“那就把他们揪上来。”

除了温迪，这些倒霉的囚徒们被一个个从货舱里拉了出来，排成一行，站在胡克面前。起初，胡克好像没看见他们。他懒洋洋地坐在那儿，有腔有调地哼着几句粗野的歌，手里玩弄着一副纸牌。他嘴里雪茄烟的火光，一闪一闪地映出了他脸上的颜色。

“好吧，小子们，”胡克干脆地说，“你们中间六个人今晚走跳板。我还要留下两个做小厮，留下谁好呢？”

“除非到万不得已的时候，否则千万不要惹他发火。”温迪在货舱里曾这样告诉孩子们，所以图图很有礼貌地走上前去。他不愿意在这个人手底下当差，便灵机一动，想到可以把责任推给一个不在场的人。尽管他有点笨，可还是知道，做母亲的总是愿意代人受过。所有的孩子们都知道这一点，并因此看不起母亲们，可是有时却常加以利用。

于是，图图就谨慎地解释说：“你知道，先生，我想我母亲是不会愿意我当海盗的。你母亲会愿意你当海盗吗，斯莱特利？”

他冲斯莱特利挤了挤眼，斯莱特利悲伤地说：“我想她不会的。”好像他希望事情不是这样。“你们的母亲愿意你们当海盗吗，双胞胎？”

“我想她不会。”老大说，他也像别的孩子一样聪明。“尼布斯，你……？”

“少废话。”胡克吼道，说话的孩子被拉了回去。“你小子，”胡克对约翰说，“你像是还有点勇气，你从来没有想过当海盗吗，我的乖乖？”

约翰在做算术习题的时候，就遇到过这样的诘问，胡克单挑他出来问，使他感到有点突然。

“我有一次想把自己叫作红手杰克。”约翰犹豫地说。

“这名字不赖呀。要是你入伙，我们就这样叫你。”

“迈克尔，你怎么想？”约翰问。

“要是我入伙，你们叫我什么？”迈克尔问。

“黑胡子乔。”

迈克尔对这个名字自然是颇感兴趣。“你看怎么样，约翰？”他要约翰来决定，约翰要他来决定。

“我们入了伙还能当国王的好百姓吗？”约翰问。

胡克咬牙切齿地说道：“你们得宣誓，‘打倒国王！’”

约翰或许一直表现得不太好，不过，这一次他可大放光彩了。

“那我不干。”他捶着胡克面前的木桶喊道。

“我也不干。”迈克尔喊。

“英王万岁！”卷毛高呼。

暴怒的海盗们打他们的嘴。胡克大吼道：“这是你们自找的。把他们的母亲带上来，准备好跳板。”

他们不过是些孩子，看到鸠克斯和切科抬来那块要命的跳板，脸都吓白了。可是，当温迪被带来时，他们竭力装出一副勇敢的样子。

我简直没法给你们形容温迪是多么瞧不起那些海盗。男孩们觉得，当海盗多少还有点迷人的地方；而温迪只看到，这艘船多年没有打扫过了：没有一个舷窗的玻璃不脏，你都能在上面用手指写出“脏猪”的字样，显然她已经在几个舷窗上写下了。可是，当男孩们围在她身边时，她当然一心只为他们着想。

“我的美人儿，”胡克说，嘴上像是抹了蜜糖，“你就要看着你的孩子们走跳板啦。”

尽管胡克是一位体面的绅士，可是他的唾沫弄脏了衣领。突然，他发现温迪正盯着他的衣领瞧，便急忙想去遮盖一下，可是已经来不及了。

“他们是要去死吗？”温迪问，她的神情轻蔑透顶，几乎把胡克气晕了。

“是的。”他狠狠地说。“全都住口！”他又幸灾乐祸地喊道，“听一个母亲和她的孩子们的最后诀别。”

这时，温迪显得庄严极了。“亲爱的孩子们，这就是我最后要对你们说的话。”她坚定地说，“我觉得，你们真正的母亲有句话要我转达给你们，那就是：‘我希望，我们的儿子要死得像英国绅士那样。’”

听了这话，就连海盗们也大为敬畏。图图发狂似的大叫：“我就要照我母亲希望的去做。你呢，尼布斯？”

“照我母亲希望的去做。你们呢，双胞胎？”

“照我母亲希望的去做。约翰，你……”

胡克在震惊过后，又怒吼起来。

“把她捆起来。”他狂叫。

是斯密把温迪捆到桅杆上。“喂，我说，小乖乖，”斯密悄悄地说，“要是你答应做我的母亲，我就救你。”

可是，就连对斯密，温迪也不肯答应。“我宁可一个孩子也没有。”她鄙夷地说。

说来也够凄惨的，在斯密把温迪捆在桅杆上的时候，没有一个孩子望着她。孩子们的眼睛全都盯住那块跳板，他们将要去走那小小的最后几步。他们已经不敢指望自己能雄赳赳气昂昂地走那几步，他们已经失去了思想的能力，只剩下呆呆地望着，瑟瑟发抖。

胡克咬牙切齿地冲他们微笑，他朝温迪走去，想要扳过她的脸来，让她瞧着孩子们一个个走跳板。可是胡克没能走到她跟前，没能听到她发出的呼痛声——他听到的是另一种声音。

那是鳄鱼的可怕的滴答声。

大家全都听到了——海盗们，孩子们，温迪；刹那间，所有的头都朝一个方向转过去——不是朝着发出声音的水中望去，而是朝胡克望去。大家都知道，将要发生的事只和他有关。演员一下子变成了看客。

看到胡克身上起的变化，那才叫吓人呢。他瘫软地缩成一小团，就像浑身的骨节都挨了痛打似的。

那滴答声越来越近了。声音还没到，一个骇人的念头先到了：“那只鳄鱼要爬上船来了。”

胡克的那只铁爪也一动不动地垂着，好像它也知道，自己不是那个正在进攻的敌人真正想要得到的一部分。落到这样孤立无援的境地，换了别人，早就闭上眼睛倒地等死了。可是，胡克强大的头脑还在活动，他的头脑指挥他双膝着地，跪在甲板上往前爬，尽量逃开那个声音。海盗们恭恭敬敬地给他让出一条路，他一直爬到了船舷那边，才开口说话。

“把我藏起来。”他沙哑地喊。

海盗团团围绕在他身边，他们的眼睛都躲避着那个就要爬上船来的东西们，他们不想去和它战斗，这是命啊。

胡克藏起来以后，孩子们一齐拥到了船边，好奇地看着那只鳄鱼爬上船来。这时，他们看到了这惊人的一夜中最惊人的事。因为，来救他们的不是鳄鱼，而是彼得。

彼得做了个手势，示意他们不要发出惊喜的叫喊，免得引起怀疑。接着他继续发着滴答的声音。

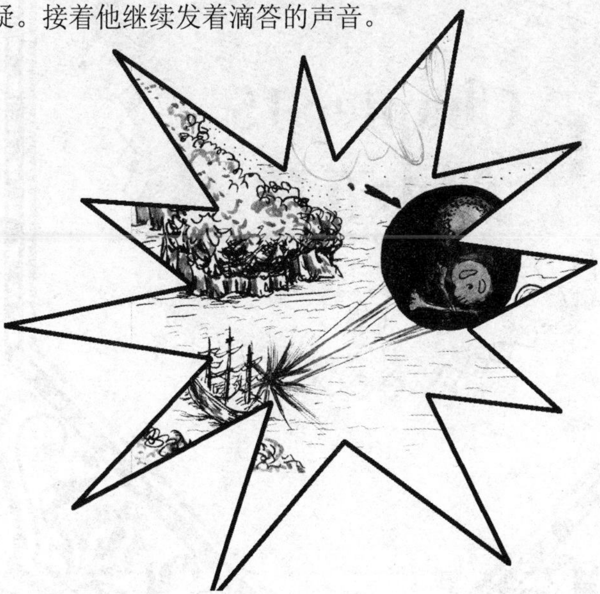

Chapter 15
第十五章

"Hook or Me This Time"

Odd things happen to all of us on our way through life without our noticing for a time that they have happened. Thus, to take an instance, we suddenly discover that we have been deaf in one ear for we don't know how long, but, say, half an hour. Now such an experience had come that night to Peter. When last we saw him he was stealing across the island with one finger to his lips and his dagger at the ready. He had seen the crocodile pass by without noticing anything peculiar about it, but by and by he remembered that it had not been ticking. At first he thought this eerie, but soon concluded rightly that the clock had run down.

Without giving a thought to what might be the feelings of a fellow-creature thus abruptly deprived of its closest companion, Peter began to consider how he could turn the catastrophe to his own use; and he decided to tick, so that wild beasts should believe he was the crocodile and let him pass unmolested. He ticked superbly, but with one unforeseen result. The crocodile was among those who heard the sound, and it followed him, though whether with the purpose of regaining what it had lost, or merely as a friend under the belief that it was again ticking itself, will never be certainly known, for, like slaves to a fixed idea, it was a stupid beast.

Peter reached the shore without mishap, and went straight on, his legs encountering the water as if quite unaware that they had entered a new element. Thus many animals pass from land to water, but no other human of whom I know. As he swam he had but one thought: "Hook or me this time." He had ticked so long that he now went on ticking without knowing that he was doing it. Had he known he would have stopped, for to board the brig by help of the tick, though an ingenious idea, had not occurred to him.

On the contrary, he thought he had scaled her side as noiseless as a mouse; and he was amazed to see the pirates cowering from him, with Hook in their midst as abject as if he had heard the crocodile.

The crocodile! No sooner did Peter remember it than he heard the ticking. At first he thought the sound did come from the crocodile, and he looked behind him swiftly. They he realised that he was doing it himself, and in a flash he understood the situation. "How clever of me!" he thought at once, and signed to the boys not to burst into applause.

It was at this moment that Ed Teynte the quartermaster emerged from the forecastle and came along the deck. Now, reader, time what happened by your watch. Peter struck true and deep. John clapped his hands on the ill-fated pirate's mouth to stifle the dying groan. He fell forward. Four boys caught him to prevent the thud. Peter gave the signal, and the carrion was cast overboard. There was a splash, and then silence. How long has it taken?

"One!" (Slightly had begun to count.)

None too soon, Peter, every inch of him on tiptoe, vanished into the cabin; for more than one pirate was screwing up his courage to look round. They could hear each other's distressed breathing now, which showed them that the more terrible sound had passed.

"It's gone, captain," Smee said, wiping off his spectacles. "All's still again."

Slowly Hook let his head emerge from his ruff, and listened so intently that he could have caught the echo of the tick. There was not a sound, and he drew himself up firmly to his full height.

"Then here's to Johnny Plank!" he cried brazenly, hating the boys more than ever because they had seen him unbend. He broke into the villainous ditty:

"Yo ho, yo ho, the frisky plank,
You walks along it so,
Till it goes down and you goes down
To Davy Jones below!"

To terrorize the prisoners the more, though with a certain loss of dignity, he danced along an imaginary plank, grimacing at them as he sang; and when he finished he cried, "Do you want a touch of the cat before you walk the plank?"

At that they fell on their knees. "No, no!" they cried so piteously that every pirate smiled.

"Fetch the cat, Jukes," said Hook; "it's in the cabin."

The cabin! Peter was in the cabin! The children gazed at each other.

"Ay, ay," said Jukes blithely, and he strode into the cabin. They followed him with their eyes; they scarce knew that Hook had resumed his song, his dogs joining in with him:

"Yo ho, yo ho, the scratching cat,
Its tails are nine, you know,
And when they're writ upon your back – "

What was the last line will never be known, for of a sudden the song was stayed by a dreadful screech from the cabin. It wailed through the ship, and died away. Then was heard a crowing sound which was well understood by the boys, but to the pirates was almost more eerie than the screech.

"What was that?" cried Hook.

"Two," said Slightly solemnly.

The Italian Cecco hesitated for a moment and then swung into the cabin. He tottered out, haggard.

"What's the matter with Bill Jukes, you dog?" hissed Hook, towering over him.

"The matter wi' him is he's dead, stabbed," replied Cecco in a hollow voice.

"Bill Jukes dead!" cried the startled pirates.

"The cabin's as black as a pit," Cecco said, almost gibbering, "but there is something terrible in there: the thing you heard crowing."

The exultation of the boys, the lowering looks of the pirates, both were seen by Hook.

"Cecco," he said in his most steely voice, "go back and fetch me out that doodle-doo."

Cecco, bravest of the brave, cowered before his captain, crying "No, no"; but Hook was purring to his claw.

"Did you say you would go, Cecco?" he said musingly.

Cecco went, first flinging his arms despairingly. There was no more singing, all listened now; and again came a death-screech and again a crow.

No one spoke except Slightly. "Three," he said.

Hook rallied his dogs with a gesture. "'S'death and odds fish," he thundered, "who is to bring me that doodle-doo?"

"Wait till Cecco comes out," growled Starkey, and the others took up the cry.

"I think I heard you volunteer, Starkey," said Hook, purring again.

"No, by thunder!" Starkey cried.

"My hook thinks you did," said Hook, crossing to him. "I wonder if it would not be advisable, Starkey, to humour the hook?"

"I'll swing before I go in there," replied Starkey doggedly, and again he had the support of the crew.

"Is this mutiny?" asked Hook more pleasantly than ever. "Starkey's ringleader!"

"Captain, mercy!" Starkey whimpered, all of a tremble now.

"Shake hands, Starkey," said Hook, proffering his claw.

Starkey looked round for help, but all deserted him. As he backed up Hook advanced, and now the red spark was in his eye. With a despairing scream the pirate leapt upon Long Tom and precipitated himself into the sea.

"Four," said Slightly.

"And now," Hook said courteously, "did any other gentlemen say mutiny?" Seizing a lantern and raising his claw with a menacing gesture, "I'll bring out that doodle-doo myself," he said, and sped into the cabin.

"Five." How Slightly longed to say it. He wetted his lips to be ready, but Hook came staggering out, without his lantern.

"Something blew out the light," he said a little unsteadily.

"Something!" echoed Mullins.

"What of Cecco?" demanded Noodler.

"He's as dead as Jukes," said Hook shortly.

His reluctance to return to the cabin impressed them all unfavourably, and the mutinous sounds again broke forth. All pirates are superstitious, and Cookson cried, "They do say the surest sign a ship's accurst is when there's one on board more than can be accounted for."

"I've heard," muttered Mullins, "he always boards the pirate craft last. Had he a tail, captain?"

"They say," said another, looking viciously at Hook, "that when he comes it's in the likeness of the wickedest man aboard."

"Had he a hook, captain?" asked Cookson insolently; and one

after another took up the cry, "The ship's doomed!" At this the children could not resist raising a cheer. Hook had well-nigh forgotten his prisoners, but as he swung round on them now his face lit up again.

"Lads," he cried to his crew, "now here's a notion. Open the cabin door and drive them in. Let them fight the doodle-doo for their lives. If they kill him, we're so much the better; if he kills them, we're none the worse."

For the last time his dogs admired Hook, and devotedly they did his bidding. The boys, pretending to struggle, were pushed into the cabin and the door was closed on them.

"Now, listen!" cried Hook, and all listened. But not one dared to face the door. Yes, one, Wendy, who all this time had been bound to the mast. It was for neither a scream nor a crow that she was watching, it was for the reappearance of Peter.

She had not long to wait. In the cabin he had found the thing for which he had gone in search: the key that would free the children of their manacles, and now they all stole forth, armed with such weapons as they could find. First signing them to hide, Peter cut Wendy's bonds, and then nothing could have been easier than for them all to fly off together; but one thing barred the way, an oath, "Hook or me this time." So when he had freed Wendy, he whispered for her to conceal herself with the others, and himself took her place by the mast, her cloak around him so that he should pass for her. Then he took a great breath and crowed.

To the pirates it was a voice crying that all the boys lay slain in the cabin; and they were panic-stricken. Hook tried to hearten them; but like the dogs he had made them they showed him their fangs, and he knew that if he took his eyes off them now they would leap at him.

"Lads," he said, ready to cajole or strike as need be, but never quailing for an instant, "I've thought it out. There's a Jonah aboard."

"Ay," they snarled, "a man wi' a hook."

"No, lads, no, it's the girl. Never was luck on a pirate ship wi' a woman on board. We'll right the ship when she's gone."

Some of them remembered that this had been a saying of Flint's. "It's worth trying," they said doubtfully.

"Fling the girl overboard," cried Hook; and they made a rush at the figure in the cloak.

"There's none can save you now, missy," Mullins hissed jeeringly.

"There's one," replied the figure.

"Who's that?"

"Peter Pan the avenger!" came the terrible answer; and as he spoke Peter flung off his cloak. Then they all knew who 'twas that had been undoing them in the cabin, and twice Hook essayed to speak and twice he failed. In that frightful moment I think his fierce heart broke.

At last he cried, "Cleave him to the brisket!" but without conviction.

"Down, boys, and at them!" Peter's voice rang out; and in another moment the clash of arms was resounding through the ship. Had the pirates kept together it is certain that they would have won; but the onset came when they were still unstrung, and they ran hither and thither, striking wildly, each thinking himself the last survivor of the crew. Man to man they were the stronger; but they fought on the defensive only, which enabled the boys to hunt in pairs and choose their quarry. Some of the miscreants leapt into the sea; others hid in dark recesses, where they were found by Slightly, who did not fight, but ran about with a lantern which he flashed in their faces, so that they were half blinded and fell as an easy prey to the reeking swords of the other boys. There was little sound to be heard but the clang of weapons, an occasional screech or splash, and Slightly monotonously counting – five – six – seven – eight – nine – ten – eleven.

I think all were gone when a group of savage boys surrounded Hook, who seemed to have a charmed life, as he kept them at bay in that circle of fire. They had done for his dogs, but this man alone seemed to be a match for them all. Again and again they closed upon him, and again and again he hewed a clear space. He had lifted up one boy with his hook, and was using him as a buckler (shield), when another, who had just passed his sword through Mullins, sprang into the fray.

"Put up your swords, boys," cried the newcomer, "this man is mine."

Thus suddenly Hook found himself face to face with Peter. The others drew back and formed a ring around them.

For long the two enemies looked at one another, Hook shuddering slightly, and Peter with the strange smile upon his face.

"So, Pan," said Hook at last, "this is all your doing."

"Ay, James Hook," came the stern answer, "it is all my doing."

"Proud and insolent youth," said Hook, "prepare to meet thy doom."

"Dark and sinister man," Peter answered, "have at thee."

Without more words they fell to, and for a space there was no advantage to either blade. Peter was a superb swordsman, and parried with dazzling rapidity; ever and anon he followed up a feint with a lunge that got past his foe's defence, but his shorter reach stood him in ill stead, and he could not drive the steel home. Hook, scarcely his inferior in brilliancy, but not quite so nimble in wrist play, forced him back by the weight of his onset, hoping suddenly to end all with a favourite thrust, taught him long ago by Barbecue at Rio; but to his astonishment he found this thrust turned aside again and again. Then he sought to close and give the quietus with his iron hook, which all this time had been pawing the air; but Peter doubled under it and, lunging fiercely, pierced him in the ribs. At the sight of his own blood, whose peculiar colour, you remember, was offensive to him, the sword fell from Hook's hand, and he was at Peter's mercy.

"Now!" cried all the boys, but with a magnificent gesture Peter invited his opponent to pick up his sword. Hook did so instantly, but with a tragic feeling that Peter was showing good form.

Hitherto he had thought it was some fiend fighting him, but darker suspicions assailed him now.

"Pan, who and what art thou?" he cried huskily.

"I'm youth, I'm joy," Peter answered at a venture, "I'm a little bird that has broken out of the egg."

This, of course, was nonsense; but it was proof to the unhappy Hook that Peter did not know in the least who or what he was, which is the very pinnacle of good form.

"To't again," he cried despairingly.

He fought now like a human flail, and every sweep of that terrible sword would have severed in twain any man or boy who obstructed it; but Peter fluttered round him as if the very wind it made blew him out of the danger zone. And again and again he darted in and pricked.

Hook was fighting now without hope. That passionate breast no longer asked for life; but for one boon it craved: to see Peter show bad form before it was cold forever.

Abandoning the fight he rushed into the powder magazine and fired it.

"In two minutes," he cried, "the ship will be blown to pieces."

Now, now, he thought, true form will show.

But Peter issued from the powder magazine with the shell in his hands, and calmly flung it overboard.

What sort of form was Hook himself showing? Misguided man though he was, we may be glad, without sympathising with him, that in the end he was true to the traditions of his race. The other boys were flying around him now, flouting, scornful; and he staggered about the deck striking up at them impotently, his mind was no longer with them; it was slouching in the playing fields of long ago, or being sent up for good, or watching the wall-game from a famous wall. And his shoes were right, and his waistcoat was right, and his tie was right, and his socks were right.

James Hook, thou not wholly unheroic figure, farewell.

For we have come to his last moment.

Seeing Peter slowly advancing upon him through the air with dagger poised, he sprang upon the bulwarks to cast himself into the sea. He did not know that the crocodile was waiting for him; for we purposely stopped the clock that this knowledge might be spared him: a little mark of respect from us at the end.

He had one last triumph, which I think we need not grudge him. As he stood on the bulwark looking over his shoulder at Peter gliding through the air, he invited him with a gesture to use his foot. It made Peter kick instead of stab.

At last Hook had got the boon for which he craved.

"Bad form," he cried jeeringly, and went content to the crocodile.

Thus perished James Hook.

"Seventeen," Slightly sang out; but he was not quite correct in his figures. Fifteen paid the penalty for their crimes that night; but two reached the shore: Starkey to be captured by the redskins, who made him nurse for all their papooses, a melancholy come-down for a pirate; and Smee, who henceforth wandered about the world in his spectacles, making a precarious living by saying he was the only man that Jas. Hook had feared.

Wendy, of course, had stood by taking no part in the fight, though watching Peter with glistening eyes; but now that all was over she became prominent again. She praised them equally, and shuddered delightfully when Michael showed her the place where he had killed one; and then she took them into Hook's cabin and pointed to his watch which was hanging on a nail. It said "half- past one!"

The lateness of the hour was almost the biggest thing of all. She got them to bed in the pirates' bunks pretty quickly, you may be sure; all but Peter, who strutted up and down on the deck, until at last he fell asleep by the side of Long Tom. He had one of his dreams that night, and cried in his sleep for a long time, and Wendy held him tightly.

和胡克拼个你死我活

每个人一生中都曾遇到过一些奇特的事，可是在一段时间内，却丝毫没有觉察到。举个例子说吧，我们突然发现一只耳朵聋了，却不知道聋了多久，就说半个钟头吧。那天晚上，彼得遇到的就是这种情况。上次我们说到，他正悄悄地穿越海岛，一个手指头按着嘴唇，一手握刀做好准备。他看见鳄鱼从他身边爬过，没觉得有什么异样，可是过了一会儿，他慢慢想起来了，鳄鱼肚子里不再滴答作响了。起初，他觉得这事有点蹊跷，不过很快他就明白过来，是那只钟的发条走完了。

鳄鱼突然间失去了它最亲密的伴侣，该是多么伤心，彼得压根儿没替它着想，他立刻想到是要好好利用这一点。他决定自己学着发出滴答声，当被野兽听到时，会以为是鳄鱼，不加伤害地放他过去。他的滴答声模仿得惟妙惟肖，可是却引来了一个意想不到的结果。鳄鱼也像别的动物一样，听到了滴答声，就跟上了他。那鳄鱼究竟是想找回失去的东西，还是以为它的好友又滴答作响了，我们永远也不会知道，因为这只鳄鱼是个很蠢的动物，它一旦有了一个念头，就像奴才一样固守不变。

彼得平安无事地到达了海岸。他的腿触到了水，却好像丝毫感觉不到那是另一种物质。许多动物从陆上到水里都是这样的，可是我见到的人类当中还没有别人像他这样。他游泳的时候，心里只有一个念头："这回定要和胡克拼个你死我活。"他已经滴答了很久，现在继续滴答下去已经不知不觉了。要是他觉出了，他早就停止了滴答。因为，虽然他是靠发出滴答声登上海盗船的，他却从没有想到过这会是一条绝妙的计策。

正相反，他自以为自己像只老鼠似的悄无声息地爬到了船边。等到他看见海盗们十分害怕地纷纷躲开他，胡克藏在海盗们中间，失魂落魄，像看到鳄鱼一样，他也不由得惊讶起来。

鳄鱼！彼得刚想起鳄鱼，就听到了滴答声。起初，他以为声音是鳄鱼发出的。他很快地回头扫一眼，这才发现，发出滴答声的原来是他自己，这一瞬间他才明白了事情的原委。“我多聪明呀！”他立刻想。于是，他向孩子们做手势，示意他们不要拍手欢呼。

就在这当儿，舵手爱德华·坦特钻出前舱，从甲板上走过来。现在，读者，请你看着表，计算下面发生的事的时间。彼得一刀砍下去，又准又深，约翰用手捂住这遭殃的海盗的嘴，不让他发出临死的呻吟。海盗向前栽倒了。四个孩子上前揪住他，防止他在落地时发出咕咚的声音。彼得一挥手，那具臭尸就给抛下海去。只听得扑通一声，然后就是寂静。一共花去多少时间？

“一个啦！”斯莱特利开始计数。

这时，有几个海盗壮着胆子东张西望；说时迟，那时快，彼得一溜烟钻进了船舱。海盗们能够听到彼此惊慌的喘息声了，可见那个更可怕的声音已经走远了。

“它走了，船长，”斯密说，揉了擦他的眼镜，“现在没有一点声音了。”

胡克把头从带褶的衣领里慢慢地伸出来，仔细倾听，看还有没有滴答滴答的余音。一点声音都没有了，于是他又雄赳赳地挺直了身体。

“现在，该走跳板啦。”胡克觍着脸喊道。他现在更加恨那些孩子们了，因为他们看到了他的狼狈相。他又开始唱起那只恶毒的歌：

唷嗬，唷嗬，跳动的木板啊，
踩着木板走到头；
连人带板掉下去，
到海底去见大卫琼斯喽！

为了把这些囚徒吓得更厉害些，胡克不顾尊严，沿着一块想像中的跳板舞过去，一面唱着，一面冲他们狞笑。唱完了，他说：“走跳板以前，你们要不要尝尝九尾鞭的味道？”

听到这话，孩子们都跪了下来。“不，不。”他们怪可怜地喊道。海盗们都忍不住笑了。

“鸠克斯，去把鞭子拿来，”胡克说，“鞭子在船舱里。”

船舱！彼得就在船舱里！孩子们互相对看着。

“是，是。”鸠克斯乐呵呵地回答，大步走下船舱。孩子们看着他离去，以至于都没有注意到胡克又唱起歌来，而他的喽罗们应声和着：

啃嗬，啃嗬，抓人的猫，
它的尾巴有九条，
要是落到你们的背上……

最后一行是什么，我们永远都不会知道了。因为，突然间船舱里传来一声可怕的尖叫，响彻全船，随后就戛然停止了。接着又听到一声欢快的叫喊，那是孩子们都熟悉的，可是在海盗们听来，却比那声尖叫还要令人毛骨悚然。

“那是什么？”胡克喊道。

“两个啦。”斯莱特利郑重地数道。

意大利人切科犹豫了一下，然后摇摇晃晃地走下船舱去。他踉跄着退了出来，脸都吓黄了。

“比尔·鸠克斯，怎么回事，你这狗东西？”胡克龇牙咧嘴地说，恶狠狠地逼视着他。

“怎么回事，他死了，给砍死了。”切科压低了嗓门说。

“比尔·鸠克斯死啦！”海盗们大惊失色，一齐喊道。

“船里黑得像个地洞，”切科几乎话都说不清了，“可是那儿有个吓人的东西，刚才的叫喊声就从那里来。”

孩子们的兴高采烈，海盗们的垂头丧气，胡克全都看到了。

“切科，”他冷冰冰地说，“回到舱里去，把那蠢东西给我捉来。”

切科，这个最勇敢的海盗，在船长面前战战兢兢地喊道：“不，不。”但是，胡克咆哮着举起了铁爪。

“你是说你要去，是吧，切科？”

切科绝望地挥舞着两臂，下去了。再也没有人唱歌了，全都在静听着。又是一声临死前的惨叫，又是一声欢叫。

没有人说话，只有斯莱特利数道：“三个啦。”

胡克一挥手，集合了他的部下。“混账，岂有此理，”他暴跳如雷地吼道，“谁去把那东西给我抓来？”

“等切科上来再说吧。”斯塔奇咕噜着说，别的人也附和着他。

“我仿佛听到你说，你要自告奋勇下去。”胡克说，又发出了咆哮声。

“不，老天爷，我没有说！”斯塔奇喊。

“我的钩子可是认为你说了，”胡克说着向他逼进，“我看，你还是迁就一下这钩子为妙，斯塔奇。”

“我宁愿给吊死，也不下那儿去。”斯塔奇固执地回答说，他得到了水手们的支持。

“要造反呐？”胡克问，显得格外兴奋，“斯塔奇是造反头头。”

“船长，发发慈悲吧。”斯塔奇呜咽着说，浑身都在哆嗦。

“握握手吧，斯塔奇。”胡克说，伸出了铁钩。

斯塔奇环顾四周求援，但是别的海盗全都背弃了他。他步步后退，胡克步步进逼。这时，胡克的眼睛里现出了红光。随着一声绝望的嚎叫，斯塔奇跳上了长汤姆大炮，一个倒栽葱，跳进了大海。

“四个啦。”斯莱特利叫着。

“现在，”胡克彬彬有礼地问，“还有哪位先生要造反？”他抓过来一盏灯，威吓地举起铁钩，“我要亲自下去把那东西抓上来。”他说着并快步走进了船舱。

“五个啦。”斯莱特利恨不得这样说，他舐湿了嘴唇准备着，可是胡克趔趔趄趄地退了出来，手里没有了灯。

“什么东西吹灭了我的灯。”胡克有点不安地说。

“什么东西！”马林斯应声说。

“切科怎么样了？”努得勒问。

“死了，像鸠克斯一样。”胡克简短地说。

胡克迟迟疑疑，不愿再下到舱里，这在海盗们当中造成了不良的影响，反叛的声音又起来了。海盗们全都是迷信的，库克森嚷道：“人们都说，要是船上来了一个不明不白的东西，这只船肯定要遭殃的。”

“我还听说，”马林斯嘟囔着说，“这东西早晚要上一艘海盗船的。它有尾巴吗，船长？”

“他们说，”另一个海盗说，不怀好意地瞄着胡克，“那东西来的时候，模样就和船上那个最恶的人差不多。”

“他有铁钩吗，船长？”库克森侮慢地问，于是，海盗们一个接一个地嚷起来了：“这只船要遭厄运了。”听到这话，孩子们忍不住欢呼起来。胡克几乎把囚徒们都忘了，这时他回头看到他们，脸上忽然又亮了。

“伙计们，”胡克对他的水手喊道，“我有一条妙计。打开舱门，把他们推下去，让他们跟那个怪物拼命去吧。要是他们把那怪物杀了，那最好不过；要是那怪物把他们杀了，那也不坏。”

海盗们最后一次佩服胡克，于是他们便忠实地执行了他的命令。孩子们假装挣扎着，给推进了船舱，舱门关上了。

“现在，听着！”胡克喊。大家都静听，只是没有一个敢对着那扇门看；不，有一个，那是温迪，她一直被绑在桅杆上。她等待的不是一声喊叫，也不是一声欢叫的啼鸣，而是彼得的重新露面。

温迪没等多久。在舱里，彼得找到了他要找的东西：给孩子们打开镣铐的钥匙。现在，孩子们都偷偷地溜到各处，用能找到的各种武器武装起来。彼得先做手势叫他们藏起来，然后他溜出来割断了温迪的绑绳。现在，他们要一起飞走，是再容易不过的事了；但是有一件事拦阻了他们，就是那句誓言，“这回我要和胡克拼个你死我活”。所以，彼得给温迪解开绑绳以后，就悄悄地让她和别的孩子藏在一起，他自己披上温迪的外衣，代替她站在桅杆前。然后，他深深地吸进一口气，欢叫了一声。

海盗们听了这声叫喊，以为舱里所有的孩子都给杀死了，他们吓得魂不附体。胡克想给他们打气，可是，他早已把他们练成了一群狗，他们现在对他龇着牙。胡克心里明白，要是不盯住他们，他们会扑上来咬他的。

“伙计们，”胡克说，准备糊弄他们一下，必要的话动武也成，但是一刻也不能在他们面前表现出畏惧，“我想起来了，这船上有一个约拿。”

“对了，”水手们狺狺地说，“一个带铁钩的人。”

“不，伙计们，是一个女孩。海盗船上，来了个女的，就不会走运。如果她走了，船上就会太平了。”

有的人想起来了，弗林特说过这样的话。“不妨试一试。”水手们将信将疑地说。

“把那个女孩扔到海里去。”胡克喊道，海盗们朝那个披着外衣的人冲过去。

“现在没人能救你了，小姐。”马林斯嘲笑地怪声说。

“有一个人。”那人说。

“他是谁？”

“复仇者彼得·潘！”这就是那人可怕的回答。说着，彼得甩掉了外衣。这一来，他们知道了是谁在舱里作怪。胡克两次想说话，都没说出来。在那可怕的一瞬间，恐怕他那颗凶残的心都碎了。

最后，他喊了出来：“劈开他的胸膛！”可是他已经没有什么信心了。

“来呀，孩子们，杀呀。”彼得大呼。转眼间，船上响起了一片刀剑撞击声。如果海盗们能集合在一起，他们肯定会得胜的，可是在遭到袭击时，他们松松垮垮、毫无准备，只是东奔西突，胡砍乱杀。人人都以为自己是最后一个活下来的。要是一对一的话，海盗们可能还更厉害，可是他们是处在被动挨打的地位，这就使孩子们能够两个对付一个，还可以随意选择对手。海盗们有的跳下了海，有的躲藏在阴暗的角落里，最后全都被斯莱特利找出来了。他都不必参加战斗，只提着灯跑来跑去，用灯光直照他们的脸，晃得他们什么也看不清，轻而易举地就成了别的孩子的刀下鬼。船上除了听到兵器铿锵，再没有什么喧闹声；偶尔有一声惨叫，或落水声，还有斯莱特利那单调的数数声——五个——六个——七个——八个——九个——十个——十一个。

当一群凶狠的孩子团团围住胡克时，我想其余的海盗大概都完蛋了。胡克像有魔法一样，孩子们竟无法靠近他，仿佛他周围有个火圈。孩子们已经把他的喽罗们全干掉了，可是，他一个人似乎就能对付他们所有的人。孩子们一次又一次逼近他，却一次又一次被他杀退了。他还用钩子挑起一个孩子，当作盾牌，这时，有一个孩子刚刚用剑刺穿了马林斯，跳过来加入战斗。

"收起你们的刀，孩子们，"新来的孩子喊道，"这个人由我来对付。"

忽然间，胡克发现他和彼得面对面了，其他的孩子都退下去，围着他们站成一圈。

两个仇人对看了好半晌。胡克微微发抖，彼得脸上现出了奇异的微笑。

"这么说，潘，"胡克终于说，"这全是你干的。"

"对，詹姆斯·胡克，"彼得严峻地回答，"这全是我干的。"

"骄傲无礼的年轻人，"胡克说，"准备迎接你的末日吧。"

"阴险毒辣的人，"彼得回答，"前来受死吧。"

两人不再多说，就交手刺杀起来，一时不分胜负。彼得剑法高超，躲闪迅速，使人眼花缭乱。他不时虚晃一招，乘敌人不备猛刺一剑，可惜他吃亏在胳膊太短，刺不到要害。胡克的剑法也毫不逊色，不过，他手腕上的功夫不如彼得灵活，靠着猛攻的办法压住了对方。他希望用巴比克早先在里奥教给他的致命的刺法，一下结果敌人的性命，可就是屡刺不中。他的铁爪一直在空中乱舞乱抓，他想逼过去用铁爪致对方于死命。彼得一弯身，躲开铁爪，向前猛刺，刺进了他的肋骨。胡克看到了自己的血——你们还记得吧，那血的怪颜色最叫他受不了——胡克手中的剑坠落在地上，他现在完全任凭彼得摆布了。

"好啊！"孩子们齐声喝彩。可是，彼得做了个优雅的手势：请敌手拾起他的剑。胡克立刻拾了起来，不过心里感到一阵悲哀，因为他觉得彼得表现了良好的风度。

胡克一直以为和他作战的是个恶魔，现在却起了晦暗的疑心。

“潘，你到底是谁，到底是什么？”胡克粗声喊道。

“我是少年，我是快乐，”彼得信口答道，“我是刚出壳的小鸟。”

这当然是一派胡言。但是，在不幸的胡克看来，这就足以证明彼得根本不知道他自己是谁，是什么，而这正是好风度的顶点。

“再来受死吧。”胡克绝望地喊。

他像打稻谷似的拼杀，频频挥动着剑。无论哪个大人或孩子，一碰到这可怕的剑，都会被挥成两段。可是彼得在他周围闪来闪去，好像那剑扇起来的风把他吹出了危险地带，使他可以灵巧地反击和进攻。

胡克现在对取胜已不抱希望。他那颗残暴的心也不再指望活命了，只盼着在死前能得到一个恩赐：看到彼得失态。

胡克放弃了厮杀，跑到火药库里点着了火。

“不出两分钟，”他喊道，“整条船就要炸得粉碎。”

这下好了，胡克想，看看各人的真面目吧。

可是彼得从火药库里跑出来，手里拿着弹药，不慌不忙地把它扔进了海里。

胡克自己表现的风度又如何呢？他虽然是个误入歧途的人，并不能博得别人的同情；但我们还是高兴地看到，他在最后关头遵守了海盗的传统准则。这时，别的孩子都在围攻他，讥笑他，嘲弄他。他蹒跚地走过甲板，有气无力地还击他们。他的心思已经不在他们身上，而已经回到了儿时的游戏场，在那里懒洋洋地游荡，或者扬帆远航，或者观看一场精彩的拍墙游戏。他的鞋，背心，领结，袜子都整整齐齐，干干净净。

詹姆斯·胡克，不能说你不是一条好汉，永别了。

因为他的最后时刻已经来到了。

看到彼得举着剑慢慢地凌空向他飞来，他跳上了船舷，纵身跳下海。他不知道鳄鱼正在水里等着他；因为，我们有意让钟停止滴答，免得他知道这个情况，这总算是最后对他表示的一点敬意吧。

胡克取得的最后一点胜利，我们也不妨一提：他站在船舷上时，回头看着彼得向他飞来，他作了个姿势，要彼得用脚踢。彼得果

然用脚踢，没有用剑刺。

胡克总算得到了他渴望的恩惠。

“失态了。”他嘲讽地喊道，然后心满意足地落进了鳄鱼口中。

詹姆斯·胡克就这样被消灭了。

“十七个啦。”斯莱特利唱了出来。不过他的计数不大准确。那晚上十五名海盗因罪受诛，可是有两个逃到了岸上。斯塔奇被印第安人捕获，被迫给印第安婴孩当保姆；对于一个海盗，这不能不说是个悲惨的下场。斯密从此戴着眼镜到处流浪，饥一顿饱一顿，逢人便吹嘘自己是詹姆斯·胡克惟一害怕的人。

温迪当然没有参加战斗，不过，她又大又明亮的眼睛一直目不转睛地注视着彼得。现在战事已经过去，她又变成了重要的人物。她一视同仁地表扬了他们。迈克尔指给她看他杀了一个海盗的地点时，她高兴得直发抖。然后，她把孩子们都带到胡克的舱里，指着挂在钉子上的胡克的表，表上指示的时间是“一点半”。

时间这么晚了，现在睡觉该是最重要的一件事了。于是温迪很快地把孩子们安顿在海盗的舱铺上睡下。只有彼得没睡，他在甲板上来回踱步，最后，倒在长炮旁睡着了。那夜，他做了许多梦，在梦中哭了很久，温迪紧紧地搂着他。

Chapter 16
第十六章

The Return Home

By three bells that morning they were all stirring their stumps; for there was a big sea running; and Tootles, the bo'sun, was among them, with a rope's end in his hand and chewing tobacco. They all donned pirate clothes cut off at the knee, shaved smartly, and tumbled up, with the true nautical roll and hitching their trousers.

It need not be said who was the captain. Nibs and John were first and second mate. There was a woman aboard. The rest were tars before the mast, and lived in the fo'c'sle. Peter had already lashed himself to the wheel; but he piped all hands and delivered a short address to them; said he hoped they would do their duty like gallant hearties, but that he knew they were the scum of Rio and the Gold Coast, and if they snapped at him he would tear them. The bluff strident words struck the note sailors understood, and they cheered him lustily. Then a few sharp orders were given, and they turned the ship round, and nosed her for the mainland.

Captain Pan calculated, after consulting the ship's chart, that if this weather lasted they should strike the Azores about the 21st of June, after which it would save time to fly.

Some of them wanted it to be an honest ship and others were in favour of keeping it a pirate; but the captain treated them as dogs, and they dared not express their wishes to him even in a round robin. Instant obedience was the only safe thing. Slightly got a dozen for looking perplexed when told to take soundings. The general feeling was that Peter was honest just now to lull Wendy's suspicions, but that there might be a change when the new suit was ready, which, against her will, she was making for him out of some of Hook's wickedest garments. It was afterwards whispered among them that on the first night he wore this suit he sat long in the cabin with Hook's cigar-holder in his mouth and one hand clenched, all but for the forefinger, which he bent and held threateningly aloft like a hook.

Instead of watching the ship, however, we must now return to that desolate home from which three of our characters had taken heartless flight so long ago. It seems a shame to have neglected No. 14 all this time; and yet we may be sure that Mrs. Darling does not blame us. If we had returned sooner to look with sorrowful sympathy at her, she would probably have cried, "Don't be silly; what do I matter? Do go back and keep an eye on the children." So long as mothers are like this their children will take advantage of them; and they may lay to that.

Even now we venture into that familiar nursery only because its lawful occupants are on their way home; we are merely hurrying on in advance of them to see that their beds are properly aired and that Mr. and Mrs. Darling do not go out for the evening. We are no more than servants. Why on earth should their beds be properly aired, seeing that they left them in such a thankless hurry? Would it not serve them jolly well right if they came back and found that their parents were spending the week-end in the country? It would be the moral lesson they have been in need of ever since we met them; but if we contrived things in this way Mrs. Darling would never forgive us.

One thing I should like to do immensely, and that is to tell her, in the way authors have, that the children are coming back, that indeed they will be here on Thursday week. This would spoil so completely the surprise to which Wendy and John and Michael are looking forward. They have been planning it out on the ship: mother's rapture, father's shout of joy, Nana's leap through the air to embrace them first, when what they ought to be prepared for is a good hiding. How delicious to spoil it all by breaking the news in advance; so that when they enter grandly Mrs. Darling may not even offer Wendy her mouth, and Mr. Darling may exclaim pettishly, "Dash it all, here are those boys again." However, we should get no thanks even for this. We are beginning to know Mrs. Darling by this time, and may be sure that she would upbraid us for depriving the children of their little pleasure.

"But, my dear madam, it is ten days till Thursday week; so that by telling you what's what, we can save you ten days of unhappiness."

"Yes, but at what a cost! By depriving the children of ten minutes of delight."

"Oh, if you look at it in that way!"

"What other way is there in which to look at it?"

You see, the woman had no proper spirit. I had meant to say extraordinarily nice things about her; but I despise her, and not one of them will I say now. She does not really need to be told to have things ready, for they are ready. All the beds are aired, and she never leaves the house, and observe, the window is open. For all the use we are to her, we might well go back to the ship. However, as we are here we may as well stay and look on. That is all we are, lookers-on. Nobody really wants us. So let us watch and say jaggy things, in the hope that some of them will hurt.

The only change to be seen in the night-nursery is that between nine and six the kennel is no longer there. When the children flew away, Mr. Darling felt in his bones that all the blame was his for having chained Nana up, and that from first to last she had been wiser than he. Of course, as we have seen, he was quite a simple man; indeed he might have passed for a boy again if he had been able to take his baldness off; but he had also a noble sense of justice and a lion's courage to do what seemed right to him; and having thought the matter out with anxious care after the flight of the children, he went down on all fours and crawled into the kennel. To all Mrs. Darling's dear invitations to him to come out he replied sadly but firmly:

"No, my own one, this is the place for me."

In the bitterness of his remorse he swore that he would never leave the kennel until his children came back. Of course this was a pity; but whatever Mr. Darling did he had to do in excess, otherwise he soon gave up doing it. And there never was a more humble man than the once proud George Darling, as he sat in the kennel of an evening talking with his wife of their children and all their pretty ways.

Very touching was his deference to Nana. He would not let her come into the kennel, but on all other matters he followed her wishes implicitly.

Every morning the kennel was carried with Mr. Darling in it to a cab, which conveyed him to his office, and he returned home in the same way at six. Something of the strength of character of the man will be seen if we remember how sensitive he was to the opinion of neighbours: this man whose every movement now attracted surprised attention. Inwardly he must have suffered torture; but he preserved a calm exterior even when the young criticised his little home, and he always lifted his hat courteously to any lady who looked inside.

It may have been quixotic, but it was magnificent. Soon the inward meaning of it leaked out, and the great heart of the public was touched. Crowds followed the cab, cheering it lustily; charming girls scaled it to get his autograph; interviews appeared in the better class of papers, and society invited him to dinner and added, "Do come in the kennel."

On that eventful Thursday week, Mrs. Darling was in the night-nursery awaiting George's return home; a very sad-eyed woman. Now that we look at her closely and remember the gaiety of her in the old days, all gone now just because she has lost her babes, I find I won't be able to say nasty things about her after all. If she was too fond of her rubbishy children, she couldn't help it. Look at her in her chair, where she has fallen asleep. The corner of her mouth, where one looks first, is almost withered up. Her hand moves restlessly on her breast as if she had a pain there. Some like Peter best, and some like Wendy best, but I like her best. Suppose, to make her happy, we whisper to her in her sleep that the brats are coming back. They are really within two miles of the window now, and flying strong, but all we need whisper is that they are on the way. Let's.

It is a pity we did it, for she has started up, calling their names; and there is no one in the room but Nana.

"O Nana, I dreamt my dear ones had come back."

Nana had filmy eyes, but all she could do was put her paw gently on her mistress's lap; and they were sitting together thus when the kennel was brought back. As Mr. Darling puts his head out to kiss his wife, we see that his face is more worn than of yore, but has a softer expression.

He gave his hat to Liza, who took it scornfully; for she had no imagination, and was quite incapable of understanding the motives of such a man. Outside, the crowd who had accompanied the cab home were still cheering, and he was naturally not unmoved.

"Listen to them," he said; "it is very gratifying."

"Lots of little boys," sneered Liza.

"There were several adults to-day," he assured her with a faint flush; but when she tossed her head he had not a word of reproof for her. Social success had not spoilt him; it had made him sweeter. For some time he sat with his head out of the kennel, talking with Mrs. Darling of this success, and pressing her hand reassuringly when she said she hoped his head would not be turned by it.

"But if I had been a weak man," he said. "Good heavens, if I had been a weak man!"

"And, George," she said timidly, "you are as full of remorse as ever, aren't you?"

"Full of remorse as ever, dearest! See my punishment: living in a kennel."

"But it is punishment, isn't it, George? You are sure you are not enjoying it?"

"My love!"

You may be sure she begged his pardon; and then, feeling drowsy, he curled round in the kennel.

"Won't you play me to sleep," he asked, "on the nursery piano?" and as she was crossing to the day-nursery he added thoughtlessly, "And shut that window. I feel a draught."

"O George, never ask me to do that. The window must always be left open for them, always, always."

Now it was his turn to beg her pardon; and she went into the day-nursery and played, and soon he was asleep; and while he slept, Wendy and John and Michael flew into the room.

Oh no. We have written it so, because that was the charming arrangement planned by them before we left the ship; but something must have happened since then, for it is not they who have flown in, it is Peter and Tinker Bell.

Peter's first words tell all.

"Quick Tink," he whispered, "close the window; bar it! That's right. Now you and I must get away by the door; and when Wendy comes she will think her mother has barred her out; and she will have to go back with me."

Now I understand what had hitherto puzzled me, why when Peter had exterminated the pirates he did not return to the island and leave Tink to escort the children to the mainland. This trick had been in his head all the time.

Instead of feeling that he was behaving badly he danced with glee; then he peeped into the day-nursery to see who was playing. He whispered to Tink, "It's Wendy's mother! She is a pretty lady, but not so pretty as my mother. Her mouth is full of thimbles, but not so full as my mother's was."

Of course he knew nothing whatever about his mother; but he sometimes bragged about her.

He did not know the tune, which was "Home, Sweet Home," but he knew it was saying, "Come back, Wendy, Wendy, Wendy"; and he cried exultantly, "You will never see Wendy again, lady, for the window is barred!"

He peeped in again to see why the music had stopped, and now he saw that Mrs. Darling had laid her head on the box, and that two tears were sitting on her eyes.

"She wants me to unbar the window," thought Peter, "but I won't, not I!"

He peeped again, and the tears were still there, or another two had taken their place.

"She's awfully fond of Wendy," he said to himself. He was angry with her now for not seeing why she could not have Wendy.

The reason was so simple: "I'm fond of her too. We can't both have her, lady."

But the lady would not make the best of it, and he was unhappy. He ceased to look at her, but even then she would not let go of him. He skipped about and made funny faces, but when he stopped it was just as if she were inside him, knocking.

"Oh, all right," he said at last, and gulped. Then he unbarred the window. "Come on, Tink," he cried, with a frightful sneer at the laws of nature; "we don't want any silly mothers"; and he flew away.

Thus Wendy and John and Michael found the window open for them after all, which of course was more than they deserved. They alighted on the floor, quite unashamed of themselves, and the youngest one had already forgotten his home.

"John," he said, looking around him doubtfully, "I think I have been here before."

"Of course you have, you silly. There is your old bed."

"So it is," Michael said, but not with much conviction.

"I say," cried John, "the kennel!" and he dashed across to look into it.

"Perhaps Nana is inside it," Wendy said.

But John whistled. "Hullo," he said, "there's a man inside it."

"It's father!" exclaimed Wendy.

"Let me see father," Michael begged eagerly, and he took a good look. "He is not so big as the pirate I killed," he said with such frank disappointment that I am glad Mr. Darling was asleep; it would have been sad if those had been the first words he heard his little Michael say.

Wendy and John had been taken aback somewhat at finding their father in the kennel.

"Surely," said John, like one who had lost faith in his memory, "he used not to sleep in the kennel?"

"John," Wendy said falteringly, "perhaps we don't remember the old life as well as we thought we did."

A chill fell upon them; and serve them right.

"It is very careless of mother," said that young scoundrel John, "not to be here when we come back."

It was then that Mrs. Darling began playing again.

"It's mother!" cried Wendy, peeping.

"So it is!" said John.

"Then are you not really our mother, Wendy?" asked Michael, who was surely sleepy.

"Oh dear!" exclaimed Wendy, with her first real twinge of remorse, "it was quite time we came back."

"Let us creep in," John suggested, "and put our hands over her eyes."

But Wendy, who saw that they must break the joyous news more gently, had a better plan.

"Let us all slip into our beds, and be there when she comes in, just as if we had never been away."

And so when Mrs. Darling went back to the night-nursery to see if her husband was asleep, all the beds were occupied. The children waited for her cry of joy, but it did not come. She saw them, but she did not believe they were there. You see, she saw them in their beds so often in her dreams that she thought this was just the dream hanging around her still.

She sat down in the chair by the fire, where in the old days she had nursed them.

They could not understand this, and a cold fear fell upon all the three of them.

"Mother!" Wendy cried.

"That's Wendy," she said, but still she was sure it was the dream.

"Mother!"

"That's John," she said.

"Mother!" cried Michael. He knew her now.

"That's Michael," she said, and she stretched out her arms for the three little selfish children they would never envelop again. Yes, they did, they went round Wendy and John and Michael, who had slipped out of bed and run to her.

"George, George!" she cried when she could speak; and Mr. Darling woke to share her bliss, and Nana came rushing in. There could not have been a lovelier sight; but there was none to see it except a little boy who was staring in at the window. He had had ecstasies innumerable that other children can never know; but he was looking through the window at the one joy from which he must be for ever barred.

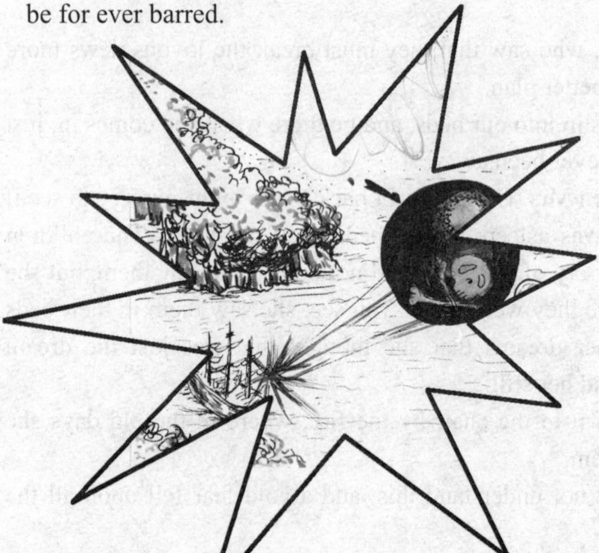

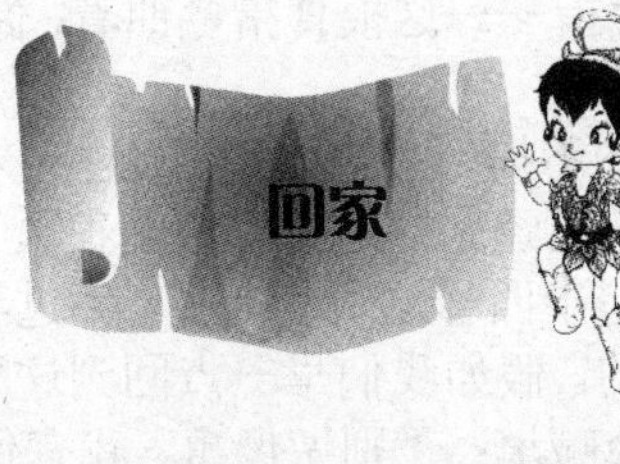

第二天清晨钟敲过三响后，孩子们就都东奔西跑地忙碌起来，海上大风浪正滚滚而来。图图这位水手长，手里握着缆绳的一端，嘴里嚼着烟草。他们全都穿上了从膝盖以下剪去的海盗服，脸刮得光光的，像真正的水手那样，提着裤子，两步并作一步，急匆匆地爬上甲板。

船长的人选是显而易见的，尼布斯和约翰是大副和二副。船上有一位女士，其余都是普通水手，住在前舱。彼得已经牢牢地掌住了舵，接着又把全体船员召集到甲板上来，做了一个简短的训话，他说希望他们都像英勇的海员一样，要恪尽职守。不过他知道，他们都是里奥和黄金海岸的粗人，要是谁敢违抗命令，就把他给撕碎。他的几句唬人的粗话水手们倒听得懂，他们发出了一阵粗重的欢呼声。接着，彼得下了几道严厉的命令，然后他们掉转船头，向英国本土驶去。

船长彼得查看过航海图以后，推算要是这种天气持续下去的话，他们将在六月二十一日到达亚速尔群岛。到那里以后，再飞回去就省时间了。

有些水手希望这船是一艘安分守己的船，另一些人则希望仍做一艘海盗船。可是船长只当他们是喽罗们，所以他们都不敢发表意见，连递交一份陈情书也不敢。绝对服从是惟一稳妥的办法。斯莱特利有一次奉命测水，脸上露出迷惑的神色，就挨了十二下打。大家都觉得，彼得眼下故作老实，为的是消除温迪的怀疑；不过，等到新衣做成之后或许还会有变化。这件衣服是用胡克最邪恶的一件海盗服改做的，温迪本不愿意做。在彼得穿上这件衣裳的头一夜，大家都在窃窃私议。他在舱里坐了很久，嘴里衔着胡克的烟袋，一手握拳，只伸出了食指——这根食指弯曲着，像只钩子，举得老高，做出恐吓的姿态。

船上的事且搁下不提，现在我们先回过头来看看那个寂寞的家庭。我们的三个家伙已经无情地离家出走很久了。说也惭愧，我们这么长时间没有提起十四号这所住宅了。不过我们可以肯定，达林太太一定不会见怪的。假如我们早一点回到这里，带着懊悔和同情来探望她，她多半会喊道：“别做傻事，我有什么要紧？快回去照顾孩子们吧。”母亲们总是这样，难怪孩子们都会利用她们的这种弱点，迟迟不肯回家。

即使我们现在冒昧地走进那间熟悉的育儿室，也只是因为它的合法主人已经在归途中了。我们只不过比他们先行一步，提前来看看他们的被褥是不是都晾过了，并关照达林先生和达林太太那晚不要出门。我们不过是跑腿的罢了。不过，既然他们离开时走得那样匆忙，连句感谢的话都没说，又何必给他们晾被褥呢？要是他们回到家里，发现父母正好都到乡间度周末去了，那不是活该受报应吗？这是从我们和他们相识以来，他们应得的教训。不过，如果我们把事情设想成这样，达林太太永远也不会饶恕我们的。

有一件事我实在想做，就是像一般写故事的人那样，告诉达林太太，孩子们就要回来了，下礼拜四他们就会到家。这样一来，温迪、约翰和迈克尔预先设想的给家里一个意外惊喜的计划，就完全落空了。他们在船上一直想像着——母亲的狂喜，父亲的欢呼，娜娜跳起来抢先扑上前拥抱他们；而他们准备要做的就是秘而不宣。如果我预先把消息泄露出来，破坏他们的计划，那该多么痛快。那样的话，当他们神气十足地走进家门时，达林太太甚至都不会去亲吻温迪；达林先生还可能会烦躁地嚷道：“真讨厌，这些小子们又回来了。”不过，这样做，我们也得不到感谢。我们现在已经了解达林太太的为人了，可以肯定，她准会责怪我们，不该剥夺孩子们的一点小小的乐趣。

“可是，太太，到下礼拜四还有十天，我们把实情告诉你，可以免去你十天的不快乐。”

“不错，但是代价得多大呀！剥夺了孩子们整整十分钟的快乐。”

“啊，如果你是这样看问题……”

“可是，还能有什么别的看法呢？”

你瞧，这女人的情绪不对头。我本想替她美言几句，可我现在瞧不起她，不想再提孩子们的事了。其实，我用不着关照达林太太安排好一切，一切都已准备妥当了。三张床上的被褥都晾过了，她也从不出门——请看，窗子是开着的。尽管我们可以留下为她效劳，但我们不如回到船上去。不过，我们既然来了，就不妨留下来观察观察。我们本来就是旁观者嘛，没有人真正需要我们。所以就让我们在一旁观望着，说几句不中听的话，好叫某些人听了不痛快。

育儿室里能看到的惟一变化就是，从晚九点到早六点，狗舍不在房里放着了。自从孩子们飞走以后，达林先生就打心眼里觉得，千错万错，都错在自己把娜娜拴了起来，且娜娜自始至终都比他聪明。当然，我们已经看到，达林先生是个单纯的人。真的，假如能去掉秃顶，他甚至可以再装成一个男孩。但是，他也有一种高尚的正义感，凡是他认为正确的事，他都有极大的勇气去做。孩子们飞走后，他把这事苦苦思量了一番，便四肢着地，钻进了狗舍。达林太太亲切地劝他出来，他悲哀但是坚定地回答说：

“不，亲爱的，这才是我应该呆的地方。”

达林先生悔恨至极，发誓说，只要孩子们一天不回来，他就一天不出狗舍。这当然是件遗憾的事，不过，达林先生要做什么，都喜欢走极端，要不就很快停止不做。过去那个骄傲的乔治·达林，如今变得再谦逊不过了。一天晚上，他坐在狗舍里，和妻子谈着孩子们和他们可爱的小模样儿。

他对娜娜的尊敬，真叫人感动。除了不让娜娜进狗舍，在别的事情上他全都无保留地听从娜娜的意见。

每天早晨，达林先生坐在狗窝里，叫人连窝一起给抬到车上，拉到办公室。下午六点钟，再照样运回家。要是我们还记得这个人把邻居的意见看得多么重，那么就可以看出，他的性格有多么坚强。现在这个人的一举一动，都引起了人们惊诧的注意。他内心一定忍受着极大的痛苦，但是当小伙子们指着他的小屋子说三道四时，他外表还能保持镇静。要是有哪位太太探头向狗舍里张望，他还总是向她脱帽致意。

这也许有点堂·吉诃德式的理想主义，可是也挺伟大的。不久，这事的原委传了出去后，公众深受感动。成群的人跟在他的车后面，欢呼声经久不息；俊俏的女郎爬上车去，求他亲笔签名；各大报刊都刊载了他的专访，社会名流也纷纷邀请他去做客，并且总是加上一句："务请乘狗舍光临。"

在礼拜四这个不寻常的日子，达林太太坐在育儿室等着达林先生回家，眼神充满忧郁。现在，我们来仔细端详一下她，想想她昔日的活泼愉快，现在那些风采就都荡然无存了，因为她失去了她最疼爱的孩子们。我现在实在不忍心说她的坏话了。要说她太爱她的那几个坏孩子，那也难怪。她坐在椅子上睡着了，看看她吧：你首先看到的是她的嘴角，现在几乎变得憔悴了；她的手不停地抚摸着胸口，就像那儿隐隐作痛似的。有的人最喜欢彼得，有的人最喜欢温迪，可是我最喜欢达林太太。为了让她高兴起来，我们要不要趁她睡着了，在她耳边悄悄告诉她，小家伙们回来了？孩子们离窗口真的只有两英里远了，正飞得起劲呢，不过，我们只需悄悄地说，他们已在回家的路上了。让我们这样说吧。

很糟糕的是，我们真的这样说了，因为达林太太忽然跳了起来，呼唤着孩子们的名字；可是，屋里一个人也没有，只有娜娜。

"啊，娜娜，我梦见我的宝贝们回来了。"

娜娜睡眼惺忪，她所能做的只是把爪子轻轻地放在女主人膝上，他们就这样坐着；这时，狗舍运回来了。达林先生伸出头来吻他的妻子时，我们看到，他的脸比以前憔悴多了，神情也温和多了。

达林先生把帽子交给莉莎，她轻蔑地接了过去，莉莎缺乏想像力，没法理解这个人的所作所为。屋外，随车而来的一群人还在欢呼，达林先生自然不能不感动。

"听听他们，"他说，"真叫人快慰。"

"一帮小毛孩。"莉莎讥笑地说。

“今天，人群里有好几个大人呢。”达林先生微红着脸告诉莉莎，可是她却不屑地摇摇头，达林先生也没有责备她。大出风头并没有使他得意忘形，反倒使他变得更和气了。有一阵子，他坐在狗舍里，半截身子伸到外面，和达林太太谈着他的这番出名。达林太太说，希望这不会使他头脑发昏。这时，他紧紧握着达林太太的手，要她放心。

“幸亏我不是一个软弱的人。”达林先生说，“天呐，要是我是一个软弱的人就糟了。”

“乔治，”达林太太怯生生地说，“你还是满心的悔恨，是不是？”

“还是满心的悔恨，亲爱的！你瞧我怎么惩罚自己：住在狗窝里。”

“你是在惩罚自己，是不是，乔治？你能肯定你不是把它当作一种乐子吗？”

“什么话，亲爱的。”

当然，达林太太请求原谅；然后，达林先生觉得困了，他蜷着身子，在狗舍里躺下。

“你到孩子们的睡房去，为我弹钢琴催眠好吗？”他请求道。达林太太向睡房走去时，他漫不经心地说：“关上窗子，我觉得有风。”

“啊，乔治，千万别叫我关窗子。窗子是永远要为孩子们开着的，永远，永远。”

现在，轮到达林先生请求她原谅了。达林太太走到孩子们白天游戏的房间，弹起钢琴来，达林先生很快就睡着了。正在他睡着的时候，温迪、约翰、迈克尔飞进了房间。

不对，不是这样的。我们这样写，是因为我们离船以前，他们原是这样周密安排好的；可是，在我们离船后，一定是发生了什么情况，因为，飞进来的不是他们三个，而是彼得和叮叮铃。

彼得的头几句话，就说明了一切。

“快，叮叮铃，”彼得低声说，“关上窗子，上闩。对了。现在，咱们得从门口飞出去了，等温迪回来时，她会以为她母亲把她关在外面了，然后她就得跟我一道儿回去。”

我脑子里，一直有一个疑问：杀了海盗以后，彼得为什么不回到岛上去，让叮叮铃护送孩子们回家？现在，这个问题终于迎刃而解了，原来彼得脑子里一直藏着这样一个诡计。

彼得并不觉得这样做有什么不对，反而开心地跳起舞来。然后他向游戏室里偷偷张望，看是谁在弹钢琴。他轻轻地对叮叮铃说："那是温迪的母亲。她是一位漂亮的太太，不过没有我母亲漂亮。她嘴上满是顶针，不过还是没有我母亲嘴上的顶针多。"

当然，关于他的母亲，他知之甚少；可是，他有时候喜欢夸耀地谈到她。

彼得不知道钢琴上弹的是什么曲子，那其实是"可爱的家"，可是他知道，那曲子在不断地唱着"回来吧，温迪，温迪，温迪"。彼得洋洋得意地说："太太，你再也别想见到温迪啦，因为窗子已经闩上啦。"

彼得又向房间里偷偷看了一眼，想看看琴声为什么停了；他看见达林太太把头靠在琴箱上，眼里含着两颗泪珠。

"她要我把窗子打开，"彼得心想，"可是我才不呢，就不。"

彼得再一次向里偷看，只见两颗泪珠还在眼里呆着；不过，已经换了两颗。

"她真是很爱温迪。"彼得对自己说。他现在很恼恨达林太太，因为她不明白为什么她不能再得到温迪。

这道理再简单也不过："因为我也爱温迪，太太，我们两个人不能都要温迪呀。"

可是这位太太偏偏不肯善罢甘休，彼得觉得不痛快，就不再看她。可就是这样，她也不放过彼得。彼得在房里欢蹦乱跳，做着鬼脸，可是他一停下来，达林太太就仿佛在他心里不住地敲打。

"啊，那好吧。"最后，彼得忍着气说。然后他打开了窗子。"来呀，叮叮铃，"他喊，狠狠地对自然法则投去了轻蔑的一眼，"咱们可不要什么傻母亲！"就飞走了。

所以，当温迪、约翰和迈克尔飞回来的时候，窗子还是开着的：这当然是他们不配得到的。他们落到了地板上，一点也不感到惭愧，最小的一个甚至已经忘记了他的这个家。

“约翰，”他疑惑地四面张望，说道，“这儿，我好像来过。”

“你当然来过，傻瓜。那不是你的旧床吗？”

“没错。”迈克尔说，可是还不大有把握。

“瞧，狗舍！”约翰喊，他跑过去往里瞧。

“也许娜娜就在里面吧。”温迪说。

于是约翰吹了一声口哨。“喂，”他说，“里面有个男人。”

“是爸爸！”温迪惊叫。

“让我瞧瞧爸爸。”迈克尔急切地请求，他仔细地看了一眼。“他还没有我杀死的那个海盗个头儿大哩。”他坦率地带着失望的口气说。幸好达林先生睡着了，要是他听见他的小迈克尔一见面就说出这样一句话，该多伤心啊。

看见父亲睡在狗舍里，温迪和约翰不禁吃了一惊。

“真的，”约翰像一个对自己的记忆力失去信心的人那样说，“他不会是一向都睡在狗舍里吧？”

“约翰，”温迪犹犹豫豫地说，“也许我们对过去生活的记忆，不像我们想的那样准确吧。”

他们觉得身上一阵寒气，活该。

“我们回来的时候，”约翰这个小坏蛋说，“妈妈也不在这儿等着，真是太粗心了。”

这时候，达林太太又弹起琴来了。

“是妈妈！”温迪喊道，向那边偷看。

“可不是吗！”约翰说。

“那么，温迪，你并不真是我们的母亲啦？”迈克尔问。他一定是困了。

“噢，我的天！”温迪惊叫道，她第一次真正感到了痛悔，“是到了我们该回来的时候了。”

“我们偷偷地溜进去，”约翰提议，“用手蒙住她的眼睛。”

可是温迪认为应该用一种更温和的办法宣告好消息，她想到了一个更好的办法。

“我们都上床去，等妈妈进来的时候我们都在床上躺着，就好像从来没有离开过一样。”

于是，当达林太太回到孩子们的睡房，来看达林先生是不是睡着了；这时候她看到，每张床上都睡了一个孩子。孩子们正急切地等着听到她的欢呼，可是她没有欢呼。她看到了他们，但她不相信他们在那儿。原来，她时常在梦里看到孩子们躺在床上，所以达林太太以为她现在还是在做梦。

达林太太在火炉边的椅子上坐了下来，从前，她总是坐在这儿给孩子们喂奶。

孩子们不明白这是怎么回事，三个孩子都觉得浑身发冷。

“妈妈！”温迪喊道。

“这是温迪。”达林太太说，可是她还以为这是做梦。

“妈妈！”

“这是约翰！”达林太太说。

“妈妈！”迈克尔喊。他现在认出妈妈来了。

“这是迈克尔。”达林太太说。她伸出双臂去拥抱那三个自私的孩子，她还以为自己再也抱不到他们了呢。不错，她确实抱着了，她搂住了温迪、约翰和迈克尔。他们三个早已溜下了床，跑到了她身边。

“乔治，乔治。”达林太太好不容易才叫出声来。达林先生醒来，分享了她的欢乐，娜娜也冲了进来。再也没有比这更美妙动人的景象了。不过，这时候没人来观赏，只有一个陌生的小男孩，从窗外向里张望。他的乐事数也数不清，那是别的孩子永远得不到的。但是，只有这一种快乐，他隔窗看到的那种快乐，是把他关在外面，永远也得不到的。

Chapter 17
第十七章

When Wendy Grew Up

I hope you want to know what became of the other boys. They were waiting below to give Wendy time to explain about them; and when they had counted five hundred they went up. They went up by the stair, because they thought this would make a better impression. They stood in a row in front of Mrs. Darling, with their hats off, and wishing they were not wearing their pirate clothes. They said nothing, but their eyes asked her to have them. They ought to have looked at Mr. Darling also, but they forgot about him.

Of course Mrs. Darling said at once that she would have them; but Mr. Darling was curiously depressed, and they saw that he considered six a rather large number.

"I must say," he said to Wendy, "that you don't do things by halves," a grudging remark which the twins thought was pointed at them.

The first twin was the proud one, and he asked, flushing, "Do you think we should be too much of a handful, sir? Because, if so, we can go away."

"Father!" Wendy cried, shocked; but still the cloud was on him. He knew he was behaving unworthily, but he could not help it.

"We could lie doubled up," said Nibs.

"I always cut their hair myself," said Wendy.

"George!" Mrs. Darling exclaimed, pained to see her dear one showing himself in such an unfavourable light.

Then he burst into tears, and the truth came out. He was as glad to have them as she was, he said, but he thought they should have asked his consent as well as hers, instead of treating him as a cypher in his own house.

"I don't think he is a cypher," Tootles cried instantly. "Do you think he is a cypher, Curly?"

"No, I don't. Do you think he is a cypher, Slightly?"

"Rather not. Twin, what do you think?"

It turned out that not one of them thought him a cypher; and he was absurdly gratified, and said he would find space for them all in the drawing-room if they fitted in.

"We'll fit in, sir," they assured him.

"Then follow the leader," he cried gaily. "Mind you, I am not sure that we have a drawing-room, but we pretend we have, and it's all the same. Hoop la!"

He went off dancing through the house, and they all cried "Hoop la!" and danced after him, searching for the drawing-room; and I forget whether they found it, but at any rate they found corners, and they all fitted in.

As for Peter, he saw Wendy once again before he flew away. He did not exactly come to the window, but he brushed against it in passing so that she could open it if she liked and call to him. That is what she did.

"Hullo, Wendy, good-bye," he said.

"Oh dear, are you going away?"

"Yes."

"You don't feel, Peter," she said falteringly, "that you would like to say anything to my parents about a very sweet subject?"

"No."

"About me, Peter?"

"No."

Mrs. Darling came to the window, for at present she was keeping a sharp eye on Wendy. She told Peter that she had adopted all the other boys, and would like to adopt him also.

"Would you send me to school?" he inquired craftily.

"Yes."

"And then to an office?"

"I suppose so."

"Soon I would be a man?"

"Very soon."

"I don't want to go to school and learn solemn things," he told her passionately. "I don't want to be a man. O Wendy's mother, if I was to wake up and feel there was a beard!"

"Peter," said Wendy the comforter, "I should love you in a beard;" and Mrs. Darling stretched out her arms to him, but he repulsed her.

"Keep back, lady, no one is going to catch me and make me a man."

"But where are you going to live?"

"With Tink in the house we built for Wendy. The fairies are to put it high up among the tree tops where they sleep at nights."

"How lovely," cried Wendy so longingly that Mrs. Darling tightened her grip.

"I thought all the fairies were dead," Mrs. Darling said.

"There are always a lot of young ones," explained Wendy, who was now quite an authority, "because you see when a new baby laughs for the first time a new fairy is born, and as there are always new babies there are always new fairies. They live in nests on the tops of trees; and the mauve ones are boys and the white ones are girls, and the blue ones are just little sillies who are not sure what they are."

"I shall have such fun," said Peter, with eye on Wendy.

"It will be rather lonely in the evening," she said, "sitting by the fire."

"I shall have Tink."

"Tink can't go a twentieth part of the way round," she reminded him a little tartly.

"Sneaky tell-tale!" Tink called out from somewhere round the corner.

"It doesn't matter," Peter said.

"O Peter, you know it matters."

"Well, then, come with me to the little house."

"May I, mummy?"

"Certainly not. I have got you home again, and I mean to keep you."

"But he does so need a mother."

"So do you, my love."

"Oh, all right," Peter said, as if he had asked her from politeness merely; but Mrs. Darling saw his mouth twitch, and she made this handsome offer: to let Wendy go to him for a week every year to do his spring cleaning. Wendy would have preferred a more permanent arrangement; and it seemed to her that spring would be long in coming; but this promise sent Peter away quite gay again. He had no sense of time, and was so full of adventures that all I have told you about him is only a halfpenny-worth of them. I suppose it was because Wendy knew this that her last words to him were these rather plaintive ones:

"You won't forget me, Peter, will you, before spring cleaning time comes?"

Of course Peter promised; and then he flew away. He took Mrs. Darling's kiss with him. The kiss that had been for no one else, Peter took quite easily. Funny. But she seemed satisfied.

Of course all the boys went to school; and most of them got into Class III, but Slightly was put first into Class IV and then into Class V. Class I is the top class. Before they had attended school a week they saw what goats they had been not to remain on the island; but it was too late now, and soon they settled down to being as ordinary as you or me or Jenkins minor. It is sad to have to say that the power to fly gradually left them. At first Nana tied their feet to the bed-posts so that they should not fly away in the night; and one of their diversions by day was to pretend to fall off buses; but by and by they ceased to tug at their bonds in bed, and found that they hurt themselves when they let go of the bus. In time they could not even fly after their hats. Want of practice, they called it; but what it really meant was that they no longer believed.

Michael believed longer than the other boys, though they jeered at him; so he was with Wendy when Peter came for her at the end of the first year. She flew away with Peter in the frock she had woven from leaves and berries in the Neverland, and her one fear was that he might notice how short it had become; but he never noticed, he had so much to say about himself.

She had looked forward to thrilling talks with him about old times, but new adventures had crowded the old ones from his mind.

"Who is Captain Hook?" he asked with interest when she spoke of the arch enemy.

"Don't you remember," she asked, amazed, "how you killed him and saved all our lives?"

"I forget them after I kill them," he replied carelessly.

When she expressed a doubtful hope that Tinker Bell would be glad to see her he said, "Who is Tinker Bell?"

"O Peter," she said, shocked; but even when she explained he could not remember.

"There are such a lot of them," he said. "I expect she is no more."

I expect he was right, for fairies don't live long, but they are so little that a short time seems a good while to them.

Wendy was pained too to find that the past year was but as yesterday to Peter; it had seemed such a long year of waiting to her. But he was exactly as fascinating as ever, and they had a lovely spring cleaning in the little house on the tree tops.

Next year he did not come for her. She waited in a new frock because the old one simply would not meet; but he never came.

"Perhaps he is ill," Michael said.

"You know he is never ill."

Michael came close to her and whispered, with a shiver, "Perhaps there is no such person, Wendy!" and then Wendy would have cried if Michael had not been crying.

Peter came next spring cleaning; and the strange thing was that he never knew he had missed a year.

That was the last time the girl Wendy ever saw him. For a little longer she tried for his sake not to have growing pains; and she felt she was untrue to him when she got a prize for general knowledge. But the years came and went without bringing the careless boy; and when they met again Wendy was a married woman, and Peter was no more to her than a little dust in the box in which she had kept her toys. Wendy was grown up. You need not be sorry for her. She was one of the kind that likes to grow up. In the end she grew up of her own free will a day quicker than other girls.

All the boys were grown up and done for by this time; so it is scarcely worth while saying anything more about them. You may see the twins and Nibs and Curly any day going to an office, each carrying a little bag and an umbrella. Michael is an engine- driver. Slightly married a lady of title, and so he became a lord. You see that judge in a wig coming out at the iron door? That used to be Tootles. The bearded man who doesn't know any story to tell his children was once John.

Wendy was married in white with a pink sash. It is strange to think that Peter did not alight in the church and forbid the banns.

Years rolled on again, and Wendy had a daughter. This ought not to be written in ink but in a golden splash.

She was called Jane, and always had an odd inquiring look, as if from the moment she arrived on the mainland she wanted to ask questions. When she was old enough to ask them they were mostly about Peter Pan. She loved to hear of Peter, and Wendy told her all she could remember in the very nursery from which the famous flight had taken place. It was Jane's nursery now, for her father had bought it at the three per cents from Wendy's father, who was no longer fond of stairs. Mrs. Darling was now dead and forgotten.

There were only two beds in the nursery now, Jane's and her nurse's; and there was no kennel, for Nana also had passed away. She died of old age, and at the end she had been rather difficult to get on with; being very firmly convinced that no one knew how to look after children except herself.

Once a week Jane's nurse had her evening off; and then it was Wendy's part to put Jane to bed. That was the time for stories. It was Jane's invention to raise the sheet over her mother's head and her own, this making a tent, and in the awful darkness to whisper:

"What do we see now?"

"I don't think I see anything to-night," says Wendy, with a feeling that if Nana were here she would object to further conversation.

"Yes, you do," says Jane, "you see when you were a little girl."

"That is a long time ago, sweetheart," says Wendy. "Ah me, how time flies!"

"Does it fly," asks the artful child, "the way you flew when you were a little girl?"

"The way I flew? Do you know, Jane, I sometimes wonder whether I ever did really fly."

"Yes, you did."

"The dear old days when I could fly!"

"Why can't you fly now, mother?"

"Because I am grown up, dearest. When people grow up they forget the way."

"Why do they forget the way?"

"Because they are no longer gay and innocent and heartless. It is only the gay and innocent and heartless who can fly."

"What is gay and innocent and heartless? I do wish I were gay and innocent and heartless."

Or perhaps Wendy admits she does see something.

"I do believe," she says, "that it is this nursery."

"I do believe it is," says Jane. "Go on."

They are now embarked on the great adventure of the night when Peter flew in looking for his shadow.

"The foolish fellow," says Wendy, "tried to stick it on with soap, and when he could not he cried, and that woke me, and I sewed it on for him."

"You have missed a bit," interrupts Jane, who now knows the story better than her mother. "When you saw him sitting on the floor crying, what did you say?"

"I sat up in bed and I said, 'Boy, why are you crying?'"

"Yes, that was it," says Jane, with a big breath.

"And then he flew us all away to the Neverland and the fairies and the pirates and the redskins and the mermaid's lagoon, and the home under the ground, and the little house."

"Yes! which did you like best of all?"

"I think I liked the home under the ground best of all."

"Yes, so do I. What was the last thing Peter ever said to you?"

"The last thing he ever said to me was, 'Just always be waiting for me, and then some night you will hear me crowing.'"

"Yes."

"But, alas, he forgot all about me," Wendy said it with a smile. She was as grown up as that.

"What did his crow sound like?" Jane asked one evening.

"It was like this," Wendy said, trying to imitate Peter's crow.

"No, it wasn't," Jane said gravely, "it was like this"; and she did it ever so much better than her mother.

Wendy was a little startled. "My darling, how can you know?"

"I often hear it when I am sleeping," Jane said.

"Ah yes, many girls hear it when they are sleeping, but I was the only one who heard it awake."

"Lucky you," said Jane.

And then one night came the tragedy. It was the spring of the year, and the story had been told for the night, and Jane was now asleep in her bed. Wendy was sitting on the floor, very close to the fire, so as to see to darn, for there was no other light in the nursery; and while she sat darning she heard a crow. Then the window blew open as of old, and Peter dropped in on the floor.

He was exactly the same as ever, and Wendy saw at once that he still had all his first teeth.

He was a little boy, and she was grown up. She huddled by the fire not daring to move, helpless and guilty, a big woman.

"Hullo, Wendy," he said, not noticing any difference, for he was thinking chiefly of himself; and in the dim light her white dress might have been the nightgown in which he had seen her first.

"Hullo, Peter," she replied faintly, squeezing herself as small as possible. Something inside her was crying "Woman, Woman, let go of me."

"Hullo, where is John?" he asked, suddenly missing the third bed.

"John is not here now," she gasped.

"Is Michael asleep?" he asked, with a careless glance at Jane.

"Yes," she answered; and now she felt that she was untrue to Jane as well as to Peter.

"That is not Michael," she said quickly, lest a judgment should fall on her.

Peter looked. "Hullo, is it a new one?"

"Yes."

"Boy or girl?"

"Girl."

Now surely he would understand; but not a bit of it.

"Peter," she said, faltering, "are you expecting me to fly away with you?"

"Of course; that is why I have come." He added a little sternly, "Have you forgotten that this is spring cleaning time?"

She knew it was useless to say that he had let many spring cleaning times pass.

"I can't come," she said apologetically, "I have forgotten how to fly."

"I'll soon teach you again."

"O Peter, don't waste the fairy dust on me."

She had risen; and now at last a fear assailed him. "What is it?" he cried, shrinking.

"I will turn up the light," she said, "and then you can see for yourself."

For almost the only time in his life that I know of, Peter was afraid. "Don't turn up the light," he cried.

She let her hands play in the hair of the tragic boy. She was not a little girl heart-broken about him; she was a grown woman smiling at it all, but they were wet smiles.

Then she turned up the light, and Peter saw. He gave a cry of pain; and when the tall beautiful creature stooped to lift him in her arms he drew back sharply.

"What is it?" he cried again.

She had to tell him.

"I am old, Peter. I am ever so much more than twenty. I grew up long ago."

"You promised not to!"

"I couldn't help it. I am a married woman, Peter."

"No, you're not."

"Yes, and the little girl in the bed is my baby."

"No, she's not."

But he supposed she was; and he took a step towards the sleeping child with his dagger upraised. Of course he did not strike. He sat down on the floor and sobbed; and Wendy did not know how to comfort him, though she could have done it so easily once. She was only a woman now, and she ran out of the room to try to think.

Peter continued to cry, and soon his sobs woke Jane. She sat up in bed, and was interested at once.

"Boy," she said, "why are you crying?"

Peter rose and bowed to her, and she bowed to him from the bed.

"Hullo," he said.

"Hullo," said Jane.

"My name is Peter Pan," he told her.

"Yes, I know."

"I came back for my mother," he explained, "to take her to the Neverland."

"Yes, I know," Jane said, "I have been waiting for you."

When Wendy returned diffidently she found Peter sitting on the bed-post crowing gloriously, while Jane in her nighty was flying round the room in solemn ecstasy.

"She is my mother," Peter explained; and Jane descended and stood by his side, with the look in her face that he liked to see on ladies when they gazed at him.

"He does so need a mother," Jane said.

"Yes, I know." Wendy admitted rather forlornly; "no one knows it so well as I."

"Good-bye," said Peter to Wendy; and he rose in the air, and the shameless Jane rose with him; it was already her easiest way of moving about.

Wendy rushed to the window.

"No, no," she cried.

"It is just for spring cleaning time," Jane said, "he wants me always to do his spring cleaning."

"If only I could go with you," Wendy sighed.

"You see you can't fly," said Jane.

Of course in the end Wendy let them fly away together. Our last glimpse of her shows her at the window, watching them receding into the sky until they were as small as stars.

As you look at Wendy, you may see her hair becoming white, and her figure little again, for all this happened long ago. Jane is now a common grown-up, with a daughter called Margaret; and every spring cleaning time, except when he forgets, Peter comes for Margaret and takes her to the Neverland, where she tells him stories about himself, to which he listens eagerly. When Margaret grows up she will have a daughter, who is to be Peter's mother in turn; and thus it will go on, so long as children are gay and innocent and heartless.

THE END

温迪长大了

我相信你们都愿意知道别的孩子的下落如何。他们都在楼下等着，好让温迪有时间解释。当他们数到五百下的时候，就会走上楼来。他们是沿楼梯走上来的，因为他们觉得这样会给人一个好印象。他们在达林太太面前站成一排，脱掉了帽子，心里恨不得没有穿海盗衣。他们没有说话，眼睛却在恳求达林太太收留他们。他们本该也望着达林先生，可是他们把他给忘了。

当然，达林太太立刻就说她愿意收留他们；可是达林先生很不高兴，孩子们知道，他是嫌六个太多了。

“我得告诉你，”达林先生对温迪说，“你可不要做半截子事。”这话里有气，双胞胎觉得是冲他们来的。

老大比较高傲，他红着脸对达林先生说：“先生，你是嫌我们人太多吧？那样的话，我们可以走。”

“爸爸！”温迪惊讶地叫了一声，但是，达林先生还是满脸阴云。他知道，他这样做很不体面，可他又有什么办法？

“我们几个可以挤在一起。”尼布斯说。

“我可以经常给他们剪头发。”温迪说道。

“乔治！”达林太太惊叹了一声，看到她亲爱的丈夫表现得这样不光彩，心里很难过。

达林先生突然哭了起来，于是真相大白。他说，他也和达林太太一样愿意收留他们；只不过他们在征求太太的意见时，也应征求他的意见才对，不该在他自己家里把他看成一个可有可无的人。

“我并不觉得他是一个可有可无的人。”图图立刻大声说，“你呢，卷毛？”

“我不觉得，你呢，斯莱特利？”

“我也不，双胞胎，你们呢？”

到头来，没有一个孩子认为达林先生是个可有可无的人。说来荒唐，他竟心满意足了‘并说，要是合适的话，他可以把他们统统安置在客厅里。

“合适极了，先生。”孩子们向他担保。

“那么，跟我来。”他兴冲冲地喊，“请注意，我不敢肯定我有一间客厅，不过我们可以假装有一间客厅，反正一样。啊哈！”

他手舞足蹈地满屋子转着，孩子们也全都高喊“啊哈！”手舞足蹈地跟着他走，寻找那间客厅。我也记不清楚他们究竟找到客厅没有了，可不管怎么样，他们总可以找到几个角落，比较合适地住下了。

至于彼得，他再飞走前还来看了温迪一次。但他并没有专门来到窗前，只是在飞过时擦了一下窗子，这样，如果温迪愿意的话，就可以打开窗子呼唤他。温迪果真这样做了。

“喂，温迪，再见了。”他说。

“啊，亲爱的，你要走了吗？”

“是的。”

“彼得，你不想跟我父母谈谈那件甜蜜的事儿吗？”温迪有点迟疑地说。

“不。”

“关于我的事，彼得？”

“不。”

这时达林太太走到窗子前来，她现在一直在密切地监视着温迪。她告诉彼得，她已经收养了所有其余的孩子，也愿意收养他。

“你要送我去上学？”彼得机警地问。

“是的。”

“然后再送我上办公室？”

“我想是这样。”

“我很快就要变成一个大人？”

“很快。”

“我不愿意去学校学那些正儿八经的东西，”彼得愤愤地对达林太太说，“我不要变成大人。温迪妈妈，要是我一觉醒来，摸到自己有胡子，那该多别扭！”

“彼得！”温迪安慰他说，“你有胡子我也会爱你的。”达林太太向他伸出两臂，但是彼得拒绝了她。

“太太，你靠后站吧，谁也不能把我变成一个大人。”

“可是你到哪儿去住呢？”

“和叮叮铃一起住在我们给温迪盖的小屋子里。仙子们会把它高高地抬上树梢的，她们夜里就住在树上。”

“多可爱呀。”温迪羡慕地喊道。达林太太不由得把她抓得更紧。

“我以为所有的仙子都死了呐。”达林太大说。

“总会有许多年轻的仙子生出来。”温迪解释说。关于仙子的事，她现在可以说是个行家了。“因为，每个婴孩第一次笑出声的时候，就有一个新的仙子诞生了；既然总是有新的婴孩，就总是有新的仙子，他们住在树梢上的巢里。绛色的是男的，白色的是女的，蓝色的是些小傻瓜，他们自己也说不准他们是男是女。”

“我会很快乐的。”彼得一只眼瞅着温迪说。

“晚上一个人坐在火炉边怪寂寞的。”温迪说。

“我有叮叮铃做伴。”

“叮叮铃可干不了什么事。”她有点刻薄地提醒他。

“背后嚼舌头的家伙！”叮叮铃不知从哪儿钻出来，骂了一句。

“那没关系。”彼得说。

“彼得，这有关系，你知道的。”温迪说。

“那好，你跟我一起到小屋子去吧。”

“妈妈，我可以去吗？”

“当然不可以，你好不容易回家了，我决不让你再离开。”

“可是他真需要一个母亲哪。”

“你也需要一个母亲啊，乖乖。”

“那就拉倒吧。”彼得说，好像他邀请温迪去只是出于礼貌。但是，达林太太看到彼得的嘴抽动了，于是她提出一个慷慨的建议：每年让温迪去他那儿住上一个礼拜，帮他搞春季的大扫除。温迪宁愿有一个更长远的安排，而且她觉得，春天要等很久才到来。但是，这个许诺却使彼得高高兴兴地走了。他没有时间观念，又有那么多冒险的事要做，我告诉你们的只不过是其中微乎其微的一点点。我想，大概温迪深知这一点，所以，她最后向他说了一句这样悲伤的话：

“你不会忘记我吧，彼得？在春季大扫除以前，你会忘记我吗？”

当然不会，彼得向她担保，然后他飞走了。他带走了达林太太的一吻，这个吻是谁也没得到的，彼得却毫不费力地得到了，真有趣。可是温迪好像也心满意足了。

自然，所有的孩子都进了学校，多数人上第三班。不过，斯莱特利先给安插到第四班；后来，又改上第五班。第一班是最高班。他们上学还不到一个礼拜，就已经懊悔，觉得不该离开梦幻岛，可是现在已经太迟了。他们也就很快安下心来，像你、我或小詹金斯

一样过普通的日子了。说来怪可怜的，他们渐渐失去了飞的本领。起初，娜娜把他们的脚绑在床柱上，防止他们夜里飞走。白天，他们的一种游戏是假装从公共汽车上掉下来；可是渐渐地他们发现，只要不拽住那根绑带，他们从公共汽车掉下时，就会摔伤。到后来，帽子被风刮走，他们都不能飞过去抓住它。他们说，这是因为缺少练习，其实，真正原因是，他们不再相信这一切了。

迈克尔比别的孩子相信的时间长些，虽然他们老是嘲笑他。所以，第一年底彼得来找温迪时，他还和温迪在一起。温迪和彼得一起飞走时，身上穿着她在梦幻岛时，用树叶和浆果编织成的罩褂。她生怕彼得看出这罩褂已经变得多么短了，可是彼得根本没注意，他自己的事，他还说不完呢。

温迪盼着和他谈起那些激动人心的往事，可是新的冒险趣事已经从他脑中挤走了那些旧事。

温迪提起那个大敌时，彼得很感兴趣地问：“胡克船长是谁？”

“你不记得了吗？”温迪惊讶地问，“你是怎么杀的他，救了我们大家的命？”

“我杀了他们以后，就把他们忘记了。”彼得漫不经心地回答。

当温迪犹犹豫豫地表示希望叮叮铃会高兴的见到她时，彼得却问：“叮叮铃是谁？”

“啊，彼得。”温迪万分惊讶地说；可就算她再怎么解释，彼得仍旧想不起来了。

“这种小东西多的是，”他说，“我估摸着她已经不在了。”

我想彼得大概说对了，因为仙子是活不长的。不过，因为她们很小，所以很短的时间在她们看来也显得很长。

还有一点也使温迪感到难过：过去的一年，对于彼得来说，仿佛只是昨天；可在她看来，这一年等起来真长啊。不过，彼得还像以前一样招人喜欢，他们在树梢上的小屋里，痛痛快快地进行了一次春季大扫除。

下一年，彼得没有来接她。她穿上一件新衣服等着他，因为那件旧的已经穿不下了。可是，彼得没有来。

“彼得许是病了吧。”迈克尔说。

“你知道，彼得是从来不生病的。”

迈克尔凑到温迪跟前，打了个冷颤，悄悄说：“也许根本就没有这样一个人吧，温迪！”就算那会儿迈克尔没哭，温迪也会哭的。

再下一年，彼得又来接她去进行春季大扫除了；奇怪的是，他竟不知道自己漏掉了一年。

这是小姑娘温迪最后一次见到彼得。有一段时期，为了彼得的缘故，她努力不让自己越来越痛苦。当她在常识课上得了奖时，她觉得自己是对彼得不忠实。但是，一年年过去了，这位粗心大意的孩子再也没来。等到他们再见面时，温迪已经是一位结了婚的妇人，彼得对于她，只不过成了她收藏玩具的匣子里的一点灰尘。温迪长大了。你不必为她感到遗憾，她属于喜欢长大的那一类人，她是心甘情愿长大的，而且心甘情愿比别的女孩子长得更快一点。

男孩子们这时全都长大了，完事了，没什么好说的。你随便哪天都可以看到双胞胎、尼布斯和卷毛提着公文包和雨伞向办公室走去。迈克尔是位火车司机。斯莱特利娶了一位贵族女子，所以他成了一位勋爵。你看见一位戴假发的法官从铁门里走出来吗？那就是过去的图图。那个从来不会给他的孩子讲故事的有胡子的男人，他就是原来的约翰。

温迪结婚时，穿着白色的婚纱，系着一条粉红饰带。想来也挺奇怪，彼得竟没有飞进教堂，去反对这桩婚事。

岁月如流水，温迪有了一个女儿。这件事不该用墨水写下，而应用金粉大书特书。

她的女儿名叫简，小姑娘总带着一种好发问的古怪神情，仿佛她一来到世上就有许多问题要问。等她长到可以发问的时候，她的问题多半是关于彼得·潘的。她爱听彼得的事，温迪把她自己所能记得起的事情全讲给女儿听。她讲这些故事的地点，正是那间发生过那次有名的飞行的育儿室。现在，这里成了简的育儿室，因为，她父亲以百分之三的廉价从温迪的父亲手里买下了这房子。温迪的父亲已经不喜欢爬楼梯了。达林太太已经去世，人们都已忘记了她。

现在育儿室里只有两张床了，简一张，她的保姆一张。狗舍已经没有了，因为娜娜也死了。她是老死的，最后几年，她的脾气变得很难相处，因为她非常固执己见，认为除了她，谁也不懂看孩子。

简的保姆每礼拜有一晚休息，这时候，就由温迪照看简上床睡觉。这是讲故事的时间。简别出心裁地把床单蒙在自己和妈妈的头上，当作一顶帐篷。在黑暗里，两人说着悄悄话：

“咱们现在看见什么啦？”

“今晚我什么也没看见。”温迪说，她有种感觉，要是娜娜在的话，她一定不让她们再谈下去。

“你看得见，”简说，“你是一个小姑娘的时候就看得见。”

“那是很久很久以前的事啦，我的宝贝，”温迪说，“唉，时间飞得多快呀！”

“时间也会飞吗？”这个机灵的孩子问，“就像你小时候那样飞吗？”

“像我那样飞！你知道吧，简，我有时候真搞不清我是不是真的飞过。”

“你飞过。”

“我会飞的那个好时光，已经一去不回了。”

“你现在为什么不能飞了，妈妈？”

“因为我长大了，小亲亲。人一长大，就忘了怎么飞了。”

“为什么他们会忘了怎么飞呢？”

“因为他们不再是无忧无虑、天真无邪、毫无心机的人了。只有无忧无虑、天真无邪、毫无心机的人才会飞。”

“什么叫无忧无虑、天真无邪、毫无心机的人呢？我真希望我也是这种人呀。”

或许这时候温迪真的悟到了什么。“我想，这都是因为这间育儿室的缘故。”她说。

“我想也是，”简说，“往下讲吧。”

于是她们开始谈到了大冒险的那一夜，先是彼得飞进来找他的影子。

“那个傻孩子，”温迪说，“他想用肥皂把影子粘上，粘不上他就哭，哭声把我惊醒了，我就用针线给他缝上。”

“你漏掉了一点。”简插嘴说，她现在比母亲知道的还清楚了，“你看见他坐在地板上哭的时候，你说什么来着？”

“我从床上坐起来，说：‘孩子，你为什么哭？’”

“对了，就是这样。”简说，深呼吸了一下。

“后来，他领着我飞到了梦幻岛；那儿还有仙子，还有海盗，还有印第安人，还有人鱼的礁湖，还有地下的家，还有那间小屋子。”

“对了！你最喜欢的是什么？”

“我想我最喜欢的是地下的家。”

“没错，我也最喜欢。彼得最后对你说的话是什么？”

“他最后对我说的话是：‘你只要永远等着我，总有一夜你会听到我的叫声。’”

“对了。”

“可是，唉！他已经完全把我给忘了。”温迪微笑着说。她已经长得那么大了。

“彼得的叫声是什么样的？”简有一晚问。

“是这样的。”温迪说，她试着学彼得叫。

“不对，不是这样，”简郑重地说，“是这样的。”她学得比母亲强多了。

温迪有点吃惊：“宝贝，你怎么知道的？”

“我睡着的时候常常听到。”简说。

“啊，是啊，许多女孩睡着的时候都听到过，可是只有我醒着的时候听到过。”

“你多幸运啊。”简说。

有一夜悲剧发生了。那是在春天，晚上刚讲完了故事，简躺在床上睡着了。温迪坐在地板上，靠近壁炉，就着火光补袜子，因为，育儿室里没有别的亮光了。补着补着，她听到一声叫声。窗子像过去一样吹开了，彼得跳了进来，落在地板上。

彼得还和从前一样，一点没变；温迪立刻看到，他还长着满口的乳牙。

彼得还是一个小男孩，可温迪已经是一个大人了。她在火边缩成一团，一动也不敢动，既尴尬又难堪，一个大女人。

“你好，温迪。”彼得招呼她，他并没有注意到有什么两样，因为他主要只想到自己；在昏暗的光下，温迪穿的那件白衣服，很像是他初见她时穿的那件睡衣。

“你好，彼得。”温迪有气无力地回答。她紧缩着身子，尽量把自己变得小些。她内心有个声音在呼叫：“女人呐女人，你放我走吧。”

“喂，约翰在哪儿？”彼得问，突然发现少了第三张床。

“约翰现在不在这儿。”温迪喘息着说。

“迈克尔睡着了吗？”他随便瞄了简一眼，问道。

“是的。”温迪回答，可她立刻感到自己对简和彼得都不诚实。

“那不是迈克尔。”她连忙改口说，否则要遭报应。

彼得走过去看：“喂，这是个新孩子吗？”

“是的。”

“男孩还是女孩？”

“女孩。”

现在彼得该明白了吧，可是他一点也不明白。

“彼得，”温迪结结巴巴地说，“你希望我跟你一起飞走吗？”

“当然啦，我正是为这个来的。”彼得有点严厉地说，“你忘记了这是春季大扫除的时候了吗？”

温迪知道，用不着告诉他有好多次春季大扫除都被他漏过去了。

“我不能去，”她抱歉地说，“我忘了怎么飞了。”

“我可以马上再教你。”

“啊，彼得，别在我身上浪费仙尘了。”

温迪站了起来，这时，彼得突然感到一阵恐惧。“怎么回事？”他喊，往后退缩着。

“我去开灯，”温迪说，“你自己一看就明白了。”

就我所知，彼得有生以来，这是第一次害怕了。“别开灯。”他叫道。

温迪用手抚弄着这可怜的孩子的头发。她已经不是一个为他伤心的小女孩，她是一个成年妇人，微笑地看待这一切，可那是带泪的微笑。

然后温迪开了灯。彼得看见了，他痛苦地叫了一声。这位高大、美丽的妇人正要弯下身去把他抱起来，他陡然后退。

“怎么回事？”他又喊了一声。

温迪不得不告诉他。

“我老了，彼得。我已经二十好几了，早就长大成人了。”

“你答应过我你不长大的！”

“我没有办法不长大……我是一个结了婚的女人，彼得。”

“不，你不是。”

“是的，床上那个小女孩，就是我的女儿。”

“不，她不是。”

可是，彼得想这小女孩大概真是温迪的娃娃，他高高举起了手中的短剑，朝熟睡的孩子走了几步。不过，当然他没有砍她。他坐在地板上抽泣起来。温迪不知道怎样安慰他才好，虽然她曾经轻而易举就能做到这一点。她现在只是一个女人，于是她走出房间去好好想想。

彼得还在哭，哭声很快就惊醒了简。简从床上坐起来，觉得眼前这一切非常有趣。

“孩子，”她说，“你为什么哭？”

彼得站起来，向她鞠了一躬；她也在床上向彼得鞠了一躬。

“你好。”彼得说。

“你好。”简说。

“我叫彼得·潘。”他告诉她。

“是，我知道。”

“我回来找我母亲，”彼得解释说，“我要带她去梦幻岛。”

“是，我知道，”简说，“我正等着你哩。”

温迪忐忑不安地走回房间时，她看到彼得正坐在床杆上得意洋洋地叫喊着，简正穿着睡衣狂喜地绕着房间飞。

“她是我的母亲了。”彼得对温迪解释说，简落下来，站在彼得旁边；她脸上露出了姑娘们注视他时的神情，那是彼得最喜欢看到的。

“他太需要一个母亲了。”简说。

“是呀，我知道，”温迪多少有点凄凉地承认，“谁也没有我知道得清楚。”

“再见了。”彼得对温迪说，他飞到了空中，不知羞的简也随他飞起，飞行已经是她最容易的活动方式了。

温迪冲到了窗前。

“不，不。”她大喊。

“只是去进行春季大扫除罢了，”简说，“他要我总去帮他进行春季大扫除。”

“要是我能跟你们一道去就好了。”温迪叹了一口气。

“可你不能飞呀。”简说。

当然，温迪最后还是让他们一道飞走了。我们最后看到温迪时，她正站在窗前，望着他们向天空里远去，直到他们小得像星星一般。

你再见到温迪时，会看到她头发变白了，身体又缩小了；因为，这些事是老早老早以前发生的。简现在是普通的成年女子了，她的女儿名叫玛格丽特；每到春季大扫除时节，除非他自己忘记了，否则彼得总是来带玛格丽特去梦幻岛。她在那儿给彼得讲她自己的故事，彼得总是聚精会神地听着。玛格丽特长大后，又会有一个女儿，这个女孩又成了彼得的母亲。事情就这样周而复始，只要孩子们无忧无虑、天真无邪。

（完）